Not Exactly Manless

Margot Sinclair

BENYA PUBLISHING

Library of Congress Control Number: 2025941902

First published in 2025 by Benya Publishing

ISBN: 978-1-968455-06-4 (paperback)
ISBN: 978-1-968455-07-1 (ePDF)
ISBN: 978-1-968455-08-8 (ePUB)

Publication data:
Margot Sinclair
Not Exactly Manless
Volume 3 in the "Not Exactly" Series

Design and layout by Scribe Inc.

Benya Publishing
P.O. Box 799
Sullivan's Island, SC 29482

www.benyapublishing.com

Preface

Who remembers the '90s? The Clintons were in the White House. The SUV was the new thing. Martha Stewart was a household name. Cell phones were clunky things a few people carried in cars.

More important to our story Charleston, South Carolina, was still Charleston. Big patches of the city were shabby and ungentrified. The old families lived in the old houses and maintained the old rituals in their kingdom by the sea.

And there was and is an underbelly of the city of organized and disorganized crime that the visitors never see.

1

"Stop it, Sparky, you dam' re-tard! You're gone hit him too hard, and then where will you be?"

Bobbi-Jean Kincaid never liked watching a man get pistol-whipped, even when he deserved it.

In the huge parking lot of the "Long Gone" truck stop on U.S. 85 right outside of Opelika, Alabama this over-large trucker jacked up on reds the way they always are had decided she was a whore and tried to drag her up into the cab of his big Peterbilt.

As it was close to midnight and nobody much was around, B-J's travelling companion Sparky Truluck had taken the opportunity to roll him for gas money and was using a medium barreled .38 on the man's face.

"Don't you get it?" grunted Sparky. "I don't like this old boy one bit. And I'm gonna teach his ass." He glared at her like he thought she'd suddenly gone substandard in intelligence.

The problem was he was starting to enjoy it too much, and B-J figured he was going to kill the man.

Real exasperated, she put both hands on her hips and said, "I hate to appear less than worthy in your eyes, but

I've never been real hot to go to prison for accessory after fact of murder."

Sparky said to quit distracting him. Told her if she was going to be all non-comprehensive to go get in the car and wait. Instead, she pulled her five-iron out of the Ben Hogan golf bag and smacked Sparky in the back of the head laying him out cold.

And there she was, confronted with Sparky knocked out and a truck driver on his hands and knees moaning and cursing and drooling blood. As she watched, the trucker collapsed like a feed bag and lay still too. There was really only one solution from her point of view. She took Sparky's car keys and drove off in his Firebird leaving him there asleep.

B-J liked to say there was no such thing as bad luck. Or if there was, you just ran from it. It never followed you for long. She was a Gemini—June 15—and liked travel and meeting new people. Spur-of-the-moment trips just fitted her changeable nature right down to the ground.

Sparky was a hoodlum. Good looking, but still a hoodlum. He reminded her a little bit of her daddy. B-J was not what you call trailer trash, but not too far above it having been brought up in a little aluminum-sided box on the outskirts of Valdosta, Georgia near the Moody Air Force Base. Her earliest memories of her daddy were being waked up in the middle of the night and carried in her pyjamas out to a wrecked car where she was told to cry a lot and act like her whole body hurt.

B-J's daddy was an insurance rip-off artist by trade—a not very successful one. Or rather he had a flurry of 19 phony auto accident claims that netted him some $156,000 and change before culminating in 20 years in the Georgia penal system. After that her daddy's face only appeared through wire mesh.

B-J was 26-years old, blond, and just as cute as a button. But her real assets were a set of 38 Double-D hooters. Men would say aw honey, them hooters. Or them gazoonies. Or them jugs. How do you live with that prosperity?

All she would say was she woke up each morning grateful for their companionship. Bobbi-Jean thought men were about the silliest dam' thing God had ever invented.

Not that she didn't want a prince charming. In fact, she was ever on the look-out for one. But long before she had heard about "female empowerment" she had had a profession that made her dependent on no one.

What she was was a golf hustler and had been since she was a teenager. She came from an extended family of pool and card sharks, and she could play those fair enough. But golf was her game.

She'd make up gambling games on the spur of the moment, give them names like Hully-gully, Alley Oop, and Stack o'lea. The bets would change with every stroke. Men would get so wrapped up in keeping track of the bets and doing the math they'd lose concentration on their game. Her hooters were a major distraction as well.

She had such a facility with numbers that her high school teacher got her a scholarship to the University of Georgia to major in math. Bobbi-Jean didn't see much point in all the little weird men with beards figuring out which way space was curved. She wanted out in a big world of flowing emerald fairways and water hazards.

And that's where she had been for the past few years.

With her looks she never lacked boyfriends and had no trouble getting tickets for sold-out sporting events. The rich ones made her right at home with soft-shelled crabs Grand Marnier soufflé.

B-J and Sparky had been headed for Roebuck Plantation just south of Charleston, South Carolina where the property developer and devastator Byron Jasper was ravishing the last untouched Sea Island. They had each worked for Byron previously and found it a good financial return on time spent. That was why B-J accepted the ride up from Mobile, Alabama where she had kept her permanent residence since dropping out of college. She liked to call herself the "touring pro" for the Chocktaw Bend Country Club.

The traffic was almost nonexistent on 280/431 past the Goat Rock Dam. In a few hours the sky would be coming up a purple-pink dawn. She'd stop for an egg over easy, grits and coffee in Macon, Georgia. Then go 16 to Savannah and 95 up to Charleston.

Byron had said Roebuck was a very high tone operation. They even had an investment banker working with them. B-J wasn't sure what an investment banker was, but he sounded a whole lot richer than ordinary bankers. She would have to check this one out very carefully. She hoped he wasn't some stuck-up jerk.

B-J had had her share of love affairs and disappointments, but generally she was so successful with men that she had no doubt she could nail down the ideal package she wanted. He'd have to be rich of course. Have a reasonably low golf handicap. Pinehurst had its place in her dreams. Kind of a nice cottage on a fairway with the dogwood and azalea blooming.

She liked to say 'Golf is like sex. You don't have to go on any old grail quest for the truth. It comes at you with every stroke.'

■ ■ ■

"You know what I hate?" said Chase Haulbase Jeffcoat. "I hate how big speculators suddenly get religion when they go bust. They author their own dire fates, and the next thing you know they've found Jesus. Born again like Jimmy Carter. Failed peanut farmer. Failed President. Failed do-gooder."

"I thought Jimmy found Jesus before he got started failing" said Bracey Jeffcoat.

Chase gave his wife a look in the dark. He didn't like being contradicted.

They were on their way to a dinner invitation. Chase was driving their BMW down lower King Street in Charleston to where it came out onto Whitepoint Gardens with a full moon throwing a trail of silver light onto the harbor. He'd park on the Battery to kill fifteen minutes, let a few other cars arrive and then drive around the park to the huge ante-bellum mansion on the East Battery. Bracey knew his habits by heart.

She was not looking forward to the evening. The Rantowles had just returned from safari in Botswana, and Hack would want to show off some vanishing species he had killed. His wife Sherry would spend the night adjusting her dress and patting her hair. She'd expect everyone to admire her William Ewan handcrafted silver with mulberry design. They'd eat okra and crab fitters. Chase would do his pitch. Bracey knew the spiel by heart.

"We need to understand what your goals are, what target we're shooting for. This is venture capital. The expectation is one dollar becomes five within your three years. This is so far beyond industry average, the average couldn't catch it riding a roman candle rocket."

Bracey would sit in a lonely silence and speculate on whether there was any man at the dining table she had the ability to steal away from his wife. She always came up with a negative.

"You'll have to accept me dominating the room tonight," said Chase. "I've got to close a deal with Hack. He's a fish on the line. I've been playing him long enough, and now I land him. He's old. I tell him he loves the action. It's his life blood. If he quits—if he lays down like an old dog—he dies."

"I'm sure that he'll adore that imagery," said Bracey drily.

Chase looked over at her. "Should I understand any better than Sigmund Freud? Isn't he the one who asked, 'what do women want?'"

Bracey shrugged and twisted the diamond on her finger. "Just to play some kind of role in her life. Mother. Helpmeet. Girl Friday. Dogsbody. Pretty much anything."

"I thought you did. You're the protocol expert on how to hobnob with South-of-Broad. Talk to Sherry Rantowles about *Martha Stewart Living* stuff. Creative ways to carve the Halloween pumpkin. Whatever. Go on in that vein. It's like some high society encryptogram code to me. Never a full sentence."

When Bracey was finished thinking about the men who weren't attracted to her, she'd brood on the loss of wetlands and vanishing wild bird species. Bracey was Audubon Society, Isaac Walton League, Sierra Club. A bird watcher. A tree-hugger. With a husband developing the last Sea Island on the coast. He had sworn to her the wetlands would be preserved, and they'd set aside thirty percent for wildlife habitat. It made good sense, he said. They were selling a natural setting.

She didn't know whether to believe him or not.

Chase parked the car against the sea wall as Bracey had expected, glanced at his Rolex, shut the engine. Through the tangled branches of huge dark oaks of the park, warm lights flickered from the windows of the row of mansions.

"I think over the next few years we'll see compensation ranges really widen among investment bankers. You'll find a real spread between serious and mediocre performers."

Bracey knew her husband was edgy. Not about his sales pitch. That was second nature. But the UVA business school had sent him a ten-year reunion notice. He was concerned with how he stacked up against his peers.

Chase looked at his watch again. "Is that the Pinckneys driving up over there?"

"No" said Bracey. "They have a Jaguar."

He settled back in his seat. "I think we need to transition out of Labrador into Jack Russell."

Bracey had figured this was coming. Chase was hyper-attuned to the dog-*du-jour* of the downtown set. It was his idea to buy the big black lab retriever he named Hector. Tied a bandana around its neck like all the in-crowd and wouldn't let her take it off. Dog never would answer to its name. Finally, one day, Bracey had yelled "Hey, imbecile!" and the thing had come running. To Chase's mortification, she had called it that ever since.

Brain-wise Chase was only so-so. If he had been born rich, he would have been put in the trust department of a bank where he couldn't do too much damage. As it was, he was born poor but athletic which was almost as good as rich in America.

High school all-star in football, basketball and baseball. This led to UVA and playing second and finally senior year first-string quarterback for the Cavaliers when injuries took better players out of action. Out of high school, the recruiting deal that was cut was that he could take the standard jock's straight-C-average into the prestigious Darden School of Business for his MBA without the usual two years of work experience. From there it was Wall Street although his class rank didn't justify it.

A fraternity brother who loved to hang with football studs had a legitimate berth at Lehman Brothers. Chase became a bond trader although not an orthodox one. In his third year he created a string of losses that threatened to grow into a black hole that would swallow the entire firm. Despite the hush-hush nature of his departure, rumors leaked, and Bracey heard.

"If you don't step up to the plate you don't get a hit," was all Chase would say.

The departure from New York coincided with Bracey's 21st birthday and her coming into the corpus of a trust fund from her grandfather. Chase got an investment banking license and used Bracey's money to set up Chase & Co. in the premises of a former real estate agency on Broad

Street. It was appropriate because about all he was doing was real estate limited partnerships.

"I'm like a patron saint to these people," he would say. "I capture the mood of the times."

In Charleston, there was only token resistance to his blandishments as he began making the rounds to everyone with over a million dollars in assets. Now in every drawing room South-of-Broad, you heard men solemnly saying, "I've learned to rely very heavily on Chase Jeffcoat's judgment."

Chase looked at his watch. "Thursday I'll have to take the 'Red Eye' to New York. Charleston has always had lousy air connections. Routing through Atlanta for anywhere else."

From day one of the marriage, Chase had been busy distracting himself from his Orangeburg hick town heritage, trying to act like he had always lived in Charleston. Out of New York, he had quit talking macho, quit saying things like money was just a way of keeping score. Now he was genteel and low-key.

Chase was clutch-your-heart, drop dead handsome, there was no question of that, while Bracey was pretty plain with an increasingly pear-shaped rear end. Her fantasy since adolescence had been a Cary Grant type man taking off her glasses, shaking out her hair and saying she looked really beautiful.

Bracey had met Chase because of a "Rides Needed" notice on a bulletin board in college at Thanksgiving of her freshman year. They were both South Carolinians and going in the same direction. She owned a Buick Roadmaster station wagon, and Orangeburg was on the Interstate before

Charleston. He hitched over to Sweet Briar from Charlottes-ville and rode the six hours down with her, talking to her intimately the way no man ever had, being super intrigued with her family. She was homely little Bracey Fanseau with a trust fund and a big house on Legendre Street, but no man had ever looked at her twice. When she pulled over in front of his parents' little brick box house, he planted a kiss on her so deep and passionate she thought she would hyperventi-late on the rest of the drive home. Twice she pulled off the road to get control over her trembling.

In Virginia, he came to see her several times a week after that and by Easter they were engaged. At first, she was so dazzled, she didn't think about why UVA football/business school stud needed to date an eighteen-year-old at Sweet Briar. It didn't really dawn on her that something was wrong until well into marriage.

During an attack of pre-marriage jitters, she confided to her mother she was worried about how Chase carried his own little jar of honey when he ate his breakfast in a restaurant. And an espresso machine on car trips.

"He's overcompensating, dear," said Isabelle archly. Bracey's widowed mother was arch on most topics. "That Orangeburg background. At least there is a comfortable six-year age difference. You won't have to put up with that ghastly premature ejaculation stage the way I did with your late father."

Bracey was mortified by her mother's frankness. What Bracey was trying to say was Chase was so certain that everything he did was right. He never discussed his motives or told her anything of his inner thoughts. He dictated the way things would be. Always with that slightly smiling handsome face. But what he said went.

Chase was saying, "I figure in ten years to sell the bank, retire on my capital. Maybe we'll go live in the Virgin Islands."

"I think it's time to end our marriage," said Bracey, trying to put some force into her voice.

"A lot of Wall Streeters do that. Start out with a vacation home and wonder why they spend time in New York at all. Move down there permanently. It's no problem to keep up with the market electronically. Shift your assets around at will."

"Did you hear what I said? I'm getting a divorce."

"No you're not."

2

For Tamzie Jerome, the easy part of coming into three million dollars was when you rush out and buy a new car which for her meant a Saab 900 hatchback sedan with a turbocharged engine and anti-lock brakes. Right after that you're all a sudden amazed at how every salesman in three states wants to share in your good fortune. Then you got charities, con-artists, relatives never-before-met, friends, neighbors and strangers on the street all with their hands out.

Tamzie had spent her life up to now as a maid for rich white people South-of-Broad, but finding a slave ancestor's diary had translated into millions from the Getty Museum in California. At age 28, almost 29, doing windows was a thing in the past.

Tamzie had been reading about using laughter to fight cancer. She had just about decided the whole situation was funny when the Bogard Street AME Evangelist church delegation showed up—the Right Reverend Otis Peebles and his three lady Bishops Albertha, Jewel and Mamie Kate. They took their time settling into chairs. Time was what they always had plenty of.

"We here to aim some shame," said Bishop Albertha.

"Focus on the positive," said Bishop Jewel.

"Community commitment ain't no sin," said Bishop Mamie Kate.

"Amen to that," said the Right Reverend.

They sat rocking and nodding. Prepared to mire themselves in protracted negotiations. Wear her down.

The Right Reverend Peebles said, "The ballgame of life is often one of swings and misses. But lemme ask you. How do you spell 'participate'? How do you say 'yes' to the Lord's work?"

Tamzie said there were right answers to both those questions, but just at the moment she was paramountly concerned with getting her windfall invested wisely to produce a steady stream of income. Then she could budget her tithing to the church.

State Senator Collier Ralston, the son of her former employer, was urging her money to Seagrass Savings & Loan, an up-and-coming thrift in Charleston. She didn't trust that sorry son-of-a-bitch. The man had nearly go to prison for bribery. She was leaving it with Merrill Lynch.

But so far it wasn't producing any big change of lifestyle. Buying nice clothes ate up most of the little she got. So Tamzie still lived in her little shotgun house on Cannon Street, still ate collards and cowpeas most meals.

Peebles rocked and nodded. He said, "We are here to give you useful information on church projects which would welcome your generous financing. Differences are inevitable as we unveil our economic proposals. But rest assured they have been subjected to screening and early follow-up review."

The church needed a new roof. That headed the list of economic needs.

Tamzie said to come down the scale a bit.

Peebles proposed new robes for the Positive Person Choir.

Tamzie said lower yet.

Peebles said, "Finance our letter-writing campaign against rap music and trash-talk TV. The growing trend of neon-lit Joe Camel billboards that serve up such controversy in the organized society."

Tamzie said how much? He said five thousand dollars.

She said, "You know the expression 'Just say no?' Well, get familiar with it."

Reverend Peebles rocked a bit more and rolled his jaw. He dwelt at length on a certain new Saab beside the house and how it was a profligate waste next to salvation, and didn't Volvo offer airbags and a $250,000 accidental loss of life insurance policy with their car?

Tamzie said she recalled a brand-new Lincoln Towncar the Right Reverend acquired with church funds.

Peebles said he knew he drew flak from some quarters, but he believed in buying American.

Tamzie said she didn't think that was the thrust of the criticism.

Peebles said he saw it as a wise investment in efficiency and saving time. His extensive missionary travel had been blasted in the past and his position was well known. He would, however, allow his spokeswoman Bishop Albertha to address the issue.

Albertha rocked and took a long time to get started. Tamzie looked at her Timex watch.

Albertha said she wanted to downplay this split of

opinion, but she saw the issue as not one of luxury auto-mobiles, but a horse race. And other congregations were widening their financial lead over the Bogart Street AME Evangelist. She said, "When the church asks for the life-blood of Jesus—everyday it hears 'Not today.'"

Peebles could never stay quiet for long. He said "I see cruelty and indifference in your calm demeanor, Sister Tamzie. And this at a time when our nation's spiritual leaders decry cruelty here in societal history."

The phone rang and Tamzie got up to answer it. Reverend Peebles' voice rose to follow her.

"I would like express my displeasure with your lacking change of heart. Here the Lord is hinting at a pardon for your transgressions. And I am a personal petition begging reconsideration."

Tamzie said hello to the phone.

"Hard-won and priceless salvation is reaching out for you," Peebles was saying in his loud preaching voice.

Tamzie put a hand over the free ear to block the noise.

A phone voice said, "I want you to fulfill the promise of your life." It was a black man's voice, but it had that ring of 'deal too-good-to-be-true' about it.

"I can sense the oblivion of damnation, sister," Peebles chided. Shouting, "Hellfire is always an option!"

"I ain't buying nothing," Tamzie said on the phone.

"We would like you to serve on the Board of Directors of the Seagrass Savings & Loan."

"What's that gonna cost me?"

"Your director's fee would be $25,000 a year."

"You living in the Twilight Zone you think I'd pay you that to sit on some old board."

"No no. You don't understand. Seagrass would pay you."

Tamzie said, "Now you talking."

■ ■ ■

"I'm only competitive with myself," pronounced Isabelle Fanseau. She was called Izzie by her friends and Icky by her enemies. The latter were the more numerous.

Bracey said, "What?" to her mother.

Izzie said "So don't begin with something you picked up out of a psychology book about mothers and daughters being at permanent draggers drawn. We've gone nearly a whole day without an argument."

Bracey wondered how her formidable mother had added mind reading to her list of things she was certain she knew all about. Izzie had been a great beauty in her youth, still was a handsome woman as they said. But she married a short man and produced Bracey who ended up with the worst features of both of them. When Bracey was little, her maternal grandfather made a pointed remark about "runtin' out your stock" that she had never forgotten. Which had made her overwhelmingly grateful for tall and handsome Chase Jeffcoat whom she now could barely tolerate.

The three of them lived in a big, historic house on Legendre, the street of big, historic houses that ran straight down to the Battery with its flash of blue harbor. It had thirty rooms, swagged curtains, and wall sconces, regency furniture. Also, Izzie's pack of twenty yelping corgis.

When Bracey and Chase left New York, Izzie had lured them into living with her, swearing devoutly that she would move out to a small house within a year and give them the big one. Four years had passed, and there was no sign of her budging.

Their overworked colored maid finished a long day of her once-a-week cleaning in a house that needed a full-time staff of five. Izzie was prowling through the rooms repositioning every little thing to exactly where it belonged. She was fond of saying, when they want to steal, they first start moving things around.

The Rantowles party had been as ghastly as Bracey had feared. The golf development Chase was putting together on Roebuck island had them drooling. Chase, the master investment banker, had crafted the deal by marrying an experienced developer—Byron Jasper—with Seagrass Savings & Loan which had a direct pipeline to as much New York mortgage market cash as required.

What he needed was bridge money between the Seagrass construction loan and the permanent mortgage financing as each extremely upscale homeowner built his three-million-dollar dream home. Smart money could double itself in under six months. He was just offering this fantastic opportunity to Charlestonians he knew and trusted.

After dinner when men and women separated in antique custom, Chase had shown the men projections of the number of annually retiring Fortune 500 CEOs. Each of them needed to sell a lavish house in Connecticut or Chicago's north shore and get the money into a house of equivalent value down South to avoid paying capital gains.

It wasn't that paying a little tax would have hurt them all that much. What was really at work was the northern real estate prices had gone up so drastically that you could build a house four to five times as large in South Carolina for the same money. And having flabbergasting square footage did their egos no end of good. Particularly when the man was having to step down from all the power and perks and helicopters and 24-hour limos that had been his whole life.

The Rantowles and all the other guests nodded like Pavlovian dogs. They liked feeling superior to Yankees who made $15 million a year.

When they got home from the Rantowles and were getting in the big four-poster bed, Bracey had told Chase that he couldn't prevent her from divorcing him. It was the time when men despise argument. All that having to stay up tense and bickering and then use sex to stifle the whole thing. But Chase was utterly unruffled. He said he thought Sherry Rantowles serving fruitcake stuffed pork loin was a bit *outré* even for Southern cuisine. Bracey said don't try to change the subject.

"Right," he said calmly. "And then what will you do? You've never been traffic-stopping beautiful. You and your big house all redolent of wealth. You think you've got some authority of history on your side. Like you're entitled to everything. Can spend your life indifferent to what I do all day. Contemptuous indifference. How did you even select me? Was there some vetting procedure?"

After he had said all that nastiness, he just waited with his calm expression.

"The afterglow of love is certainly a delight," said Bracey.

She rolled over and lay with her back to him. Seething. Wanting to pick up something and hit him with it. When she finally drifted off, he was still awake with the light on reading spreadsheets.

Now, the scene was still vivid as she sat watching her mother tidy the room and complain about the servant problem. Izzie's clothes typically were of the deepest greens and the darkest blues. She was in green today with little Gucci pumps with snaffle-bits.

"Chase is being uglier than usual," Bracey said. "He said you and I both think the world's some big mirror held up for us to admire ourselves in."

"I'm sure he didn't mean that about me. Chase and I get along famously. He's the son-in-law I'd always dreamed of."

Bracey bit her tongue. How many times would it take for her to learn to never seek her mother's alliance. The woman always turned on her. When she was a kid it would fill her with such rage and despair, she'd slam every door in the house and scream she was going to kill herself.

She said, "Okay, we had a major fight. He was ugly. One more of his multitudinous acts of ass-holerey."

Izzie said she couldn't pretend to understand Bracey's idiom. She presumed her daughter learned to talk with that vile mouth in New York. It certainly wasn't part of the curriculum at Ashley Hall.

Bracey said how could she put it? Marital grid-lock? They hadn't had sex for nearly a year. There. It had come spilling out. And she didn't feel overwhelmed with embarrassment the way she normally did.

Izzie said, "Well, you read in Ann Landers that many men prefer cuddling to actually 'doing it'."

Bracey said she thought it was the other way around.

Izzie said she wouldn't know herself. She never gave such things much thought. She and her late husband were both intoxicated when Bracey was conceived.

Bracey said, "I'm down to the worst case scenario. I'm going to divorce him."

Izzie gave her a look. "No you're not."

3

"We talking million-square-foot distribution facility," said Grady Troxler. "Initial investment of, oh, mebbe $70 million with a ass-load more to follow."

Lunch in the director's room was fricassee of red-clawed crayfish with tarragon and a French wine called *Nuit de* something. Looking back, Tamzie Jerome would always remember the slippery slope that got her mixed up with Seagrass Saving & Loan.

When Tamzie had found her ancestor's diary—a slave freed before the Civil War—that she sold to the Getty Museum for three million dollars, life as a maid for white folks was history. However, making the transition from low-life to high-life was anything but easy. Friends weren't friends anymore, and hundreds of strangers had their hands out.

Unlisting her phone number didn't seem to stop the sales calls, so she finally ripped the cord out of the wall. All her neighbors on Cannon Street trying to borrow and steal made her flat-out hostile to the poor and fearful of losing her good fortune.

Merrill Lynch had her money in "mixed growth and income" stocks, but there wasn't much growth and mighty little income. She was starting to get grateful that the son of her former employer kept asking to steer her money to the newly formed Seagrass Savings & Loan which had the backing of all the smart money in town. He said, "The style here is nothing radical—we refine old-fashioned ideas."

They wanted to get her funds in a 90-day C.D. where it would "work for her." Grady Troxler, the Seagrass President, said their investment approach was both innovative and conscientious. Mostly, Tamzie was amazed at how little income three million dollars brought in. Which was why she was only too glad to join the bank's Board of Directors and get the $25,000 a year in director's pay which Vineyard Dupree described as kind of a voucher for some private fun.

She did ask why they wanted her.

Vineyard, the Seagrass attorney said, "You ain't brain dead is the way I see it."

Vineyard was a real good-looking black man dressed in dark suits with vests and wine-red neckties. He talked law-school educated, but he was always gazing at her with hooded eyes contemplating carnal acts in a darkened bedroom. She liked being a sex-object as well as rich and powerful.

"I don't trade on victim-status no more," said Tamzie.

She asked what her job was. He said largely to be a cheerleader for the area economy. Go to groundbreakings for new industry, ribbon-cuttings and corporate meetings.

She said she thought directors were responsible for overseeing the working of the bank. He said you don't try to dominate the process. But you won't be marginalized. You'll be more than allowed to reinvigorate debate.

Mostly the board meetings seemed like a bunch of

loud-mouth white men shooting the shit. Today was no exception.

The big property developer Byron Jasper said he was through being a prisoner of the nay-sayers. He was personally tired of personal attacks on the land industry, making it out to be evil incarnate when it espoused such an articulate commitment to growing the local economy. It was sweet justice that the partnership of local business leaders and everyday workers was sharing in the prosperity. He was personally motivated by the wallet in his back pocket and saw nothing wrong with that approach.

The chairman of the board, state Senator Collier Ralston, who had nearly gone to jail on bribery charges, congratulated Tamzie on assimilating the win-win attitude of Seagrass S & L. He said she had been waiting in the wings for too long, and now it was time for her to sample the champagne of life.

This made her uncomfortable because in her previous existence, she had cleaned house for his momma old lady Ralston who was a rich old drunk with a big mansion on Legendre Street. The Senator's best buddy was Chase Jeffcoat, the investment banker who steered the best deals to Seagrass so they could lend money to them. Both these men kept telling Tamzie that Seagrass was the "upper-end" place to "grow" your assets.

When they got down to business, Seagrass President Grady Troxler started out saying, "The prime thing about this Board is we're all family." Then he said the thrift's progress had been all uphill, but they had turned a corner and there was light at the end of the tunnel. He talked about cash-flow carry-throughs and amortization schedules and other stuff Tamzie knew nothing about. She'd kind of cut her eyes at Vineyard Dupree in his fancy tailored Italian suits and think damn he was one handsome man. He didn't have any trouble giving her a look back and holding it for way too long.

Troxler said the mood of the day was jubilant. The bank's third quarter earnings were $1.3 million, up 17 percent from the year before. This beneficial event culminated from a 25 percent spike in loans and an extremely low volume of past due loans at 2 percent of assets. In this most recent quarter, assets rose 18 percent to $450 million while deposits grew 15 percent to $375 million. Regulatory approval was well underway to open a second branch in Eutawville. He said he could sum up by saying they were getting the job done. He felt good about all this. Upbeat.

Tamzie was looking at Chase Jeffcoat, the investment banker. He looked like a male model in Vogue or Bazaar. This interracial dating thing was catching on nationwide. You could see it not just on the street but in the Calvin Klein ads. Tamzie was thinking of pictures of Robin Givens on Donald Trump's yacht. Hanging out with investment bankers and Charleston old money and new money, she was moving in just such elevated circles.

Byron Jasper said all this jump-starting the economy was never more apparent than leading indicators of new housing starts at Roebuck Plantation. As the nation's population moved to hug the coastline, planned developments like Roebuck mirrored the overall economy. Byron wasn't on the board, but he seemed to be at all the meetings. Roebuck was financed by Seagrass.

He gave a report on his project saying there had been some impediments, but the back nine of the golf course was intact and ready for play. The whole thing was revived with some real courage and a quick infusion of about four million bucks raised from limited partnerships. The Seagrass loans were safer than ever.

Some other white man said it was a jungle out there, and even though he was bullish on the local economy, you couldn't never relax your vigilance.

Troxler said we're playing to win. We've got both a ground and an air game. We need it and we want it bad. He was proud of a real outstanding show of character on the part of the staff over the past quarter.

Vineyard Dupree said that's the understatement of the year. This banking talent team was all your consummate professionals. He had never seen such determined team effort. Everyone did their homework. Troxler had put together the optimal mix of veterans to give you a core of talent and newcomers committed to winning. None of them would stop short of the mountaintop.

Suddenly all of them were looking at Tamzie so she said she guessed her feelings were the same. She took a quick peek at her new black Ferragamos to reassure herself she looked good.

Further discussion moved to a vote on hiring two people she had never heard of named Sparky Truluck and Bobbi-Jean Kincaid as "equal access agents" of both Seagrass and Roebuck Development. Byron Jasper said Sparky had been useful in the past doing a variety of chores. The employment contract was voted on by unanimous voice vote.

On the way out of the board room, Byron said to Chase

Jeffcoat, "I mean we talking hooters on that gal." He cupped his hands in front of his chest. "Look like they done been hooked up to a air hose."

Outside in the parking lot, Tamzie couldn't help but notice that Vineyard's red BMW was parked right next to her Saab, and he was idling around waiting to accidentally run into her. He didn't waste any time making a move.

"You a visual poem, sweet-heart," he said.

She said wasn't that a wedding band she saw on his finger? He said he and his wife Shereese were split up planning a divorce, and in the meantime, they had an arrangement. It was called what she didn't know wouldn't hurt her.

Tamzie said, "Let's go back to that poetry motif."

■ ■ ■

"Are you in some day-late-and-dollar-short contest?" Byron Jasper sounded real put out over the phone. He had wired Sparky Truluck money for a plane ticket to Charleston, but the jist of the situation didn't make him happy.

Sparky had trouble hearing with all the noise in the Atlanta airport concourse and the ringing he had in his ears since his head had connected with a golf club. He wore shades against the bright light.

He said, "It's funny how set I am in my ways. I like to get through sometimes a whole week with no life-threatening surprises. Then I give your big hooter pal a ride. Bitch talking high stakes gambling like she was Jimmy the Greek. Up and cold cocks the shit out of me. When I finally locate her, she's gone need a safety net like the federal government has never even dreamed of."

Byron said he always liked an eloquent argument but to lay off on B-J. He'd talk to her, recommend a behavior improvement. And he'd try to round up the missing Firebird.

Sparky was right royally pissed at being smacked upside the head with a golf club and losing his Firebird to boot. It was also something of a wake-up call. Reminding him that there were sharp edges in his world no matter what his score card with women.

He said, "That's okay for now 'cause this is business and I recognize I'm in a business landscape. But you make it clear to her that my personal hatred has both a past and a future."

Byron said they needed him to get busy working with some folks who were reluctant to sell their property. "If they don't see it our way then we use you for some community renewal. Get in there and psychologically liberate them from their damn ol' fixed prejudices."

Sparky said, "When it comes down to mean-spirited behavior, I'm your boy. I had me an abusive stepfather. Got me morally disconnected from the main-stream and well on the road to a life-time of trouble and bad deeds."

Byron said from past experience he knew Sparky could claim that mantle. He was a real original Peck's bad boy.

"I defy stereotypes all right," said Sparky.

"Myself, I'm predisposed to gastric problems," said Byron. "So let's keep the overt violence more on the convert side of things. What I don't know won't hurt me."

Sparky said just have a ride waiting for him. Then he hung up without saying good-bye, the same way big deal corporate execs did.

Over in 14-G, a good-looking blonde was sitting in the row of seats facing a wall and working a laptop computer. Business traveler type gal in a suit. Sparky flopped down on the floor right at her feet, crossed his cowboy boots at the ankles, sat with his back against the wall.

"You ever hear that song *Midnight Rider*?" he asked. The girl glanced at him and then clamped her eyes back down on the computer screen.

"Got me one last silver dollar. You know the words. Had Robert Redford in the movie. Some folks say I look like him. What do you think?"

She didn't take the bait on that one. Just kept typing real fast. Probably faking it.

Sparky reached in his jeans pocket and pulled out a silver dollar. Held it out between his thumb and forefinger. "Well, that's me. I'm the Midnight Rider. And this here's my bottom dollar. Always keep one in reserve."

The girl gave it a quick glance.

"When I get to my air destination, I got to get my car out of long-term parking. I figure this dollar cause it's a silver one is worth maybe seventeen-eighteen bucks. I can negotiate with the gal what runs the little booth. Or somebody picking up their luggage who forgot a present for his kid. Problem is I figure it'll take at least twenty to shake my car loose."

The blonde opened her purse and got out four dollars, thrust it to him still without looking up.

"That's great. Thank you kindly. I'm gone be in Charleston awhile. You see some crazy dude driving around wearing shades you know that's me. The Midnight Rider."

She kept typing.

"You need, say, some automotive repair done right, then you look me up. Or maybe golf lessons. I'm gone be working out at Roebuck Plantation. Landed me an executive position. I'm doing business travel right now, and that's a fact. I tell you what, the telephone sure do beat the hell out of this airplane business."

"Fuck off, will you?" she said sharply.

"Shore. Shore thing." Sparky got up and walked down the concourse, bought himself a four-dollar Miller beer in a tall paper cup. Thinking he should have asked for more money. Get some fries with ketchup.

4

"There's NOT always two sides to every issue," said Isabella Fanseau, Bracey's mother, waving her left hand with all the diamonds on it.

They had just been to the bank trust officer who claimed their income was dropping because the stock market was bad. He went over the same thing three or four times, Izzie had been willfully obtuse. As though acting dense and impatient would make him come up with more money.

The trust officer hesitantly suggested ways of economizing. Food and vet bills for twenty corgis were very high. Izzie didn't take the hint. She said her newest dog Bitsy had a harelip and needed surgery.

He said the city's new assessment on South-of-Broad property had put the tax bills through the roof. Perhaps a smaller house on James Island. Izzie raised an eyebrow contemptuously. She said she considered the house a trust for her daughter. She was going to deliver it intact. It was the Fanseau heritage.

Living with her mother in the big mansion on Legendre Street was not easy on Bracey. Sure, there was plenty of space as Izzie had insisted, and sure the house would be hers one day, but life was awfully stifling.

The officer said she couldn't continue her present lifestyle without dipping into capital. Izzie said then by all means do that. If it was so simple, why was he wasting their time?

He said at 59 she was still a young woman. She couldn't reduce her capital and expect her money to see her out.

Izzie said he would just have to arrange things. That was why she was paying him. She swept out of the office with Bracey trailing behind.

Izzie had been to a wedding on Hilton Head Island the day before. Ever since, she had obsessed on the cost of the wedding—a minimum of $50,000—and where the mother of the bride got her face-lift. She used words like "cockamamie" and "beyond the pale" to describe the wedding, "ghastly" and "all too evident," the face-lift. Bracey could tell her mother wanted a face-lift very badly. It was that time of life for her, and Izzie felt her social status simply entitled her to certain things.

Izzie led her daughter into "Got Lotta' Rocks" on King Street. It was a tacky name for a jewelry store, and it was run by . . . well, Jews. Or Jewish people as everyone said now to try to show sensitivity. Izzie never shopped there because of the tacky name and because the owner talked in a "whataya whataya" voice. Worse, his name was Isador called Izzie for short. Bracey's mother took it as a personal affront.

"Well, I know what I'm going to do," she said. "I'm going to buy myself a little present."

Bracey reminded her mother of what the trust officer had said.

"He's just exaggerating," Izzie insisted. "They all do."

Bracey watched in horror as her mother perused the trays of diamonds while a clerk hovered unctuously. Izzie said Bracey had best learn to evaluate jewelry or she would never make informed purchases.

Bracey rolled her eyes. She had been taught to parrot the four Cs of diamonds—clarity, color, cut and carat—when she was six years old. She had no interest in jewelry.

Izzie said she never bought a diamond that was less than VS in clarity. Then moved on down the counter. Bracey's relief was short-lived as Izzie picked out two citrine bracelets. Citrine is a semiprecious yellow stone. It's created by heating yellow quartz. They were $1,200 each. She told the clerk to send the bill to the bank trust department. There was a nice man there who handled all her major expenses.

Bracey thought she would choke. "You can't afford $2,400 for a pair of bracelets."

"Of course I can't," Izzie said breezily. "It'll just make him work harder."

She bought Bracey a gold-leaf pin with a fresh-water pearl in the middle. She said she didn't want her daughter to feel left out. She said Bracey always sulked when she felt slighted in the least way.

Bracey swallowed the insult as she always did.

Out on the sidewalk Izzie seemed like a woman with a purpose. She announced that everything was going to be straightened out anyway. She had decided to take an interest in old Blake Huston. He had a great deal of very valuable real estate. She was thinking of stealing him away from his present company. He had far too much money to waste it on whatever he was wasting it on. He needed to be taken in hand.

"It seems a shame to let it all be squandered," she said. "The man's practically ga-ga and could fall into the clutches of unscrupulous people. Or maybe escheat all that land to the state when he dies. Or let it go to that . . . *extremely illegitimate* Rannie Ralston."

Bracey couldn't figure how someone could be extremely illegitimate. It seemed like you either were or you weren't. And everyone in town knew that Blake Huston had fathered Rannie when her mother—Mary Canty Ralston—was married to someone else. Blake was a notorious blackmailer by trade, now crippled but still mean as a snake.

Father and daughter had reconciled to the extent that he now lived with Rannie's mother right down Legendre Street. They saw him being wheeled out for his daily airing by the maid. Mary Canty and Blake were not married. He was not going to hand over his wealth that easily.

She asked just exactly what it was that Blake Huston owned.

"I've told you," said Izzie. "A great deal of real estate. I have it on the best of authority. And however coarse it sounds from the mouth of a realtor, they're not making any more of that stuff. There's a profound truth there."

Bracey said where was the real estate? Izzie waved her hand vaguely towards the south of town. The citrine bracelets clacked.

"I can't see any reason on earth why Rannie should have it," said Izzie. "She earns a gracious plenty practicing law. She must allow us our more traditional means of seeking out security."

"Us?" said Bracey.

"You're exactly like me, dear. You just can't bring yourself to admit it."

Bracey cringed at the thought of a squabble with Rannie Ralston, probably the most feared lawyer in town. Rannie was rumored to have murdered a bail bondsman in a dispute over some buried drug money. Then there was that awful period of her smashing her car into other motorists who irritated her. And her litigation was as creative as it was vicious.

Once on an airplane flight she had had to sit behind some poor loony who kept leaning over the seat jabbering at her. She sued the airline for intentional infliction of emotional distress and forced them to settle with her for $50,000. She claimed she had a phobic fear of flying, and the added stress had prostrated her for a month causing a loss of income.

Even the senior partners in the big firms—men with 50 hard-charging lawyers under them—got off the sidewalk when she walked by. She remained unmarried at 33. Although she had a sexual look about her in a flame red-hair way, there was an aura of the Gorgon Medusa. You almost expected her hair to turn into serpents.

"You can't just fleece that man of his property," Bracey protested.

"I'm going to marry him. There's a distinction."

Bracey knew for sure her mother was deranged. The wedding on Hilton Head, the high cost of a face-lift, it had all sent her around the bend. "The man is eighty years old," she protested. "He's had a stroke and sits all day paralyzed in a wheelchair."

"Yes," said Izzie. "He won't live long at all. I'm sure I can see to him in that regard."

■ ■ ■

"Well your continued hanging around here freeloading is at an end!" yelled Tamzie. She had been suppressing her fury for the past hour and now it just leap out of her.

The whole gang of neighbors went out in a huff leaving her alone with a eat-up 29th birthday cake and a tub of melted ice and empty Colt Malt Liquor cans floating in it. What had prompt their departure was her refusal to buy half-pints out the back door of her neighbor who would buy a case of them and then mark them up fifty percent for those who need a drink after sundown and don't get to drop by the liquor store in time.

Deewayne Mazyck from up the street stop down at the curb and yell back at her, "I'm gone have the IRS launch an inquiry of you. Report your ass for tax evasion!"

"I don't mind you doing that if you don't mind dying!" Tamzie yell back at him.

"Yeah I hear you," he say. "They gone be only too glad to see me coming with felony information. Un-huh."

Week before, Deewayne thinks he can just snow her blind. Comes on with how about we get a doctor to prescribe some mutual physical therapy with bed rest afterwards. She say, in your dreams. The fool wearing a jacket with NFL on it like he had even finish high school let alone play college and pro ball.

Tamzie look around at the mess they leave in utter disgust. She should have known hosting her own birthday was a mistake. If folks don't care enough to give you a surprise, then they're not worth having over.

The moment they all come through the door it was where's the steaks and Chivas Regal? Tamzie got plenty of money now and need to loosen up and entertain in high style. They ain't coming over for no cut-rate vittles. Nossir. Not them.

Oh sure, it was all funny and laughing around, but when it came clear she wasn't feeding them dinner they started getting downright shifty. The old ones saying their hypoglycemia level was up, and they couldn't just eat cake without a few meat courses beforehand. At least a Family Bucket of chicken. Others asking for updates on what exactly her monthly income was now Merrill-Lynching sending her checks. What were her underlying economics? Would she finance a loan they need in whole or in part? Help them make up some surprise shortfalls?

Despite their health handicaps, they get through the cake and beer easy enough, but then they want her to buy those half-pints to keep the party going. And it was the same old ding-dong refrain. Opportunity done knock at her door, not theirs. They got unexpected bills coming in. She need to implement a sharing policy. Spread that stuff around.

That was when she decide they were house guests who had done stayed too long and they could just get their asses out. If they thought she was a meal ticket they ain't too encumbered by brains.

Evil old woman next door selling marked-up liquor

without a license. She seemed to architect a strategy of snooping around whenever Tamzie came back to the house carrying a bag or package. Just invite herself in and flop down. Say how her back hurt and did Tamzie have anything strong to drink to ease the pain. If not, she could step next door and sell her some.

Tamzie looked around at her little biddy shotgun house with the water stained wallpaper. Her momma Mozelle had work herself to death to get them out of the Jackson Street projects and into a real house.

All Tamzie had known was a life of cast-off clothes and hanging her underwear on coat hangers over the tub because they never dream of a washer-dryer. When the money had come in, Tamzie had a lot of bright expectations of what she'd buy, how she'd live. She read ads with words like "sumptuous" and "quiet luxury" in them. But mostly she thought about romance. Find a real man who'd do everything right and in style. Rock-solid.

Tamzie's father had just been a man who came by drunk on Christmas wanting a free dinner or else when a girlfriend kicked him out. The only good memory she had of him was in first grade when the kids all went on a field trip on a big yellow bus. They stop at a light, and she look out the window. There was her daddy down in a hole digging for the water department. She yell at the other kids look at my daddy down there tearing up that street! Ain't he something!

He hear her and come over to the bus and give her two dollars for the trip. For that one little moment she thought she had the finest, best daddy in the whole world. The week after that he went to sleep drunk on the railroad tracks and a train come along.

Tamzie's momma kept her locked up at night over in the project. She'd say ain't no men gonna come around lick in your ear. Tamzie would lie in her bed at night and listen to the drunks and heroin addicts screaming outside, breaking bottles on the basketball asphalt. She'd dream about Michael Jackson and going with him to Monte Carlo to meet a European king and queen. Wear a dress with a long dark bodice and glide when she walked. She never got very far with that dream because when she was sixteen, along come Debone who marry her and eat up and plunder about ten years out of her life.

Debone had a slow hand, you could say that for him. He'd get her so worked up making love, when she went over the top you could measure it on one of those earthquake reader seismographs. Other than that, he didn't have much to recommend him as a husband and father. He was fond of beating her up as a way to settle any difference of opinion. Or try to pour draino down her throat. He lied, stole, cheated. He killed three men and went to prison for one of them. His idea of a job with a future was rising to chief enforcer for a dope dealer. Tamzie ended up scrubbing in the same big Legendre Street house her momma had work and die in. When Debone got shot to death, Tamzie took it calmly.

Tamzie found a somehow missed Colt Malt Liquor and sat down to savor it. It didn't take much effort to conjure up the image of Vineyard Dupree. It just kind of hung there in front of her. She stared at it like she was hypnotized.

The upside was worsted wool suits and Brut cologne and a red BMW. College degrees. An office with MacIntosh computers being typed on by foxy secretaries with six-inch nails.

The downside was he was married. Her momma Mozelle wouldn't have cared for that. Or Reverend Peebles. The Ten Commandments was right strict on that subject.

The face was swimming now. Going in and out of focus as though beckoning her.

A third of black men were in prison or on the street playing midnight basketball, drinking out of brown paper bags. That didn't leave very many to go around. A girl pretty much had to make her move on impulse. No letting well enough alone.

Other women never had any trouble stealing her husband Debone away from her until he was run out of money. Then they send him back. Tamzie could pay her own way. She wasn't after money.

"You best believe it," she said to the wallpaper.

5

The funny thing about Grady Troxler was Bobbi-Jean Kincaid had met men just like him before. He was actually a type.

It wasn't just the hairspray and the immaculate knife-edge creased suit. The weak chin. The way they always wore their suit jacket while working. The obsessive neatness of the objects on a mostly bare desk. The kind who collected stamps as kids and never got dirty on the playground. Or had an ant farm.

Sure, that was repulsive enough.

But there was a nastier characteristic lying there.

What they'd do was talk real low so you couldn't hear them until you moved in close. Then you'd find they were talking, flat, hard, mean and dirty. They'd be using words like twat and cunt and pussy while staring a hole through you. Whack-o psychotic was what it was.

A lot of insecure women would get so frightened they'd fall under their power like with a hypnotist or a dentist who's got your head down lower than your feet and moving in with that drill. Bobbi-Jean was not insecure. A 38-double-D bust had cured her of any problems in the self-esteem area way back when the growth spurt took off in 9th grade.

Grady's office occupied most of the second floor of what was nothing more than a typical dumpy Savings & Loan building. Although its only view was a mall parking lot, he called it the Skydeck and had it done up with fake marble floors and wood paneling.

Grady had her sit in a chair beside his desk. Not in front, but close to him.

She moved the chair further back. He was about as appetizing as a cup of microwave coffee with a cigarette butt floating in it.

He made a tent of his manicured fingertips and began his low mumble talking behind his hands all the while giving her the steel-eyed glare.

She twirled a bit of blond hair around her finger. Said, "I'm sorry, I guess I'm going deaf or something, but I just can't hear a word you're saying."

His eyebrows came closer together. He raised his growl a bit, but not much.

Bobbi-Jean looked around. The office was decorated in Clemson University purple and orange. She looked at a watercolor print of the football stadium with a sunrise behind it. Then she reacted like she suddenly realized Grady was saying something. Cupped a hand behind her ear. "Say what?" She sounded almost serene.

He got audible. "I don't dumb things down for cunt-fuck bimbos. You're shit-fucking late arriving in Charleston. You're shit-fucking late for your appointment. You're real far below expectations, you big tit, cock-sucking bitch. Your job—other than swinging those big tits in front of high-balance customers—is to be sweet and cuddly with key people. Does that mean put out? I didn't use those words. But I'm the 800-pound gorilla around here who does whatever the fuck he wants. And if you expect to be on the team you better pay some heavy fucking deference to that."

It all came out like gray gunmetal. Flat. No intonation.

Bobbi-Jean was nonchalant. "If you're going to use that trash mouth, I'll just get up and leave. I'm sure I can find a man who wants to be nice to me with no trouble at all."

His voice went up high, loud, and angry. "You sorry shit blow-job bitch, I got an emerging impulse to GET UP AND SLAP THE LIVING DOG SHIT . . ."

He caught himself and brought it down to a normal tone. The man was real tightly wound. And goodness, all those violent threats out of such a little runt.

"Now you don't mean that, Mister Grady Troxler. I know you don't. My understanding was I was the ladies' golf pro. Teach interlock, overlap grip. Stance and posture. Back-swing and follow through. Do you know anything about golf? You look kind of like out-of-bounds and balls in the water to me. Anyhow, I'm accustomed to what you call your substantial autonomy."

Grady sneered. "You cross me and I'll fucking strip you down to the bare essentials."

Bobbi-Jean acted like she hadn't heard. "By the way, what's the point spread on the Clemson-Carolina game?"

"How the fucking shit should I know or fucking shit care?" he spat.

That one actually floored her. She kept looking at all

the Clemson stuff, university seal and orange tiger paws everywhere. Lampshade. Armchair. Framed aerial views of the campus. Crewel-work picture of the oldest building.

Byron Jasper was coming into the bank. You could hear him booming at the tellers all the way upstairs into Grady's office.

"Hey there, sweet thang! How's my line of credit? Is the whole dam' world in a conspiracy to keep me in poverty?"

Bobbi-Jean left Grady snarling and went down to greet Byron. The man could be such a goof. One time at a baseball game she had sat there in the stands shelling peanuts and eating them. Bet him $500 she could throw a peanut past first base. She had glued ball bearings in one beforehand. He never did figure it out.

Byron had a lime green golf outfit and a face that looked like ruddy good health at a distance but up close was the culmination of a lifetime of heavy drinking. He did have that deep-burned golf course suntan and a flashing gold Rolex Oyster on his wrist.

"You sweet-britches honey dahlin'! You're mercifully heah! Lordy, transition is always a challenge, but now I got you standing there like some embodiment of lady luck."

She flashed her most endearing smile. Did her patented little trick of making her eyes all wide and elated. "Oh, Mister Byron Jasper!" she shrilled in a breathy way.

"That's my name! Don't wear it out" He spread his arms wide for a big hug. "Come here and let me squeeze up to that charisma on your chest."

She told him he was still one hell of a man and ooo-wee was she glad to see him. You could have filled a jam jar with that Southern honey accent. Then she submitted to a thorough hugging.

Byron went, "Oh sweet mercy! Give me some moral ratification for all my naughty thoughts. Them gazoonies are so big they must need underwire rigging in that bra." He looked all around at the bank tellers with a fat smile on his face. Just so pleased.

Bobbi-Jean knew why she was on the payroll. (One) She was a scratch golfer, and (Two) Byron Jasper wanted in her pants. There was no particular order to it, both just twisting around inside his head like coiled snakes. And the sex part just jumped on the brain of every man she met. Even cold-fish slime like Grady Troxler.

Foul-mouth she could work around. But there was something wrong there, she knew. Clemson produces your engineers. Chemical. Textile. Ceramic. Some architects. Even a few aggie boys still. And it's let in girls who do God-knows-what. But it's not known for bankers.

And there's not a Clemson grad alive who wouldn't know the spread on the Carolina game.

■ ■ ■

"I can't be involved with this," said Izzie Fanseau through the bathroom door. From the scratching noise Bracey figured she had at least three of the Corgis with her.

Bracey had a fever of 102 and couldn't seem to stay off the commode. In a way, it was a welcome exile. She said, "I'm not asking you to be involved, Mother."

Izzie didn't hear. "I simply cannot afford to be sick for

the next three weeks. I'm going to be very busy and every minute is crucial."

Bracey mumbled no one had asked her to be involved.

"If your father were alive, he would have absolutely nothing to do and could devote his idle time to nursing you. A male presence is vital in a house."

Bracey felt like death was the long-term prognosis. She wondered if it had been brought on by the news of Daniel Island in the upper end of the Charleston harbor that had remained simple farms and forest due to lack of a bridge. Now they had one.

"Preferred" volume builders had been selected. Small town charm they promised. Seven thousand residences were projected. A park was to be named Etiwan for a tribe of Native Americans who were comfortably no-longer existent. The city of Charleston called it the "newest tax source."

The first settlers will be like pioneers, the developers boasted. Despite all the fiber-optic phone and cable TV systems that seemed to be the first stage of any housing boom now.

It was inevitable as soon as the freeway passed over it. Can't stop progress, they droned. Water and sewage is the top priority they vowed, as though there were some unusual twist here.

Her husband Chase was in the same business. He was just working his destructive will south of town on the last Sea Island. Make every one of them into mini-versions of Hilton head. He had promised her the wetlands would be preserved, but she knew he was lying.

The EPA seemed to have strict rules, but all developers

knew you could fill in ten acres or less a year and nobody cared.

"I've been with Mary Canty Ralston," said Izzie. "She was boring me to death telling me about her Miles Brewton silver. I'm surprised somebody hasn't stolen it by now. All the Redcoats and Yankees that have plundered through this town. Not to mention those despicable little housebreakers we get nowadays with the melting furnaces right in their vans."

"You've been scouting Blake Huston, haven't you, Mother? Trying to figure how to get him free of their house long enough to work your designs."

"He's just an old sweetie. Nobody understands him the way I do."

Sweetie had never been applied to Blake Huston before. He came from Southern gentry broken by the Great Depression. Lacking an inheritance, he had taken an interest in history and dug up dirt on prominent families, made a successful career as a blackmailer. Vicious. Evil to the core. Pit viper. You heard those epithets more commonly.

Izzie said she thought Blake would be very happy in their home. She was sure he had plenty of personal objects he'd want to bring from his plantation, and she had no objection. That valuable manuscript collection of his. Antique furniture. He was virtually camping out at the Ralston's. No man of his background should be treated so poorly.

Bracey had seen a hundred domestic dramas like this. Old people who used their wealth as power right up to the deathbed. They were weak, and it was the only weapon they had. With her mother running loose, it was little wonder they felt insecure.

Izzie jerked open the bathroom door and five yelping corgis rushed in, moiling about, chasing their tails in the narrow space. One went right to the wastepaper basket, began trying to eat a pink plastic Bic safety razor.

"You're sulking as always. You shouldn't hate your mother. It's really the same thing as hating yourself. Here. I want you to have a present. Two citrine bracelets. Aren't they lovely? They're very valuable so be careful of them. It's $2,400 on your wrist. Now you get well soon. We have so much to arrange."

6

"She done sold my Firebird?" said Sparky. It shook him, and he was not a man easily rattled. "Here I had me a period of high mobility. Now I'm deeply curtailed."

He looked around at the near empty dining room of the Roebuck Island Club. Two acres of white tablecloths. Coon waiters in red jackets standing off at a distance. A couple little groups of realtors and clients talking golf scores.

Byron Jasper shook his head in wondrous memory. "That Bobbi-Jean, she sure got her some premium grade hooters. If I owned her, I'd register them under about six patents. Protect the design."

Sparky said, "I grant you they can sure concentrate the eye. Kept me distracted just enough to let her put a sand wedge in the base of my skull."

Byron agreed those knockers distilled the whole idea of sex down to its prime ingredients. Sparky said they were getting off the topic which was without his Firebird he was fucked up, down, and sideways. Was he supposed to rob a lemonade stand?

Byron said, "Hey, any miracle drug is going to carry along its unwanted side-effects as baggage. We need a little 'give' on both sides."

When the lunch special came, they both stared at it in wide wonder. Sparky had to get the menu back and read it close to figure out exactly what it was.

Mélange of tiny vegetables.
Goat cheese with herbal salad.
Stewed mushrooms with egg cracked over them.
Ragout of matchstick artichoke slices flavored with coriander.

He said many called him old fashioned, but he subscribed to the belief that if it ain't fried it ain't food. Byron agreed the meal wasn't exactly what you'd call cardiovascularly challenging. But this was the kind of image the club needed for the monied Yankee set. Sparky said later on he was going to go locate him a chicken box, take a feedbag voyage of nostalgia.

He pointed a fork at Byron. "My focus may seem a bit myopic, but I need me a set of wheels. In the worst way."

Byron dug into his meal. It tasted as bad as it looked. "This has been addressed and addressed. I got you a damn rental. Now don't confuse business with friendship. Eat your rabbit foot and shut up."

Sparky thought yeah, he'd shut up. Sharks are real quiet. They make no noise at all in the water.

Byron had moved on. Talking about Roebuck Island Plantation. He said, "I tell you, this has done moved my sorry-shit life from mess to miracle. It's the best I been in on. We got a crack sales force. Bringing in the buyers. They talk, Yankees don't understand shit, but that's okay. It soothes them. Gives you an air of control. Damn CEOs run billion-dollar companies. Can't fathom a regime fee contract."

Sparky looked around the near-empty room again. Looked at his watch. It was 12:30. Prime eating time. If turnout was critical, he reckoned sales were flatter than a pancake.

Byron brought up the name Grady Troxler, President of Seagrass S&L. the major finance vehicle for Roebuck. Said, "Tight asshole of a man. We can work in the same building but still have trouble communicating."

Sparky agreed first impressions marked him down a real shitheels. Kind of boy had a stamp collection when he was little. Or maybe an ant farm.

Byron said, "I got to explain over and over to the boy you can't just loot a Savings & Loan the way you could back in the 80's. The best-laid plans can shatter against a FSLIC wall."

Sparky grinned big, poured on the charm and humor. "That's a dam' shame," he said. "Growing up in this country you always had a sense that anything was possible. That the future was all go-go-go." He made a futile gesture. "And to find out here as I approach mid-life it's all hype."

Byron laughed big. "You got to have your quasi-legitimate investment. We get Roebuck Island pumped up, sell it to some sucker quick before the debt roof caves in. If we miss the timing, then the loans are just gone. Maybe Seagrass dies under an avalanche of bad debt. We all shrug, go 'who me?'"

Sparky thought sure, let Byron have his big-cheese status. He'd get beyond the short-term trauma. Move on to the fulcrum of his agenda.

Byron yelled across the near-empty room at a waiter.

"Ain't chall got a cheeseburger back there somewhere? A draft beer?"

The waiters didn't budge.

"Ain't they something?" said Byron. "Little pocket of them blue-gums over on Roebuck being moved off way too slow. Had to hire them so we could say we were making jobs in the area. We got us a tame nigra boy acting as lawyer for Seagrass. He ain't exactly a shining ornament in the brains category, but he sure puts a social face on the whole thing."

Sparky agreed. "Yeh, you got to be aware of the social dimension these days."

The two were real good buddies. For the short run.

■ ■ ■

Tamzie was sure tired of dating men who wore clothes with Oakland Raiders stamped on them. Dudes who carry handguns and end up doing fifteen years on manslaughter. So it was kind of natural to accidentally run into Vineyard Dupree who wore a suit every day and had a profession and all that went with it.

Vineyard was standing on Broad Street where all the lawyers have their offices talking to an actual white client, both of them wearing suits. Left that client and came right up to make small talk about Seagrass S & L and how pleased he was to have her on the Board. This led into him asking her to drop by his office at six when business had closed down and he'd take her for a drink.

What else he said during the invitation was he was going to personally work with Seagrass on improving her asset position. Get her out of that low-return mess with Merrill-Lynch. Tamzie was thinking on that later as she rode the elevator up to the 6th floor in the old People's Building, a big old 1905 bank building on Broad Street where so many lawyers seemed to roost.

Tamzie was on some millionaire's marketing list that must have been faxed all over the U.S. of A. White dude had call that afternoon from New York trying to sell her a half-timbered, thatched roof doghouse for $6,500. While she was putting together an impressive collection of clothes with designer labels, she knew too much of that ye olde doghouse shit and she'd be impoverished in a hurry.

At six o'clock, the secretary was gone, and Vineyard was sitting at her desk working on the word processor. He said come right in and didn't she look fine all dressed up. Just wondrous what a big infusion of money could buy.

Tamzie said her love affair with buying things had cooled off, but she couldn't resist the fur jacket. It wasn't classic fur because the mink got married with suede, silk and Swakara lamb.

He said it took guts to face the anti-fur activists.

She said there weren't any of those in Charleston, and anyhow *faux* furs were bad for the ecology. They were made out of petroleum by-products.

Vineyard said, as quick on the feet as she was, she ought to have been a lawyer. Or maybe a prize fighter the way women movie stars were taking up boxing now.

Tamzie smiled feeling coy. She was thinking how mockingbirds do a mating dance. Dodging back and forth being all cute.

Things were progressing real mellow when the over-size

black client dude barge in, and Vineyard said, shit why didn't he lock that door.

The client had big shoulders on him and fists the size to knock down a mule. Bib overalls and muddy work shoes. It was that little bit of blue thread tying off a twist of hair, keep off the haints, that said he was from down off the islands.

He didn't beat around the bush, straight off saying he'd come for his money and wasn't going to take more putting off shit.

Vineyard pull back his French cuffs, examine a slim wristwatch and said, "Right off hand I'd say your timing is not the best. I'm due to take a meeting with an assortment of local dignitaries. I'll have my secretary set you up an appointment."

In reply, the client take a hardball stance. "Look'a here. How 'bout I whup the shit outten yo' sorry lawyer ass?"

Vineyard looks him over kind of cool. Not flinching.

"Now ain't that something," he said. "You getting all inflamed by distortions. Let's just go ahead and get this over with before anything of bad consequence takes place that you might come to regret." He got out his big office checkbook. "I swear I give up too much, man."

The client said, "Un-huh."

Tamzie stood there uncomfortable while Vineyard wrote out a check to Omonio Reese for $15,000. The client signed a deed that said "Quit Claim" across the top and went out. Vineyard said don't walk off with my pen. It's special. The client gave it back to him.

Vineyard held it up for Tamzie to see. Say, "The Cross

Townsend writing instrument with the Art Deco design. Superior craftsmanship."

The client was going out again. "Don't try to cash that at no liquor store," Vineyard said to his back. "You got to take it to a real bank. On Monday morning when they open up. The one with the name on the check."

The elevator doors closed, and he was gone.

Vineyard locked the door this time. "Let's hope we got that episode of acrimony behind us."

He said clearing land titles on Roebuck Island was the hardest work of his career. What happened was black folks would die without wills and without being formally married or anything. That had been going on since just after the Civil War when they first start to own land. So you had hundreds of folks who had scattered to northern cities to seek out and buy off.

And they all expected to get rich. Saying will there be enough that I can invest some and spend some on a new car too?

Tamzie said what about the ones living on the land at current? Where do they go with only $15,000? She was right aware of finances since her three million wasn't producing any lavish Aretha Franklin lifestyle.

Vineyard said, "We all live in a world of uncertainty and fear. The trick is to manage the change."

As he led her back into his personal office, he said, "Currently I'm exploring strategic options with regards to your investment portfolio."

They both sat down. On the wall he had diplomas from Howard University and South Carolina School of Law. A photo of him as a young man looking like a Black Panther with leather jacket, mirror shades and a 'fro. Another one of him in madras Bermuda shorts standing next a big bill fish and a fishing boat. She guessed that was his new lawyer image. The fish was stuffed on the wall with that plastic look that stuffed fish always got.

"The very notion of an investment is being transformed. Static investments—buy and hold strategies—are an artifact. It's a no-promises climate."

He pulled the pint bottle of Old Harper and two glasses out of his desk drawer. "Let's toast the success of the initial stage of our long-term cooperation."

Tamzie clinked glasses with him wondering if this was his way to get out of paying bar prices for a drink out somewhere fancy.

Vineyard said, "What do you say to the Mills Hotel for dinner? A little 'Steak Diane.' A half-way decent red wine."

Tamzie thought about all the men with one cigarette behind an ear. Buying one beer in the store. No watch, asking you got the time to nervous white men on the street. She told herself she had been around the dudes with the fake Raider clothes for way too long. This man was a big-time attorney. Corporate lawyer working for an S & L None of that two-bit hang around the bail-bondsmen criminal stuff. A year ago, even with Civil Rights laws and everything, she would have never dared go in the Mills.

"Things are looking good," said Vineyard. "It's an end to that old Southern world of systemic discrimination. Folks like us got our financial futures just racing along like Kentucky Derby horses busting out of a starting gate."

Tamzie was thinking, man, you look as good as two sniffers of brandy in front of an open fire. How does your wife let you out of her sight? The woman got to be blind and brainless.

7

"At age 18 I ran off with a lady yodeler from a carnival," said Blake Huston.

His voice was slurred from the stroke and three stiff drinks of Maker's Mark. Bracey could barely understand what he was saying.

"Parents tracked me down, trussed me, and dragged me back to college. I was designated to do well and glorify the family. Or shore up its deteriorating fortunes really. The old man came with a horse whip, and I got a good exercise in alibi construction."

Blake clawed some bread into his mouth with his bad hand. As he chewed, half of it fell out. "She was a rare beauty. And could she ever yodel. What a posterior she had on her. Talk about a seat of power."

With Mary Canty Ralston wedged into the back bar at the Carolina Yacht Club doing her afternoon's drinking, it had been safe for Izzie Fanseau to launch her inaugural move in man stealing. She went down to No. 1 Legendre, intimidated the black maid, and wheeled Blake up to No. 15 for the traditional Charleston "dinner" which was a big mid-day meal served at 3 p.m., a time that dated to plantation days. Pork chops, apple sauce and potatoes.

Three green vegetables. Fresh biscuits. The old man ate like he was ravenous.

Bracey had advised extreme caution. Her mother answered she didn't want to hear a jumble of pious criticism. She had her life to lead and intended to be responsible for her own financial destiny. Bracey should learn to play a more constructive role.

Blake Huston seemed vague and disoriented. He drooled a lot out of the dead side of his face. He cackled at his stories. Talked without noticing any response Bracey or Izzie made. Laughed openly about blackmailing "Old lady" Huger in 1947 over "niggra blood" in her family tree. "A touch of the tar brush," he cackled. "That always scares the underpants off them. Gets them looking for that little kink to the hair. Too much purple in the fingernails."

"That's always a give-away," Izzie agreed.

"They go sprinting for the check book. Put some notation on the bottom 'for services rendered' or some such bull-feathers."

Bracey decided Blake was virtually deaf. She sat squirming at the unexpurgated history of his life, thinking the meal would last for an eternity.

Izzie was beautifully turned out in midnight blue. On her wrist, one of the citrine bracelets. She said Bracey wasn't wearing it and she had nothing herself—this from Izzie with a virtual bank vault of jewelry.

When her mother got up to fetch the dessert—an English trifle with extra-thick whipped cream and heavy lashing of sherry—Bracey followed her into the kitchen. She said she couldn't believe Izzie was actually carrying through with her marriage designs on Blake Huston.

Izzie said, "Constancy in a campaign is my strong suit."

Bracey warned her mother that provoking Rannie Ralston was a dangerous course of action. Izzie said nonsense. Rannie's brother was on the Board of Seagrass along with Chase. The Ralston's had a vested interest in the success of her marriage to Blake Huston.

Bracey pointed out there was no love lost between Rannie and her state senator brother. Rannie told everybody in town he was a brainless, spineless twit, and a disgrace to the legislature. And there was that awful incident of him being caught in the FBI sting naked in bed with a woman who was passing him a bribe. Rannie got him off on technicalities while telling everyone in town he was guilty as hell.

Then a bell went off in Bracey's head. "What do you mean vested interest?" she said.

Izzie explained to her real patiently that Blake Huston had a big plantation out Highway 17. More to the immediate point, he also owned 800 acres of prime land right smack in the middle of the planned golf course of Phase 2 of the Roebuck Island development. It would be a very nice use for the land. Not like that wasteland of tract housing the city had planned for Daniel Island.

Bracey had never seen a developer's map of Roebuck with Phase 2 marked on it. But the undeveloped end of the island was rich in marsh, a prime breeding area for birds. Chase had promised her the wetlands would be preserved.

She asked what the property was worth. Izzie said how should she know? Many million of dollars no doubt. Ask Chase. He knows all about it.

Bracey felt like the life was draining out of her. Her

mother and husband were in league in this berserk scheme. She fought to hold onto her temper.

She railed, "Instead of 'provoking' I should have said 'infuriating' Rannie Ralston. You'll receive more than just a letter and a phone call on this one."

Izzie said, "You're always striving for a near-hysterical atmosphere for things. I merely want to marry the man. Should a woman my age be denied every pleasure? Is poverty my legacy?"

Bracey said a less charitable description might be outright plundering of his property.

Izzie said marriage contracts had held that aspect since the dawn of time. Whatever the veneer of romance, they were primarily a business venture. That was undeniable. Even those with a very short shelf life.

Izzie intended for him to die in short order. That was part of the plan. For Bracey, it raised the specter of her mother actually doing something violent if all didn't go to schedule.

Izzie took the trifle into the dining room. Bracey sat for a long time alone in the kitchen mulling a course of action. None came to mind. She pushed open the swinging door to finish clearing the table.

The spectacle she saw was striking to say the least.

A dish of trifle was set untouched in front of Blake Huston. Her mother was standing leaning over him. She had her blouse open and one breast bare. Blake Huston was sucking on it. Izzie caught her daughter's shocked eye.

"Would you excuse us please, dear? This is a personal matter."

■ ■ ■

"Shore," said Byron Jasper. "I can set you up in one of them little fairway condos. Any one you want. But there are better offers out there on the banquet table of life." He stood holding the pin on the eighth green admiringly as Bobbi-Jean sank a fifteen-foot putt.

B-J was doing her usual dazzling self-possession routine while being hit on heavily by Byron Jasper the real estate developer. She wanted out of a motel and into one of the Roebuck condos, but she also wanted title to the real estate so she was being extra nice to Byron.

"You best believe it, sweetheart," he said. "I ain't just got great looks, but depth and sincerity as well. Lemme free-associate here a moment. Hefty bank account. Flashy car. Big square footage in a house back in Dallas. Do them kind of affiliations turn you on? Set off a detonation in that heart of yours?"

B-J smiled indulgently. "Can we have a drumroll here, please?"

B-J had no problem in the shrewd defense area. She'd just yack and let the conversation drift in odd directions, keep him off his point until he wanted to explode with frustration.

She said, "I had me a Dallas boyfriend once who had a real low golf handicap and enough oil in the ground to last to the trump of doom. Anyhow, he just went whole-hog on France. Once he gave me a box of prunes that had been drowned in Armagnac and stuffed with foie gras. You know what that is? It's like liquor and goose liver. I mean the French think we'll eat anything."

"You're cremating me, dahlin'. I gotta know if our relationship is gonna meander into you being my live-in."

B-J looked him over. Byron was not even approaching her idea of a romantic dream. At fifty-something he was getting those long hound-dog earlobes, the nose hair and spare tire of an old man. Her voice went innocent and tentative. "Why Mister Jasper, why would I do that?"

"Hey, even your ungifted lip-reader can catch my drift. I'd sure like to get into a gratifying relationship with those twin big lungs of yours. And it may not hurt to mention—and I swear to you it's the gospel truth—I am hung like a dam' cruise missile. And we're talking very limited refractory down-time for a man my age. Sweetheart, just you talk dirty in that sassy tone of yours—hang them Hall of Fame Hooters down in my face—and I'll perform like Godzilla going through Tokyo."

B-J gave him a smile like she was the central enigma in all of life's great female mystery. She had enough money that she didn't need to rush into anything. A car lot in North Charleston had been willing to pay $4,000 for Sparky's Firebird without a title document. That was adequate seed money. Entrepreneurs like to run each venture as a separate corporation so one bad deal wouldn't sour the others. B-J had taken a page from their book and never dipped into savings when she set off in a fresh direction.

Byron missed an easy two-foot putt. It rimmed the cup and just sat there staring at him. He snatched it up, said that was a gimmie anyhow.

Then he got impatient. "Sure, I got me an edge of immodesty. But a man unpublicized can't get his gameplan out there for examination. But sweetheart, I'm here to tell you you ain't giving me a trace of satisfaction."

B-J knew for sure she had herself a moron dangling from the bottom rim of the bell curve. She said, "You know sometimes when I get to dreaming about how things might be ideally, I think I'd like to just kind of drift back into the past. You know? When golf was more basic and didn't have little electric carts and designer clothes."

"Sure, sweet-thang. I got reverence for tradition and gravity and all that. I'm loyal as a dog to it."

"But you lived back in those times. I guess you know all about it."

Byron gaped at her. Then blustered on. "Sure, we got us a age differential. Why I can remember when *Deep Throat come* out. But there ain't no gulf that money won't bridge. Am I generous? Just ask my three ex-wives. Damn bottle-blondes ever one. They get positively jubilant when my name comes up."

B-J asked if he was proposing marriage. That threw him off his pace and he digressed into how his ex-mates had a fierce rivalry over his wallet that he didn't need Tammy-Jan to get prominently in the middle of. While she was his manifest destiny and everything, it was best to keep her a well-arranged secret for a bit.

As he did this, they walked over to the ninth tee, and B-J slapped a perfect shot that hit well and just rolled and rolled. Byron said wooo-eee hum-dinger! She was playing off the men's tee, and he'd give her a half-stroke a hole.

Byron bent down to tee up his ball.

B-J smiled with her little air of detached bemusement. "I don't need any courses in victim advocacy. You know what I think of marriage? It's what them Alabama D.A.s call L-WoP. Life without parole."

"Love-thang, that enlightened attitude of yours mitigates all guilt. We on the same cotton-picking wavelength. I want to *rendez-vous* with you forever."

"You don't happen to have $355 on you?"

"Say what?"

"I just need that particular amount in a real hurry."

"What for?"

"I got a car insurance payment."

He looked mystified. "You don't own a car."

She smiled sweetly. "I need one of them too."

Byron shanked his shot real bad off into the woods.

8

When the waiter brings over the *caipirinhas*—Brazilian drinks of sugarcane, rum and lime—Vineyard Dupree was saying, "You ever notice how in a book when there's a black domestic he's always dignified? As in a dignified black man waited on their table."

"What's it suppose to say?" said Tamzie. "*A coon darkie jig an' amble over with the watermelon cart?*"

They both laugh, enjoying themselves around 8 PM in the Tanganyika Club, a near ancient negro nightclub dating back to the Chittlin' Circuit in 1949. The walls got African shields and pictures of Red Foxx back when he was young and had done stand-up there. The new Brazilian cuisine and drinks was an update for contemporary sensibilities.

Tamzie had her hair dyed sort of a rusty red and done in long, tangled ringlets like Tyra Banks who everybody say she look like. She could tell Vineyard liked what he saw, the man checking out every inch of her body.

Tamzie and Vineyard had both grown up in Charleston and were sharing background history. He said despite the usual migration of black talent to Atlanta or D.C. he had chose to make his way as a home boy on home ground. All the lily-white corporations were bowing down to diversity and need him to lend an air of social responsibility by billing them big hourly rates. He called it a nutrient-enriched soil.

Tamzie said, "Sound like plain old bull-shit to me," and they both laugh, the drinks making them feel just fine.

In fact, they make her feel so good she agree to let him manage her money. He say he was honored and it awakened a new dimension within himself.

He said first off she need to get out of the old neighborhood and into a suitable dwelling unit. Probably a condo out at Roebuck Plantation would be ideal for her new upscale lifestyle. Take up golf and tennis.

Tamzie told him she owned the Cannon Street house free and clear. She couldn't afford to pay on a mortgage.

Vineyard said that was no problem. One of his specialties was managing Section-8 housing. He'd have a tenant moved straight in.

Tamzie said you mean the poverty housing? He said no shit. Federal HUD largesse at its finest. She said she couldn't do that to Cannon Street. It was bad enough them all being working poor without having that shit dumped on their heads.

He said what had they done for her not lately but any time? She had to learn to follow her affairs in the market. The way Section-8 worked was your lawyer filled out some forms to qualify your property. HUD so dumb you could charge $5,000 a month, say it was the market rate, and they never question it. He would take his standard management fee. There was plenty of fat there for her to buy a condo.

Tamzie said, "$5,000 a month?" doing the times-twelve

math in her head. She couldn't believe anyone would be fool enough to pay rent like that for her little shotgun house.

Vineyard said federal programs were there for folks to access their entitlements. Look at Colin Powell, an avowed Eisenhower Republican getting his TV station. Charles Barkley turning out Republican. And Sammy Davis, Jr. before him. It only made sense. Did the Democrats have the interest of the middle-class taxpayer at heart? It's one IRS gouge after the next, and Tamzie needed to get some interest deductions or she'd be eat up come April tax time.

Tamzie studied her drink. She said it was a crying shame the way wrongs are now called rights. Nobody has any sense of moral indignation.

Vineyard said it's time the black middle class backed workfare and letting law abiding citizens carry concealed guns and take other issue stands of this caliber.

Vineyard laid his hand over hers and said, "We'll put all this business subject behind us and talk about lighter matters. I just bought me a six-pack history of rhythm and blues that is stunning. CD number 2 totally devoted to drinking songs. Amos Milburn wailing 'One Scotch, One Bourbon, One Beer' and 'Bad, Bad Whisky.' They say drinking songs were big in the early '50s."

"Sure," said Tamzie. "The music hung on even up when we was kids. You remember Brownie McGhee's brother Stick who record 'Drinking Wine Spo-dee-o-dee.' Later redone by forgettable white folks."

"My true music roots," said Vineyard, "age 13, begin with Randy's Record Shop, advertised on WPAL, with the Rev. J. Herbert Hinkle singing 'I'm in Debt and I Can't Pay'."

Tamzie laughed. "And John R., the dee-jay, offered a set of lint-free towels, for $9.98, plus mailing, write to TOW-ELS, that's T-O-W-E-L-S. And his other major sponsor was White Rose Petroleum Jelly, and John R. advised all us 'you babies' to keep a jar in the glove compartment."

Vineyard laughed, "He also offered it in 50-gallon drums."

The waiter brought two more drinks. Vineyard took Tamzie's hand in both of his. "You a real visual-arts resource."

Tamzie said she was low maintenance when it came to make-up. "I go understated. Other than smoky eyes, maybe a little blush. Touch of high-lighter to the cheek-bones to catch the light. I don't try to match my make-up to my clothes."

Outside, rain was drumming down on the roof. The lights went low. A singing act was beginning using lasers, dry ice smoke and psychedelic videos. A montage of best-known hits of Motown.

Vineyard said that sure evoke nostalgia. Here he was sitting with a heavenly body dropped out of the sky.

Tamzie said "You sure turning in a stellar performance."

Vineyard did a mild double-take. Said, "Stellar. Stars. Heavenly body. My, my, you are quick."

He reached across and toyed with Tamzie's necklace. She was wearing her black Tahitian pearls that look more gray than black. He said, "I'd like to get on with the arduous process of seduction. Yes, I could sure participate in that trend."

Tamzie said don't get your hopes up. She said time is

not of the essence. But she gave him a real slow smile looking up through her eyelashes.

■ ■ ■

"Glad to see you got none of that Perrier," Sparky told the
big spade bartender in the T-shirt with the sleeves torn off.
"I mean think about it. Folks paying two ninety-five for a
glass of water and a lemon wedge. Where are their brains?
I ask you?"

The rain had let up when he got out of his rental Chev-
rolet Caprice and walked into the "Get-Down Lounge"
way up a dirt road on St. John's Island, two islands over
from Roebuck. Just a tin-roof shack without even indoor
plumbing, which was just as well because who'd want to
get trapped in there taking a leak, get rolled.

Sparky ordered a Miller and looked around the smoky
room. His was the only white face in it. The spade popped
the top on the bottle and slapped it down on the bar.

"Is this what you call a monogamous relationship bar?"
said Sparky. "Or are some of these couples intent on illicit
sex? Headed for a hot-sheets motel. Or figuring on rocking
a mobile home off the blocks?"

The bartender said, "You got bidness here or you just
trying to collect on your life insurance policy?"

Sparky said he was looking for a dude name of Ono-
mia or Omonio Reese. His lawyer had sent him out with
more papers to sign. "Did you know he come into a bunch
a money? $15,000 to be exact. Just thought I'd share that
bit of info in case the boy run a big tab here or something.
A man needs to stay on top of those accounts receivable."

The bartender thought on that and said he'd locate Omonio. But don't make any sudden moves or get cute with the customers. Most of them tended to go armed and the white race was not their favorite.

Sparky raised both hands and said peace brother. When he was in his early twenties, he had done time at the maximum-security penitentiary in Angola, Louisiana. Joint was eighty percent gigantic big blue-gum spades out of a swamp. Any one of them could have killed him with a casual blow. He had learned to work around them in the five years he spent there.

What he did was grin and act all friendly. Then he'd do something so on the edge as to defy belief. Their nervous systems couldn't take a whole lot of high-octane stress. Put that stress on, and they'd just get confused and shut down. Eating fatback and salt gave them all high blood pressure.

That high-yaller spook Vineyard Dupree was a real trip. Acting all self-important. Sparky saying you bet, he'd deliver the ordnance with real precision. The boy had probably never ordered a professional hit in his life. Sparky intended to have oodles of fun with him.

About then, Omonio came staggering over, big field hand of a nigga with bib overalls and his tractor cap pulled sideways on his head. The boy was bad drunk, maybe on drugs as well.

Sparky shook hands. "Just call me the Lone Stranger. Man, I feel like Robinson Crusoe among the cannibals."

Omonio said, "Say what?"

Sparky told him about lawyer papers and how they had

to sign them so he could get that ol' check cashed without some banker giving him a hairy-eyeball run-around. Told the bartender to not drink his beer. They'd be right back.

As he led Omonio out to the car in the pitch dark, said watch your step now, there's big mud holes out here. All this rain. Is this kind of a seasonal thing? Or is it always this bad? Not that it really matters too much. You gotta think philosophical about all the knowns and unknowns in the universe.

Omonio said, "Murrhmuh."

Yes, the boy was bad drunk. But he understood that $15,000. Sparky popped the trunk on the Chevy. Man, it was dark out. Bar of light coming out of the door of the "Get-Down," but that was it.

The trunk light showed the Ithaca pump action just lying there all innocent. It's not guns that kill people as they say. Sparky pulled on a set of gloves. Omonio starting at him as he said you got that check on you? I got to register the check book number. Lawyer Dupree had a whole bunch on his mind and neglected that little chore. Have to say I'm pretty pleased with how open-minded you are about all this. Guess with all that money you got room to ease into the future.

He reached down in the trunk. "What I got here is a mixed blessing."

Sparky picked up the shotgun, shell already jacked into it, and laid it on Omonio's chest. Look of animal awareness jumped into the man's eyes.

"Just think of it as life-changing," said Sparky. He pulled the trigger. KA-WHOOM!

Omonio pitched backwards in the dark and lay still on the ground. Sparky couldn't see his eyes in the dark, but they had lost all focus.

As he drove off, he was thinking how easy it was to own someone. Fools get into crime and don't have the guts to kill on their own. Ought to know you can't get good help these days.

Yes indeed, he was going to have lots of fun with Vineyard Dupree.

9

"These big-name brokers you were using are like a silent epidemic of thievery," Vineyard Dupree told Tamzie. He was looking mighty fine in a double-breasted suit with peak lapels. Tape deck playing Smokey Robinson's *Cruisin'*.

Vineyard was driving her down to Roebuck Island in his red BMW to see the property he had picked out. He called it whimsical but moderately priced. He was vague about how moderate. In the one-fifty to two hundred range he said.

Tamzie had joined an abs-buns-thighs class, and her body hurt over every inch. Scrubbing floors for old lady Ralston had never been so bad. Little white college girls bouncing around like they made of rubber.

Vineyard was saying Seagrass S & L maintained a core basic research capability that put Smith, Barney—Merrill Lynch all of them to shame. Folks at Seagrass go at investment deliberately. You work with them, it's no load, no fee, one-stop shopping. An investment advisor is family, or if not, the closest thing.

Outside of Charleston lay a maze of little tidal creeks with bridges, roads that took you onto the marsh-ringed islands. When you got past the trailers and cinder block houses with signs saying pitbulls for sale, you pass tomato fields and patches of forest.

Up through the 1960s the black folks picked tomatoes in summer, gather oysters in the winter. Shuck and pack in little oyster canning factories. It was the old way of getting by. The oyster business was about gone now. That just left tomatoes and welfare.

Tamzie was beyond that now. Sure, her three million didn't put her up on a Bill Cosby, Magic Johnson level, but she was sure enough beyond poverty.

Passing the little houses, she felt guilty about leapfrogging over their heads into the rich white world. Living on a golf course and a beach for why? It wasn't like she needed to maintain a year around tan.

Vineyard was saying companies like Roebuck Development were key to the future of a backward state like South Carolina where prisons were the only growth industry. Everybody trumpet the small business guy, but when it come down to it, he's out on a limb on his own.

She thought about Reverend Otis Peebles and his three lady Bishops all with their hands out. Saying give us a new understanding of God's will through opening your checkbook.

Well forget that. It wasn't like they was a bunch of Haitians. They didn't live in tin shanties with raw sewage in pools out in the yard. Peebles driving around in that shiny Lincoln.

Tamzie just didn't need all the aggravation. Rat-like smiles wherever she went. Tantalizing over her wealth. Some drunk on the street would yell hey baby gimmie some of that stuff, and she didn't know if he was talking money or poon.

Tamzie closed her eyes and sat back in the seat, letting the car hurry her to a new life of luxury. Her Donna Ricco dress feel like it belong on her body.

At the gate, Vineyard waved at the uniformed security guard and drove on through into a golf course world. Not much had been built yet for how much land there was. Here and there big houses sat among the palmetto jungle.

Vineyard said there's no detectable environmental damage. Ain't no polar bears here. No snail darters. So Roebuck could build right up to the edge of wetlands. Once his legal firepower consolidate title on all the property, they'd have a green light for community-minded building. Make jobs for the whole region.

He said as a member of the South Carolina Bar he also had a real estate broker's license, so he was officially selling the place to her for Roebuck Development Company. He may as well take a commission. It was all Seagrass loan money anyhow.

Tamzie asked why she can't use her money? He said cause it's tied up making more interest than she's paying Seagrass on her loan. There's a fake name on the loan documents because as a director, she shouldn't be accepting loans from Seagrass. But if you can't dip in and help yourself a little bit, what was the point of being on the Board?

Tamzie said, "What would bank examiners say about that?"

He said, "We talk frequently."

She said, "What's that mean?"

He said, "What's *what* mean?"

She said, "Lemme ask you a hypothetical. What happens if shit hit the fan and come full circle?"

Dupree said, "Let me frame that succinctly. Those concerns are unfounded. You got that state Senator Ralston on the Board. The man is wired in with congressmen, U.S. senators. Tamzie Jerome is traveling with a power crowd. Got all the cover she could want or need. What we really got to focus on here is gainsharing and not downside risks."

Tamzie liked him being in charge. Liked hearing him say good things going to happen. Pending verification, she figure to just roll with the flow. Let her path be covered with rose petals.

The property he show her was in a little nest of condos clustered around a golf tee. Set up on pilings. Cedar shake shingles. He had a key and took her inside. Said the wall color was "dusty apricot." He had pick it out personally with her in mind.

And Lord even without furniture it was sure enough nice. Fancy kitchen with everything built into the walls. Carpet all nailed. Deck for alfresco dining by firefly light. Sip that California merlot.

Tamzie walk from room to room all impressed. Sun shining in. View of grass and trees. Birds be up singing in the morning. Bye-bye Cannon Street. You is now past gone history.

Vineyard put his hands on her shoulders. "We could formalize our relationship by you getting naked."

Tamzie pull back smiling at him. "I thought you'd get around to revealing that frame of reference."

His hands go right back. "I can understand that you might clutch at this point. But I'm used to leading off strong and with consistency. And you just the essence of carnality."

"My momma always say men don't like nasty women. They don't stick around for a diamond anniversary."

"You need to disown that point of view," said Vineyard. "It's a psychology thing. What men like and what they say they like are different. So why don't we just get innovative and go against stereotypes?"

Here in this new house Tamzie felt like she'd assumed a secret identity. She let him move in close. He whisper to her ear, "We having a right fruitful round of negotiations."

■ ■ ■

"When business and pleasure meet," said Chase Jeffcoat the investment banker.

"Sounds like that could become a giant trend," Bobbi-Jean replied.

She was looking at this big handsome hunk wondering if he was some predestination event for her eternal love life. The man looked like he might be the love child of Richard Gere and Cindy Crawford. It would take serious will power to keep from doing a face-down in his crotch and letting him know too soon just how trashy she could be. In her experience, men wanted you to act all innocent first and then imagine their expert loving had turned you into a wanton, out-of-control harlot.

Chase had driven her down to the exclusive gated community of Roebuck Island Plantation with its courtyard homes, villas, and luxury condominiums. It was like she had some special radar guidance system just built right into her body that drew men zooming in on her, even men this overwhelming, drop-your-step-ins, handsome. Tits and ass were that all-power duo at work.

The car radio said a tropical depression was off Puerto Rico, called it a Tropical Teaser. B-J knew selling golf resort property in the South was a business of serious timing.

January and February were too cold anywhere but in Florida. Come summer, heat and bugs were unbearable throughout the region. And then in Fall you had those terrifying hurricane threats. Although cooling waters usually caused a storm decline after mid-October, hurricane season didn't officially end until Nov. 30. Which gave the Roebuck Island Company a narrow window of opportunity between terror and cold to get that property moving.

Chase rode her around in a golf cart, showing her the big wealth on display. Tennis shop and pavilion. HarTru tennis courts. He said the Golf, Beach & Raquet Club was the focal point, the centerpiece of island life. It was designed with jigsaw decorative eaves like colonial houses found in the West Indies. Since most of their owners would be retirees, it was important they were proximate to the Medical University in Charleston. But they'd have concierge on-site health care as well.

B-J was thinking this man would get straight A's in any test of rugged good looks and suave debonair carry on. Listening to the vibrations of his voice was pushing her into a just-ignited melt-down.

Roebuck was strongly committed to having planted buffers along property lines and at least 5% of the surface of all parking lots. The "Links at Roebuck Plantation" had been designed by one of the world's great names in golf course architecture. Homesites on the ocean were running $2 million, on the golf course $500,000.

This was just the start. In a year when they opened Phase 2, prices would double. Chase said the economic benefits of it would be truly regional.

B-J said this sure was an exclusive enclave if that was the right word. Chase said she was right on both counts. He called Roebuck an American success story and said he was understandably proud of what he had created.

B-J told him she was raised in a tin siding job near an Air Force base. Clothes made out of remnants. She said, "Golf got me out into a world I never knew existed except in magazines. Pictures looked so pretty I kind of figured it might all be a put-up job. Turned out to be real though. Pinehurst. Indian Wells. Palm Desert."

Chase said he had been born poor too. His daddy ran a gas station in Orangeburg. But a refusal to compromise had brought him right far along.

B-J said, "That's a mouthful. Folks out here seem to have all the money anybody'd ever need for a whole life-time. I see all this and get downright envious. And yet other times I think all I want in life is to be at home fixing dinner for my man." She gave it that little baby doll pout.

Chase said maybe they should go have a drink at the club, talk about a timeframe for her realizing her dreams. B-J said, "Well, they say liquor is bad for unborn children, but I'm right talented at not getting knocked up."

She had been trying to be semi-intellectual around Chase, but that just blipped out. Maybe learning he was a son of a gas station caused her to relax.

That kind of forthright trash talk startled him right down to the roots. "On a personal level, I'd like to say . . ." The words choked in his throat.

A big lump in his trousers was visibly demonstrating his dirty thoughts. B-J put her hand on his erection. "This is like the first horn of a dilemma."

His face turned as bright red as a Monterey sunset. "Horns of a dilemma," he said. "I know you went to college."

B-J said she had for about three months, but that going-to-class business took too much time away from her golf. And the girls there were either ugly ol' rad-libbers or else getting brainwashed into one of those shave-your-head religions you see in airports. Sometimes she'd read a big ol' doorstopper of a book—Stephen King or James Mitchener goes to Hawaii or something—but that was about it for her education.

She said, "In many ways it's easier to not be a college graduate. Must be no fun to go back to one of those reunions and have people see you fat."

Chase blanched. He said his business school reunion was coming up this Spring. Then he said, "You can reverse aerobic decline. Just avoid sedentary living. Keep those muscles burning oxygen. Work the diaphragm. Keep the lung function strong. Some guys are into heavy jogging or even rock climbing, but orthopedic injuries are a high price to pay for keeping your heart strong. Golf has less joint strain than racket sports."

B-J just cocked her head to one side to let her blond hair hang over an eye and smiled. She had seen a movie star named Veronica Lake do that on an old movie channel and liked it. She knew she had Chase totally flustered.

Reminding him that she was still in the prime child-bearing age. Instead of acting like a still potent stud, he was letting out his fear of aging. Now to whip the saw in the other direction.

She looked off at the snack truck that was going up the tree shaded road towards the club. "You know it's funny," she said. "Whenever I see one of them Frito-Lay trucks, I always read it crazy. I read it Free-to-Lay. You know. Like free to get laid." She laughed.

His mouth was hanging open.

B-J told Chase she really needed a car. Not one of those rental jobs. But titled in her own name. So she could be visible for the business.

Chase was hesitating. Time to squirt in a little controlled anxiety. "Mister Jasper has already paid for the insurance. I'm real grateful to him. Especially with that mean old Sparky Truluck being so nasty about what happened down in Alabama. That was so bad I don't even want to talk about it, him beating that trucker up and forcing me to hit him like I did."

Chase got all authoritative. "I can handle all that. You don't need to go to Byron Jasper for money. Let me underline that. Don't stoop to getting indebted to him. He's not as nice as you might think."

B-J said, "You're so cute when you get all masterful and bombastic."

Then she just smiled up into his eyes, took a deep breath to raise the combined size of those knockers, and let it all say thank you.

10

The sun came through the office window on the picture of Vineyard Dupree's Howard University diploma. Sparky was sitting in the client's chair telling the joke about negroes abolishing all holidays except Martin Luther King's birthday and September 15.

Behind the desk, Vineyard stared at him real sullen. "Okay, I'll bite. What's September 15?"

"That's the day the new Cadillacs come out!" Sparky slapped his knee and laughed out loud.

Vineyard's lips were tight. "You know I'm preoccupied busy. Maybe you got a few things to say to me. So you could go ahead and get to the point."

Sparky got up and walked around the office, taking his time looking at the picture of Vineyard next to the big bill fish. Kind of sensing the tension.

Finally, the skinny yellow spook couldn't hold it in anymore. Just bust out with, "I can't believe you were dumb enough to tell that bartender you came from my office. Knew all about the $15,000. Me denying and lying about everything. Never closed a deal with the man. Things just in the negotiation stage. I've had cops sitting in here all day yesterday because you got shit for brains."

"No need to have a hissy-fit," said Sparky. He was looking out the window down to the cars parked on the street now. "That your BMW parked down below? The red one?"

"Uh, yeh."

"You know what I always heard growing up about folks your color and driving? You always drive either too fast or too slow. Never the right speed. And you'll load up a car with six-ten folks but always look comfortable. But you know what I really love? It's how a spade'll get out of his car double-parked and leave the flashers on. Just walk away to do some business like he's got diplomatic immunity or something."

Vineyard stared at him. He was stymied and knew it.

"Probably smells like fried chicken inside it," said Sparky.

"Nobody's asking you to ride in it."

Sparky looked around the room like he was hearing voices. "They ain't? Here I thought you boys was real concerned about how I lost my Firebird to that cheatin' and lyin' slut you got working for you out at the golf course."

Vineyard said he had nothing to do with that. Sparky'd have to see Byron Jasper if he wanted a new car. He was sure there'd be money in the budget.

Sparky shook his head all amazed. "We got to face up to the wage disparities between black and white in this country and do something about it. Sure, we may disagree on this or that aspect of my policy, but the big issue here is fairness. I need the loan of your car. That's all. Half-way respectable set of wheels for a man of my responsibility to ride around in while I do business." He paused. "How do you get that kink out of your hair? Put the marcel iron to it?"

Sparky grinned watching the spook touching his hair

looking startled. Not able to keep up with the flow. And everybody thinks your coloreds know how to shuck and jive. He started up again.

"I could list my positive accomplishments. Sure. But you don't need that. You're sitting here all flushed with the excitement of the recent day. Your land project moving right along. Knowing you'll have future adversity, but old Sparky can manage it okay. There's dynamic to this team."

Vineyard came around the desk like he might actually try to take a poke at Sparky. Trembling with anger. Sparky looked down at the lizard skin shoes with lifted up red heels. "Man, you know how to dress, I give you that. But what I'm wondering is do you know what happened to the $15,000 check? If the cops should get hold of it, it might tie you to the killing. You can imagine what they'd think. You lying to them and the lies all written up in their report."

Vineyard went so pale Sparky thought he'd like to turn white. When he handed over the car keys, Sparky said to relax, man, he was just borrowing it for a few days till he got something worked out with Byron. Car'd come back good as new. Full tank of gas and everything. Run it through a car wash.

He paused in the doorway having a final thought.

"Now I don't want to encourage resentment here. But when you wake up one morning and find out how easy it is to own people, well, it affects your outlook."

■ ■ ■

"It seems quaint I suppose," said the head accountant at Seagrass S & L. "But we insist on old-fashioned notions of community. Putting something back in instead of just taking out." He was looking down at his hush puppies the whole time he talked.

Bobbi-Jean thought the head accountant looked about as boring as an evening spent in a laundromat. Some girls specialized in fleecing such hapless men, but she had never sunk that low down the food chain. She had a moral compass after all and kept her virtue basically intact.

They were standing in Grady Troxler's office with all the Clemson decorations. Grady came in telling the accountant to go address some fundamental problems and not let the door hit him in the ass on the way out.

The little man blushed furiously and scuttled away like a land crab. Big sweat stains marked his armpits. He was sure whip-broke.

B-J's high school math teacher had said with her numbers-sense she should become a CPA. Have a profession. Never be out of work. If that was true, what was the little turkey so scared of?

Grady did his low, gravel voice mumble. "You juicy, dripping cunt. Murmur. We gotta reduce a level of distrust between us."

B-J took a cautious step backward thinking here we go again. "The disenchantment is just downright mutual," she said.

He mumbled more saying he wanted to slam her up against the wall mumble mumble work her ass up high murph murgle jam it to her standing up.

She said she had previously explained how if he didn't clean up his mouth she was going to walk. She got up and walked.

"Nobody dares quit me," sneered Grady. "I pride myself on a loyal workforce."

B-J kept walking. She wasn't worried, but it was an odd remark, and it made her think about the whipped dog look of all the staff. She wondered what he had on them.

On the banking floor, a big banner proclaimed: "*We Are Committed to Excellence in All We Do and Say.*"

A framed, blown-up news story had Chase Jeffcoat saying Grady Troxler was providing the kind of honest, tough-minded leadership that this nation's economy so very badly needs. "His biggest asset is he's committed to excellence and to people."

Byron Jasper bulled through the front door of the thrift with a couple of his contractors. His mood as high as ever. Clemson had just won over UNC 17–10.

"Talk about your personnel!" he boomed. "They are playing the most physical football I ever did see. I swear they gone have their choice of bowls. Gator or Peach. They pick."

"Virginia's got 'em beat in the rankings," somebody argued. "Hell, they beat Clemson 22–3 *at* Death Valley."

"This bowl business ain't all rankings and records," Byron argued back. "It's ticket sales and fans. The gate. And they are one bodacious *tour-de-force* in that arena." Then he spotted B-J.

Byron said, "Sweetheart, you look as good as a tray of bourbon balls." He gave her a big hug, squeezing up against her boobs as much as possible. "Lordy, if I could put you nekkid on pay-per-view TV, I could retire."

B-J figured there's no time like the present and lifted

his wallet from his hip pocket, sliding it smoothly into her tote bag. "You just got the most infectious enthusiasm I ever did see," she cooed.

"Mercy, I drank so much last night I feel like I'm recovering from a near-death experience. Been spent like this month's rent money. Round about two AM I rallied in overtime play and managed to make it through to the bust of dawn."

"That's always the moment of truth," she smiled.

"Hell, honey, there ain't nothing I like better than a goal-line stand."

In what was supposed to be a deep conversation, he told her she was a heartbreak ballad in a honky tonk barroom. His life up to now had been basically leftovers, but the servings had suddenly got extremely generous.

B-J left him going up to Grady's office in the Skydeck and stood out front of the thrift going through his wallet, pulling out two charge cards. With this new financing in place, life had turned to the flip-side where there was always a better tune.

Sure enough, in the parking lot she ran into Chase Jeffcoat who was looking just as fine as she remembered. Wearing that chalk-stripe three-piece suit like some Dallas banker who went to London a lot. She'd sure like to give him a full body massage with oil.

"You're looking rather well," he said, stiff, a little nervous as usual.

B-J acted all perky because she was feeling perky. "Life is like golf. Some days you break par and some days you don't. But you always show up full of the best intentions."

"I don't want to fuel your expectations," he said, "but ..." He dangled a set of car keys.

He kind of pointed with his chin towards a spanking brand new forest green BMW roadster that they made in the factory up in Greenville now. It was one of the first on the market. Even showed up in a James Bond movie although it didn't do anything much in the action.

B-J knew an emotional outbreak was expected. "Ooo-eee!" she shrieked, clapping her hands together like a child. She said she'd just love to get behind that wheel and give him a ride just about any old place he wanted to go.

He said do you like it?

She said, "I am like, Wow! I mean, imagine such a present just come out of the blue like that!"

Chase ran his hands along the shiny body and talked about sleek curves and precision timing in a suggestive way. Then he held her shoulders and put his forehead against hers saying, "I'd like to believe we could be a partnership that works."

B-J waited. He was practically divorced was what was coming next. All the men she met were.

"I'm everything but divorced from my wife," he said, gazing out over the parking lot with a sad look in his eyes. "Our current status is not what you'd call serene."

11

"I am Missus Chase Jeffcoat," Bracey bristled, being very clear about each word. The security guard at the gate to Roebuck Plantation was insistent she had no pass to be on the property.

What was wrong with him? She was driving a Range Rover. She had a black labrador with a blue bandana tied around his neck on the seat beside her. It was all the right accoutrements. Did he want to see her house with the pineapple flag hanging from it? Maybe Chase didn't want her coming in. The thought so exasperated her, that she snapped, "Open the gate, you foolish little man!"

Obediently, he raised the gate, and she drove on through.

A wave of guilt passed through her. It was her mother's voice that had come out of her mouth. And the guard was a black man. "Yezum," he had said when she got all peremptory and officious. Bracey was inhabited by an evil spirit.

"Shut up, Imbecile!" she snapped, taking her anger and guilt out on the whining dog.

She parked in the empty lot at the club house and got out. No dogs allowed on the course, but she didn't care. Nobody was playing. Imbecile ranged in wide elipses on the fairway barking and chasing crows that took flight and sat in treetops to mock him. The trees cast blue shadows of afternoon on the grass.

Chase always said a golf course was a better use for land than asphalt as though those were the only two alternatives. Which was probably true. In the same vein of logic, Bracey accepted the NRA and redneck deer hunters as a positive sign there was some forest habitat left. Still, it never failed to amaze her how men who worshipped deer hunting would gape in awe at the latest parking lot and mall that was the biggest in the southeast or the state or the county or wherever. Go golly gee whiz ain't that something else? And won't all that new construction make for jobs.

The NRA membership declined, and liberals applauded as though the country was becoming more civilized. This in a nation with a constant murder rate and growing massacres in the workplace.

The number of hunters nationwide had dropped by several million, but the statistic was only analyzed from the point of view of declining retail sales of outdoors gear. No one could openly admit the numbers had fallen because the land was disappearing. Boys no longer grew up near a wood where you could shoot squirrels with a .22. They all lived in suburbs and hung in malls. Or gritty industrial cities where they argued over tennis shoes and killed each other with handguns.

The disease cut across social class. She could be sitting at a mahogany table in the best houses in Charleston and watch the men's faces light up with greed at the thought of subdividing an old plantation.

It was premature to gauge the impact, they always said

as they scraped and gouged the earth. To the contrary, the impact was all too apparent. The habitat was polluted or just plain gone. The marshes and thickets were no longer filled with birds. The National Audubon bird count would come at Christmas. As usual they would find fewer than the year before. Just thinking on it was like drinking a cup of bitter tea.

The Huston property lay beyond the golf course, a big acreage of loblolly with tangled palmetto jungle in the wet places. The pines were just now getting up in height. Had probably been logged in the 1940s. Chase would pluck out the palmettos and sell them to malls which liked them because there were no leaves to blow away by men with little power packs.

It was so quiet she could hear a pinecone drop on the soft ground.

Beyond a broomsage field, a little tin-roof shack trickled wood smoke into the sky. An old colored woman was milking a nanny goat in the yard. In the old-time island life, goats and cattle roamed free. Now Roebuck would raise hell if that goat got onto their golf greens.

A quail whistled its clear "bob-white." Bracey wet her lips and whistled back. The colored woman looked up like she had detected the difference in the two.

Feeling like a spy, Bracey slunk back into the trees and walked on. On the edge of the marsh a great blue heron took flight with a cry like a heart breaking.

Bracey sat on a tree trunk feeling her aloneness, thinking about Hansel and Gretel lost in the forest. Despised by a stepmother, their father too weak to protect them. As an only child, Bracey didn't have a brother to die of starvation with. She guessed it reflected something of a mother-daughter agreement on population control. Izzie had borne her in a premature labor filled with pain and anxiety and afterwards swore she would never repeat the sordid experience.

A flock of red-winged blackbirds settled in the reeds. The females and males flock separately like humans with their hen parties and boys' nights out. Bracey thought about the bones of things that have died among the marsh grass and lie in the pluff mud, picked over by little fiddler crabs.

The November sun set at five taking the weak light to bed. A great horned owl hooted for its mate.

The first star rose.

Bracey made a wish that she could be in love or at least be a more self-reliant spinster, got confused between the two choices and just gave up. Feeling shivery and lonely, she shoved her hands in her pockets and walked back to the car.

Imbecile had dug up the eighteenth green looking for a mole.

Oh dear God.

Bracey looked around frantically. There were no witnesses. She hustled the dog into the Rover and drove away.

When Bracey was a girl, she read *Little Women*, wondered if she was Jo or Beth. As a teenager she read *The Prime of Miss Jean Brody* and figured she'd turn out a self-reliant spinster. Maybe have one love affair during a holiday in Italy.

When Chase married her, she was so certain of losing

him that she booked their honeymoon in Rome. Fatalistic. Just so it could be that one love affair when things didn't work out.

It had worked out almost like that. Matrimony hadn't settled her life. It was just the one short holiday affair.

Back in Charleston on Legendre Street, Omar was feeding the dogs in groups of three. If he let them all out of the house at once they'd fight.

Her mother and dogs. Ordinarily a woman obsessed with dogs would wear tweeds and gum boots. Go to field trials. Mother and daughter might have found some common ground. Instead, Izzie collected Queen Elizabeth Buckingham Palace dogs and dressed like a fashion plate.

When Omar saw Bracey, he said evenin' Miz Jeffcoat.

Bracey was always self-conscious around servants. Even those she had known all her life. She didn't have an Isabelle Fanseau's instinct to command.

Omar Temple Gillyard. His mother had borne him in the kitchen of the local Shriners Lodge during the annual banquet. Named him in commemoration of the event.

Omar said, "Law, your momma's in a state. She done cuss me, unh!" He laughed like it was the funniest thing on earth, flashing a set of big white teeth. "She just cuss me and cuss me."

Bracey never knew whether it was an act or not. How could he possibly find her mother amusing? How could he be so servile?

God the guilt.

12

"My books are my best friends, I always return to them." Tamzie kept murmuring that to herself. She had heard a celebrity say it on a Barbara Walters interview, and she liked its ring. Besides, her fortune derived from an ancestor's diary. It was Tamzie's favorite book of all time.

The Fall Tour of Homes South-of-Broad was the closest thing to an A-list party that Tamzie could just walk into by paying a fee. Vineyard had griped a lot about the $40 each to see a bunch of old slaveowners' houses so she had paid for both of them.

Things had sure change for the best in her life. Coming back to tour the Ralston mansion where she had work so many years. In the old days she would have been breaking her back all week getting the house spotless and putting away loose stuff somebody could thief. And then on this night be standing around in that maid's costume with orders to make sure nobody lean up against nothing and broke nothing or it would come out of her pay.

She had been watching the Psychic Network on TV and had even phoned in some right expensive calls for a personal reading of her inner psyche. All the news was good news. The voice said successful men and big money was all in her future.

So Tamzie was feeling and looking good all decked out in vest, bolero jacket, short skirt and Pappagallo's cap-toe slingback. Vineyard wore an Armani suit like that stud use to on *Miami Vice*. She didn't care for those long fingernails of his, but that was small stuff to change about a man.

The lights were on the big houses like palaces lit for a ball. On the sidewalk outside the big Ralston Mansion at No. 1 Legendre, the old white women in their full-length furs were milling around talking about the trailing ivy.

That was when Tamzie sees Omar Temple Gillyard who worked for the Fanseau woman up Legendre Street. He had six of those ugly looking misbegotten dogs all tangled up on their leashes. Taking them out for the evening stroll and crap.

"You lookin' good, gal," he said to Tamzie. "Buying in all the best places now I hear."

"My love affair with buying things done cool off," said Tamzie. "But I like to keep up appearances."

Deep beneath her dark skin, a red glow of embarrassment was burning because she used to think of Omar in a marriage-minded way. In church on Sundays, the light would shine down through Jesus in the window and seem to land a ray smack on top of Omar's head. When the congregation stood up to sing hymns, she'd be craning her neck to get a glimpse of him and convinced she could pick out his baritone from the rest of the voices.

What she was mostly thinking was she should have worn a bra. Her nipples were standing up like twin dogs begging for table scraps.

Omar didn't notice though, being distracted by the ugly

short-leg dogs, saying to them, "There you pretty thing, you. Get on over here now, Cleopatra. Settle down, Racer."

In his Italian suit and snazzy shoes, Vineyard just kind of looked down his nose at Omar. All Tamzie could think was she want to be elegant like Diana Ross with straightened hair kind of swept back with a bit of crinkle still in the mass of it and slinky dresses that cling to her like a fish skin. And a high-tone lawyer type man like Vineyard to just make love to her all day every day. Never let her off her back except to go out to beauty salons and exercise classes.

They said a few more things and went on with the group into the house. Tamzie thought the docent woman at the door looked awful close at their little tags what say they had pay the eighty dollars. Like maybe they trying to sneak in or belong going around to the back door with the help.

Inside, old lady Ralston be drunk like always and going on about the history of her New Milford lettuce-leaf pottery, the French empire clock and the famous painting of Adam and Eve with the serpent's head that of Abraham Lincoln.

Old lady didn't even notice the two black faces standing there as she yack about the Lost Southern Cause and the Yankee vandals with their big cannon name "Swamp Angel" what knock the cupola off her house in 1864.

Now she on the Miles Brewton handcrafted silver. Miles worked from 1696 to 1743 blah blah blah. How many hours had Tamzie spent cleaning that silver?

"I would never eat with machine-made silver," said old lady Ralston like some kinda queen she think she is.

Room by room they go hearing about the house's pedigree and how each piece of furniture got a story to tell. Tamzie was thinking, yeah, she could tell about polishing this one and upholstering that one and the empty liquor bottles shove under that one over there.

"I am not a total slave to the past," said old lady Ralston, leading them up the big stairs. "I imposed my own taste on the house."

Tamzie thinking what is this shit? Everything just stay the same like some ancestor did it.

"I arrange the furniture to manipulate the mood. That mirror I hung there in a burst of creativity."

Down below, the new maid Lobelia push the cripple old man in the wheelchair. Now that's a story for you, think Tamzie. Old bastard hump old lady Ralston way back when they young—neither of them married to each other—and get her with the red bitch Rannie who grow up to be the meanest lawyer in town. About a year back Rannie learn he's her real daddy and bring him into the house. Tamzie was sure glad she don't have to take care of that old demon. We talking man who practically invent evil.

They were up to the first landing where the stairs jog right and the big window look down on the spike fence along the street. Tamzie was thinking any minute now old lady Ralston would recognize her and ask how she was now that she owned three million dollars. Tamzie'd say her public persona was low-key, but she had a busy social calendar all the same. Which was why she hadn't dropped by for drinks.

What happened instead was she yell at Tamzie in that familiar shrill voice saying, "Tamzie, thank God you're here! Go down in the street and get those rubbernecks off my Jaguar! They think they can plop their fat butts down wherever they choose!"

The woman's voice was so urgent and crazy that for a split second Tamzie got jerked back into a former time and felt like she been caught sneaking a drink of liquor in the kitchen. Two worlds hit in a wham-smack collision. All the white women turned to look at her, and she got confused and half-twisted around there on the landing for a moment of vertigo.

Then she was falling, Boom-boom-boom down the stairs in a sprawl of arms and legs.

At the bottom she lay there dazed momentarily. Her first conscious thought was the polished floor was cool beneath her cheek.

"Tamzie, get up from there this instant!" shrilled old lady Ralston from the top of the stairs. "You're making a fool of yourself! Go out and see to my car!"

Tamzie didn't really hear it. Or rather she did, but she had so many years of abuse from the old bat under her belt it was water off a duck's back. She wanted Vineyard to lift her up gently and rub her shoulders. That was all she wanted in the whole wide world.

What he did instead was whisper, "Don't move. Charitable immunity is done been abolish in South Carolina. We got us a good slip-fall."

He wouldn't let her budge until EMS came and transported her. Then he followed the gurney out.

"I want you to go see Doctor Dupree who's like a relative of mine by marriage. Get you a good permanent disability report."

■ ■ ■

Bracey Jeffcoat knew the tour of homes was as much a celebration of social position for the homeowners as it was a money raiser for the Historic Charleston Foundation. Tourists were beckoned by night into what they imagined was a serene and gracious world that exalted the traditional virtues of womanhood. Meditative. Tranquil. Women defined by the inventory of their china cupboards. And both hosts and visitors just ate it up. Loved taking a warm bath in the myth.

Chase always went on the tour. He said the men were exiled from their own houses and gathered in groups in the yards to talk. Good chance for him to make a pitch. It really irked her how everything he did was a raiding party out for scalps.

He had denied there was a Phase 2 for Roebuck. Said it was only in the haziest stages of speculation. Whatever Izzie was up to—well, Bracey knew no one could control her mother.

Down the street at Number 1 Legendre—the Ralston mansion—an EMS ambulance was flashing its lights. Bracey wondered if Mary Canty Ralston had finally had a stroke. The woman was such a lush.

In the news that day, South Carolina was shocked that running a radioactive landfill for the entire nation hadn't turned out to be the expected cash cow.

"It's going to get down into the aquifer," Bracey warned her husband. "We'll have poison in the water for the lower state and all of Georgia."

"You know that's unsubstantiated rumor," he argued. "Pseudo-science."

Skip Rightenberry the loud-mouthed realtor with the bad toupée came out of the dark, pursuing Chase to be in on investments. "You can run but you can't hide," he said, all cheesy grin. "I'm bird-dogging you." The smell of his breath said he was fueled on bourbon. He lent new meaning to the term "dirtbag."

Chase said he had been out of the office lately. He let others do the maintenance-type research. He spent his time pursuing new ideas.

Skip said, "Roebuck Plantation."

Chase shook his head like a tolerant parent. He always said when you've never had a loser, they come in droves. Begging. Demanding. Posturing.

He told Skip he and Bracey were out for a social stroll. Getting out while folks toured their home. He really couldn't concentrate on business just now. Skip needed to call the office. Set up a meeting.

Skip said, "Roebuck. I want in big time. I want an opportunity to play on the next level."

Chase kept that unemotional measured tone. He counseled Skip get into Daniel Island. City and state government were helping out on that one. It was lower risk.

Skip said baloney. The math don't add up. Daniel was too big and there was too much politics. All that blending of public and private funds meant politics would be the 800-pound gorilla. Developers'll be jacked around by local land-use plans. And wait'll HUD announces a major public housing project and condemns the land for it. They're laying back waiting for the richest neighborhoods to get built. Put a big crime zone right smack in the middle. Values will plummet. Fuck everybody over good.

Bracey realized she was hearing Chase's words being fed back to him. Skip Rightenberry was hypnotized by greed.

Chase said he had some other projects where he was predicting a sound increase in capital-gains realizations. They were unparalleled really. More tailored to Skip's needs.

Skip said, "Roebuck. I am a hog for it. I understand it. I believe in it. I worship it. It's me. Roll them dice. If they come up snake-eyes, you'll find me working down at McDonald's saying 'you want extra cheese on that?'"

Chase said his conscience couldn't live with causing Skip any losses.

"Screw it," said Skip. "This country's built on risk. I can snap back. There's always federal handouts to be seized by the audacious."

Chase said there was room for another half million in investment but that was it. Skip said he'd take all of it. Tell the others to move over and let the big dog eat. Chase said be realistic. That position had been promised to a lot of very dear friends. Skip said whatever was available. He said is there a glut of money in this town? Do I have to beg you to risk the cash I busted my buns for?

"No," Chase said quite seriously. "Not Roebuck. You don't like to operate without a safety net."

Skip really got mad at that one. "Are you trying to test our friendship? I bankrolled some of your first ventures. I go back to the origins. You were one more bright boy out of college and now you go highfalutin' investment king on me. Am I a fucking ugly duckling or a swan?" He stamped his feet on the ground like a kid pitching a tantrum in Toys 'R' Us.

Chase put up both his hands and laughed. "Don't go into meltdown. You're in. I'll give you the half million." He flashed that magnetic grin like light coming out of his soul.

All rejuvenated with joy, Skip whooped and slapped him a high five. "I say let's not regress; let's progress. Backing you against the wall is one productive catalyst."

Chase was all indulgent. He said, "Makes me think of a Milan Kundera quote. 'Stupidity is not ignorance but the non-thought of received ideas.'"

Skip blinked at that, having no idea who Milan Kundera was.

Chase told him, "Seagrass S&L is completely behind the project. And I tell you, nothing determines the integrity of a thrift so much as the character of its President. Grady Troxler is a memorable figure. He's like a glorious remnant of what community banking once was. Responsive. Dedicated to local interests. And there's a remarkable integrity to his investments."

Skip said, "I feel deployed and poised for the future. Paradigm shift, here I come"

Chase warned, "It may turn spooky during the winter months, but it's easy to hang tough when you've got the right company. Come spring when we've all cashed in, we'll share a little Château Margaux."

Bracey had seen Chase pull this routine more times than she could count. He always said the facts never catch up with greedy dreams until it's too late. For wannabe high rollers, merits are too complicated to ponder much, and details are boring.

Her mind was somewhere else.

Izzie was up to something. That morning she had gone for a facial with cleansing, exfoliating, extracting and hydrating. Sounded like an ordinary activity, but she had a grim sense of purpose about it. Bracey knew the look. Set jaw. Eyes straight ahead. Off to a bravura performance.

Somebody was pushing a man in a wheelchair down the sidewalk on the other side of the street. Away from the huge Ralston mansion with its big stable block and servants' quarters behind.

OH migod! Her mother was wheeling Blake Huston down the street in the dark. Pushing him along with the kind of tense poise of a shoplifter as she goes out the door of the store. Knowing she's on the threshold of no return, no excuses. Wondering if a loud voice will challenge her.

13

"Mother this is dumb with a capital D," said Bracey. "Outrageous with a real big O."

"I've never approved of your vocabulary choices," said Izzie, doing her face before the vanity in her bedroom. A dozen corgis lounged on the pink satin bed. For her wedding, Izzie was beautifully dressed in a way that Bracey could never quite achieve. She wore a boxy jacket with a stand-up collar and three-quarter-length sleeves.

"We're going to have to face the Ralstons on the street from time to time," Bracey argued. She was dressed in double-crepe silk and an abstract silver necklace. Her mother had bought it for her in exchange for the first citrine bracelet. She had barely given the bracelet to her before she coveted it back.

Izzie was wearing both bracelets. She said one didn't look right on its own. She'd pay Bracey for the second one sometime soon.

Although long used to her mother's antics, Bracey could not absorb this turn of events. "You're not offering a rousing defense of this union, mother. It's absolutely breathtaking in its deviousness."

"Don't perform against type, dear. Go right ahead and

bring your jealous, spiteful self. If spleen venting is therapeutic, then you'll soon be filled with perkiness and *joie de vivre*."

"You're not hearing a word I say," Bracey declared. "You're so adept at changing the focus."

Izzie leaned into the mirror, said her lipstick was starting to bleed into the little lines other lips. She was thinking of getting collagen injections. If you got a tummy-tuck they could make the collagen out of your own skin so there was no danger of allergic reaction.

"It goes down after two months, mother," Bracey said disgusted. "Have to refill. You'll become like an addict to it."

Izzie moved close to inspect her daughter's face. "You really need to go for a cosmetic-surgery consultation. At least have a light chemical peel. Get some alpha hydroxyl cream. Women used to have the sense to stay out of the sun. Now sun damage sets in before you're even a teenager."

Izzie led her daughter down the grand staircase. Ancestral portraits on the wall conveyed all the rightness of history and family pedigree.

Bracey was thinking, what's wrong with this picture? When she was a girl, her mother spent her days getting dressed up in the morning, going out to lunch, and playing bridge in the afternoons. There was the Book-of-the-Month Club. She was just mother. Not a thoughtful and decent person, but still mother.

Somehow, she had become a creature of exuberance and virile grace. Congratulating herself on her age defying looks. No cottage cheese thighs. Just long, lean muscles.

Blake Huston sat watching "Gilligan's Island" on TV propped by pillows covered with a flowering magnolia print. Izzie pronounced it a touching vignette. She turned down the sound and told her daughter that Chase would be performing the marriage ceremony.

"I adore Chase. He's intellectually engaging. Very protective of me. He understands the rules of discretion of our class."

It dawned on Bracey that South Carolina had so cheapened the marriage ceremony that a notary public could perform it. And Chase was a notary. You sent off $200 every seven years.

Izzie arranged a silver bowl of hydrangeas on a Regency table. "Do my eyes look all wide with girlish delight? Blake's just the most darling man, and I know this whole match was fated from the beginning. We're really just too perfect for each other. He will save me from a world of men in iridescent suits."

Blake was reaching out his feeble, claw-like hand trying to turn the TV back up. On the screen, the Skipper was slapping Gilligan on the head.

"It's trashy, mother. That's what it is. Just plain trashy."

"Well you can drop the little Miss Innocent act. What's the worst case scenario you can imagine? That he lives on 'til he's 110? That would be a pity. But things can be arranged. Life with your father was an endless round of being overworked and underappreciated."

She talked like that knowing that Blake was virtually stone deaf.

"You need therapy, mother. You really do."

"I'm sure I bear a large measure of responsibility—God knows I indulged you—but you are a spoiled only-child category all unto itself. I will not acknowledge your nasti-ness on this happy day."

Chase came in smiling, exuding his confidence, think-ing he was defusing the tension. He was carrying the Fanseau family *Bible* and the *Book of Common Prayer* as though he had acquired a new self knowledge.

"Been out shopping for a new identity?" asked Bracey. "Buy a parson's dog collar? Get the sheet music to the 'Bridal Chorus' from *Lohengrin* so you can pick it out with two fingers on the piano?"

Izzie said ignore her. She has an unhoned instinct for meanness. She cost me my youth.

With the TV flickering in the background, Chase actu-ally read through the standard "dearly beloved we are gathered here" service. Chase who said you either had to be a "niche" or a "global" player and changed what he was depending on his customer. Chase who scoffed at the idea of earning your age times a thousand dollars. He had taken time out from the pursuit of an exalted dream of vast wealth to play Parson Notary Public.

When he did the "speak now or forever hold your peace" line, Bracey looked about nervously, expecting Rannie Ralston to kick in the door. During the responses, Izzie would say "of course he does" in place of an "I do" on Blake's part.

The marriage license presented a minor difficulty. Izzie had to guide Blake's hand as he signed it.

"I want a special treat for this," Blake demanded petu-lantly. His breath smelled strongly of Maker's Mark.

"Shush, dear," said Izzie. "It's only two o'clock. We'll be romantically intertwined later on."

Bracey was thinking she knew she had been switched at birth. Someone else was her real mother.

The phone rang, and Chase was called away to report to the realtor Skip Rightenberry about the status of his bridge loan to Roebuck Plantation.

Something hit the window with a thwack. Bracey went and looked out in disbelief. Old Mary Canty Ralston was outside throwing sticks at the house. She was a notorious drunk. A silver flask was a constant companion filled with her special mixture of Irish Mist, Crème de Menthe and blended scotch. Now she was so drunk she could barely talk.

"Dam' shit-asses!" she slurred up at the window.

Appalling.

Izzie looked down on her adversary from a tall window. She might have been Marie Antoinette watching the peasant mob advance on Versailles. "The detractor arrives," she said. "They say alcoholism runs in families. Her progenitors were legendary drunks. She's such a disgrace at the Club. Creating endless scenes. And afterwards a mass of denials and memory lapses."

Mary Canty was bellowing now. "You sorry shit white trash! I'll 'do not disturb' your ass!"

For Bracey, the horror of what her mother was doing paled beside this. It was a forewarning. A grim indicator of trends to come.

Chase announced his return by popping the cork on a bottle of champagne. He seemed to be relishing the moment.

"Fuggin' worm turns!" the voice shouted from outside. "Human misbehavior! Gobs 'a shit!"

Izzie turned away from the window to accept champagne poured into a glass of vintage crystal. "It's my wedding day," she said magisterially. "I don't need acrimony."

"What I'm wondering, mother, is how you'll explain to your bridegroom that you sleep with the dogs."

"I don't need to think about that now. I'll deal with it tonight." She waved an airy hand of dismissal, making the bracelets clack.

■ ■ ■

When Tamzie moved into the Roebuck condo she ditch every bit of her old furniture and redecorate from Southeastern Galleries. Some fruit from Roebuck come around saying he want to help her with her "horticultural plan." He suggest she plant Japanese andromeda, Persian parrotia and Chinese pistachio.

He said Yoshino Cherry trees would soften the edge of the forest. Tamzie took one look at the price of all that and said she still had one foot in the past. She figured American dogwood and azaleas would be fine for her to accessorize the yard.

On that one foot in the past subject, Cannon street was outraged by the Section-8 new neighbors, and she got a lot of angry phone calls saying these hoodlum teenagers of the family so bad that the old folks got to get their groceries before school let out at 3 o'clock.

Tamzie said the city got public housing right up the end of the street. You got a crack house around the block. Addicts standing out there drooling. What was new?

They said that's up the street. She argued it's two blocks away. They said we got to have some pride.

Tamzie unlisted her phone number.

Reverend Peebles catch her on King Street and ask how her change of life pan out. She said it survive the birthing process. He condescend right smart telling her up front she all self-involved now and dealing with folks not part of her community. She tell him his loss of leadership in her life was self-evidence.

He warn to look out her money don't run out of gas. Reverend Peebles always get in the last word.

Tamzie met her new neighbor right across the fairway, a real nice white girl name of Bobbi-Jean Kincaid. She was like a golf pro/real estate saleswoman. It wasn't hard to guess that with tits like the woman got, she must sell for a living.

Tamzie took some golf lessons but was a mess at it. Spent most of her time in the trees. In *People* magazine, you'd see these pro basketball players out playing golf. But then they were pro players. Had all that hand-eye coordination. Mostly Tamzie like to putt because she had some background in miniature golf. One afternoon Vineyard catch her out on the green.

He said the best thing about Roebuck was the security system. Insurance investigators couldn't get on the premises and make a movie of her playing golf.

Tamzie ignored that. She wasn't stooping to insurance fraud even to get at old lady Ralston. She said there didn't seem to be a whole lot of new building going on at Roebuck.

He said we got a resurgence coming up. Come spring she would be amazed. And she'd just be lounging around the big club pool wearing a dental floss bathing suit. Tamzie didn't swim, but she liked the idea of the suit. She'd look like one of those beach bunnies down in Brazil.

Vineyard said her doubts about those big-name investment companies, Merrill Lynch and all of them, were well founded. They would flat-out bamboozle the unwary. In one of his more militant stances he had told a couple of them brokers their stonewalling should cease or else he was thinking of suing their ass off. Sure lucky he had come along to bail her out of her mistakes.

But it was cool. They had hand over all her accounts, and her budget anguish soon to be at an end. Get that pulse restored to a lifeless balance sheet. Every day he was having shirtsleeve sessions with the Seagrass asset guidance team. No false modesty, but those boys pretty amazed with his performance. Say his argument always insightful, his conclusion provocative.

She asked what the hold up was. He answer problem was just some mutual fund prices were gyrating here as the tax year come to a close. He was waiting for them to settle down so she could buy in at the bottom of the market. It was worth the wait.

She said don't rosily his predictions. He said way cool. They charismatic enough on they own. But since her money's a bit short, she need to get that Doctor Dupree check-out. Wear a neck brace for a couple weeks.

He can get a quick settlement for maybe twenty thousand dollars out of old lady Ralston's insurance carrier. Tide her over a bit. His fee was one third of any settlement.

It was a lawyer industry standard although some crooks would hit you for forty percent. You had to be alert for them.

She said she was wondering when he would invite her to go to his church on Sunday. She knew he went to St. Marks which was the high-tone Episcopal church that dated back to the time of freed blacks before the Civil War. All the members had real light skin and the minister was white. Vineyard parading her in that church, dark as she was, would be the test of his love.

He said well there was this little problem with his estranged wife. She showed up there most Sundays along with her family and cousins. It might make for some unpleasantness. Didn't want Tamzie marooned among a bunch of hatred.

Tamzie had to concede she could imagine that.

He said, "In the meantime, how about some less aggressive therapy?"

A voice in Tamzie's head murmur a misapprehension, but she pay it no mind. Life held too many sparkling highlights of promise. She wasn't about to look at the world through doomed eyes.

She got naked with him in her condo and joined that issue right forcefully. The man had magic hands and knew all her preferences.

14

"We don't need no habby-tat in North Charleston!" boomed the crass yokel voice on the car radio. "We don't need no bears! No mountain lions!"

Bracey cringed. While she drove, she was listening to the local radio show "Feed-Back America." Its format was area boosterism and railing at pointey-head bureaucrats in Washington.

A new airport had been constructed in North Charleston. The mayor of the city was now determined to level the massive acreage of woods around it for business development. In the process he had run up against the EPA which ordered him to preserve a few pathetic patches of wetlands.

No one—absolutely no one—had proposed that the garish asphalt sprawl of the city needed a park, a lung to breathe. That woods could be made into hiking and riding trails, picnic spots, an outdoor concert area.

"Your position on this wetlands bidness is a strong one," said "Battling Bob" Dawtrey, the show host.

"Bob, I'm jus' a ole country boy," said the mayor.

Uh-oh, she thought. Here it comes. That line always

precedes some monstrous crime against nature. It's supposed to imply simple virtues and common sense, but it's a cover for an almost pathological hatred of trees, grass, and birds, anything that doesn't broaden the tax base.

"I see a bunch a' swamp, I want to throw out a drag line and drain it out. The whole shootin' match."

New airports are always justified on the basis of the old one being unsafe because of business encroachment around it. So they trash a green-field site with the airport and then begin to immediately jam the businesses up around it. An asphalt cancer was eating America while the filthy mob cheered it on.

Bracey drove through the bumper-to-bumper traffic of the Savannah Highway past Food Lions and car dealerships with giant American Flags. Fast food. Decrepit old people tottering across six lanes of traffic. Derelicts pushing shopping carts full of tin cans. Vacuous underclass teenagers headed for video arcades with screwdrivers to break into the machines.

At the close of the show, "Battling Bob" led the listening audience in a prayer for the local economy while "Shenandoah" played low in the background.

"Dear God we ask you to give us the capability to be excellent promoters. Help us mature and come together as a team. Let us take care of business. We don't rule out an upset, Lord, but give us an opportunity at hand to give our every effort for the goal."

By the time Bracey pulled into the parking lot at Seagrass S&L she was so depressed she had to sit and close her eyes and try to picture something nice. Nothing readily came to mind.

Inside, Grady Troxler was waiting for her behind his big desk in what he fatuously called the "Skydeck." Chase had told her she had to meet with him immediately, right now, this morning. It had been an urgent message and he'd hung up abruptly afterwards.

She had thought Chase would be there waiting, but he wasn't. She was alone with the thrift President.

Grady said to shut the door. She did. He said sit down here next to my desk. She did that too.

Grady always gave Bracey the willies. He was so perfectly groomed and pressed in his wool/linen gray suit and Bill Blass tie. So oily in his manner. The unctuous smile that seemed to hide the dirtiest, smuttiest thoughts.

It was difficult to understand the man, he talked in such a mumble. But the gist of what she heard was she was to borrow money from Seagrass and then turn around and lend the identical sum to Roebuck Plantation.

She asked what for? He said they needed a bridge loan. It'd be paid back inside of six months. She'd then pay back the loan to Seagrass. All just paperwork. He'd take care of it, and she wouldn't have to give it another thought.

He spread out a whole bunch of papers—loan origination applications, loan contracts, mortgages, promissory notes—Seagrass to Bracey Jeffcoat—her to Roebuck Plantation—a whole ornate transaction already prepared. Lacking only her signature in key places.

The loan was for $3,000,000. Good God! It took her breath away.

Bracey asked why? He said he'd already told her. He sounded impatient now. Almost mean. All the smooth oilyness gone.

Bracey had put in barely a year in college before she married Chase, but college doesn't really teach you anything. You either have a brain or you don't. And Bracey was no fool. Also, she was a good listener. Married to Chase, she had to be.

She knew there were limits to how much a bank could lend to any one business venture. Common sense told you to not put all your eggs in one basket. Seagrass was up to the limit of what they could put into Roebuck Plantation. This was a straw loan to her to disguise it from the Federal Reserve bank examiners.

Grady held out a pen for her use.

Bracey said she needed to talk to her husband. Grady said Chase knew about it. Why the fuck did she think Chase sent her down here today? His voice was harsh and punitive.

When she recoiled at his language he said, "Lemme express my feelings without holding back. You worried about the state of the bank? Fuck it. Fuck the depositors and the horse they rode in on. It's all insured with the FSLIC. If we go belly-up the taxpayer picks up the tab. Nobody gets hurt. They want a match? Then I got one for them. My ass and their face.

"We're trying to return America to the roadway of economic growth. Be an energizing force. But why do I have no inner peace? Should I worry about low birthweight infants? The feminization of poverty? Should I put a rubber band around my money instead of a silver money clip? Get dragged down in guilt and paranoia?

"Sure, I can wrestle with all that in my spare moments.

But right now we got to get rid of your goddamn deficiencies and work on improvement, you little hoighty-toighty twat bitch."

Nearly paralyzed with horror, Bracey signed next to the 'X's. But that didn't end it.

As she tried to leave, he backed her against the wall muttering to her in his unbelievably foul-mouthed way. "You little refined taste bitch. You crook your pinky finger when you sip tea? I bet you got a twat on you like a kumquat. You wanna smear it all over my face? I bet you'd like that. You are moanin' for a bonin'. I can smell it on you."

He jammed his hand down between her legs and began to work a finger in the side of her underpants.

"You like this dynamic on display? You want, I'll give you a bifurcated system. One in front, one in the rear."

Bracey's knees were buckling. He had wormed his finger inside . . . *inside her vagina!*

Oddly, Bracey felt more embarrassment than fear. In fact, she hadn't been so mortified since sorority initiation when all the pledges had to lie naked on the floor one after the next and pretend they were having sexual intercourse. Cynthia big butt had used a dildo on herself which was a device that Bracey had never even heard of at the time, and it set a new standard against which all the rest were judged. When it was her turn, Bracey fainted and hit her head which mercifully kept her from having to do it.

As Grady's finger went in deeper, her whole body flushed red and hot. *Oh dear God she was lubricating! She was actually responding to him!*

He leered, "You like it don't you? It'll give your pussy a transformational change. Work through your frustrations."

Bracey tore away and fled in horror down the marble stairs, almost slipping and falling. Everyone seemed to be staring at her as she crossed the banking floor. She was nearly in tears. *The vicious, vulgar swine.*

She sat in her car in the parking lot breathing heavily and trying not to pass out. With shaking hands, she dialed her mother on the car phone.

Wheezing, barely able to talk, she told Izzie she thought she, Bracey, needed to get a lawyer and go to court for an alimony order quick. Meaning immediately. Yesterday. It was already too late.

Izzie wasn't paying any attention. She said she had celebrated her new fortune by having Botox shots to get rid of frown lines. Now she had to remain perfectly still for six hours so the botulinum toxin—which paralyzes the muscles between the brows—didn't drift and cause drooping eyelids. No lying down, nothing. Just sit perfectly still.

Bracey said aren't you listening? Chase's business is in real trouble. The whole thing may fall apart tomorrow.

Izzie was blasé. "Don't worry dear. Your father has assets enough to see us through."

"My *father*?"

"Yes, your father. Blake Huston."

"He's not my father!"

"Well stepfather then. Whatever. If you take that sullen attitude, I'm sure he won't be generous with you at all."

■ ■ ■

Bobbi-Jean always felt things looked brightest when you've just come into a pile of money. Using Byron Jasper's charge cards, she had gone to Talbot's and bought $2,600 worth of winter wardrobe.

She had pretty much patented the act of talking too loud about the nice man who had told her she could use his cards. Just so generous and sweet. The shop owner or manager or whoever could catch that a mile off and would always come out to personally attend to her, bring out whole racks of accessories to go with the clothes. Never question her signing a man's name.

B-J'd be saying how it really adds to the luster of a man when he trusted your financial good sense like that. It just cemented the whole identity of the relationship. Made her heart instantly accessible.

The clerks and manager would be exchanging knowing looks at this point. Trying to feel morally superior to this girl who was well into the pipeline of general whoredom.

B-J would say she liked candle-lit dinners for two and everything, but she sure kept the atmospherics in perspective. Married men with hormones in overdrive were pretty familiar to her. She was buying all this and afterwards she was going to get her some tee-niny little underwear at Victoria's Secret.

As the clerk pinned the hem of her new skirt, B-J thought about Grady Troxler and Clemson football.

Following three straight victories in the Atlantic Coast Conference, the Clemson Tigers were ranked not just in the top 25, but No. 24 in the AP poll. To be eligible for bowl invitations, they needed another win.

B-J had asked Grady if he was concerned about how the passing game shut down in the second half and what about Sunday's injury report on the defensive line. And how about the QB missing those reads on the play-action passes in the third quarter? Grady just kind of stared at her and muttered. He looked like an android. Or a pod man from *Invasion of the Body Snatchers.*

B-J just went all chatty saying she had picked some very nice wins, Valparaiso over Aurora, Linfield over Lewis & Clark, and Slippery Rock over Rock Haven. Grady didn't seem to have heard of any of those institutions of higher learning or to have had any bets down on them. She also mentioned the Canisius-Iona game, Marist-St. Peter's and Midwest State-Prairie View.

He was blank on those too. The man did not know jack-shit about college football.

Even more telling, he did not have the little DeColores or Iptay decals on his rear car window which showed he had given major money to the Clemson athletic program.

That telltale sign was what prompted B-J to phone up the records department at Clemson and confirm her suspicions. Grady Troxler had not graduated from Clemson. He had never even attended Clemson.

So he was a liar and crook. She had known that going in. Liars and crooks were all Byron Jasper hung out with. Well, she'd let them worry with fucking folks out of serious money. She was manless right now and that always took priority. And that good-looking Chase Jeffcoat seemed like a super worthy stud target, and she maybe better lay in some Bl and some Dex just so she didn't get wore out subduing him.

B-J got brought back to the extreme present by a loud BAM outside the store.

She looked out the big plate glass window onto King Street to see a girl sitting with her face down on the steering wheel of a Range Rover crying. She had side-swiped a couple of parked cars and rear-ended an Acura in traffic backed up at the red light. Always a Samaritan, B-J interrupted her shopping spree to go outside and see if she could help.

Traffic was stopped all the way up the street. People gathering on the sidewalk. There wasn't much damage to the Acura, the driver getting out and looking at a crumpled bumper.

The girl had her face in her hands now sobbing almost uncontrollably. She didn't seem to be physically hurt. A big black Labrador with a blue bandana around his neck was howling.

B-J put her hand on the girl's shoulder and said, "This analysis may not qualify for a Nobel prize, but I'd say you're right upset."

15

"Doctor Dupree will see you immediately," said the receptionist at the chiropractor. A roomful of waiting patients looked at her. Tamzie felt pretty good. This was the kind of treatment she'd like to get used to.

Vineyard's lawyer business cards were setting in a little glass dish next to the receptionist's window.

It felt good to have a man just take charge of her life. He said her new investments were coming online a bit slow because the thieving bandits she had working for her before had give them up slow. Dragging their feet. Claiming the computer down. So he had got her over to Seagrass to take out a loan for about six months of mortgage payments on the new condo.

The nurse tell her to take off all her clothes and lie face down on the examination table. Tamzie was thinking she'd lie there freezing to death, but no, the door open right away. First class treatment.

Doctor Shereese Dupree was African, but real light skin, kind of a cocoa butter color. Tall, slim and foxy looking. She had extra long fingers too except for the thumbs which are short and stubby like they been cut off at the front knuckle. Strangler's thumbs, the old folks call them. Spooky.

And the way she talk is not what you call refined.

"That's a convincing high ass you got on you, gal-girl," she said. "No wonder you got a positive self-image." She give Tamzie's rear a big hard slap that make her yelp.

Then she run her hands over Tamzie's body. Say, "Uh-huh. We got us some tight rhomboids and trapezius. And that old sternocleidomastoid—unh-unh."

Tamzie lay still not wanting to ask what that was.

The doctor said, "What I'm about to do is as easy as A-B-C. So listen up. A-is-for-asshole as in dumb asshole you. B-is-for-bitch as in one mo' bitch think she on top of things. C-is-for-catastrophe which about to land on the unsuspecting."

Tamzie start to get up, but the doctor take hold of her shoulders and slam her face onto the mat with hands that feel like their previous career was unloading trucks.

"There's ain't a thing wrong with you. It's fake like all a' Vineyard's clients. But there's gone be plenty wrong when you walk outta here 'cause trouble just come looking. Woo-ee. I'm gone have me some mean-spirited fun and violate every Hippocratic oath I ever took."

Wham! Tamzie take a two-fisted blow square between her shoulder blades that nearly whomped the breath out of her. She gasp, "Hey, I ain't no crash-test dummy for you to hammer on."

She would have jump up, but the doctor pinch a nerve in her neck that paralyze her with the most excruciating pain she had ever known existed.

"Did he tell you I was a relative? He always does. I'm his wife. And lemme tell you, being married to that sorry sum-bitch is a grueling schedule of deceit, suspicion and sneaking-round—do you know what I'm saying?"

"His wife?" Tamzie gag.

"My husband who's supposed off on a Continuing Legal Education trip but really spending the night between the sheets with a ho-bitch. Or seeing clients late, he's really hittin' skins."

Tamzie said, "But I ain't . . ."

The doctor said, "You in denial? That shit don't move me. You probably already learn that love with him ain't exactly a volcanic eruption of thrashing bodies and passion colors behind the eyelids. The real message get brought home when you find $250 cashmere sweaters in shades of lilac charge to your name. He always think that's a relevant gift for his efforts on a girl's behalf. But that ain't even a fraction of the equation what about to hit your pocketbook.

"But don't let me be too long-winded here. It's time for you to squawk."

The stumpy thumbs go into Tamzie's back so deep she thought they'll rip out her lungs. She still can't seem to scream. She can barely breathe and at the moment that take priority.

Over the next ten minutes, Tamzie get run over by a Mack truck, then a steam roller, and have a refrigerator fall on her. She still can't scream because her body's too paralyzed. When the beating is over, the doctor say if Tamzie will excuse her, she got an office full of patients waiting.

"But lemme tell you a little hint about fuckin' round with Vineyard Dupree. Right now, you can't see beyond your clit. But lemme tell you, it's a road to ruin, and there's no redemption at the end. And that's the truth."

Tamzie isn't sure how she manage to get dressed. She can barely hobble out to her Saab. She felt like she been expertly beat up by a team of L.A. cops from the special beating niggaz squad.

She force herself into her car and sit there trying to get her brain organized. Her fingers don't seem to want to work the car keys. This is when she discover that both her car phone and her American Express Gold Card are missing. She tries hard to remember when she last seen them and finally settle on the night before with Vineyard Dupree. When he had slept over at her house.

■ ■ ■

Rannie Ralston crossed her sensual, silk-clad legs with an easy grace, then uncrossed them. She was dressed in a soft winter knit in a dove gray.

Bracey Jeffcoat toyed with her hair, then forced her hands into her lap, fighting to keep them still. This was her house. She had to be in charge. But she didn't feel in charge.

Rannie stirred the sugar in her cup of tea, set the tiny silver spoon on the saucer with a little clink.

A clock ticked in the silence.

Bracey wanted to drink her own tea, but she had a morbid fear it would make her have to run to the bathroom. "I'm sure mother will be disappointed she missed your visit," she said.

Rannie gave a sickly smile. "Me too. But I guess she's busy at Krogan's. Architecting her jewelry expansion program."

Krogan's was the society jewelry store in town. If your husband wanted to confess an affair he went there and bought something first.

There was six years difference in age between Rannie and Bracey. Their grandmothers had been formidable competitors on the Charleston social scene. They entertained *comme il faut* and kept perennial gardens filled with narrowleaf zinnias, joe-pye weed, Moonbeam coreopsis, pennisetum and climbing roses, the colors echoing in muted good taste. Time and changing social habits had eroded the importance of that.

Rannie and Bracey had been raised well versed in the old traditions, but there the ways parted severely. Rannie was an unrelenting career attorney. She ran over her opposition with a flair that would impress F. Lee Bailey. Bracey was a rather unornamental wife of an investment banker who marketed dubious investments. Bracey liked to watch birds.

Bracey's mother Izzie still clung to a doctrinaire belief that a woman's place was in the mansion ordering domestics around. Or out buying things. Bracey hadn't exactly intended to be a clone of her mother. It had worked out that way by accident. Maybe it was predestined. Now she was just trying to keep afloat by treading familiar waters.

Bracey felt like she was drowning in manure. She was reasonably certain she had participated in a crime at Seagrass. She was terrified that people would learn what Grady Troxler did to her. Slavering over her. Calling her juicy tidbits. Ordering her to assume the missionary position.

Trying to flee from the degradation, she had had a wreck. Chase was furious about paying the deductible under the insurance policy. But while she sat there crying, waiting for police and a towing service, the most extraordinary girl came and held her hand.

Her name was Bobbi-Jean Kincaid, and she worked in some capacity for Roebuck. She was nice and all bubbly with sympathy and helpful advice about car engines and tow trucks. She just yacked away like they had known each other for years although Bracey had never met anybody—never even dreamed of meeting anybody like her. Given how nice the girl had been, Bracey felt unbearable guilt at the thought, but Bobbi-Jean was as common as they come. A girl who would own paintings of Elvis on black velvet.

"You know, scumbags are funny," Rannie said, smiling to herself. She sipped her tea.

"Yes?" said Bracey.

"Back at Halloween a cop got inside an apartment to make a bust by wearing a clown costume. Everybody inside thinking it was funny. Maybe like one of those balloon-a-gram greetings or something. He makes the arrest. Then, you know what this state-of-the-art dirtbag says?"

Bracey hated when people would ask questions and make you say 'no, what?' Rannie was patiently waiting. So Bracey said "No, what did the dirtbag say?" She used the vulgar term since Rannie seemed to be giving her a short course on life above Broad Street.

"He said 'Man, you got me under false pretenses. That ain't right. How can the children of this community ever trust a clown or a cop again? The poor kids won't be able to get their candy at Halloween. It's a sorry state of affairs I tell you.'"

Bracey said nothing. What was there to say?

"You know what he was wanted for?"

"No."

"Armed robbery."

"That's very interesting."

"I guess the point I'm making is every scumbag thinks he's got the moral high ground. The old 'Yeh, but he hit me back first' routine."

"Yes."

"Fuck up your life. Then externalize the problem. Blame everyone else for it. Blame society."

"I guess," said Bracey. She felt like an idiot child. She had never been able to deal with women who used casual profanity. That Bobbi-Jean girl . . . just appalling.

In all her distress at the car wreck, Bracey had let it slip out that she had just passed an unpleasant hour with Grady Troxler. And the girl had said "That man. I bet he's got a dick so ugly it'd make you cringe."

"Marrying for money," said Rannie. "It's a patented formula for success."

Bracey chewed her lip. She shifted gingerly in her chair.

"Here's Izzie Fanseau with a sudden ravenous awakening of her sleeping libido. Soon she'll take a fetishistic interest in real estate. But it'll always be for the best of reasons."

Bracey sat frozen like a bird before a snake. Rannie was smarter, tougher, richer, and better looking. For a solo practitioner she had unparalleled clout on Broad Street. She was going to make a gruesome example of them for daring to spirit her father out of the Ralston house and into the Fanseau. Already, she had quietly put out the word that Fanseau and Jeffcoat enemies were now her friends. It was the topic of the day at the Yacht Club.

The tension made Bracey want to scream '*what are you going to do to us*'?

Rannie said in her experience, get excited at the pre-orgasmic level, it gives you an atomic climax. Muscle tension. Blood flow to the genital area.

Bracey gaped at her.

"If you're going to be fucked," Rannie said.

Bracey said, "Wh . . . ?"

Rannie said she really must be going.

Bracey said, must you? Her voice came out a croak.

Rannie paused at the front door and looked back into the cavernous house. "I'm tremendously disappointed in your mother," she said. "But I'm sure I won't disappoint her."

16

"I'm on a new diet," said Rannie Ralston the meanest attorney in town sitting back in the big high-back chair behind her office desk. "It's all sauerkraut. It would make anyone lose her appetite. Maybe rhubarb would be worse."

Tamzie kept telling herself she didn't have to take shit off this red bitch. She had more money than her. Well, at least as much. You couldn't tell how much the Ralston house was worth.

But here she was summoned down to Broad Street just like back when she was a maid for the Ralston family about to be told she was taking a pay cut or working all day and all night both instead of just days.

Tamzie had worn her Prada loafers and carried the Hermès bag to give herself courage. They weren't working very well. The Calvin Klein dress didn't help neither.

When Tamzie was a little girl, her momma Mozelle would bring home Rannie's cast-off clothing. In sixth grade, Tamzie got a round red skirt with a black telephone appliqué and big looped phone cord on it. She went to school, hair done up in cornrows, thinking she was about the classiest black girl in all of Charleston.

That was why she had dressed up so. Let the red bitch know she was on her level now. Didn't take charity. Although as the minutes tick by Tamzie get to thinking maybe she'd take about any charity offered.

The red bitch Rannie Ralston just sit there conveying power and sheer meanness. She was the super-hardball mortal combat of Broad Street. And she looked awful good in that pearly gray suit. Probably shantung silk. And shit, check out those slingbacks. You just knew they ran $200 a pair at Bob Ellis.'

She was saying, "I try to snatch a few spare moments to exercise. Work on my pubococcygeus and other pelvic floor muscles. The principal benefit of a strong pelvic floor is heightened orgasm."

Tamzie can't believe the red bitch was talking to her like that. She said she herself was enrolled in a buns-and-abs class, but it was killing her.

The red bitch look thoughtful. "That reminds me of a client I have. Married to a man for fifteen years then ups and knifes him to death. Claims amnesia. Says she has no idea how the steak knife got in his back."

Tamzie knew there was some ingratitude message intended. There it was. That evil smile spreading across her face.

Rannie's voice crooned. "Of course, you're not going to sue my mother over your little fall down the stairs. You've got a full range of movement. Anyone can see that. Besides, I've had an insurance investigator following you for days. Making videos."

Tamzie gape at her.

"It's an almost elegant life you have now. Certainly a blameless one. I confess I'm envious. You clipping coupons while I keep on in my workaholic ways. I see you've taken up with that Vineyard Dupree. Doing some rather acrobatic maneuvers in bed with him."

Tamzie almost jump out of the chair at that one. Rannie raise a hand to shush her. "I know. It's an invasion of privacy. Relax. We'll never use that film. And I've never told you we had it. Just a little party amusement I'll show my friends over the years." She shook her head with a sad smile. "Vineyard Dupree. Well, you know I'm not one to play down the risks."

"What's wrong with him?" said Tamzie, real belligerent. The red bitch sitting there dressed fit to kill. Big Lucite ring on her finger. Looking better than Tamzie ever hope to. Saying she got naked movies of her.

Rannie smiled negligently. "Well, let's say he's generally dismissed by the County Bar as a lightweight." Before Tamzie can rebut that, she goes on.

"And, of course, his ethics are somewhat troubling. You know what a major part of his practice is? He lines up men in prison with disability benefits from Supplemental Social Security. They can get up to $458 a month for drug addiction and alcoholism. He takes a cut."

Tamzie ask what's wrong with that, and the red bitch say just that it's illegal. Tamzie say, oh. The red bitch say, think about it. They're already being supported by the state. They in jail. Tamzie say, oh yeah.

"Then he turns them in to the feds and collects a reward. He juxtaposes the two activities in an artful way."

There was that damn smile again. "Are we engrossed yet? Do I detect a curious reticence to discuss Vineyard? I suppose that small time crook sold you a house with a clouded title."

Tamzie said, what you talking about, and the red bitch flip on one of them computers on her desk and tap some things on the keys with long wicked black-red fingernails painted in Chanel metallic vamp. They look like they been sunk in human flesh, gouge the blood out of some poor soul.

Various screens change places with each other on the computer, and then up come the deed Tamzie got to her condo. The mortgage. The note. She had bought them all as a corporation—Jerome, Inc. somehow Rannie had figure that out.

The red bitch say, "Vineyard's always one to sell you a major stake in his own debacles. Plus, it gave his debit column something of a face-lift. He was the owner of the condo. Bought it on spec and sold it to you. Did you know that?"

Tamizie was really being run round in circles on this one.

The red bitch say, "Everyone knows he doesn't do title checks. He nearly got disbarred for that a few years back. Only kept his license by solemnly vowing to stay out of real estate practice. Don't imagine you'll ever get money out of him when you find out the depths of his screw-up. No malpractice insurance company will touch him. He's flying bare."

A long pause. Big crease between her eyebrows showed she was thinking. She tap the computer keys again with those bloody nails. Some more screens come up.

"Oh my God. Seagrass isn't so stupid as to let him do their closings!" Rannie bust out laughing. She sound like the undead down in a cemetery at night. The big toenail staring out of her open-toe shoe was the same blackish-red.

Going down in the elevator to the street Tamzie can barely stand. She's dizzy and her knee joints won't seem to lock. As she had went out the door, the red bitch sniff the air and say, "You've always favored somewhat bold fragrances haven't you." Then she do that laugh again like she seen in a crystal ball that Tamzie about to get gallstones, cancer, and a broke back all in the same day.

On Broad Street, Tamzie breathe the air trying to get a grip. She look at her Prada loafers but they don't inspire great confidence.

Up the street near the bank Vineyard Dupree's standing. Some good-looking sister talking to him real intent like maybe she wanted to eat him like raw oysters on the half-shell. Her body language intentions are so obvious she might as well have been naked in a strip club and lap-dancing all over him.

Vineyard's wearing double-pleated pants and a canary yellow sweater. He's far off, but the sweater sure look like cashmere.

■ ■ ■

"You're looking a trifle discombobulated about something," said Izzie Fanseau. She was lolling in an old-fashioned claw-footed bathtub with a faint wisp of steam rising off the surface of the water.

Bracey was struggling to cope with the rapid changes around her. She could not keep the near-hysteria out of her voice. "Rannie Ralston will go ballistic. The sheer underlying sadism in that girl is terrifying."

What had happened was Izzie had summoned her

daughter into the bathroom and casually announced she was going to have Blake Huston declared incompetent and herself appointed as his commitee. She'd have total control of his property. It was only too appropriate. She was his wife.

"That certainly lets him see where he stands in the pecking order," said Bracey acidly.

"I don't see anything wrong with it. Just gives him less to fret about. It's not like I'm locking him off in a bin somewhere. He'll stay on here."

"You haven't been married to him for two weeks."

Izzie said marriage is a hit-or-miss proposition. Blake hadn't done badly.

Bracey agreed he had had no difficulty adapting to sleeping with the corgis. They seemed to like him too. They'd all lie in bed watching "Gilligan's Island."

Izzie said the lawyer for Seagrass—Vineyard something or other—can you believe that name?—was handling the whole matter. He apparently had some sort of general private practice as well as his corporate work. She paused and said he was a "colored gentleman" but seemed competent enough. At least Chase considered him to be, and who was she to question his judgment?

Bracey thought of course Chase was behind it. She asked what would they do if it blew up in their faces? Izzie said getting Blake's assets producing income was her first priority. She couldn't assume worst case scenarios.

Bracey said, "Yes, frugal budgets are not your *forte*."

Izzie gave her the gimlet eye. "My eyebrows are professionally shaped. What does that make me? A sybarite? I'm a good-looking woman. No face-lifts. I did have a chemical peel. I floss regularly. Still have my teeth. I'm not a cat lover with the smell of litter box everywhere. I have no drug or alcohol problems. No migraines. Don't live on megavitamins. I think Blake got a very good deal in me."

Izzie stood up dripping from the tub telling Bracey to hand her a towel. Bracey averted her gaze. She felt fairly certain that mothers didn't typically appear naked before their daughters. Maybe Tallulah Bankhead did. Or Joan Crawford.

Izzie said Hilton Head was simply ruined. They have a population of 50,000 people down there now. And outlet stores. Can you imagine such a thing? For women to come in buses. In the rental condos they only give you one roll of toilet paper and no coffee filters.

Bracey said, sure, show the selfishness and snobbery beneath the tempered steel. Izzie said, what did you say? Bracey said, nothing.

Izzie toweled herself vigorously. Her large breasts jiggled. "You were always mean-spirited and insecure as a child. I can't imagine where I failed you."

Bracey pouted, defiantly arrogant in her own small way. She said she would be missing dinner that night. Izzie asked how can you possibly do that? It's important that at least once a day a family gather to break bread together. Bracey said she was going to an Audubon Society meeting.

"Following your inner voice or whatever it is you're doing."

"Yes."

Izzie shook her head in despair. She said, "You just don't have the family feelings I do."

17

"Clemson can move the dam' football," vowed Byron Jasper. "I tell you what. We talkin' textbook blocking. I mean they got the personnel."

He hit his nine-iron shot up onto the green, it bounced bad and rolled back to the lower edge leaving him a 25-foot putt.

"They've sealed a bowl invite," said Chase Jeffcoat. "If they beat South Carolina, it's Gator. If not, Peach."

The day before, in near freezing winds, Clemson had rolled over Duke 34–17. The stadium at Death Valley had been packed. Now on Sunday in the Lowcountry, it was just plain warm and nice without a cloud in the pure blue sky. A perfect day for a golf threesome with Bobbi-Jean Kincaid. They had the Roebuck links all to themselves.

B-J was feeling good having won $500 betting with bookies picking Air Force over Army and Auburn over Georgia.

Byron said, "In the game of life I don't play just to end up in the top ten. I play to win. My only regret is more twos aren't ones."

When they teed up on the next hole, B-J was yacking about the 54-hole Super Seniors Championship at Myrtle

Beach. She said it featured the top money winners in the 60-and-over division and the famous names in golf just made her go shivery all over. The money did too for that matter.

Five of them, Stockton, Murphy, Jim Colbert and Isao Aoki had already pulled down more than one million bucks for the season. A whole bunch more could hit a million if they placed well. J.C. Snead. Lee Trevino. He is one good looking Mexican. Graham Marsh. Hale Irwin. Tony Jacklin.

She wondered out loud if she just had some weird thing for older men. Or at least older golfers with all those years of success behind them.

This succeeded in goading them into making over-large bets to show what big-time hot-dogs they were.

"Anythang I win from you, sweet-britches," said Byron, "I forgive in toto if you just let me kiss them purty laigs."

She said the Davidson College Invitational tournament was going on for colleges, and a real handsome young stud had come in first on day one with a 73. And that was on a very wet course. She wondered aloud if she had a thing about young golf studs.

That got Chase to pressing his drives which brought out his slice something marvelous. He'd always say he mis-judged the wind. He triple-bogied three holes in a row completely eliminating himself from contention.

Byron's shoulder was hurting like hell, and he was mak-ing noises about stopping the play. B-J said Super Senior Miller Barber just made her underpants all sticky. Byron said he was motivated by pain and played on.

Facing a par-saving putt, he choked. Three-putted and

blamed a hunk of mud on his ball. He said his luck had just plain gone in the tank. And anyhow it was time for a new set of clubs.

Off the seventeenth tee, his ball went whang off something in the fairway that sounded like metal, flew at a crazy angle off into the rough. When they got up there, they found an actual bowling ball kind of protruding slightly from the grass.

Byron cussed a blue streak saying those dam' dirt contractors will cover over any old kind of shit when they build stuff. He got on his cellular phone to address this lack of golf course quality with the utmost urgency. Then cussed out whoever it was came on the phone back at the clubhouse showing how important he was.

On the eighteenth, his extra, extra long driver, a 56-inch Killer Bee snapped when he was leaning his weight on it. No offense to the club. Byron was a right hefty boy.

Just as the light was going behind the trees, B-J sank a 15-foot birdie putt on the 18th green.

Byron pulled out his wallet in a more restrained manner than he had been playing. Said damn if he hadn't lost a wallet and a whole bunch of charge cards the other day. Thought it was when he was drinking brown liquid in a bar somewhere. $450 he counted out saying, "Sweetheart, you done robbed the train."

Byron wanted her to meet him at the Sheraton on the interstate going into Charleston. Motel buffets were his idea of the high life. Also, he said he wanted to have a few afterwards in the bar, listen to the lounge bop and see where it led them.

B-J lied smoothly and said sure, she'd give him a verbal

commitment on that one. Later on, she'd swear he told her another hotel, say she waited for hours, and act really put out with him.

Byron said ten-four for now and went into the club house bar for the first of about forty-five drinks he'd have that night. You could hear him booming football talk at the other drinkers, telling the lady bartender she looked as good as a gumbo sandwich.

On the way to the locker rooms, Chase got her off alone and asked had they really been betting or was it just in fun? B-J said, he was just a perfect darling and more fun than six-ball-wild snooker, but where she came from, a bet was a bet.

Chase said he was cash poor at the moment but had something better. He produced two bracelets of what looked like yellow stone. Almost gold in color but with less red in them. It was citrine, he explained, a semi-precious stone.

He said this was his $450 plus a couple of thou more. He figured he could lose to her maybe five more times based on the inherent value.

B-J said, he sure was special. She slid them onto her wrist and rattled them around a bit. She said, she knew he was married and all that, so she had to react to this without thinking too hard on the morality angles.

Chase made eye contact all sincere and serious like the on-air personality of the best-looking news anchor you'd ever hope to see. He said all the polyrhythms had gone out of his life before she arrived on the scene. No melody lingering on. Contentious wife. More than discontinuity in their thinking. She had huge mood swings, was prone to hysteria.

Of course, he was lying like they all do, but Lordy he was one dazzling handsome stud. That big house he lived in sure beat your average Jaycee's suburban ranch. And him owning his own investment bank he had built from scratch was better than some born-rich Yankee with money that got handed down from Henry Hudson or somebody.

She gave him a sultry look up through her eyelashes and said she liked the idea of being on his agenda. Up to now her love-life had filed for Chapter 11 protection due to involuntary heartbreak.

When he held her shoulders and kissed her, she thought she would just ooze down into lust jelly. She knew she was going to put ladylike inhibition tendencies on the back shelf and just take her pants down and do him. Win, lose, or draw.

■ ■ ■

"So there she was two eye-lifts and a face-lift later," said Izzie. "Striving desperately to look as young as the bride and still packing away the salmon mousse like she was starving."

Chase Jeffcoat laughed appreciatively and carved the cornish hen on the sideboard.

Bracey thought she was going to let loose with a primal scream. Her mother was still obsessed with the Hilton Head wedding and who had done the plastic surgery on the bride's mother. Her own recent marriage had been no landmark in her life, nothing to make her pause and take stock, wonder if her greedy schemes were sinful. And now she was blithely ignoring the astonishing event that had just dropped like a big rotten egg.

Izzie had just had her husband Blake served with the incompetency proceedings right in the middle of dinner. Process server, a cute young College of Charleston girl, came to the front door. Izzie let her in.

Blake was so busy leering at the girl, he didn't seem to grasp what had happened. She said, have a nice evening and left. Made a little heart-shaped movement with her hand.

"Bride and mother," said Izzie, "had one of their sharper little exchanges over how the wedding cake should be cut."

Please just shut up, Bracey was thinking.

That was when the phone rang, and Bracey went to answer it. It was Grady Troxler, President of Seagrass S & L. The word 'dreck' came to mind. Also 'arrested adolescent.' 'Anal retentive.'

He said, he thought she'd want to know it all went through. She said, what went through? He said, the loan. But more than that, he had an august personage he wanted her to meet.

She said, meet? Meet where? He said, between his legs.

She was silent. Shocked.

Grady said, he was going to let her steal him from his wife. Learn the role of homewrecker. They'd do some high-kicking, toe-tapping old favorites. A little dial-twirling on those nips of hers. Do a Junior League luncheon in her twat. Snuggle in there. Give it an indelible stamp. Do some fantasy form tongue work.

Bracey was weighing the pros and cons of screaming uncontrollably.

"I beg your pardon . . ."

Grady gave out a throaty chuckle. He put his voice low. "You social blue book bitches are all the same. Ice maiden mentality gives you a steady pulse. Dense cunt hair 'cause you never shave it. Vacuum-packed, sealed-up pussy. All that old-money risk-aversion.

"I'll teach you the gritty edge. Give you an orgasm that'll empty the vaults. Get you started with some loving on impulse. Soon you'll be begging for year-round dicking. You've got a lot of potential in that area. You'll fall in love with the bone. Be like a kid eating hash browns with chocolate cake."

Her hands were trembling. "Do you want to speak to my husband?"

"Let's not take a step backwards in our relationship. I intend to get you naked. Showcase your talents. Stick my expandable hardware about eight yards up you while a radio plays big band sounds for the seniors. And afterwards I'll gift-wrap you in a mink coat. You'd like that. Yeh."

Bracey said she was really kind of busy.

Grady chuckled. "I'm reluctant to point out that you're up to your neck in major banking fraud. Yeah, I know. What a fucking downer. Like Santa just handed you a lump of coal. But I make an effort to educate and inspire. Regular dicking is like a continual impact. A quest. An ongoing mission. Teaches you to make smart choices. Learn the social dynamics between genitals.

"Sure, you're a little confused right now. But a fancy-background bitch like you has got unique needs. Go dirt road on you. Chocolate highway. Teach you to sing high-end falsetto. Get all frothy. Have an orgasm like an avalanche."

"I'm really quite satisfied with my long-distance telephone provider," she said and hung up. She had both hands clamped on the receiver holding it down like she was afraid it would jump up and bite her.

She sat back down at the dinner table, shivering, sweating heavily.

Izzie was gone. She had wheeled Blake out to fall asleep in front of the TV. The summons and complaint lay there at his place unexamined.

"You're driving a car straight for a cliff," she told her husband in a tiny voice.

"Is that the prevailing feeling?" he asked blandly. His fork clinked down on the plate. He wiped his mouth with the thick napkin.

He said, he was never one to avoid a dialogue. Talk to him.

"You think you can make this family a proving ground for corruption. Enlisting my mother in your enterprise is like a Hitler-Stalin Pact."

Chase said he offered Izzie meaningful financial incentives. "And there lies the crucial difference in our points of view. In any choice between you and me, your mother will choose me. Nettlesome, but there you have it."

Bracey sat limp staring at the food on her plate. Outmaneuvered and outmuscled.

She told Chase he had no shame. Clubbing Blake Huston into submission with the fear of the madhouse. Chase said Blake Huston spent his life as a blackmailer. He should feel right at home with the drama.

"There's only one fly in the ointment," she said. "He's got a daughter who believes in ritual male castration. She's already paid me a visit. We had a little chat on the subject of impending doom."

18

"You giving the term 'impulse shopping' a whole new meaning!" shouted Byron Jasper, storming onto the practice putting green next to the club house. "I'm gonna be arrested for misprison of a felony after I don't turn myself in for strangling you!"

Red in the face and real pissed off, Byron was waving credit card bills that had arrived that day. Bobbi-Jean tapped an eighteen-footer right up to the edge of the cup where it hung and then fell in with a clunk. She had earlier admitted to having possession of his Visa and Master-Card, but convinced him he insisted on her using them. He spent so much time drunk that the numerous memory lapses stymied him there.

Byron was close to a meltdown. "Five thousand god-loving after-tax dollars! There are those gals who will fuck for you just to gain access to your charge cards, but I ain't got fucked! I mean I has been more than fucked! Fucked over is what it is! I swar to fucking Jesus I am not a cussing man, but goddamn you little sorry-ass thieving bitch, I'd like to whip the tar out of you!"

B-J just looked at him with those serene blue eyes. "Is this true?" She said preposterously.

Byron cussed and ranted and picked up handsful

of golf balls and flung them around. He said the name thieving cunt fit her for more reasons than one. Said she shocked even the most jaded and beat-down, beat-up, pussy-whipped, whip-broke victim of thieving cunts.

Finally, B-J said, she was real sorry, but Roebuck was just going to have to revamp its revenue sharing. She couldn't live off what she was being paid.

He stood there round-shouldered and heaving for breath.

B-J had a basic understanding of marketing and product development, and in that vein had herself a set of rules she had adapted from some sales literature.

1. *Figure the target buyer's immediate need*—Byron wanted to get laid in the worst way.

2. *Assume limited life cycle for your product*—clean him as quick as you can and move on.

3. *Stay close to target and innovate as needed*—and this was where she had an idea.

She called him "Mister Jasper," said she always respected his work, tried to be chief cheerleader for him. It wasn't easy with that foul-mouthed Grady Troxler undercutting him at every turn. An unruly realtor sales force rejiggering the accounts. Backstabbing. Widespread snafus. But she tried to take an independent role. Do some initiative on her own for his and his alone betterment.

Byron was starting to calm down. On a sober day, his attention span might have matched up to a kindergarten kid's. He said, "Long before 'female empowerment' got to be such a buzz term, I believed in it."

B-J smoothly tapped a long putt right up to the edge

of the cup and said she couldn't help but notice things weren't going ideal.

He admitted there was some evidence of slower than expected sales. His sales force was kind of a roster full of question marks. But come December, all the needed tax breaks, deduction of mortgage points and such would speed things up.

B-J said, "Well, conventional wisdom would have it that real estate sales come to a screeching halt about Thanksgiving until New Year."

He said, "Yeah, you're right about that."

"Well," she said, "some people might say this was kind of contrived. But I'm looking to generate a big play."

B-J told him she had grown up with a girl who had hit it reasonably big posing for naked pictures, now was in management for a major skin magazine. It was a time when a network sports commentator had said women weren't very good at golf because their boobs got in the way. This blooper had caused quite a ruckus in the press.

Byron was following right along. "Yeah, yeh," he said.

What she proposed was a Pro-Am with D-cup honeys paired with semi-famous men pros. There was no lack of young women who could half-way shoot a half-ass round of golf. Wanting to get married to pro athletes had so many of them taking up the game. Not just skin magazine centerfolds, but Laker/Cowboy/Raider kind of cheerleaders.

Byron spoke in a prayerful whisper. "You . . . you could arrange such a thing? Stock-pile that young talent?"

She said your most obvious sponsors were indisposed one way or another. Snap-on Tools was being hammered by radlibbers over their girlie calendars as if women worked in the auto repair shops of America. Hooters Restaurant chain was fighting for its very life against a bunch of ugly dykes in the Justice Department. Cigarette companies jumped on by health nuts.

Byron said, "*We'll* sponsor it. Roebuck its own damn self. Hell, yeah, we're in!"

By the time B-J began brainstorming potential names for the tournament—Big Girls—Goodbodies—PowerChest—Byron was hyperventilating.

"PowerChest," he breathed, cupping both hands in front of his chest. "There's something there that just captures your every emotion."

Byron was a believer. An unabashed play to the American male. The singular allure of a set of twin whopping great bazooms that made each and every one of those girls the personality-kid.

"Sweetheart, you a locomotive what can't be stopped. A pillar of strength in every crisis. You are fantasy come to town. You are flowers sprouting up in spring. I am so wracked up with love for you I feel like the Handicapped Professional of the Year."

B-J said, "Listen, do you have some other charge card I can use for a few necessaries? The two you gave me before seem to be max'ed out."

■ ■ ■

Vineyard said he done told Tamzie he cut up her charge card, now come on back here in the office and let's shut the door. Don't pay no mind to that old woman out there.

An ancient black woman sat in the waiting room, hat with veil square on her head, purse held on her knees. She made a gentle rocking motion in the chair. You could barely hear her hum and croon to herself.

Otherwise the office was empty. Vineyard always sent his secretary home at three. Said he run a low-cost structure.

Kind of reluctant, Tamzie follow Vineyard back into his office. She had her hair straightened out like Salt-N-Pepa did getting an award at the Grammys. She said she know he don't cut up her card until after he buy himself a cashmere yellow sweater.

Vineyard said he cut it up and was getting her issued a new one with better value add-ons. American Express is a lot of baloney. And as to that sweater thing, he figured it's 'bout time she buy him a present. They been going together long enough. So quit being so straitlace and come on back in here and close that door.

Tamzie look back at the old woman silently rocking back and forth. She had seen her there a lot. Vineyard said don't pay her no mind. She's got some money coming for her land, but it's all tied up in escrow. She come in from Roebuck Island every day despite him telling her it's a wasted effort. But she got a ride with somebody who work in town. Just wait out there until her ride leave at the end of the day.

Tamzie looked at Vineyard's bi-colored pinstripe suit, tone-on-tone silk tie, thinking how she would have dug that at one time. She ask, did he not search her condo title the same way he not search the others? That was a matter of big speculation with her.

Vineyard didn't take kindly to this new dimension in her thinking. He said, "Who's been telling lies on me?

Whoever slander me gone get slap upside the head with a major tort lawsuit."

Tamzie say, Rannie Ralston say it.

Vineyard say, oh. Well she ain't worth messing with. Besides her brother on the Seagrass Board. Got to be nice to her. Now come on in here where I got the home team advantage. It's Miller time. Let's you and me kick back.

The old woman rocked, looking straight ahead at the wall. Waiting like she could wait to the end of time.

Vineyard said quit fretting about this Madonna-whore complex and let's just do the whore bit. Kamasutra time for young Miss Jerome. He had his hands running up under her skirt now, using the other to try to get her away from the door, stop blocking it so he could shut the thing. Tamzie said, when would her new investments get on-line? He said, he got her covered. The Seagrass asset guidance team and he done found common ground. For a while there, they at sea level while he up on Mount Everest. He pull them half way up the slope.

She slap his hand off her breast.

"Come on now, Tamzie. None of this no glove, no love shit. I ain't got no social disease."

Tamzie look at the picture of Vineyard wearing the Afro. She decide he was trying to look like Jimi Hendrix.

Just then Vineyard get an unexpected visit from bad news. A big fat, money-demanding black woman come in. Fat meaning gravity-defying fat. Woman as big as Tamzie's Auntie Eula Mae in Cainhoy. Maybe bigger. Money-demanding meaning give it to me right now, no more sorry-ass excuses. Her temper flaring as she come through the door.

Tamzie step back out of the way staking out a claim to being an innocent bystander.

The woman loom there like a big question. Hands on hips. Say, "We at the juncture of the truth, lawyer-man. You ain't gone defuse this time-bomb without a cashier check."

Vineyard get a sly look on his face, and Tamzie had more than an inkling, she knew for sure that God had designed the man deceitful.

"That money's held by Seagrass. They all backed up with paperwork and government HUD forms. Fannie Mae. Jimmy Mac. All that mortgage stuff that pervade so much. I don't have any day-to-day responsibility for that."

The woman say don't give me none of that shit. All Vineyard's career crookedness gone come to an end with her full stop.

Vineyard said, "Don't get overexcited. You ain't suffer any apparent damage."

She said, "No more'n you, and you gone be a shock-absorber for my fist upside yo' haid. You already done cut a check to Omonio Reese, and now you got a green light to give me the same one all over again."

Vineyard said, ohhhh you related to *that* man. The problem is he's now history.

She said, she ain't some subsidiary. She's the widow. Takesha Reese.

"I know, and I'm terrible sorry," said Vineyard trying to recover from his ignorance. "I'm willing to let you experience out your grief. But I got to open an estate for him. Put that check through probate."

She said, don't give me no negatives. You cast around

in that check book of yours and come up with the money or you gone see some retribution from hell.

She took a step forward. Collision loomed now.

Vineyard warned, "Back off, woman. You starting to make me feel mortally threatened."

She said, "I'll do more than that. I'll flat-out cut off your oxygen supply." She come at him reaching out with big hands for some hand-to-hand combat.

Before she close the gap, he back up, say don't make me send out an expeditionary force. She keep coming.

He reach down behind his desk, snatch up a clear plastic shield and a whippy looking rubber stick both like cops use in riot control. He crash into her with the shield and give her a big loud pop with the baton on her thigh. She let out a scream like living death, and he pop her again. She grab two hands on the shield and try to jerk it away from him. He can see her screaming ugly face right through plastic shield. The view ain't too pleasing.

They shimmy back and forth like a tractor pull, first three steps one way, then three the next. She's screaming like a scalded dog. Vineyard yelling, he ain't bowing to pressure, and she keep this up he's going to hurt up on her, make her addicted to prescription pain killers.

The dispute boiled out into the hall and slam up against the elevator door. Vineyard beat the woman with the stick until she give up and take her screaming with her down the elevator.

Tamzie's breathing kind of heavy at the violence. The old woman still rocking, not quite seeing it but surely not missing it.

Vineyard come back in, saying that Takesha woman just learn to appreciate some stark reality. Lawyering ain't a branch of social work. He show Tamzie the shield. Say it's made out of clear urethane or acrylic or some shit. Toss it in the corner. Then show the rubber stick. Say it was 26″ hard rubber baton. A semi-flexible striking tool. He toss that in the corner. Then give Tamzie a close-up eyeballing.

"Ooo-eee, baby, you look like sex arousal. Flush cheeks. Breath coming heavy. Bright eyes of desire. C'mere to me—unh."

Tamzie ask what the hell that be all about? He owe that woman money? Vineyard say, "Don't pay no attention to that meretricious bullshit. You know me, sugar. I speak softly and carry a big dick." He laugh, his arms still spread wide wanting her to walk into them.

Tamzie cock an eyebrow before she head out the office. "I'm starting to think there's a lot less to you than meet the eye."

His voice had whine in it. "Girl-friend, you my best-kept secret. You can't walk out like some dislocation. Come back here, let me burnish up my image with you."

Tamzie look at the top of the desk where they had actual made love on. "You ain't up to your previous best," she said.

In the outer office, the old woman was still rocking.

"Come on, Auntie," said Tamzie. "I'll drive you home. The lawyer ain't behaving too well."

19

Rannie Ralston uncovered the fact that through three shell corporations, Chase & Co. Investment Banking owned a 60% interest in Seagrass Savings & Loan. Federal banking law forbade this kind of controlling ownership.

Investment banks put together deals. Like Roebuck Island Plantation. Their fee comes from the deal going through—not whether the deal ultimately makes money.

The S & L was supposed to take a professional view of loan projects Chase brought them for financing. With him controlling the majority of voting stock, he could adversely cloud their judgment.

Rannie went straight to the SEC about it.

Worse, she called a TV press conference to announce her actions and warn investors with Chase & Co. It was a slow news day, and three channels had both shown up and put it on the six o'clock report. Just a few soundbites, but Rannie proved herself a master of savage biting.

She sat behind her office desk in a power suit with an American flag showing. She looked like a red-haired Demi Moore playing Janet Reno. She had the moral high ground and wasn't inclined to hold back.

She said these violations were done by both accident

and design. Which was to say Chase was both incompetent and crooked.

She said Chase Jeffcoat was a spineless opportunist and a parable of everything that was wrong with the nation's finances.

By seven, the phone in the Fanseau mansion started ringing. People who had investments with Chase seemed to watch TV news.

From the dinner table Bracey and her mother could hear Chase issuing a load of fervent denials. "Could you say I've betrayed a public trust? Of course not. Haven't even tarnished it."

After about three calls, Chase took it off the hook. He flopped back down at the dinner table. Izzie and Bracey stared at him in a pregnant silence. Bracey had learned the interrogation technique from her mother. He looked from one to the other uneasily.

"I'm not Mother Teresa. You can't nurse lepers and achieve a measure of success." He waved his hand vaguely as though the house were a product of his work.

They both said nothing. The phone suddenly made that awful beeping noise to tell you it was disengaged.

Chase started like he had sat on a tack. "The issue has garnered a little interest. Sure. Some nervous nellies always panic."

"Is there truth in what she says?" asked Izzie coldly.

"Sure, there were some underlying contradictions. Put two banks together. A mutual accommodation. That's all."

Izzie said she felt certain everything Chase had done was honorably intended and entirely appropriate. She refused to spurn him at a moment of crisis.

Chase said he was glad the straw poll was in his favor. He said he'd end this misery in a bit, have the fiasco behind him.

His explanations remained disturbingly ambiguous. Izzie said she wondered what other undisclosed facts remained in his business dealings. For example, would their income be affected?

Under this pointed questioning, Chase acknowledged, "We're going to be on a pay-as-you-go basis here for a bit. Any income benefits will be derived from a tight rein on costs and not from any dramatically higher revenue."

Izzie paused, her lips pursed. She said she personally would have to sidestep any belt-tightening. At her age she couldn't be expected to economize.

Chase said, he'd reshuffle her portfolio. Get it back to the target percentages.

Izzie said, she hoped he would. She sounded very cold.

Chase tried his investment spiel. He said Phase 2 was moving ahead. The SeaSide Pointe at Roebuck Island. It would be quite probably the most aesthetic and challenging golf course outside of Pebble Beach. Some colored people owned a patch of it. But they were selling out. Vineyard was clearing the title.

He said, in one way it was a sad refrain. The loss of the old Sea Island culture. He had a sentimental attachment to the past, but he was the chief fiduciary of Chase & Co. His mandate was significant improvement in his clients' balance sheets.

Izzie said what would he know about the Sea Islands? He was from Orangeburg.

Now she sounded both cold and distant.

20

Sparky Truluck thought it was funny as a crutch seeing that crazy red-haired lawyer bitch on TV, and then the camera would break to Chase Jeffcoat jabbering in terror.

"Aggregate figures are never reliable and ought to be discarded in public policy issues."

Whatever in hell that meant.

You couldn't mistake the lawyer bitch's meaning though. She said, "Sleaziness has certainly achieved its most refined form in Chase Jeffcoat."

Sparky went on foot out into the woods on the far side of Roebuck Island. A tiny shack with a tin roof and a goat in the yard sat on the edge of a broomsage field. He kicked in the door and used his flashlight inside.

The spook Vineyard was a heck of a lot more polite on this job. He was starting to get the picture that this was a partnership with Sparky very much the managing partner.

Sparky liked to think he was enlightened. Didn't expect the poor booger to do any kind of Step 'n Fetchit routine. Just don't try to high-hat him. Go all uppity lawyer nigga on him. That was all. At least for now.

Like any successful crime, arson had its rules. You just needed to avoid at least two of the three red flags the investigators tend to jump on: speed of flamed devouring the building; fire staying close to the ground; a series of multiple burns.

With an old kerosene heater, it was easy as pie. Just punch a hole in it with a ten-penny nail. Let it all drain out. Toss a match as you exit. Whoosh.

The flames started to lick up the newspaper glued to the wall for wallpaper. Hanging there was a framed picture you saw in pretty much every colored house. Portraits of the Kennedy brothers and Martin L. King. Caption "They Died for Freedom." Fire glowed on the glass.

The goat was bleating at Sparky outside in the growing light of the blaze. Chewing on something.

Sparky walked back in the dark through the woods, the fire at his back. He figured he'd drop by Byron Jasper's condo for a beer. Say boy was he whipped. Tough day at the office.

■ ■ ■

"Mistuh Dupree say they got title to the land anyhows," said the old woman. Turn out her name was Jacquilla Gillyard.

"All the others done sold so I got no choice. He being nice to give me something for it. I been coming in each day sitting and waiting all patient to see the color of my money."

Tamzie was driving the old woman home. She had heard about that kind of power play. Get one heir to sell out his share. The new owner could then force the rest to sell.

During the Civil War, the Yankees had captured most of the coast at will. Only Charleston and Wilmington up in North Carolina had held out. The whites had abandoned their plantations on the islands and slaves flocked there for the protection of the bluecoat army. After the war, the Freedman's Bureau had gotten many of them title to the land.

That title turn into an unholy mess-up because nobody died with a will. Couldn't afford $50 for a lawyer. So every child and every grandchild and great-great grandchild living had a little piece of undivided interest.

"Come in with them gunnysack of oyster," said old Jacquilla. She was reminisce about the old days on the islands.

"Used to work down on Lady's Island. Had ten-eighteen cannery up and down the coast. Down to Beaufort. Oyster shucking plants. All close up now. Water's gone dirty with sewage. Got million dollars homes sitting on it.

"Got mechanical pickers that harvest every single one. You need to work them oyster bed by hand. Find a little two incher this year, you shove it in them mud. Come back next year she be nine-ten inch. Can't use no grabber. Got to use you eyes and hands.

"Men today don't want to get they hands dirty. Want to hang out in them bars. Deal them dope."

From way off they could see the glow of the fire and realized her house was burning. It was something everybody on the islands was accustom to. No fire protection. Old wooden houses. Kerosene heat and bad electrical wiring. If no electricity, kerosene light.

Old Jacquilla just kind of gasp and suck on her fist.

They keep driving to the fire knowing the worst. Tamzie stop her car in the big ring of light. The old woman cry out and fall on her knees on the ground. Tamzie think she have a heart failure from the shock. But no, she was crying and hugging her goat. That and a little bit of sandy ground was all she had left in the world.

She said she knew the white men come and burn it down. They want her land for a golf course. Tamzie said that can't be true. It just can't be.

Tamzie finally get her back in the car and say she'd take her home to her place. There was plenty of room. Bring the goat too. Just shove her up in the back seat. The goat don't seem to mind getting in although it start up eating something which Tamzie was afraid was the seat cover. She couldn't see in the dark.

Near the Roebuck clubhouse she see Vineyard Dupree driving past in a brand-new Mercedes SL. His face went up in her headlights.

He didn't stop. All intent on getting somewhere.

Nobody was coming to the fire. The Roebuck folks didn't care.

Tamzie got a real unnerving thought. She suddenly wondered if you could buy a new car with a charge card.

21

"Lord, we ask you to be with the Federal Reserve and keep that discount window open and interest rates for home financing low."

Both hands in the air like a tent preacher, Byron Jasper was leading the sales force in prayer. Sparky watched them, all heads bowed inside the main administration building at Roebuck plantation.

"Let me learn something new every day and do the very best I can. I'm where I want to be right now in my career, Lord, and my loyalty ain't in question nor under scrutiny. I'm finding my rhythm.

"We thank you for the new private investment that paid off the golf course note to Seagrass. There was no great panic getting going there, Lord, because we're professionals. But we're sure grateful for that infusion of cash.

"We ask you to get us up on our hind legs selling and selling hard. Help us bring in a bonanza or die trying. And Lord, if you must take me, let me go out on a winning note."

After that heart-warming and inspirational moment, the sales force dispersed, and Sparky told Byron he seemed full of civic-minded self-confidence as well as a tad hung over.

Byron said he really tied one on. "I swear I got a problem with substance abuse. I can't seem to abuse enough of it. Bar shuts down and ever' dam' one of them gals looks good. End up with one got her hair so teased up you need to stand on a box to get to the top of her head."

Sparky asked what was the life saving outside source of funds that paid off the golf course? Byron declined to elaborate, only saying they "skinned some booger gal."

The other good news was B-J Kincaid had come through, and what they were billing as the PowerChest Championship for a $70,000 purse was scheduled for the weekend after the Clemson game.

Sparky said not to turn things lackluster, but if he was going to have to buy his own set of wheels, he needed himself a retroactive raise. That got Byron out of his good mood in a hurry. Kind of truculent, he said to quit holding your dam' hand out and go see Chase Jeffcoat. Ask him to take a leadership role on the issue. He seemed to be brimming over with BMW Z3 roadsters.

Sparky said, "Not getting much B-J ass are you?"

Byron said obviously he was not where he wanted to be in that drama. Said horniness ain't something you turn on and off like a water tap. And he was tired of her little off-putting ways.

Byron asked what Sparky was doing to earn his keep, and he said, keeping his nose to the grindstone.

Sparky went out and got in Vineyard Dupree's red BMW and drove away from the long fairways and pine forests up to Charleston and picked Vineyard up at his office. Together they drove over to the county hospital where the welfare cases go for their medical care. Waited outside double-parked here and there, according to what security cops came by eyeballing them. Sparky smoked his way through a pack of Marlboros. Vineyard fidgeted and said he had important things needed attending to.

Sparky said how was he supposed to recognize the cunt? He left unsaid the 'you all look alike' comment, but he figured Vineyard knew he was thinking it.

As usual, Vineyard just couldn't seem to handle these uncooperative troublemakers living out there on the swamp edge of Roebuck. Had to hew to the old pattern and come crawling to the white man for help.

Making conversation, Sparky said, "You know that black box on an airplane? The one they say's indestructible. Survive any crash. What I'm wondering is how come they don't make the whole plane out of the same stuff?"

Vineyard didn't appreciate his humor. Sparky was poised to ask him how come there were interstate highways in Hawaii when she came out the emergency ramp. Waddling along. Big fat colored gal. Takesha Reese. Wearing a pink nylon jumpsuit in extra-extra whale-tail size. Omonio Reese's widow. Been having Medicaid-financed rehab for wounds inflicted by Vineyard.

Vineyard said give him the car and Sparky go deal with the mean-ass bitch. She'd been calling the grievance committee up at the state capital about the little altercation they'd had in his office. Telling lies on him and wasting his time writing explanatory letters about his trust account.

Sparky said what was he supposed to do? Follow her on foot in this big city? Out here in the medical complex wasteland?

He started the engine. Vineyard said what are you

going to do? Sparky said as a professional courtesy he would demonstrate what he was going to do.

The fat gal was jaywalking across the street now which was perfect. Sparky gunned the engine and bounced her off the hood, bounced her over onto the pavement before she whapped down on her back and lay prone. Three cars slammed on brakes to avoid running flat over her.

She lay there screaming that her whole body was busted. Vineyard was screaming too although his were more like shrieks. No specific complaints about anatomy.

Sparky said, why didn't Vineyard stick a sock in it? He had no call to overdramatize it so much.

Sparky got out, Vineyard behind him, both leaving their doors open. The fat Reese woman stopped screaming as Sparky's shadow slid over her. Sparky squatted down and talked to her in a real low monotone, nearly a whisper.

"When you get your fat ass out of a body cast you ought to think about moving to New York. Maybe Philly or Baltimore someplace. Seek out the nightlife, better welfare benefits. Quit bothering folks around town here."

Bystanders, other car drivers were gathering. Somebody said an ambulance was on its way from right across the street in the county hospital.

Sparky stood up and stretched. Said, "Man, there's no perfect solution for the insurance company on this one. None of the parties looks good worth a tootle. Worst durn contributory negligence mess you're ever gone see. Her jaywalking, not looking around, head up her ass. My chauffeur here all distracted, seeking out a street address, head up his ass. Probably driving too fast for conditions."

Vineyard said, "Chauffeur? What? I wasn't driving!"

■ ■ ■

"Slander, intimidation, outright theft," cackled Blake Huston. "I used them all. Whole bag of tricks."

Bracey pushed him in his wheelchair down the sidewalk of Legendre Street. It was hard work with all the roots of ancient trees that broke up the cement. At the bottom of the street was Whitepoint Gardens with the giant live oaks and the harbor. Her mother had no difficulty shoving this chore off on her. Omar is busy with the dogs, and you're not doing anything, after all. Take notes on the crazy things he says for the commitment proceeding. And try to call him 'father'.

It was true. She wasn't doing anything exactly. Her assignment for the week from Chase was to get rid of Imbecile and buy a Jack Russell. She hadn't made a move to do either one. Izzie liked the labrador in the way she liked all dogs. So Bracey was caught indecisively between two impossibly strong wills.

At breakfast, Bracey had read aloud from the newspaper style section that twin sets were back in fashion.

"They were never out of fashion," Izzie said flatly.

"I can live without a resurgence," Chase asserted from behind the *Wall Street Journal*.

An air of permanent apology seemed to cling to Bracey. Often, she apologized in advance. Her mother was about the only person she ever argued with, as Izzie was so quick to point out. And then she argued ineffectually.

Younger women seemed so much bolder. Little College of Charleston girls with tattoos of barbed wire around their ankles out drinking in bars with the guys. They seemed like they'd just point their lithe little bodies at a man and steal him away from whatever girl he was with. No shame. No big strain or effort.

That Bobbi-Jean Kincaid girl she met in the wreck had been on the news being all bubbly and overtly sexual. She was organizing a golf tournament at Roebuck that something called ESPN had picked up on. Some kind of cable TV business. The tournament was featuring girls from porno magazines. "Playmates" and "Pets" and things, she called them.

If ever Bracey needed evidence that Roebuck was floundering, there it was. The idea was so unbelievably tacky even Myrtle Beach probably wouldn't touch it. She had told Chase they might as well have a wet T-shirt contest. He had been all flip. Said, they were considering that next.

All the business journals Chase subscribed to frothed at the mouth about environmentalists. Occasionally, Bracey thought about writing them angry letters, refuting their idiotic positions point by point, but Chase said not to. He had a name to defend. Chase & Co. Investment Banking. Like he was about to be on the cover of *Forbes*.

"I plucked them clean like chickens," said Blake. "The only limitation was the size of their bank balances. Some ancestor got too touchy-feely with the negroes and left 'em wide-open vulnerable for generations to come."

Thoroughly depressed, Bracey obsessed on drastically plummeting numbers of songbirds. The shorebirds were virtually gone. The next generation would never see a sanderling, an avocet, a piping plover.

In the news that morning, the City of Charleston announced it was annexing 6,900 acres of virgin land north of Daniel Island. Planning the urban sprawl Bracey had known was coming.

All the usual political rhetoric and media lies were spewed out. Unquestioning berserk allegiance to growth. Its economic development guaranteed the city's future blah blah fiscal solidarity blah blah stable framework to move into the 21st century.

They wanted automobile plants of all things. Turn the city into a Detroit. A decade of high wages, and then an eternity of depressed slums, the ground poisoned with heavy metals.

It would generate millions in tax revenue of course. Farmland was capped at $12,000 a year. And there it was.

Exercising latitude and administrative discretion, the state environmental agencies would rubberstamp it, the inevitable deal struck. They knew how to game the system. South Carolina's impact studies were always carefully limited to the deer population state-wide. The impact on that would be negligible.

There was a rank insanity to it all. The desperate wild-eyed greed. The crazed obsession that untrammeled growth would permit them to rip off a few more dollars than they otherwise would. Gain a slight edge over a neighbor. Until one day the water supply got maxxed out.

At No. 1 Legendre, Mary Canty Ralston had fallen down drunk trying to open her gate. She lay there passed out and snoring. The car engine of her late model Jaguar was still running.

Bracey bent to try to revive her, then thought, Oh my God, what if Rannie finds us? She'll blame this on me. Twist it into a lawsuit.

Nearly frantic, she wheeled Blake Huston around and shoved him as fast as she could back up the street. One voice was telling her to run. Another said the old woman would die, and it would be on Bracey's conscience. Bracey slowed down, indecisive.

"Nobody could make a serious effort to stop me," Blake cackled. "They were scared shitless."

22

Roebuck Plantation was hosting a big outdoors promotional Barbeque with the Red Clay Ramblers playing a whole bunch of different instruments and pigs smoking over fires. As night fell, everybody drank a lot of alcoholic beverages and talked big money without restraint. Under the light of a Tiki torch, Sparky Truluck had himself a cold beverage and read a newspaper about a house on Roebuck Island that burned down. It appeared to start in the kitchen and destroyed the interior, roof and side walls.

"So what was left?" Sparky said, looking around, but nobody was listening.

There was no immediate cost estimate for damage. Police and fire officials were looking for leads but couldn't determine what had caused the fire. Arson hadn't been totally ruled out.

Sparky was feeling pretty good having that afternoon run over the foot of some old bat trying to make a citizen's arrest of him parking in a handicapped spot. He told her he had left his cripple certificate in his other car. When she didn't swallow that and started writing down his license plate number, he just backed up right over her foot. Left her screaming on the ground. What made it especially funny was he was driving Vineyard Dupree's very visible red BMW.

Right after that he returned the car to its rightful owner. Vineyard was having plenty of insurance problems Sparky didn't want to be mixed up in. That fat Takesha gal was real messed up. Confined to a metal brace and a body cast for two months. The bills were going to be out of sight.

The party was a strange mix of retired Yankee CEOs, Charleston gentry and the rough-edged crowd that develops big tracts of real estate.

Byron Jasper had rented a Rolls Royce everybody was taking turns driving around in waving champagne bottles. He wore a top hat and tailcoat with tennis shoes and blue jeans. "I never have a problem paying that ol' sin tax," he was telling anybody who'd listen.

As the moon rose over the ocean, the noise and revelry grew unabated. All the retired energy and talent of those Yankee CEOs mixing with Charleston investors, Yankees blathering away about a world they had left behind or were on the verge of leaving behind.

"Sure, I know the bottom line's always with us, but we gotta rethink how we measure success."

"This endless round of cost-cutting will block all product innovation."

"I don't care what it is—land speculation, big construction, you name it—fact is, you're in a knowledge management industry."

"We operate with a nimbleness that would be impossible in your more bureaucratic, top-to-bottom managed organizations."

Sparky wandered among them hearing snatches about instrumented feed-back programs and how you gotta look at not just quantity but quality of growth.

The band was playing *Highway's Built For Love* which was a good country tune but came to a kind of unrousing finish. Byron Jasper grabbed a microphone and stood there like some slack-jawed yokel. He was drunk as a skunk.

"WHAT A ROMANCE CLASSIC THAT WAS!" he shouted way too loud into the amplification.

"Shut the hail up, Byron!" somebody shouted back.

"Yeh, shut yore dam' ass!"

Byron went straight on. "I SPEAK FLUENT TEXAS RED-NECK, I TELL YOU WHAT. BUILDING ALL THEM CON-DOS DOWN ON THE GULF COAST. I'M ROAD-TESTED. I FEEL LIKE STANDING RIGHT UP TO THE MICROPHONE AND SAYING I FEEL LIKE JUMPING UP AND DOWN AND HOLLARING FOR THE SHEER CUSSEDNESS OF IT!"

The Yankees tried to ignore him. One was saying something about fishing for yellow fin tuna way out on that blue water. A really excellent experience the other agreed.

"ILLEGAL I GET NERVOUS WITH. BUT IF YOU'RE JUST TALKING IMMORAL—THEN WE CAN SWING!"

Chase Jeffcoat was hitting on B-J big time. He slurred, "I wouldn't want to rip your panties off without going through the proper procedures."

B-J said, no you sure wouldn't and pushed him off.

He wallowed back on her. "This is what you get when preparation meets in a head-on collision with opportunity."

Byron was telling some pointless story. "THERE I WAS

COHABITING WITH A LA-Z-BOY, A SIX-PACK AND A WIDE SCREEN TV. AND HE COME BUSTING IN SAYING HE WAS GONE BEAT THE BLEEPING DOGSHIT OUT OF ME!"

Sparky wandered on in the lantern-lit night. Steaks were sizzling on a big grill. Big mothers. T-bones and rib-eyes couple inches thick. He figured that was for him. The chipper little gal in hot pants and a chef hat said, "How do you want your steak, sir?"

Sparky smiled real nice and said:

"I want it blood red

Nigger lip thick

Pussy tender

And lightnin' quick."

She looked like he had slapped her right across the face.

That was when Bobbi-Jean Kincaid came up holding a plate of three-bean salad and BBQ and said to quit being so mean to folks and listen to what she had to say. Sparky turned on her.

"It sure crystallizes my feelings of pissed-off-ed-ness to see you in action. Doing that little thing with your walk. You are the biggest damn piece of work since God gave woman tits and taught her how to tease hair.

"SO I TOLD HIS WIFE I WOULDN'T WANT TO VIOLATE ANY SUBSTANCE ABUSE POLICY, BUT I'D SURE LIKE TO GIVE YOU THE BIG ENCHILADA!"

B-J said, she tried to make her way through the minefields of life with charity and grace, but anyhow listen up. She had been talking with Doris Troxler—you know— Grady Troxler's wife? The Seagrass president?

"She told me, like, a really weird story. She had gone to one of them woman-fest outings where they camp out and look at their vaginas in mirrors and stuff. And they did this chant—'I've got *the pussy.*' It was supposed to make them strong and secure in their self-worth. And then they could go home to their asshole husbands and take a firm stand on picking up dirty socks off the bedroom floor and putting down the toilet seat and such."

Sparky asked how did it work out?

"She goes back, and when he's giving her shit, she says, 'Grady, *I've got the pussy.*' Except it doesn't work."

"How come?"

"Without missing a beat, Grady says 'You've got *a* pussy, bitch. There's plenty more out there."

"The man did have a point."

"Yeah, but I think she's kind of lonely."

Sparky looked B-J over wondering what she was up to exactly. He looked at the woman Doris. She was about a six on a ten scale. Blouse full of medium size knockers. Hair she had gotten some fag to fashionably turn stringy and the color of brass. No cigarette. Holding a drink and not drinking like she was afraid liquor would make her have too much fun. There was potential lying there.

Sparky said to B-J, "You know I think I'm going to enter you in a field trial. See if you win Best Bitch."

He looked back at Doris. There's nothing quite so instantly sobering as the smell of poontang on the hoof. It just sheds that seductive spell of liquor replacing it with the lure of cunt wool.

Sparky straightened up, went right over to her, said,

lemme buy you a cold one. Said, he wouldn't look real close at that wedding diamond she was wearing because he could tell she was in the mood for a little extra-marital romancing, and that was a matter of intense interest to him too.

Her eyes went wide. The lids didn't twitch.

Byron was still going strong. "I TOLD HER YOU'RE BEAUTIFUL LIKE YOU ARE. DON'T CHANGE. STAY OAT-MEAL!" He brayed with laughter.

Making foreplay talk, Sparky told Doris how when studding a mare race horse you got to have another horse called a "teaser" bite her on the neck. That gets her all hot and lathered for the stallion to come on and do his thing.

The woman's eyes did sure bulge like a frog's.

Sparky put his hand against a roof post and leaned down low and close over her. "There's some more glamorous than me, sure, but if we can just work out a exit strategy, I'm your stud-hoss all night long. Got me a proven track record in that arena."

She sounded half-strangled when she said, "I . . . I don't know."

Sparky gave her his best grin, "Well, you've got the pussy, sweetheart. You call the shots."

■ ■ ■

"The South of France," said Chase Jeffcoat. "I don't know why they call it that when they're talking about the Riviera. But they do."

B-J agreed. She said that was like saying "down South" when you meant Florida.

In the morning, Chase was strutting around B-J's condo like his dick had grown a couple of inches during the night. Sure enough, he was every bit as beautiful naked as she had imagined he would be. He could have been Robert Wagner back when he was married to Natalie Wood. Problem was, when she got him in that big whitewashed iron four-poster bed, he had passed out inside her and nothing much got accomplished.

B-J brushed her teeth and figured on getting him back in bed and working to a serious mutual orgasm. She liked the thought of going with him to the Riviera. Play the course at Villefranche. Go topless on the beach and show off her assets to their best advantage.

She came out of the bathroom just as pleased with her buck naked body as a 38-double-D cup can be knowing she's always the center of attention. The floor vibrated as she walked across it, and she asked how come the construction quality was so shoddy. Chase said he'd been on them about that. Too much dead-weight in the organization. They think kick-backs are a God-given right.

That made B-J ask him just what it was Sparky did, and he said he didn't know exactly. Supervise maintenance. Negotiate leases. Stuff like that.

Chase made French roast coffee. He had a special way he wanted it done and took over the chore. Said his wife never could master it. She couldn't master much of anything except watching birds.

B-J thought about Chase's wife and how funny it had been running into her by accident. She seemed like a bird watcher.

The girl sure couldn't take a lot of stress, breaking down

and crying over a little fender-bender. B-J had cracked up her first car—a flame red Camaro—when she was sixteen playing chicken with some yahoo football players in her high school. Rolled and totaled it. Crawled out from the wreck, shaking glass from her hair, laughing drunk and ready to give a blow-job.

She couldn't imagine how the plain-Jane-bordering-on-mud-turtle she had met could have managed to nail down a stud like Chase Jeffcoat. That Bracey—was that her name? weird—was not your heavy-hitter bewitchment female. Didn't look like she could get even half-way horny let alone zap a man with a sleepy look or give him a Wonder Woman work-out in the rack.

They sat down with their coffee on a chintz covered couch. B-J tucked her feet up under her. God the man looked good. The little gallery of windows let in a flood of light that seemed to put a halo on his head. She thought she'd like to have a photo of him in the buff. Make it into one of those 2,000-piece jigsaw puzzles. Spend hours putting it together.

Chase told B-J she needed a better coffee maker. All authoritative like he couldn't believe she wasn't aware of the not up-to-speed inadequacy. She said she just adored surprise presents.

Staggering away from the party the night before he had been telling her all kind of drunk sweet nothings. Saying he wanted to mediate the rift between her legs. And he bet she worked her thighs with rare fluency.

That was just before he tripped over what turned out to be an automobile bumper that seemed to be working its way up through the grass on the fairway outside her condo. He sat there moaning in pain, cussing Byron Jasper for burying junk under the golf course, saying he needed to get an MRI exam for his swollen joint, see if there was any structural damage. Sitting down had let the booze creep over him, and B-J was virtually carrying him the rest of the way into her bed. There as before mentioned, he went right to sleep without catering to her needs or presumably his own.

Now he seemed just as sweet and nice as he asked if she wanted a renewed commitment.

She said, does that mean I get to kiss all down between your toes and then you lay that Mister All-America bod of yours down on me? If that brand of ecstasy was what he had in mind, then she was raring to go.

Chase grinned knowingly and sipped his coffee. He said, he was thinking of getting Chase & Co. a jet. Not in the super-rich range. Saudi Prince with his own Boeing 727. But something he could land out here at Roebuck on the executive airport they were going to build. Maybe a Gulfstream III or IV. Charter it out to defray some costs. Or maybe an amphibious Grumman Goose. Land on the edge of the marsh. It would be handy going down to Florida, the Bahamas, check on investments. No, he'd better get a G III. He needed to go back to his business school reunion. Show those cocky fuckers for once.

B-J knew he was just trying to get his dick hard, and for the sheer perversity of it, decided to jack him around. Maybe it was to teach him to not criticize her home appliances.

She said, she had a sometime-back boyfriend who ran a big Fortune 500 outfit. He had his pet Lhasa Apso flown around on a Gulfstream. The board of directors sure got pissed at that, so he cut it out. Another boyfriend had a Falcon 900. He claimed it cost $17 million but he was always bragging about something or other he had just bought, and you couldn't believe a word he said. Much like his promises to marry her.

She looked a little sad. Then forced on that smile like life was a bowl of cherries for a brave girl with a low golf handicap. But it sure shook Chase which was the effect she was after.

"I hate men who lie to women," he said so firmly you'd almost believe it.

She said, "In the event of a divorce, who gets that big old historic house you live in?"

23

"I always say if you need a knife, it ain't barbeque," said Sparky Truluck.

Doris giggled nervously. She was still having trouble getting used to her new sexual freedom.

They were eating Melvin's take-out and driving along the shore at Folly Beach where the erosion was cutting in so bad the road looked threatened. Sparky drove Doris' pale gray Cadillac Seville which was a car more to his liking. He had read Cadillac was pursuing the youth market. He was in his mid-thirties. They advertised using PGA golfers. It all made sense from the perspective of a man in management at Roebuck.

Doris would feed him from the styrofoam box, he'd lean over and open his mouth for a forkful. Take a swig of Dr. Pepper to wash it down, put the can back between his knees. He had returned Vineyard's BMW with a little surprise inside it just to let that booger know he was still alive and in control of their relationship.

In the middle of the little beach town, Sparky turned right and began going up Folly Road back towards Charleston. For a couple of miles, it was marsh and seafood places on pilings and then finally an unbroken strip of busy commerce that led to the bridge over the Ashley River.

Sparky always figured pussy was pussy. In that regard he was like spades. 'Overweight' was not in his vocabulary. Sometimes he'd go for women past menopause.

As it turned out, Doris was an okay fuck. She just lay there at first. Then after a while started to make little movements. Then it got a grip on her entirely outright. Strapped him on big time and made the most ungodly noises. Yeah, old Grady was sure overmatched by Sparky's equipment. He and Doris had been together several nights now in one of those golf course condos, and she was improving considerably. Even looked better. Less like a whipped dog.

Sparky had seen those old Cary Grant movies on the movie channel where Cary would take a woman's glasses off, shake out her hair and she'd be beautiful. Doris didn't quite reach that level, but she was at least a six on the old ten scale, and she was getting to where she could sure intensify that thigh action when the moment called for it.

He told Doris her learning skills were pretty solid which was a compliment he half-way meant. He said, he hated it when women wore metal things in their hair at night and greasy gunk on their faces. He liked to keep her naked beside him at the dinette table in the morning while he sucked down that caffeine and Marlboro. She had responded positively to those minor requests.

And Sparky didn't blink an eye when she let out she had informed Grady they were getting it on. She said she felt like she had made a career move and was super excited about it. Now when she told Grady she had the pussy he didn't know what to do. He was reduced to sputtering and saying Sparky was the worst kind of hired hoodlum, and she needed to set some base standards as to how far she went with him.

Sparky said well give Grady some credit for raising important issues. He said mostly he declined comment on the exact details, but he was indeed a hired hoodlum.

She said, was this for true? All kind of breathless like a promise of future vitality between the sheets.

He said, yes, he had a stable work history in that area. He was not interested in drug-related crime. Dealing cocaine held no lure. That brought those mandatory sentences you couldn't plea bargain out of none too well. But he had a right rounded product mix ranging from hired muscle in debt collection to strike breaking to removing market competitors. Typically, he'd style somebody's hair with a pistol barrel. Break some legs. If needed, he'd take an old boy out permanent.

Doris asked did it bother him? Did he sleep okay?

He said he didn't feel responsible for the out-of-wedlock teen birth rate any more than he did the thieving of special interests from the treasury in Washington. If American society was in a race to the basement, a downward spiral, whatever, well he couldn't worry about the fact he was exploiting it.

"But what about going to jail?"

He said the high prisoner numbers in the U.S.—up 700,000 in ten years—was a testimony to his skills. Those dumb fucks were behind bars while he was out here at the staging points for all kinds of lucrative markets.

She said she couldn't imagine him behind bars. All the terrible things men did there. He said it's nothing now. Wait'll next year when that no parole rule kicks in. Stick a knife in another con, they'll have nothing to lose. Society won't take much comfort in that development.

Doris' lips were kind of parted and wet looking.

They drove on across bridges that looked down on marinas full of boats. Over to the peninsula Charleston and parked in a high-rise garage that had a plaque saying a historic building had once stood there but been replaced by this important municipal facility. Walked up King Street with the antique shops. Sparky knew women liked to look in stores, and he was willing to tolerate that up to a point. He did draw the line at antiques.

Across from a Greek café with chickens roasting on spits in the window was an indoor mall with luxury retailers. Doris got that surge look in her eyes women get and pulled him inside. She seemed changed, like she had taken an assertiveness training course or something in the last ten minutes.

Sparky let her buy him clothes at Banana Republic. He said he was conservative with his money. Invested in a mutual fund. Didn't expect to end his days warehoused in some state institution.

Doris had a bunch of charge cards and was all free and easy with them the way an established woman is supposed to be when she's in an adulterous relationship. It deepened the meaning of what they were sharing.

Then she stopped in front of the Victoria's Secret window. Sparky felt the little tug on his arm that held him there. They had a bustier outfit on display called "The Merry Widow." Boob lifters. Lace-up back. Cathouse red.

"Do you think I should . . . ?"

Sparky laughed, "Whoa there, Nellie. Here you go venturing out with that instant gratification stuff again."

What he meant was yeh-boy, let's go for some quality time and bonus nookie.

■ ■ ■

"I don't need me no two cars," said Tamzie flatly.

Tamzie and Vineyard rode down to Roebuck in his red BMW. Bickering the whole way. Her demanding her American Express credit card back. Him swearing he had cut it in two with scissors right after buying the Mercedes SL she had seen him in. He swore the SL was three years old. A real discount bargain but a lot of good life in it yet. Some business had depreciated the hell out of it on their taxes. He got it cheap out at Autobahn Motors that had all those used executive type cars.

She said Vineyard had joined the list of disappointing men in her life she would never forget.

Vineyard said, "What about me? My expectations for this relationship ain't exactly where they should be."

Tamzie look at him like she know he's crazy. Him sitting there in a single-breasted silk sports jacket and linen trousers, open-neck black shirt.

She had old Jacquilla Gillyard living in with her. Start out feeling sorry for her but getting to wonder now. This demand, that and the other coming out of her. The goat out in the yard eating up plants. Now she got Vineyard confessing he used her card in some major way, and she got to wait with dread for the bill to come in.

She say, "I figure you for the long heralded man of my dreams, find out you got a wife who could paralyze Mike

Tyson if she get the jump on him. But the real measure of my non-expectations is you using my charge card to buy a car. This blow my mind big-time."

Vineyard said, he was prepared to address that. A key man employee of Roebuck Plantation had borrow his Beemer for awhile leaving him an attorney without wheels. But now he had it back. Said there was no point in having regrets. She could just take up payments on the SL. He'd sign the title over to her. She needed a second vehicle anyways.

She tell him again she had no money. He said, no problem. One of the Amex advantages was 45 days of insurance on any item purchased. She could take the car into the woods, torch it, and get her money out.

She said she don't like to go into the red without compelling reasons. If he want to pay off the car and sign it over then she might persuade herself to not ask the State Supreme Court what it thought of his ethics.

Vineyard said, his ethics so high they raise the bar for everyone else. Say, Tamzie Jerome was really learning the system to being a badass. In fact, she was notable among badasses he had known.

She said, "You trying to flatter me or is that just another piece of your routine? Act like I've won and then you pull something else afresh."

He said, he was coming to accept, maybe even enjoy, being dominated by her.

Tamzie feel certain he's laughing at her. "You gone be a dark-horse candidate for the flat of my hand upside your head."

At that point the wheel on the car start to wobble something awful and Vineyard pull over knowing he's got a flat tire. Nothing but trees and tomato fields around them. Big bare sky up above. Vineyard seem to have never change a flat before and have a lot of trouble finding the jack and putting it together.

And then along come the county cop who pulls up behind them. Tamzie thinking oh shit here it come. Niggas don't belong in a BMW so he's going to roust us.

Cop got out, hitching up his gunbelt, big gut hanging over it. Looked right out of *Heat of the Night.*

Vineyard was looking at a wallet he had found in with the spare tire, going through the identification in it. Suddenly he turned ash gray and fell over in a dead faint. Boom. Just like that. Stretched out on the dirt.

Tamzie was stunned when the cop help bring him around, change the tire for them, say there was no reason for a lady like her to get dirty. While he was working, she looked at the wallet. It belonged to someone named Omonio Reese. That name sound familiar for some reason. Vineyard snatch it out of her hands and shove it in his pocket like he afraid it might bite them both.

Tamzie is further amazed when the cop escort them down to a little country grocery and buy them each a slushie and stand around shooting the breeze, making sure Vineyard was okay to drive. Then he come out with it. Say, weren't they part of Roebuck?

Tamzie said she was no media darling and wonder how he know. He said cops are paid to notice things.

What it was, he was thinking about retiring from the force. Cop work was not what it used to be. Want to start up a security guard service, and weren't they hooked up with Roebuck? What was the payroll for their security force out there? Hinted he could be persuaded to take over the account as the cash cow of his coming security enterprise.

Tamzie thought she never would get used to being important. The white man actual wanting her to use inside influence for him.

Vineyard seemed distracted, fidgety, like he was contemplating a nervous breakdown. He kept his hands in his pockets scratching his crotch like the crabs eating him up.

Then Tamzie remembered who Omonio Reese was. Her rapport with Vineyard became a real dwindling asset.

24

"They may as well run a wet T-shirt contest, Mother," Bracey had said with disgust.

"What on earth is a wet T-shirt contest?" Izzie asked.

"It's too complicated to explain."

The coming PowerChest Tournament had been the feature on the sports segment of the local news. And that right behind the latest bombshell exposé on Roebuck on the hard news. Still Izzie couldn't get it through her head that Chase's financial dealings were teetering on the brink.

When Rannie discovered that Byron Jasper was barred from the banking and securities business in Texas, she went right to all three local stations to make it public. She said, question marks were raised in her mind about the links between Byron and Chase Jeffcoat and loans made by Seagrass S & L. Even the most charitable reading of the situation made her think something slimy was hidden under a rock.

Her gall was vintage Rannie Ralston. Anyone else would have been leery of a libel suit. She was daring them to bring it on.

Unlike Chase Jeffcoat, Byron was not shy about talking back through the TV medium. Bracey and her mother watched his big jowly face fill the screen on the eleven o'clock news.

"None of that snafu in Texas was my own fault. Somebody always wants to sue. Nobody asks a lawyer about justice. Just how deep are the victim's pockets. I had my (bleep) chewed off. Whole teams of lawyers done arthroscopic surgery on my (bleep). We ought to modify the lyrics to that old Beatles tune to 'I wanna hold your wallet.'

"Sure, I don't have the eloquence of these smart mouths who get into that tearing down of the venture capitalist. That's the trendy thing now. Energy and enterprise ain't looked on kindly."

When asked about his current projects, he said, "I've done awful well given the education I don't have. I admit to some bumpy rides. The stress level ain't bad. I get good production now. I'm gonna recommit and take the game up a notch. You got a winner in town name of Byron Jasper. You'll know I'm finished when I suddenly get religion."

That was when the doorbell rang, and Izzie said who on earth at this hour and answered it to find a cop with a warrant and a Department of Social Services woman. They had come to investigate an anonymous neighbor's report of abuse of the elderly.

Izzie said blandly, "Well I guess I should be insulted. I'm not that elderly. But most of the abuse I take is standard mother-daughter stuff."

The cop said very funny now please step aside. He recited by heart the federal and state statutes that permitted them to just waltz in based on casual information.

Bracey heard it all from the next room and knew what was on the agenda. She came out and said there's nothing wrong, really. The house was in order. All the utilities working. Everything fine really. Honest.

"We have a different version of things," said the DSS woman. She sounded real sour. Like everyone told the same lie and she was inured to it. Figured they'd find a crack baby battered to death in the bathtub.

They asked to see Blake Huston and followed Bracey and her mother up the stairs. Sure enough, Blake was lying in bed in his pyjamas asleep with ten dogs while the TV flickered soundlessly across the room. *Baywatch* was on, little nubile blondes in high-cut swimsuits capering on a beach. The DSS woman woke him up by shaking him. The dogs sat up and started barking in a nightmare cacophany.

DSS asked Blake if he was in pain.

Blake seemed disoriented. He said, "It's a long time between drinks."

"You have to shout at him," said Bracey. "He just seems out of it because he can't hear you. And he just woke up."

The dogs kept barking. Bracey thought the bed was like a seal rock in a northern ocean.

The DSS woman yelled was Blake hungry or thirsty?

"The stock market's just an investment dart board!" shouted Blake. "You can't trust those bozos!"

Izzie said of course he couldn't understand. Poor man was perfectly ga-ga. But as to abuse, dogs were nice companions for the feeble-minded. And she slept in the same bed. What was wrong with it? Was there a suggestion of something perverted?

Bracey said her stepfather had had roast beef with

new potatoes for dinner. Broccoli. A glass of milk. Banana cream pie. He ate with a considerable appetite. She didn't mention the eight drinks of bourbon.

DSS seemed stumped. In a vaguely threatening tone, the woman said she intended to write a full report.

"I'm sure you will," said Izzie. "There's more than a whiff of corruption about this. The fine hand of Rannie Ralston, concerned neighbor, seems evident."

"I'd think long and hard about that!" Blake yelled at their backs as they went out.

The dogs were still barking.

■ ■ ■

Vineyard had take to avoiding Tamzie and only pick up the phone by mistake. He said, the market was giving off strong buy signals, and he was moving her money in. Just jog in place a bit. She had hired him looking for a total return over a complete business cycle. This little down-market cold streak she had to ride out. Now he had to go. Got an office full of clients.

Tamzie said just hold on. She had come by Broad Street looking at the Mercedes 500 SL Vineyard wanted her to pick up payments on. She said it looked brand new. He said, no, they just detail it. Spray in that new car smell. Thing had a quarter of a million miles on it.

She report she hadn't gotten any money that month, not even the Section-8 rent money she expected. Vineyard say, yeah, they late on sending that. He'd call the regional HUD office and get on them. The seesaw moves. She'd be up next. Now 'bye.

Tamzie couldn't really go downtown anymore, see folks she knew. The old gals selling sweetgrass baskets and flowers around the federal courthouse. Her friends who work in the big houses out strolling the white babies. And you could bet they remembered her much-publicized good fortune.

Trying to run a charity for old Jacquilla Gillyard didn't help her conscience much. Ordinarily the woman live off fatback and collards, but get her in a Harris Teeter and suddenly steaks and shitaki mushrooms get in the cart. Snuff cans were smelling up every room of the condo. Copenhagen Skaol. She liked the heightened nicotine in it. *As the World Turns* on the TV every day. Gospel music blaring on a tape recorder.

All the same, seeking for a bright spot amid the misery she went down Legendre Street and saw Omar out walking the ugly corgis. He act like she had only gone yesterday. Just start in chatting about this and that.

"I see the anti-smoking crowd want to outlaw cartoon camels. And cigarette ads that show physical beauty in smokers. How they gonna advertise?"

Tamzie laugh for the first time she can remember. "I guess they can show my Auntie Eula Mae from up in Cainhoy smoking a Camel. The woman weigh close to 300 pound. She'll flat out display some freedom of choice for you."

Omar laugh. He sure seem to like them ugly dogs. It was like they had become family to him. He say, getting out like this cut down on mid-life male hypertension.

"Besides, I don't default on my obligations. Them dogs pretty much depend on me. I could stuff mattresses in the factory. Work maintenance around the bank buildings. But I'm where I want to be, and there's no doubt where my loyalty lies."

Tamzie ask what the gossip be, and Omar say, the white folks in an uproar because of Chase not suppose to own part of a Saving & Loan. What they ain't find out yet is he stepping out with a gal other than his wife. That Jeffcoat marriage about to collapse under a mountain of recriminations.

Black servants down South-of-Broad always spotted the love affairs first. In one famous situation, a banker who fly to New York a lot figure he be safe having his affair up there. Somebody's third cousin who work in the Waldorf-Astor assistant bartending happen to mention it on a Christmas visit, and it get all over town same as always. The banker man don't know whether to shit or go blind.

Tamzie laugh. "Maybe he need to focus more on his core business instead of all this gettin' down to bidness."

Omar say, "I'd be happy to balance work and family. Only you lost all interest in me lately."

Tamzie look down at her feet uncomfortable, so he change the subject.

Omar say oystering was getting bad. "Use to go out Robin Creek in the John boat come November, haul in ten-twelve bushel a day. Now it down to four. If you lucky. Oyster shell getting so scarce you can't hardly seed them bed.

"All them restaurant want Texas Gulf oysters. They don't come in jagged clusters like ours do. Texas oysters all smooth and round and lay down flat on a plate. So you can count out an even twelve."

Tamzie shake her head. She say, "That barometer what serve notice of things to come has been set out for all to see."

Omar say, he was right grateful to her taking in his auntie. She said Jacquilla Gillyard? He say, the very one.

Tamzie hadn't made a connection between them. Sometimes it seem like half the black folks in Charleston named some form of Gaillard. Gilliard. Gillyard. Or else Mazyck. Them white families must have had them a whole bunch of slaves at one time.

Tamzie say, if he was family, then Omar's got a claim to the property out at Roebuck. He say he hadn't checked on any internal documents or formulated the laws of probability, but yes, it seem likely.

All the loose ends tried to make connections in her head. Omonio Reese shot dead. Takesha Reese run over by a car. Jacquilla's house burned down.

"I got to express some strong worries," she said.

"How's that?"

She said, she don't want to be overharsh in her warnings, but maybe he need to keep that information close-to-the vest. Seems like property holders end up getting hurt. A large bogeyman was hanging out there, and he seem to work for Roebuck Plantation.

25

Bobbi-Jean was in Grady Troxler's office on the Skydeck saying, "That real cute quarterback for the Gamecocks—the one with the long hair and earring and everything—he's just got the best poise in the pocket. Just holds onto that ball until you're sure he's sacked. Then lets fly. Zoom-bap like a bullet on those short passes. It sure makes for big plays."

"Bull-shit," argued Byron Jasper. "We're looking at a season-ending loss for Carolina. The fans are already talking basketball."

Grady Troxler stood staring at the two of them just as ignorant of football as ever.

It was Wednesday. Clemson was seven and three for the season and the betting line had them a four-point favorite over South Carolina which was four-five-and one. Kickoff Saturday was 12:32 PM at Williams-Brice stadium in Columbia.

"I don't need to manufacture excitement about this," said B-J. "How about you, Mister Troxler?"

Grady said Clemson would run away with it.

"What score do you figure?" asked B-J. "Fifty to nothing?"

"Easy," said Grady. "Maybe worse."

B-J said. "Well I tell you what, Mister Clemson Tiger

Troxler. How about I take Carolina and twenty-five? Fifty large. No pissing and moaning."

Like every mark ever born, Grady half-way knew he was being manipulated. The year before, Carolina coming off an equally lame season pulled a 33–7 astounding upset over Clemson right in Death Valley with the tiger fans painted orange and howling like wild animals. Same Carolina quarterback. The long hair and earring boy. Even Grady knew that, it had been talked about so much around Seagrass.

"Shore," said Byron, perked up by the enormous size of the bet she was proposing. "That's fair. When Clemson-Carolina comes up, you throw the win-loss column out the window. This is pure-T rivalry, and anything can happen. When that first kick goes off, they're both O-and-O again."

Grady's jaws clenched so tight they seemed to be vibrating. B-J knew he was calculating what he could do to her if he won. The power he'd have over her. All his gutter dreams.

"Hello-o-o!" B-J said. "Earth to Troxler. Gonna put your old money where your fan loyalty is?"

He stared at her like a question was posing itself. Then said okay, deal, in a real little voice like he didn't want anyone or hear.

"Aww-riiight Christ-a-mighty!" whooped Byron, making them shake hands to solemnize the wager in that time-honored way.

Grady's hand felt like a clammy fish and looked sure enough like whitebait.

B-J and Byron left this important business conference

and went outside. Byron said all confiding, boy did you take that dumb fucker, but what he really wanted was to express a larger satisfaction with how their relationship was developing, learning to forge alliances spur-of-the-moment and such. Skinning Grady in tandem.

B-J agreed if this was any indication, the sky was the limit. They were gold dust twins.

What she was thinking was, God the man had gone to seed. Flab. Dark circles under his eyes. He looked like a candidate for an instant heart attack.

She had been between the sheets with Chase Jeffcoat now, and the boy had performed on a semi-stud level with a lot of initiative and poise. He seemed to know pretty much everything he was supposed to do, and what he didn't know she had no trouble teaching him. A little trouble hovering over her because his back was bothering him, but on his side, he was a class-A, smooth-as-silk dream.

Byron said he wasn't denying her permission to rub up against him by way of thanks for him helping to hustle Grady. He reached for her, but she did a little twist and got free.

"You don't have to be so sanctimonious about your tits," Byron grumped. "You want me to curtain off a room so Chase Jeffcoat won't see you?"

B-J said, oh Mister Jasper, Chase was just being a lovesick puppy and she felt she had to be polite to him because she was devoted to Roebuck.

She said, "I mean the man uses words like 'leit-motif' whatever in hell that is."

Byron said, "Well have I got b.o. or something? I'm in

ambulatory condition. My heart's pumping good. I don't feel out of place in my own skin. Got a degree of polish on me."

B-J said he was a real attractive man, and she knew she ought to be oozing gratitude around him, but she was concerned about . . . well, she better not say.

Naturally he set in pressing her. She toed the ground and said, everybody had his limitations.

He kept saying what is it? What's the problem? You can tell old Byron. We're practically joined at the hip emotionally.

Byron said if it was something painful, well, he hated to pick at scabs, but he felt she had to let it out. All the advice columns took that position. Ask Abby. Ann Landers.

B-J winced and shuddered. Said, the thought of blood was what it was all about. She ought to be strong. She had endured the harsh realities of the women's pro tour where you really needed a protector.

He said, whose blood? He said, he had to cry foul here being shut out like this.

She chewed her lip a bit and said she couldn't talk about it. Hurried off like she didn't want him to see her cry.

He called after her, "What? What is it? How do I raise my profile on this? Who stands to benefit from making my sweet babydoll unhappy?"

Looking at all this trickster behavior from a moral standpoint, B-J felt okay. Working Byron to her advantage fell into that gray area where women tried to get ahead in their jobs without submitting to undue sexual harassment. A working-class girl has to walk that fine line or she'll end up with cum on her teeth and nothing to show for it.

The central fact in very recent history was that old slimeball Grady Troxler was in a big bet and had $50,000 laying out on the table.

■ ■ ■

Tamzie tell the secretary, "I'm tired of this he's in court shit! Tied up with clients! In a closing! You get his ass on the phone or I'm gone come down there and use that cop riot gear on both you two! Even if he come on and ack polite I may still come down there and put a halt to his whole process!"

Vineyard pick up the phone sounding like he's afraid she can crawl through the line. Tamzie light into him saying she getting over-due mortgage notices on her condo from Seagrass when she's on the Board and their boss and what kind of nerve was that? They know she's got no income and can't pay them because they managing her money and giving her nothing. She's got a welfare case woman living in her house eating the refrigerator bare and she's had about all the shit she can stand for one lifetime.

Vineyard say, what's that mean for him exactly?

"You in a I.Q. funk or what? I catch you out in the open, I'm gonna give you a dose of brain reformation!"

He say not to worry about her mortgage. He'd get Troxler to cut her a loan. Enough to pay the mortgage for a couple of months. Plus enough extra to pay on the second loan for the same time. While this was going on, he'd backload her investment. Get it reconfigured. Square it all up.

She say, what was this 'reconfigured'? You can wrap catfish in newspaper, but it still smell fishy.

Vineyard say, "Be an armchair Monday morning investor. Keeping me bleary eyed. Sure. Right-on. I'll change my approach. That strange device Excelsior on my banner. I'll straighten up Seagrass. Meantime I'll confirm the availability of other options."

Tamzie say, he damn well better.

He say there's one other problem.

Tamzie take a deep breath and ask what's that?

He say her tenants, the Section-8 folks in the house on Cannon Street. She recall them? Well they up to bad ways. Beat and rob the old woman next door. The one sells half-pints of liquor at night.

Tamzie hung up the phone feeling like she been kicked in the stomach. Things were getting desperate, and the days of champagne and lobster for relaxation were gone. Prada, Jean Muir and Azzedine Alaia had wave bye-bye too.

26

The temperature had shot up to a warm 74. Tamzie sat in Grady Troxler's marble office on the Skydeck trying to get some answers. She had serious money problems. She was becoming like a stereotype of destitute.

Troxler don't show much genuine concern. He was all memory lapses and changing the subject. He said, "This is not a career lull for me. I'm dealing with staff changes. We're trying to fight this state-wide building code in the legislature. There are 20 counties and 111 municipalities in this state without inspection programs. They believe in the free market and *caveat emptor*. They're the last of Americans who know you can't live in a risk-free world."

Tamzie sit up taut with disapproval, say she had trouble with all this eye for the future. She was interested in the right here now. And right here now her income was down to a dried-up trickle that barely stirred the dust.

Grady said the past year'd been a difficult one. He said, her investment's being reconfigured. She say what do that mean? He said what are you, invincibly ignorant or something? Sounding pissed.

She say all his smart talk was hard to keep up with, but she knew for certain she was a big customer of the

Seasgrass trust department and that ought to count for some respect.

Troxler said, "Fuckin' eight-foot jigaboo goes to play basketball for thirteen million a fucking year. That's a big customer for some bank down in Miami wherever. That's what we're trolling for in depositors. What're you? Three million? You ain't shit."

Tamzie rear back like she been slapped. Say, she was on the Board. She was like his boss. He say horse-apples and dog dookey. You come in here with scare tactics and misrepresentations. Think you can spook me into pledging to commit more time and resources to looking after your piddley pile of money. He laugh, say "spook," that's a good one.

Tamzie grip the arms of her chair, trying to keep control and not let a gridlock of fear clamp on her like a cage. She had worn her Bruno Magli shoes for courage, but they weren't working. She said, "I'd like for this hysteria to go no further."

Grady said, who's hysterical? Tamzie said, she was.

He said, "So go outside and placate yourself." He said, "Your investment counselor, Sapsucker Dupree, he figured he couldn't operate you cost-effectively. You all the time wanting this, wanting that. Throwing yourself at him. Trying to wreck his marriage. This commercial venture cropped up. He bet the farm on it."

Tamzie feel like her wrists been slashed. Vineyard telling low dirt trash on her. Love and pain felt the same at that nosedive point. She said, where did the money go? She'd like to get an acquaintanceship with the details.

He said, don't try to embroil him in her messy disputes,

extended legal wrangles, whatever. He could watch all that on Court TV.

Tamzie repeat the question. This time she enter into what she was saying with a real intensity.

Troxler shrug. "Roebuck Plantation had an overdue note to the thrift for the golf course. Three million bucks. Flat-ass delinquent as hell. They were coming off a weak October. Things are picking up in November. Housing unit sales gains aren't so skinnyass meager."

Tamzie said, real slow, "He lent it to Roebuck Plantation? All my money? So they could pay you off?"

"Not me personally. The thrift. Kind of a bridge loan on your part until Roebuck gets permanent financing."

Tamzie ask was Roebuck paying on its debts? Troxler say not currently. Except for the golf course loan from Seagrass. That was now paid up due to her money.

The doom news was making headlines in Tamzie's brain. Agony of decline they said. Harsh light of media and public attention focus on nugatory asset balance sheet. Tamzie sucks wind on financial front. Poor House desired destination. Flash cameras did glaring publicity.

Troxler chuckle. "Ol' Dupree, he's a work of uneven quality all right. But it's a bad news, good news kind of thing." He leaned forward, his voice falling to a murmur.

"The good news is what I'd like to do is take that good-looking negress black body of yours and make it an enterprise zone. Contrary to popular belief, this white man has got a prize-winning cock and balls on him. And I am true to my root."

He laugh so loud she can see his back molars.

Tamzie gape at him. She had never known night riders. The Klan was something her momma Mozelle talk about. Martin Luther King was shot dead ambushed when she was about three years old. All the same, there's a heritage of fear you never quite break out of. She hadn't exactly been expecting blue-eyed soul in Grady Troxler, but this was a whole other category of scarey white man.

He's giving her a fever scowl, his eyes glittery yellow, his voice turning silky.

"Strap you on. Do some pile-driving. All improvised. Churning. Non-stop effort. Then—ba-boom-lift-off. Culmination? When I get through, you'll be so wrung out you'll be staggering drunk and disorderly. But next day you'll walk all sprightly."

The whole time he was talking, he was taking a bird dog statue—dog on a point with the tail straight out, one front foot in the air—and he chipped that bronze tail into the surface of his desk making little nicks. Chip. Chip. Chip.

Ugly thoughts streamed through her head. Omonio Reese shot dead. Takesha run over. Jacquilla's house burned down.

Tamzie stagger to her feet. She feel like she was locked up in a detox center all shivering and shaking while neon lights played behind her eyes. She couldn't even see Troxler, the man sitting there being a reptile, talking at her.

"Yeah, you dark bitches are notorious for your contrariness. And here comes that trait surfacing again."

Defiance wasn't working too well. Her voice barely came out. She said, "Robert Redford, maybe under the right circumstance, we achieve some sublime. That Robert De Niro what marry the black gal. But you yourself, Grady Troxler, ain't no burning bright ethereal vision of white manhood."

■ ■ ■

"It ain't the best defense Clemson's ever had," said Sparky. "But it's gritty. I tell you what. They only allowing 16 points a game."

Doris asked what that meant. Sparky said, what did she think? The other team only gets 16 on the board.

The bar waitress brought over two Palmetto beer longnecks and cute-butted around a bit while Sparky ordered crab dip and a big plate of french fries and gravy off the menu.

It was a half-way decent bar in Charleston with booths along the wall and a horseshoe shape where you could sit and watch sports on TV while you drank. From where he was sitting, he could watch the TV and the good-looking honey bartender with the barbed wire tattoo on her bicep and mostly ignore Doris and her ignorance.

Doris asked was Clemson doing well then? Sparky explained the Tigers were coming off big wins over Georgia Tech and North Carolina. Clemson was 5-2-0 in the conference and 6-3-0 overall.

Doris said was that good?

Sparky drank his way half through his beer and looked around for the honey waitress with the fries and a backup Palmetto. He said, yeah it was good, and what had him flat-ass stunned was the Clemson-Carolina game November 18 wouldn't be televised. Jefferson-Pilot Insurance what put together the Southeastern Conference's television package said it had dropped plans to broadcast the hallowed event this year.

Doris asked why that was. Real patient, he explained the decision is based on audience levels. Or what them dam' fools projected as audience levels. Which was what had him baffled. This was the first time not televised since Clemson joined the Southeastern Conference back in 1992. And everybody knew Clemson could put some dam' sixty minutes of football together, I tell you what.

Doris said well maybe they could go for a walk on the beach that day. Do something romantic.

Sparky lifted an eyebrow. He said it was yet to be determined whether or not the game would be available on a pay-per-view basis.

Sparky always figured that even the best fuck will fade with memory. Porking Troxler's wife Doris had its moments. She sure liked to open up and let out the naughty aroma. What had him most amazed was how she started to wear crotch-less underwear. Just all ready to do him anytime anywhere. They'd be driving somewhere in the car and he'd look over and see she had her legs spread, had slid a couple of fingers up herself. It was like the woman just could not get enough of it.

Sparky had heard of nymphomaniacs before, but never actually met one. Oh sure, there was plenty of bored wives liked to sport-fuck. Get drunk at a roadhouse in the afternoon. Bang just for the sheer unadulterated adultery of the thing. No ulterior motives. Had to watch your wallet, but otherwise they weren't angling for marriage or a paternity suit.

And damn-straight, Doris sure loved that bone. But the ecstasy moments were getting diluted with female complaints. He could understand that Doris had been a little oppressed, depressed whatever married to old fuck-brain Grady. Rotary clubs. Opening events for things Grady lent money to. Grady jerking off in a sock in the bathroom instead of putting it to her. But Doris sure could spew out some bunch of whiney stories. Women were like that. They all made you to listen to their hard-luck shit.

Now she was starting to get in little digs about Sparky smoking. Correct him in this or that way. How he ate at the table. Whether he tipped the waiter enough. Well, as the preacher says, we give God all the glory. And it's getting to be *adios* motherfuckers time.

It was a core value question really. Did he just dump her flat-out or keep boning her until he had located a replacement muff? Horny was, after all, his middle name.

Doris had been thinking hard like she had something unpleasant to unveil to him. She said, "I don't like football because my husband has become a gambling addict."

Sparky said horseshit. The man didn't know a tight end from a tight asshole. How would he know how to gamble?

Doris said he had wagered $50,000 with that Bobbi-Jean creature. And given her some off-the-wall number of points. He was such a dildo-head.

In getting over her backward shyness, Doris was starting to talk trash-mouth like that.

Sparky said, yeah, B-J. The one with tits so big they're like a distortion of the idea of tits. Yeah, he knew about that bet. It was kind of out of character for the geek. Doris said she didn't like Sparky admiring other women.

He was about to tell her she could quit editorializing about his shortfalls. And she could go lay on her back and finger herself until she got a herniated disk. But his pants were staying zipped up until this unfair criticism of his performance shut down permanent.

He was about to say all that, but Doris said her husband was up to something strange. Sparky said, the man is strange. He's a fucking Martian.

Doris said no, it was more than his little closed-up hyper-suspicious paranoid world. OR it was that multiplied by some.

Sparky said he knew your own country was the last place to look for a prophet, but did she mind being a little clearer. Doris said, okay, the bare facts were Grady had become very security conscious. Built into the architecture of the Skydeck was a strong room where he could lock himself in. It had an outside secret entrance so he didn't have to go through the main bank building. It was painted over to make it look like the outside wall. Paint uncracked because he'd never actually exited that way. It was for an emergency. And unknown to everyone else, he had started to spend a lot of time there lately.

"So he sits in there and pulls his pud," said Sparky. "Flogs the bishop. Has a cheap date. Whatever you call it." The fries were coming and hot dam' there was a stack of them. And look at all that dark gravy.

"No," said Doris. "I think it's where he conceals the records of all the money he's stealing."

Sparky put his hunger on hold and looked at her real close. "What money?" he said.

27

"How about you get some of that Sweden vodka?" old Jacquilla Gillyard had say right forceful as Tamzie went out of the house. Tamzie told her, you crazy? Pay three times the price? She was stopping by a pawn shop with a Tahitian pearl necklace on her longer route to the Poor House.

Every day she'd get up feeling good in the bright sunshine, birds singing, then an aftertaste of yesterday's fear and doubt would come over her like a hangover.

Poverty just ran all unabated. She had let that Vineyard Dupree get her another couple of loans from Seagrass. One to pay on the mortgage which said on the application it was for "property improvement" Another one they call a "thirty-day signature loan" for personal and household use. All of it basically lies. She was coming to view dishonesty as trade tools of her life. But the cash wasn't stretching out none too far.

The goat had finally created a stink eating a neighbor's azaleas. Gang of white wives come over to "express concern." Tamzie had apologize all up down and sideways. Tie up the goat to the porch where it sit and bleat all day. Her fighting with Jacquilla because the woman want to bring it in the house.

Tamzie's newspaper horoscope said she should pick up

the pace of her financial ambitions, but she knew that was dead wrong. She was starting to get a first-hand look at why rich white folks always so tense. They got so much to lose, and it seem like you could lose it so easy.

The first big warning that shit was starting to really hit the fan she got when Senator Collier Ralston resign from the Seagrass Board and deny ever voting on anything. Each board member receive a certified return-receipt letter with this news in it. It was a flat-out lie, but he was a state senator and his sister was that mean red bitch lawyer. It made the rest of the board members feel kind of naked and hung out for all the world to see. Tamzie knew that because she got weird phone calls from all of them at late night hours.

Around Seagrass, secrecy got more hush-hush than usual, and document shredders did some heavy work. Grady Troxler sat alone in the Skydeck office silently going through file after file, pulling out this, putting in that. Nobody was allowed in. Nobody.

On the day of the next meeting of the Seagrass Board of Directors, Rannie Ralston wasn't on the agenda. She just walk in, stiletto heels clicking on the oak parquet floors. Sit at the head of the long table with Grady Troxler way down at the other end. She had that awful smile on her face that Tamzie knew all too well from having worked for the red bitch's momma so many years. She looked like she was fixing to drown a sackful of kittens.

Rannie lead off saying, "I won't stay for lunch although I'm told you have quite a spread. I'm on a diet. Egg-white omelets, poached fish, skim milk, blanched vegetables. Disgusting."

They all stare at her.

"So. Let me tell you what is about to happen. The SEC is forcing Chase Jeffcoat, his shell companies, whatever, to sell his share in Seasgrass. That means a major audit. You know what auditors call a mess like this place? A pig. Or a fucking pig to be more precise. They talk like that.

"Now I know what goes on in these cozy little financial gambling dens. Illegal transactions. Conflicts of interest. Self-dealing. Excessive compensation. Lousy loan documentation. Preferential terms on loans to officers and directors. Phony financial reporting. Stacks of loans gone sour that you've just buried. You use the depositors' money like your own piggy bank. And dipping in just gets easier and easier. Up to your elbow, up to your shoulder."

Tamzie's big loan to buy the condo come to the forefront of her mind. After that come the extra loan so she could make the payments. That one loom pretty large too.

"They'll find you're teetering on the brink of insolvency. Loans going bad so fast Troxler can't keep track of them. From the looks of what I see posted out there on the bank floor, what you're paying for deposits, you're losing money on every transaction."

Grady made some protests. He said, "We have innovative financial strategies. Sure, some of them are complex. The regulators won't penalize us for that."

Rannie just stare at him with that unshakable will. "Whether you're on booze or heroin won't make any particular difference. Wildly imprudent or illegal. Who cares? They'll dig. They'll find the skeletons. When the horror becomes apparent enough, a Cease & Desist Order will get issued. You'll just stop business while they dig still deeper. Then they'll call you in for individual chats. They'll squeeze you out like lemons."

Grady said, "We had a $3 million profit this quarter before loan-loss provisions. We got new records in cash flow."

Skip Rightenberry mutter, "Yeah, Grady, you tell her." That man hate Rannie with a passion. Over the years she had sue his ass a whole bunch over shady real estate transactions. She put it out on the street he was a grudge-fuck for her.

Rannie take plenty of time, meeting the eyes of each member of the Board. She was born evil and spend a life refining the state of that art.

"You don't have the slightest understanding of what Grady just said, do you? Have you ever wondered why you're here? Hmm? You were selected because each in his or her own way is . . . how shall I put this delicately? A dunce? What Troxler said is you did so-so except for the massive hemorrhage of losses on bad loans."

Tamzie look at Vineyard Dupree. He had turn a shade of yellow like he just got jaundice.

Sorry shit-ass. Her romance with him had start out like a clear night with moon and stars. Now he just sit in a room and ignore her. Had taken her fortune and reduce her to clipping buy-one-get-one-free coupons out of the newspaper. Save thirty cents on this or that.

Rannie had brought all the joy of a hospital burn ward. She said, and you know what's especially cute? You don't have director's liability insurance.

Skip Rightenberry bluster what do you mean no

insurance? He say that to Grady Troxler who say back that concern's unfounded. Skip says meaning what?

"Meaning you don't need it."

Rannie laugh good at that one. "Oh, don't you? What happens when the feds, some minority shareholders, whoever, sees what you've rubber stamped, and they sue you? Yes, you have civil liability for all this. And since I've managed to capture some headlines, call it bragging on myself, whatever, they'll hire me as their attorney. And then . . . I shall hunt you each and every one . . . into the financial gutter."

The whole table suck wind on that one. Sit there mute. Afraid to talk back. Afraid to even run for the door.

Rannie nibble thoughtful on the end of some reading glasses. "Of course, initially what will seem most frightening is the criminal penalties. Nice Damocles sword hanging there. The pressure of that will snap one of you. Someone maybe calling the feds right now. A weak link in the conspiracy chain. A terrified appraiser who faked those appraisals so Seagrass could lend more money than a project was worth. Perhaps one of you skittish folks on the Board getting insider loans. There's quite a jail sentence attached to that, at least for middle class wimps like yourselves. A hardened killer would think it was nothing. Say he'd do it standing on his head. But then . . . you're not him."

At that point the fear just crawl all over Tamzie, jump on her and eat her up.

"I ain't done nothing wrong!" She bust out. She half-way stand up out of her chair. "Not leastways that I meant to!" She flop back down, her mind racing. Why did she leave

Cannon Street and want to learn to play some dumbass golf game? Trying to end a manless streak?

Then come that voice purring with poison. "Dear Tamzie. So in over your head. I don't think mother will be needing you back in service. Unless you've decided to do windows again."

Tamzie sat frozen to a pillar of salt like Lot's wife. She can hear her momma Mozella saying "That red bitch is meaner'n a nest of copperheads. Don't on no account never poke her with no stick."

She start to pray silently. Lord, stave off these wolves. Dear God, get me out of this unholy mess and I'll go back to church and give them Bishops money. Well, depending on how much money I got. Or manage to hang onto. I swear I'll go visit the sick and shut-ins. And if I get my money back it'll free me up for more good works, and I swear I'll never try to steal another man. I swear it was just an evil phase, and it's all over and that Doctor Shereese Dupree can have her sorry-ass husband back with my blessing, and I'll live manless to the end of my days.

Now Rannie said to the group, "I'm told if you cooperate with the D.A. and roll over onto the rest, you might only draw a couple of years. Get an early release program. If you're the first in line to squeal. They call it a 407(M)(2) investigation should you need the code when you talk with them. I can give you an 800-phone number."

Tamzie look around. Everybody seem to be writing down 407(M)(2). Even Vineyard.

Grady Troxler growl, "I'm going to stop short of calling what you've said here a threat. But you can bet for sure I'll consult an attorney about it."

Rannie shrug. "So you hire a lawyer. I am a lawyer. What does that get you?"

He was real mad now. "I don't intend to laugh off these accusations! If we lose business due to your irresponsible actions, I'll hold you personally and individually responsible!"

Rannie tap her front teeth with a long, blood-red nail. "They say there's a lot of truth in truisms. Let me give you one."

She pause a beat.

"You're all fucked."

■ ■ ■

"Are you ready for football!" Byron Jasper howled at the giant TV screen. Jefferson-Pilot had caved under sports fan outrage and agreed to televise the big game.

Byron could do a gridiron game up whole-hog right. Cole slaw, honey baked ham and three cases of Red Dog beer. Every kind of dorito, frito you name it. Hot dips. Bourbon and blended scotch for those who like to get into serious drinking early.

There were about fourteen-fifteen Roebuck contractors and real estate salesmen there in his condo drinking and cussing and telling Clemson-Carolina jokes. If a tornado hits Clemson it does nothing but improvement. Hoo-haw. In Poland they tell Carolina jokes. Whoop. Har.

Bobbi-Jean Kincaid was the only female present, but she wasn't one to feel out of place. Everybody was talking TDs, career sacks, QB sacks, wrecking crew defense, school record holders. B-J said she couldn't figure why interceptions and fumbles, just because they were both called turnovers, were the same thing. She said interceptions don't just take more skill, they're more valuable. And fumbles are just plain dumb luck.

Grady Troxler stared at her blank faced. His lifetime football attendance record was about zero.

Being ignorant of the game, he couldn't come to grips with the fact he had spotted B-J so many points that Clemson just wasn't going to win big enough no matter if some Roosevelt Brain Trust came down out of heaven and took over the coaching for them. Or Conan the Barbarian played offensive tackle. Or the whole Carolina backfield sashayed off to San Francisco to become fags.

"I got to keep my fuel intake at an optimum," Byron bellowed, powering down a couple fingers of Wild Turkey. He gave a series of body shudders as it settled in. "Ooo that's nasty stuff. Somebody hold a gun on me and make me take another drink."

B-J knew something unfortunate had happened at the Seagrass Board meeting that morning, but Byron was a full-time optimist. Put the bad cards at the bottom of the deck. Play innocent and take your fun where you get it. And I mean dammit—it was Clemson-Carolina and an over-flow crowd of close to 75,000 filled Williams-Brice Stadium. It was that old gambler spirit, and she had a plenty of it herself.

What was particularly funny from B-J's perspective was that at first Clemson looked like a bunch of preschool kids running around with a load in their britches. Receiving the kick-off, Carolina went on a 90-yard opening drive for a 7-0 lead.

"I ain't believing this shit!" yelled Byron who had some minor money on the line. "Or any of the rest of that shit the world hands out!"

Grady looked like he had swallowed a bunch of bird shot or a sack full of ball bearings.

In the second quarter, Clemson managed to score, tying it up. Otherwise their offense stepped on their dicks a lot, stumbled and fumbled and farted around. Defense saved them, digging in and stopping Carolina flat-ass cold two times at the Tiger 3 and the 5.

Byron perked up a little, saying he personally had big questions about the Carolina quarterback's mid-range passing accuracy and what that would mean over the course of the game.

B-J would have said that's it. That's the game right there. Nobody can get over those big mothers. But she enjoyed watching Grady sweat. His deodorant failed majorly as they say, and nobody wanted to sit too near him. He was all to himself on one side of the room and everybody else on the other. B-J sat in Byron's lap and let him feel her up. She figured she owed him a little attention. He purred like a big old tomcat with an open sack of liver vittles.

Carolina stalled out again at the Clemson 10 but booted in a 27-yard field goal to go off the field at half-time 10–7. During the festivities, Grady went out and put his head under the faucet in the kitchen sink and held it there a long time. This seemed out of character for such a compulsively neat and orderly person as himself.

In the third quarter Clemson nailed a field goal to tie it 10–10. Then damn if Carolina didn't get shattered up against another goal line stand only to flip out a four-yard pass for 17–10.

Then they fell apart. Grady missed this sea change because he kept getting up to take a piss even though he wasn't drinking anything. While he was out, Clemson zapped a 56-yard pass to tie at 17–17.

Grady came back all excited at the news. Then on their next possession, Clemson moved the ball 80 yards in ten running plays with the Carolina defense looking like a bunch of cripples that had lost their wheelchairs. 24–17.

Williams-Brice Stadium was roaring, and everybody in the little room was whooping and yelling and throwing crushed beer cans around. Byron hollared, "Goddammit all them sumbitches may be starving in Bangladesh or some booger place, but this is American football, and the right boys are winning!"

After that, everything the Gamecocks tried got smothered like an avalanche had fallen on them, and from there on the game was never in doubt. A team of wild-ass tigers rolled a ground attack over Carolina like Sherman going through Georgia. With 8:40 left, Clemson scored again making it 31–17.

Grady couldn't seem to let loose and yell or scream or anything. He was holding tight to the chair arms, his muscles so rigid his whole body was shaking. He might have been getting the final voltage in an electric chair.

Byron said, I tell you what. The only thing that'll make them hoodlum Clemson players happier than winning here today is if they make armed robbery legal.

Grady started hunching his shoulders, blowing on his hands, twitching, flicking, jerking around like a man with palsy. "Tigers're whipping their asses," he said. "I mean big time."

"Them Gamecocks is taking a pounding," Byron agreed.

Yes, that was self-evident. But Clemson was only leading by 14 and B-J had 25 points to the good. Grady had no feel for the time remaining on the clock or the rhythm of the game.

With three minutes to go, the Carolina fans were emptying out of the stadium just as Clemson went over the goal line again making it 38–17. Everybody farted around some more, but it was over. No miracle play. No 90-yard runs for another TD. The end. Finish. Load up the bus and go home.

On the screen, the Clemson coach, soaked down with a bucket of ice water by his players, was babbling how he was proud to be there, proud to have worked with his personnel, and proud to be an American at such a perfect moment in South Carolina history.

Yes, B-J figured, it was a happy day, and nothing said it better than money.

Grady sat there looking waxy faced like he had been embalmed and everybody was supposed to file by his coffin and say my don't he look natural.

B-J kind of patted her hair on both sides and said she hated to bring it up, but they had themselves a little friendly wager. However frustrating that might be to him.

Grady got argumentative. Scoffing at first, saying she couldn't be serious about a bet that size. It had been a joke. She said no, she had been dead serious. Hadn't she, Byron? Byron wagged his head in assent. Said get with the program and pay the little lady what she's owed.

Grady disputed the number of points he had given Carolina. B-J said liar, liar, pants on fire.

Then predictably, he got mean and dirty. Said, "I've got a rigid system between my legs I'd like to stick up your ass."

She said sticks and stones might break her bones, but words didn't hurt worth pitty-pat. It did no good to make a huge stink. Honoring a wager duly made was gentleman-like and important to future trust. Grady had been hitherto peerless in that regard and ought to not get his moral compass out of whack.

At that point he bolted out of the condo, gunned his Buick LeSabre engine and scorched off like a bat out of hell.

Byron said, he didn't know. The way municipalities were starting to rely on speeding tickets as a source of revenue, he figured Grady would have a $500 fine on top of his big debt.

B-J was feeling so good about things that she agreed to a nonprejudicial walk around the front nine with Bryon. The rest of the boys stayed behind to finish the beer and get into the scotch.

Byron said he dabbled in a woman's emotional life with a healthy dose of caution. But he needed a flicker of understanding of what was bugging her. He kept being all Mr. Diplomat, not grabbing at her ass the way he usually did.

He said, "I'd sure like to facilitate our pairing off. This enforced celibacy is taking a health toll. I ain't all precision-minded on the issue. I'm open to the power of suggestion."

B-J admitted their relationship had just gone all stagnant. She suggested maybe Byron would like to find another girl with a higher-rated opportunity for true romance.

He said no, he had no interest in other girls. And further it was time for a radical overhaul of her attitude. He was going to have to put some overt pressure on her. This kind of revenue sharing they had with her running up all those humongous bills on his charge cards . . . well, it had to go one way or the other.

B-J said, "Well, I guess I'm going to have to let it all out so you can see where I'm coming from. It's kind of an embarrassing disclosure, but I had me a boyfriend who's doing time at Raiford, you know,—down in Florida? Anyhow, I get these weird letters from him where he's all infatuated one sentence, pissed off and threatening the next. He feels like he's an incumbent lover or something. That's kind of a stripped-down version of my bad luck story."

Byron asked what he was in for. She said the boy has a whole assortment of anti-social grievances. Fuck-ups he did that he blames on other people. Byron said, yeah, but precisely what did he get sent off for? She said beating a man half to death.

They were arguing over a dog crapping in a yard. She couldn't remember which one owned the dog. But he was just real hardcore violent. Always getting fired from jobs for punching out supervisors and things. It was a wonder he hadn't been jailed before, but witnesses were usually terrified to come forward.

Byron wondered out loud, so why had she gotten mixed up with him? She said she belatedly asked herself that every day that went by. A college professor guy one time had said it was "nostalgia for the mud" whatever that meant. She thought it was just girls needed a man so bad they'd pick a sorry one just because he was available.

Byron said, he knew it was no fun getting rude mail—bill collectors sent him enough to know that pain—but the old boy was locked off. No body busted out of Raiford.

B-J said, there was a problem there. He had like a scheduled date for getting out on good behavior. Lord knows how he managed to behave himself. But he wasn't even getting community-based supervision because it was a first-time offense. Just being cut loose. As always, what the public and judges never heard were all the violent acts he never got arrested for. And now he thinks he can just waltz up here and restake his claim.

She shrugged helplessly. "And that's how it is. Like the prevailing climate or something."

Byron said, this was a real fiasco.

B-J agreed. "It's a right bitch."

He said it added a glum overtone to his hopes and yearnings. After thinking some, he asked how this criminal deviant had found where she was.

B-J said she guessed golf news. The PowerChest Tournament had in its own way backfired on her. Now she'd really need that bet money from Grady Troxler, and she sure hoped he paid up prompt.

28

"You get that full volume ass of yours over here to my house," growled Grady Troxler over the phone. "Right now. In the dark of night."

"Urn, where is that?" Bracey asked. Everything west of the Ashley River was a mystery to her. All those ghastly suburbs that just went on and on forever. Each bearing the name of a destroyed plantation.

"Your biddy tits aren't exactly a fashion trend. But I'll serenade them just the same. You'll learn to get it wet on cue like a Pavlovian dog."

Bracey, her mind reeling with horror, thought "get it wet?"

It was nine PM when Grady Troxler ordered her over to his house and finally gave detailed directions when she insisted she had no idea of where his subdivision was. Said wear a fur coat with nothing under it. She said she didn't own a fur. That was another generation. Or women of a certain, well, different social milieu. New Yorkers who went to Miami. He said, oh. Well, then get your underpants off. And make it wet when you come through the front door.

She said, 'it'? And then checked herself. Realizing with mortification what he meant.

She stood holding the phone dazed and adrift. Not hanging up. Not talking. Heavy breathing on the other end. Could there be such stark differences in the human race?

He said, "The old 'silence-means-consent' routine, huh? Yeah, you're up to your neck in shit. Doing straw loans for that clean-cut, hard charger of a husband. The feds'd love to know about that in detail. The question is whether you can be part of the solution, help find a way to crawl out."

Mechanically, Bracey got into the Range Rover, doing what she had always done with first a mother, then a husband, now Grady Troxler. Meekly accede. She even took off her underpants.

Bracey had only thrown herself at two men in her life. At age 12 one night after cotillion she impulsively kissed Chip Cotesworthy in the dark walking home on Tradd Street. She was wearing white gloves they way the girls did, and she remembered vividly holding his face in her gloved hands to keep him still.

Like all the ratty boys in their neat little blue blazers, he was carrying "crackers" that season. Little round firecrackers that went off with a loud pop when flung against pavement. He chased her all the way home jeering at her and banging those wretched things at her feet.

When she was 18 at a UVA fraternity party she got tipsy and wrapped her arms around a boy with a foolish smile on his face. He threw up on her. That had been pretty much her romantic life up to Chase Jeffcoat.

The word "assignation" buzzed in her head. The Italian prince with exquisite manners she would meet on holiday at Lake Como. The British army captain with dash and *élan* who had traveled central Arabia.

Instead she knew it was an exercise in self-punishment for sins she couldn't fully comprehend. Life was strong-arming her out of one iron straitjacket and into another.

Bracey could always remember in vivid detail every ugly and embarrassing thing she had ever done. The moments of joy and grace were faded. Day after day of dying to be a decent person was a blur.

As she drove through the streams of headlights and wet pavement, she could only get her mind from Grady Troxler by thinking of something more depressing. Someone had shot a bald eagle up near Ridgeville. It was at the raptor center with blood loss, shock, broken bones held together by pins. Eagles don't do well in captivity, and there was a 50–50 chance it would die. Most of the damage was done as it flopped around wounded on the ground.

The human trash would shoot anything. Red-tailed hawks. Great horned owls. They were compelled to destroy every last one.

Bracey turned off the boulevard and tried to read the street names. All of them out of a developer's grab-bag. Greensleeves. Highland Glen. Loch Lomond. Bonnie Lane.

The house was too big for the lot, what realtors call a tract mansion. Dormers. Arched windows. That cheap blow-on stucco that the termites get behind so badly.

Grady met her at the door wearing a smoking jacket and ascot like a caricature playboy saying, "I'd like to work in a beauty parlor. Do bikini waxes. Rip the shit out of them when I yank out that cunt hair." He chortled with a slurping noise. Teeth bared in a fierce leer.

Bracey stood there on the threshold trembling. Behind him was a slate-floored foyer. Deep-crown molding. On the wall a print of big-eyed children in front of the Eiffel Tower.

"That's particularly offensive," she said, so dazed she wasn't sure if she meant him or the picture.

"Nothing's wrong with you that a good screw won't cure," he said. "It'll give you a real learning experience."

A low groaning coursed through the house. As though someone were in feverish delirium. A death scene in a play or opera.

Bracey caught her breath. She said, what on earth is that noise? Was someone sick? Was it catching? Should she come back later?

Grady got very tense. Pulled his nose several times. "It's nothing."

"It's not nothing."

"Okay, it's my wife."

"Wuuuhhh-hunnnhhhh!"

It dawned on Bracey. The sounds . . . the woman was experiencing an intense pleasure.

"What is happening to her? Is she . . . is she masturbating?" She couldn't believe she had said that. But she couldn't quite believe any of the nightmare she was living through. Did the man expect the three of them to get in bed together? Was it that kind of degradation he had in mind?

He ducked his head. "She's murrrmurr."

"What?"

"murrrrmurhph."

A voice screamed out from the back room. "OH GAAADD! Why doesn't my husband do this to me?"

Grady steeled himself, barely moved his lips as he spoke. "She's having sexual congress. With Sparky Truluck. An employee."

Bracey let out wild peals of insane laughter. A dam had burst inside her. She laughed and laughed and couldn't stop laughing.

The woman kept shrieking through the closed door like she was in critical condition, ready to explode from sheer joy. "OHHH WUHHH OOO GAAADDD JEEEZZUSSS!"

Grady didn't care for this at all. He talked through clenched teeth and pursed lips. It didn't come out very coherently. "You get your wide ass in here. We're gonna continue this recent trend. Create things for each other."

Bracey shook her head 'no'. She was laughing so hard she couldn't speak. God, the man was such trash. You could spend a whole life celibate if he were the only man.

His voice rose. "What do you mean 'no'? You turned into a dyke activist on me? You get your wide ass in here. I'm going to hook you up with the biggest teaching tool you'll ever see. Give you so much encouragement up your twat all that profound need will come busting free like water down a sluice gate."

She kept laughing, tears running down her face. "Sorry, no can do," she stammered out between gasps of air. She laughed more. "The old ardor has cooled."

A little desperate edge crawled into his voice. "You don't have to do it in front of them. Another room. Totally private. Just make a lot of noise. Send out a sensational message."

Bracey wiped her eyes again. "Sorry, you're just not at your persuasive best."

■ ■ ■

"Used to eat squirrel brains and egg," said the old woman. "Now they won't give me eggs." She paused and looked thoughtful. "Funny. I never ask about squirrel."

Tamzie found the county home a real unhappy place. Everybody old and sick and senile. All the nurses with an attitude because they so tired and wore out.

There were so many forms to fill out to get Jacquilla Gillyard admitted it was like you supposed to go to college to learn how. The whole time she wrestle with filling in them blanks, an old woman resident sat in a plastic-covered chair nearby talking at her. Cocoa-colored like she had faded with age. Arthritic hands and knee joints. Darned stockings fallen down to her ankles.

"Last day of shrimp-baiting season," she said. "My grands say the catch all bad cause of September raining so much. Flush them big shrimp out to sea."

List all current sources of income say the form. Me, myself and I think Tamzie and not much of that. Then she was thinking if I admit she living off me they liable to decide that's okay and make me keep her. She wanted to break the pencil in half and chew up both pieces.

The old woman say, "Catch pretty good up around Bull Bay. No river outlets up there."

Tamzie realize who the old woman is. Luevenia Parsons. Woman from the civil rights marching days.

Tamzie had seen movies of the movement. Long lines of black folks marching on Selma, Alabama—Oxford, Mississippi. No bands or drums. Just African rhythm. Swaying and clapping. Carrying the gospel sound onto the streets and highways of America. Fighting down segregation.

Luevenia was a certified hero of those days. They still celebrated Luevenia Parsons Sit-down Day in the black churches of Charleston. A kidney dialysis center was named for her. The Mayor would bring her out for events.

Tamzie was thinking she'd like to put a civil rights march smack through Grady Troxler's Skydeck office. Sit in there until he straighten out her money.

She got to thinking on this. Wondering if there was something there that could be of use. She had to talk kind of loud to be understood. She say to Luevenia she want to hear about the glory days. What it was like. How it went down.

The old woman's head snap around like she hear a distant bugle. Her eyes roll back in memory, and her voice rise up.

"We had them stamina. Oh Lordy yes. Bruise them shins. Slap them feet on them ground. Clap them hands and sing them songs. Eye for eye and cheek for cheek. Prune that vine. Bring in that justice harvest."

The woman don't lack for enthusiasm. Twenty-five years roll away. A natural energy come back into her.

Tamzie tried to reduce the problem to the essence. She say, suppose, just suppose the black race under attack again. Evil white bankers driving good folks off of Roebuck Island. Needing someone to speak up loud in defense. A voice to be raised.

Luevenia stood up on shaky legs and slowly began to totter up and down the room. "Open up them amazing doors. Gonna intrusive. Gonna march them march. Gonna make us a presence in the name a' freedom."

She reached the end of the room and started back again. Everyone was staring at her. The woman could do loud.

"I ain't got no hoarse voice. I ain't cold. Ain't tired. Ain't sluggish. We gone correct the abnormal. Ain't no over-the-counter Medicaid cure. We gone go through this city like a dose a' ole time castor oil. Gone raise that butt and raise them feet. Gonna march, Gonna float. Gonna soar. Gonna fly. Gonna march to Kingdom Come for Glory Hallelujah!"

The nurse came boiling in furious. "What did you give her? Did you give her liquor? Pills? What?"

Tamzie said no, she was just trying to cheer her up. Talking about the past bye gone days.

Luevenia was still going strong. Pumping her fist up and down.

"No mean cop dogs gone stop us. No firehose gone stop us. No National Guard gone stand in our doorway. Gone march over Jordan. All working together. All praying and swaying together as one mighty flood tide army!"

Afterwards, Tamzie went out and phoned up a list of old civil rights activists she knew of around town. Most of them seemed to be deaf or bedridden. Some wanted loans of money. Nobody seemed real anxious to come out of retirement. She wondered how you get in touch with Jesse Jackson, Al Sharpton, them heavy-lifting brothers.

She had her next good idea and call up Greenpeace where an answering machine come on. Real quick Tamzie say there's a nuclear power dump being planned down at Roebuck plantation. Some banker name of Grady Troxler think it's a good money-raiser.

29

As the acknowledged daughter of Blake Huston, Rannie Ralston had no trouble persuading the probate court to allow her to represent him in the issue of his commitment. At her request the judge signed an order for an emergency video deposition and threw Vineyard Dupree off whatever small equilibrium he ever had.

The deposition was held in Rannie's office on Broad Street. Bracey and Izzie were both present as petitioners in the action. Yes, that was an unpleasant surprise for Bracey. Discovering her mother had signed both names to the pleadings.

Vineyard sat at the long table shuffling papers and looking very disorganized. He seemed like a would-be card cheat who didn't know how to stack a deck.

Waiting for Rannie to arrive, Izzie chatted with the lady court reporter about how she was going to get collagen injections to rid herself of smoking lines in her lips. She said some people were allergic to Zyderm because it was made from cattle protein. Zyderm was the name of the collagen. It dissipated over time and required maintenance injections two or three times a year.

The court reporter said that was nice. Her voice didn't betray a whole lot of enthusiasm.

Rannie swept in, saying she hoped Vineyard wasn't offended at her defending her own interests in the matter.

"Well, heh," Vineyard laughed. "I've always heard a man who represents himself has a fool for a client."

Rannie sat down, gave him a malign smile like she was about to play a game of shark and goldfish. "I'm not a man," she said. "In case you haven't noticed." Pause to shoot a dagger right between his eyes. "You pathetic nincompoop. And if you think I can't handle this and represent my own best interest and remain cool under fire . . . well, you are the ignorant, inadequate, half-wit I always took you for."

Vineyard got all stiff and reminded her of the ethics ruling on courtesy that had finally come out of the S.C. Supreme Court. This had been prompted by actual fist-fights among overly aggressive attorneys. Rannie said her recollection was Vineyard had made a tasteless crack about women in the workplace. Vineyard ducked his head and shuffled the papers in his file.

Never daunted by displays of rudeness, Izzie played grand lady. She said she was sorry circumstances had to be like this. She and Mary Canty had always been such close friends.

Rannie said, "I find it hard to believe your sincerity."

Bracey was not filled with a lot of confidence. She wondered uneasily if she needed her own attorney. Was bringing a spurious commitment proceeding a criminal offense?

A secretary rolled Blake in on his wheelchair.

Getting going, Vineyard asked Blake Huston the standard question of are you under the influence of drugs or alcohol or is there any other reason you are unable to respond adequately to the questions he was about to ask.

"Ran off with a lady yodeler from a carnival!" said Blake real loud. He licked his lips at the salacious memory.

The video camera and sound were running, the reporter typing away. Blake had never looked so bad. Huge liver spots on his head. Red veins spider-webbed on his nose and cheeks. Vacuous wild eyes.

Real pleased, Vineyard said to Rannie, "Well, here we are joined in litigation articulating our competing claims. Letting them be valued and weighed by the legal system. I would hate to delay or derail the process . . ."

Rannie bluntly told him to just get on with his meaningless line of questioning. She had a narrow defense. Blake was just fine and dandy. But there should be some intriguing testimony on that subject.

Bracey wondered how any woman could be as hardnosed as Rannie Ralston. What would Rannie do if a Grady Troxler ordered her to get "it" wet?

Vineyard asked a variety of questions on everyday events to test Blake's grip on reality. Birthdays. Names of three former wives. What he ate for breakfast.

In reply, Blake rummaged through his brain for every off-the-wall vicious and vulgar anecdote he knew. Busting virgins. Knocking up Rannie's mother while her putative father was passed out drunk in the same bed. Many of the lurid tales were open admissions of blackmailing, rape, larceny, and other blatant criminal behavior. None of them were responsive to the question. Doubtless he had been one shrewd operator in earlier years—all the underpinnings of his immoral behavior were laid bare—but none showed any current ability to manage his financial affairs.

After a ghastly half hour of this, Vineyard made a hopeless gesture and said your witness.

Rannie smiled, "Shall we uncover the real story?"

Rannie knew her father was deaf. She put into the record that she would be posing her questions in writing and proceeded to do just that.

How old are you?

"Eight-nine this January!" Blake shouted in the overloud voice of the hearing impaired.

At that point, Vineyard's case bit the dust.

Rannie asked Blake about "Gilligan's Island," and they sat through dozens of plots. He liked Mary Ann over the movie star, but the millionaire's wife was "a damned good-looking bitch."

Why did you marry Isabelle Fanseau?

Bracey cringed.

"She lets me suck her titties." He slavered and hacked up phlegm at the lusty thought.

Even Rannie was a bit thrown by that one.

Tell us about your property on Roebuck Island.

No misty-eyed reflection on old plantation days. Instead he told about the Depression and the bottom falling out of the cotton market "driving the darkies north like Hebrews in flight out of Egypt."

He was cackling. "Land wasn't worth a tootle back then. Nobody wanted to live on a stinking hot, pluff-mud marsh. All that air conditioning and golf was later. They made it into what they called a two-county landfill. Really nothing more than a dump. Barges came down from Baltimore, Newport-News. Refuse from off the Charleston navy base. Fuel oil. Mercury. Cadmium. Lead. Pesticides. Toxis sludge dredged off the bottom of Charleston harbor. I clipped Roebuck for $3 million selling them a poisoned garbage pit. Made them pay cash."

Izzie was staring at her new husband. Bracey thought there might have been admiration in her eyes.

Did Roebuck Plantation know of this prior use?

"Of course they did. They grabbed at it in a heartbeat. Covered a lot of it over with dirt themselves. It's all part of land development scams. Borrowing and juggling. Keep the balls up in the air. Get the hell out of Dodge before they come down."

"That lends a certain irony," said Rannie. "Scamming the scammer." She turned to Bracey beaming with pride. "That's my Dad." Somehow, he heard or else read her lips. "You didn't fall far from the tree, did you?"

■ ■ ■

Byron was drinking a Bloody Mary with raw egg and Tabasco for a fierce hang-over. Mixing up your drinks all night—rum and bourbon and Southern Comfort will do it every time.

He said he needed a neurologist, diagnostic services for his split-open head, maybe neonatal care. He felt like a calf got born in his mouth.

Sparky said he believed he'd have a beer. Thanks for offering. He went into the fridge in Byron's condo and popped the top on a Blue Ribbon. Held to the enamel by magnets was a nudie fold-out of a Penthouse Pet who was coming to play golf. Byron had actually drawn a crude dick pointing at her snatch.

Byron lay stretched out on the couch, a towel of ice on his face, Yelled at Sparky in the kitchen, "What have you done to that colored boy? He comes whining round here. Afraid to deal direct with you. You scare him shitless with some redneck rhetoric?"

Sparky came in and sat down, gave him the full-face frank and honest look. "Vineyard? I'm shaking him down for money. Put the wind up him with some mostly illusion fears."

Byron sat up and slapped the ice-bag down on the glass-top coffee table. Said, "Goddammit I knowed it! What is wrong with you, boy? I thought you had some conventional wisdom in that head of yours."

The exertion of a temper tantrum hurt him a lot, and he lay back down.

Sparky swigged his beer. "We need to finalize some incentives here. Get me over this personal economic dislocation. All these useful functions you squeeze out of me . . . I'm like one-stop shopping for whatever needs ironing out."

Byron looked heavenward seeking divine guidance. "Help me, Big Guy," he said. "I don't need to be fucked with so early in a hangover."

Sparky chatted on. "We did pretty well down on the Texas Gulf. Buried how many bodies? Three? Four? You refresh my memory of the exact count."

"I don't remember none of that," moaned Byron. His

eyes were closed. He desperately wanted to be alone and hassle-free.

"What's the matter? Remorse set in? Got amnesia? Brain languish?"

Byron said, he had to reiterate he didn't remember anything of the sort. No highlights. No lowlights.

"We stimulated some economic growth, but we distributed the benefits too," Sparky observed. "As we went along."

Byron said Sparky was going to get his cut out of Roebuck. All in due time. He got up like he was going to show Sparky to the door. Sparky got up. Byron slugged down his drink, staggered a bit at the impact. Steadied himself against the back of a chair.

Sparky put his fingertips against Byron's chest, gave him a little push. The man didn't push back. He was looking kind of scared.

Sparky pushed again. Said, "You indifferent, hostile, what? I feel like I'm left here sitting without a guardian. The trend seems pretty clear. Everybody uses old Sparky and then shits on him. I got to hump that nagging Doris Troxler just to have a half-way decent car to drive."

Byron gaped at him. "You got to . . . ? No. Don't tell me. I don't need more evidence of how assertive you done got."

Sparky said, he liked to think he leapfrogged over problems. Didn't beat his head on brick walls. He wasn't auditioning for a role in a play. Life was for real. While Byron was running some big-tit golf promotional gig, Sparky was engineering the underbelly work. Getting his hands dirty.

Byron was mumbling. "We got ends and beginnings

here. Things got to be moved off my desk. Vineyard crawling in here like a whipped yellow dog. Making me a middleman. I ain't comfortable with that kind of confusion. This ain't some mom-and-pop operation."

Byron held out a piece of lined notebook paper with a name on it and two addresses, one a residence, the other a workplace, a house on Legendre Street. The name was Omar Temple Gillyard.

He said he wanted Sparky to front-burner it. They needed Phase 2 in the worst way.

Sparky said, so now his job approval rating goes up again.

Byron insisted his credibility was always apparent. When you looked past the little differences of opinion, they was always best asshole buddies. Pissed up against the same tire in the parking lot.

"Well," said Sparky, "call it the general decline in civility or whatever, but the price was $2,000 up front."

Byron griped about it, said son-of-a-bitching thieving cocksucker, but he pulled out hundred-dollar bills. Counted five of them. Said that was all he had both on him and to his name. So don't browbeat him. Seduce him. Whatever. Sparky'd get the rest later along with his cut of the total profits.

Sparky said that would only fund the mechanics of the operation itself. Gas money. Ammunition. Then he asked how Byron wanted it done. In private or in front of a sellout crowd? Make an example to others.

Byron collapsed back on the couch with his face in his hands. "Private, for God's sake. Lord, I don't need to reflect on this. What you do out there on the high seas I don't want to know about."

Sparky folded the five bills once and scratched the side of his face with it. Watching Byron like a big wad of blubber. Thinking, yeah when it came time to shake the boy down it wouldn't be hard a-tall.

30

"Travis is just about the most awful, meanest sumbitch that ever drew breath and spit," said Bobbi-Jean Kincaid. "He collects all this Nazi regalia stuff. Lugers and daggers and badges and everything. Goes to gun shows all the time. And he's got this fully automatic rifle that's illegal as hell, but he's got it just the same."

B-J and Byron Jasper were going through the old open-air market in Charleston with the tourists, pawing through long tables of flea-market stuff, crafts and sweatshirts. Seashell filled lamps. Woven baskets. Jewelry.

Byron allowed as how the boy sounded like right severe company. He had phoned the prison in Raiford and been told sure enough parole was happening any day now. Travis Swails had successfully graduated from a program that steers inmates of his nature to an early release. Byron had argued the statistics on recidivism until he was blue in the face, but it didn't sway their decision.

It hadn't been hard for B-J to get a parole list and select a name at random. And she knew Byron was something less than the Sherlock Holmes of modern detective work.

The news made Byron gloomy, queasy and morbid. He was in and out of a doglike servility. Every now and again he'd show his fangs, and she'd wonder if maybe he could get out of control and turn dangerous. He'd ask her a detailed question about her boyfriend, she'd catch his eyes studying the nuance of her reaction. She'd give him her best guileless smile and make up something which even as many lies as she told she had no trouble keeping straight.

He said, "You're sure making it hard for me to continue a personal tradition of making love to perfect 10s."

"Oh buy me this, Mister Jasper!" she shrieked. "Oh be such a perfect dahlin' and buy it! I'll pay you back when that awful Grady Troxler chokes up what he owes me!" She held up a framed mosaic of Elvis made out of little bitty colored seashells mounted on black velvet.

Byron reached into his pocket slowly for a thick roll of cash. Kind of a lukewarm blessing on their deadlocked relationship. "It ain't easy keeping you under the salary cap," he griped.

She hugged him and gave him a big kiss on the cheek. Said she was so grateful because so much of her good work went largely unnoticed. She just adored the picture because she felt like her life was a great big old collage too.

She said her boyfriend was just a bad-ass impediment, and she couldn't see a way to overcome that disability. Her number-one criteria in a love affair was quality balanced with safety. It just made Byron and her shacking up together kind of a nonstarter. But she figured the PowerChest Pro-Am was not just a way to lift them past the winter months, but an actual roadmap for growth out at Roebuck.

Byron dry swallowed thinking of the girls who were coming. He asked when the list of names was arriving and what months they were featured in magazines and such. He had heard you could down-load all kinds of dirty stuff off the internet now, but when it came to computer literacy, he was pretty much an at-risk child in the woods. Was there media kits that came with these gals? Color glossies that showed frontal nudity? Beaver shots?

She said let's not get too much in the realm of supposition. You're not reading a guide to spicy food restaurants. Most of these girls come with real strict contracts about what you can say to them, where you can touch them. It was a narrow perspective, she admitted, but you couldn't get around it.

"I swear I can't take being muzzled up." Byron complained. "I got a history of extremist behavior when I get frustrated."

B-J gave him an angel face and said she deserved to be booed for not giving full attention to his personal needs. But cheer up. He could do more than just hug two of those sweethearts while he addressed the media, handed out victory cups and such. Some of them would be free agents. He could watch them getting dressed behind two-way mirrors if he wanted without it being a breach of contract. Take them out on dates. Get off on the heartaches and triumphs.

This seemed to hearten him considerably. "Ooo-eee!" he whistled. "Lemme follow my instincts."

She said like all girls they responded to those landmarks of affection. Surprise presents from jewelry stores. Being taken to nice hotels with the amenities, the ones with tiny bottles of shampoo and real glass drinking glasses instead of plastic. Unabashed, spend-with-both-hands, glitter and glitz. The kind of thing he was practically an art director of.

"I'll be following that scent at a kind of half-run," Byron vowed.

"Oh lordy!" B-J shrieked. "I declare I'm gonna die if I can't have this!"

She held up a little stuffed alligator with a clock in its belly.

Byron's attention had been diverted by a big mob of black folks gathering on East Bay Street. B-J kind of inveigled the wad of money out of his hand and peeled off a couple of hundred-dollar bills.

"They fixing to have a riot?" he wondered out loud.

"They seem kind of old for that," said B-J. She looked at the fat wad of money thoughtfully, at the two C-notes in her other hand, then shoved all of it into the pocket of her jeans.

■ ■ ■

Vineyard was saying into the telephone "Yeah, sure, I knowed them Section-8 folks all had criminal records. Well, Tamzie Jerome, maybe next time you better think twice before you hire me to do something for you."

Pause.

"What you mean what's going to happen? Your neighbor gone sue your ass off. Don't you got liability insurance on the place?"

Pause.

"Well, don't yell at me. I can't be expected to handle everything. You a big girl."

Pause.

"I done told you I don't know nothing about Omonio Reese or his wife. None of that."

He hung up.

Sparky sat in Vineyard's office browsing the *Post & Courier*. When the conversation was over, he said, "You know this ban on Sunday deer hunting is some shit, ain't it? How do the deer know it's Sunday? I mean think on it. You're the lawyer."

Vineyard was pondering heavy about something. He looked up kind of off hand, said the tradition was rooted in the old Blue Laws. They preserving some peace and tranquility during church hours.

To which Sparky said, well that's all well and good for Christians. But there's other religious affiliations. What about all them deer hunters named Ginsburg? Feinstein? Mohammed? Kungfu Phat?

Vineyard went over to the window, grunted and strained to lift it up. The building was built in 1905, so old you could still do that. Pigeons moved away on the ledges. Sparky said what's the problem?

"That bitch Tamzie Jerome threaten me. She on a phone somewhere near by. Say the fire next time's coming in about under five minutes."

Sparky said what's that mean?

"Didn't you go to Sunday school? It's like what's coming worse than Noah's flood."

Sure enough, something was going on down in the street. Vineyard leaned out trying to see.

There was just a moment there when Sparky thought how easy it would be to give him a shove. Watch him go screaming down. Splat. Go out and tell the secretary he just started acting crazy, jumped without warning. Was he having emotional problems?

"AIN'T NOBODY TIRED!"

What the hell? Somebody down there with a big bull horn. Sparky shoved into the window to look too. Some kind of a parade. Decrepit looking old black gal with the bull horn whipping them up. So old she was being held up by two other old biddies.

"AIN'T TARD! AIN'T COLE! AIN'T HONGRY!"

Sparky said what the fuck? Is that a civil rights demonstration? Those things ain't been around for years. Well, maybe up North where they got the real race problems. Boston. New York.

Vineyard said, who are all these people? There must have been seventy, a hundred-fifty black folks, maybe two hundred. Then coming up to join them a mess of squirreley looking white people in beards and those Birkenstock sandals. Girls in long skirts and Doc Marten boots They had a sign that said, "No Nukes."

Sparky thought, no nukes?

A cop came up and started arguing with them about parade permits. Gang of plaid-shirt white hippies, all linking arms in the front ranks, giving him shit eight ways from Sunday. And the old black gal just bellowing into the horn.

"NO DOGS GONNA STOP US! NO MEAN COPS GONNA STOP US!"

A cop on a horse rode up. Then a TV news van. That was what they were waiting for. Soon as the camera was out pointed at them, they just suddenly surged forward down the street.

The black ones were singing gospel. "I know He won't leave me now that's He's brought me this far." It wasn't a hard tune to pick up. The whites came in on the chorus.

It didn't take long for them to get past, there only being a couple hundred. They were just gone down the street with the mounted cop riding along side. The cop on foot was left there with a stooped-over arthritic old black man he was trying to arrest. His arms so crippled they looked like they'd snap off if the cop cuffed him.

"Yeah, bust the colored man," said Sparky. "Ain't that something?"

The crowd was down the street in front of the mayor's office now raising hell. The bullhorn was more faint. The black woman was leading them in singing "We Shall Overcome."

"What's it mean?" said Vineyard really puzzled.

"I reckon we're just a hopelessly racist society," said Sparky. "Mandatory sentences for the black man with his crack. But the white professional does powder cocaine and gets probation."

Vineyard looked at him like he was crazy. "I mean what they doing down in the street?"

Sparky shrugged. "Who cares? Or at least not in the light of America's larger social issues. Folks your color undertake your mundane commercial activities. Go shopping. You get treated like a potential armed bandit casing the store. It sure enough hangs a restraint on your upward mobility. But we waste our time looking for sinister biases, prejudices, and here you are defying the labels. Go to law school and have an office and everything."

"Are you crazy?" said Vineyard. "Jerking my chain? What?"

"I try to keep a serious outlook on life," said Sparky. "What I need for you to do is get out of that current lawyer-like skin. Kind of revert. Reach back into the old subconscious and remember the old skills. Your ancestors what were Watutis. Ubangis. Or Zulus or whatever. The ones the driving-force behind boiling up missionaries in big iron pots and eating them."

Vineyard went into the whine. The what 'chew talking 'bout, man? You bothering me. I ain't got time for this shit.

That was when Sparky unloaded. Told him tomorrow, the next day at the latest, they were going to clear title to some land in Phase 2 Roebuck Plantation. Said in an affected voice, *the Links at Roebuck.*

Vineyard looked ready to jump out of his skin. "I ain't killing nobody."

"Sure you are," said Sparky. "You get caught, what the fuck, you got a valid excuse. I forced you into it. Had a check you wrote to Omonio Reese you didn't want brandished about. Yeh. That's a story a jury would buy into."

Vineyard said yeah that's just persuasive as shit. Sparky said, well, it's true you ain't O.J. Simpson.

Then added, "Is it the case you dark folks grow them long fingernails to show you ain't a manual laborer?"

The spade looking at him, knowing for sure he was dealing with a crazy white man.

31

"You stop by and buy us a heating blanket at Kerrison's Department Sto'," the old biddies had say like some chorus as she go out the condo.

Tamzie got both Jacquilla Gillyard and Luevenia Parsons living in her condo now. She had made the mistake of having Luevenia over for a little post-march libation, turn around and the woman pass out asleep on the couch. Fine. She let her stay the night. Tuck her up in a quilt. The next morning Luevenia feeling poorly. Need to lay up in the bed some. Somehow, she never leave, and Tamzie now sleeping on the couch. But Luevenia always perk up when dinner set out on the table.

Omar's Auntie Jacquilla with that goat, now Luevenia feeding the feral cats down in the swamp. Got fifteen of them coming up to eat sardines. The neighbors come over in a delegation and say it's got to stop. The yowling at night was enough to wake the dead.

The fallout from the big demonstration was the Mayor was a little mystified. Roebuck Island was not in the City of Charleston, but there was too much noise to avoid the potential voter impact. In a calculated political strategy, he issued a statement saying compromise was the essence of good government, and he intended to appoint an investigatory commission. Get all interested parties hunkered down at table together. Take timely action that would benefit both sides of the issue.

On behalf of Roebuck Plantation, Byron Jasper issue a press release denying any nuclear dump being planned, swearing they'd treat all the black folks fairly, give them jobs, grow the economy. He say he ain't going to shoot himself in the foot to spite his face. You can't do a nuclear dump in secret. Too many agencies get involved and wreck everything in toto he was trying to achieve.

As to the sitting down at a table business, Byron appeal to give the developers a chance. Don't set our house on fire and then offer to sell us a garden hose. They were putting money in traffic signal maintenance and making sure the water system remains privatized. While they welcomed public scrutiny, they needed freedom to apply novel solutions to problems as they come up.

What he said to a reporter that didn't make a none too coherent quote was, "The flat-out bald-faced effect of all this, and that's the crux of the problem, is God-awful. And that's just a crying dam' shame."

Grady Troxler figure his way to adjust accordingly was summon the Board into the big meeting room in the Skydeck and ask them to vote to cash in his stock options at the agreed favorable rate. He said he had work diligently and suffered all the anxieties that go with the corporate environment. The options were in his contract. He wanted them now if he wasn't to quit in frustration.

Tamzie speak up and said, no, she wasn't going along with it. Every head at the table turned to look in her direction.

Tamzie the uppity niggah with the civil rights protest

over Phase 2 of Roebuck. Tamzie who need to be back on them knees scrubbing kitchen floors where she belong.

Back ago when Tamzie was real young, fresh out of high school she had figured she was too good for the maid business and had taken upwardly mobile employment cleaning chickens in a poultry factory. Management had a system of snitches who would sit in the stall next you in the restroom, listen to make sure you were actually peeing and not just taking a breather. It was amazing how quick it had brought the meanness out of her.

Within a week, she had ratted on somebody, gotten a little pat on the head and a piddly reward bonus. Also a good case of being scared wondering if her victim would retaliate. From there on it got worse and worse. Meaner and meaner, more and more scared, until finally pushing a vacuum cleaner look like heaven, and she up and quit.

She felt like that now. Knowing she had create that demonstration in town. Knowing they all knew and didn't care for it one bit. Knowing the only chance to get her money back was to get meaner and meaner. Just like she was taking on the whole chicken factory management.

Grady started talking about what a serious banker he is, all moral rectitude and concern for the marginally credit-worthy. How he had been born with nothing and managed to deal honestly with poverty and suffering around him in the world.

"The reality of all this set-back is I'm being told I have a lot to learn about banking. We got a bunch of stuff to work on. Teaching me to react to situations and capitalize on them."

That was when Tamzie butt in just like a smart-mouth

kid in school. She say what about the bank auditors coming around? What were they going to think of what they found, his educational experience?

Her question threw him, so he lash out at her. "Now you listen here, you brick shithouse mullatress . . ." Then he check himself like maybe he had undergo anger control counseling. Dismiss her with a hand wave. "I'll go one-on-one with a damn bank regulator. It's part of my game plan."

At that point, Bryon Jasper who wasn't on the Board but always sit in being a cheering section for Grady came out with, "We're okay. Bankruptcy's like the end of a football season. You start all over again with everybody at zero."

Grady silenced him. He couldn't afford at this point to stir a backlash form the Board. Said, "Let me rebut this claim. Not even in idle moments of gloom, nobody's even contemplating bankruptcy. I'm optimistic and upbeat. Poised for a comeback."

Skip Rightenberry, the realtor with the toupee and the habit of kissing ass when he thought the thrift was making him money now said, "Okay, you're the versatile big man. But bankruptcy's the culmination of some real downer shit. If we're going to tread this ground, we need details." His voice lend a hint of some previous life bankruptcy disasters he had been mix up in.

Some other Board members chime in with righteous muttering and disapproval.

"Ain't exactly been a success," said one.

"Can't win for losing," said another.

It was getting to be a forceful scene. Tamzie had sure split the once happy family into warring factions. The Board wasn't a devoted Troxler following no more.

"I don't need this double-teaming," said Grady. "It's not easy cleaning the stables all day and never getting to ride the pony. There is nothing frivolous about my management."

That was when the door opened, and that little ofay honey Bobbi-Jean poke her head in. "I don't want to interrupt anything important, Mister Troxler," she said, "—all your policies and procedures—but I really need my $50,000 from the Clemson game bet."

Every mouth in the room fell open at that triple whammy.

Well, that sure erode some public trust. The Board dig in and get up the courage to vote against Grady's stock options. Grady looked stymied as hell. Tamzie just know he was pissed off inside. She had the image of that chicken factory again and not much ray of hope that the meanness would let up.

■ ■ ■

"I've told you I had nothing to do with that demonstration on Broad Street," Bracey insisted to her husband.

Chase gave her a snide look from his armchair. He was wearing a corduroy jacket with leather patched elbows, drinking a single-malt scotch. He said, "Well, you may as well have. They're after the same objective. Take the land from me without paying for it."

Bracey said, "All zoning laws do that after a fashion."

Chase gave her a look. "All this criticism is out of line with reality. They've got scattershot growth out on those islands now. Let it keep going and it'll be wall-to-wall trailer parks. I offer controlled growth, and the tree-huggers fabricate lies about me. Nuclear waste dump. What am I? An idiot?"

"Well there's some kind of poisonous landfill out there," Bracey argued. "It came out in Blake Huston's deposition."

Chase gave her another look. Finished his drink. He said, "It's nothing you need to worry with."

For the first time she could remember, Bracey didn't feel threatened by her husband's contempt. With Grady Troxler no longer calling her, she felt she had quit hitting herself in the head with hammer. Or worse. Escaped a dismemberment in one of those drive-in movie horror things. Chainsaw Massacre Part III.

It also made her wonder about the nature of courage. Whether something magic had happened that allowed her to simply walk away from Grady without fear. Or was it just discovering that he led a more desperate life than her? I mean, my God, another man in bed with his wife, and Grady was apparently afraid to do anything about it.

Chase mused aloud. "I feel like I'm going through a metal detector at the airport. And it's calibrated so sensitive it picks up the metallic strip on my charge card."

Bracey said, what was that supposed to mean?

Chase said, he was all wrapped up doing the divestiture of his interest in Seagrass. Her mother was taking the opportunity to badger him for new heating and air conditioning, a modern kitchen.

He added, "The wine of life is gone. The Chablis has turned acidic and the burgundy tannic. Everyone lies to you. Serve you sparkling wine and call it champagne."

Bracey looked out the tall window where the garden was bright with Goldsturm cornflowers. In spring it would be a riot of foxglove and columbine, daffodils and blue phlox. When she turned back, Chase had opened a lush color brochure of Christie's real estate offerings for Nantucket. Homes of warmth and stature. It listed a Hyannisport estate for $1,995,000.

Bracey asked if he was moving north. He said no, it was just an idle moment of fantasy. He was thinking maybe Florida. Fisher Island. You could declare bankruptcy but keep a principal residence. She said, bankruptcy?

Chase looked at her blandly. He acted as though he had never made the slip.

"You know," he said, "these football bowl games are getting such commercial hype names it blows me away. FedEx Orange Bowl. Nokia Sugar Bowl." He laughed. "Poulan-Weed Eater Bowl. I mean I ask you."

Virginia had a good team that year, and there was talk of a bowl invitation. Chase seldom if ever talked about football, however. He once said he had put that phase behind when he started his MBA. He didn't want to be a failed jock living in the past. Some kind of ineffectual laughing stock.

Bracey said, "You know that money I borrowed from Seagrass and loaned to Roebuck? Do I have a mortgage on the Phase 2 land? It seems like I would. The way you and Grady want everything to look so official to cover up your fraud."

"Look," Chase said. "Let's get one thing straight. You don't own anything except a lot of debt and a peck of trouble. You sure don't own me. You'll never own a man. So you be a real good girl and hope nothing bites you."

32

"I always had trouble letting someone do oral sex on me," said Doris Troxler to the "marital difficulties" counselor. "The lips of my vagina, or I guess you'd more properly say vulva, are kind of long and floppy. I was, well, frankly ashamed of them."

Sparky couldn't believe he was sitting in on this. Little office out in a faceless office park over west of the Ashley River. Doris had insisted on it. Grady and her were trying to work out their differences. Here he was boffing the man's wife almost nightly, and he had to listen to their fucked-up emotional problems.

The counselor looked like Mr. Rogers off the TV show. Button-up-the-front sweater he had done one button off so it hung funny. Sick smile. Calling them "good people" like some Methodist youth minister.

Doris said, "You see there just are no books that show photos of a healthy vulva. The medical profession is so male dominated. It's a patriarchy really. So you don't know if yours is okay or not. When this all came just rushing out in a big purge like thing, I was on a local talk TV show. A lot of the women in the audience were quite helpful. Wanted to let me see theirs. And there was like this medical sexologist on the show. And afterwards she examined me and said I was fine. Plenty of people have flappy lips on their vulva."

Sparky said he'd like to interject at this point that he figured eating pussy was like that first drink of scotch. You just know right off it's an acquired taste.

Three heads swiveled in his direction. Stared at him in a moment of silence. He raised his hand shoulder high and waved. Said, 'Hi'

Doris said, she had colds a lot as a child. Allergies. Whatever you called them. Her father had them too. Hay-fever. He used to mow the lawn with wads of Kleenex stuffed up his nostrils.

Her parents were distant, cold and demanding. Her mother was openly envious of her. It was impossible to please them. She felt she had turned to an affair with Sparky—a close business associate of her husband's—because he was so ruthless, a killer really.

The counselor, head shrinker, whatever the fuck he was actually raised an eyebrow at that. Sparky made a pistol out of a thumb and forefinger. Said, bang bang shoot 'em down.

Grady asked, is this true? Sparky said the hell you think? You pay me don't you?

"It's a sordid story," said Doris. "Grady is obsessively private. You won't catch him baring his soul. It's kind of morbid. He sleeps in underwear and socks."

"Yeah, sure, I'm a self-indulgent asshole," muttered Grady. "The wide-open banking of the '80s was all my fault. I created it on a whim. The whole freaking federal deficit you can lay at my doorstep."

They went on and on. Who had stuck a tack under whose ass. Doris whining about rejection and separation and personal criticism she got all the time. How Grady nagged her to go to a fat farm. The counselor talking about confidence building, sharing and mutual trust. How its absence brings unparalleled anxiety. What a fucking twinky.

Sparky quit listening after awhile, thinking instead about how funny it was going to be to make Vineyard pull the trigger on someone. He was a real trip that boy. It was so easy to fuck with his mind. He'd probably puke his guts up once he had capped the dude. Collapse in a seizure. Sparky had bought a tape of gangsta rap music to play in the car.

"Do you think you can discipline your passion?" asked the counselor.

Sparky tuned back in. Said, say what? He could barely keep the smirk off his face as the counselor outlined a proposed "fidelity contract." It had all kinds of "party of the first" part shit in it. It even had Grady contractually bound to give Doris whatever foreplay she wanted as well as a Nordic Track exercise machine.

Sparky said sure whatever they wanted. He'd swear on a picture of Jerry Falwell if that made them happy. Anything to get out of this bunch of yackety-yack crap.

"Really super," enthused the counselor. "Now let's all shake hands. Partners? Yes? Okay, good people, let's get this program up and running!"

Outside the office, Sparky took Grady aside and said, shit, he didn't know. Maybe he had changed his mind. He reserved the right to do that. That Doris got a pussy on her about as spicy as Aunt Jenny's chowchow. Tell her to be ready around seven tonight. He'd come by to pick her up. And have her wear that big mink coat but be naked under it.

Grady looked like he had swallowed a dam' hop toad. Or just learned he had pancreatic cancer.

■ ■ ■

"You sure give the term 'lying shit-ass' new meaning!" yell Tamzie at the top of her lungs. She was dressed in bright crayon colors that reflect her anger.

Vineyard kind of cower back in his office chair, both hands raised to ward her off in case she start swinging heavy objects. He said, "Don't let's attack the emotional side of things."

When the charge card bill come through for $98,000 for a new Mercedes SL 500, Tamzie decide that Vineyard had really gone over the top. A lying profit-taking bastard was what she called him. She ask how he manage to get such a bill on one card? He admit he have to get the limits raised before he did it. Move up from gold to platinum with no preset spending limit. But it was cool. Like he say, he had cut up the card and was putting her into a better deal.

She had seen herself all slinky and gay with this man. Laughing white teeth under a big white moon dappling the ocean. Barefoot, holding her shoes, her gown hiked up as she wade in the surf. Now he got her so frustrated she can't think.

"What I want to know is just why you need a second car?" she demand. "And why me? Why my charge card, dear God Almighty?"

Vineyard shoot his French-cuffs and said he previously explain how he lend his BMW to Sparky Truluck who was a troubleshooter for Roebuck Plantation. That left him without wheels, and it's vital a man of professional standing need to get about, make courtroom appearances on time. But it's okay because he have the BMW back now.

She said he get it back just in time to run over Takesha Reese. He said that was an accident. Time to move on from that tragedy. He'll just sign title to the SL over to Tamzie. They go out to Autobahn Motors whenever she want and fix the paperwork for financing it through a auto loan company. She'll have a nice second car. Something sporty for those jaunts to the North Charleston coliseum to watch ice hockey.

Tamzie said she don't need and can't afford no $98,000 second car. Vineyard and this car ain't the only dark cloud in her sky. She sick and dam' tired of underdog standing and being scared idiotic of what was going on at Seagrass. Threatening lawyer letters coming from her old neighbor on Cannon Street saying they got to reach a mutual agreement on damages or go to court. She got not just one now but two old biddies living off her, eating her out of house and Frigidaire and fighting over which soap opera to watch. Both of them making a mess and saying why don't she hire a maid to clean up behind them.

That was when Tamzie notice the cot in the corner and the heap of dirty clothes and shaving stuff. She realize Vineyard living in his office.

"Your wife finally kick your ass out?"

Vineyard said, through no fault of his own. He thought she was in the process of discovering she's a lesbian.

Anyhow it's a message of reconciliation between him and Tamzie. Can't they break this negotiating stalemate and get back in love?

Tamzie said she'll break a stalemate over his head. Every time she even think of him she need a Tanqueray palate cleanser to get the taste of him out of her mouth.

He said don't she remember the good times? They play hard and play with enthusiasm. They have some right good physical nights of love making.

Tamzie said he try to love her up again, she going to give him some physical infirmities. She say what she just don't get is why did Vineyard let that ofay bastard have the BMW in the first place?

Vineyard kind of duck his head and not say anything for a while. Finally, he admit he was scared of the man.

"I think he kills people," he said.

"Yeah," said Tamzie. "What you mean is you know he do."

33

Approaching the 7th green on a right stout 440-yard par-4 at Roebuck, B-J said, it sure was funny how those brown streaks were appearing in the fairways. Chase said, it was nothing. Winter was coming on. She said, yeah, but in winter all the grass turns yellow-brown, not brown-brown, and not just in wide swaths. He said, it was nothing. Ignore it.

When he missed an easy putt for a double bogey 6, Chase paused and looked off at the tops of the trees. Said, yes, since she asked, he did have something disturbing his concentration. It was those perceived violations of SEC regs that had him down.

"I thought I was astute," he said. "But I now find I'm naïve in so many ways. Clinging to outdated notions of honesty and public service."

She said, that's some kinda pisser, ain't it?

He said, "Welcome to the brave new world of self-parody."

B-J said she didn't understand that, but then there were just so many things girls don't understand. That's why she was coming to increasingly rely on him. Like him promising to make Grady Troxler pay up on the Clemson bet.

Chase said, that was reassuring of her to say, but of

late he was all mired in mordant reflection. Wife and mother-in-law screaming money, money, money. Investors on his back night and day with a litany of insults and demands.

"I find myself clutching at quiet moments like this. But I'm not going to dig down into the pit of victimhood. I'll work out a schedule of concessions with the SEC. They don't heed expertise. What it'll do to Roebuck . . ." He made a helpless gesture.

B-J gave him a little dismayed look. She said you mean the airplane has got engine trouble, and you're not sure if it'll make the field or crash and burn.

Chase said yeh, something like that. No tidal wave of panic. Still, she was right. An engine had flamed out.

He looked off at those trees again. The course was empty as usual, so no one was pressing them from behind. He could look at trees all he wanted.

B-J thought a girl always gets some warning blips on her radar screen. And now this roundabout approach to something was building up. Made her wonder if this little love affair wasn't a synthetic enchantment.

Chase said he had to concede the Roebuck vision was off schedule. They should have been on Phase 2 by now. Manifold evils had jammed them up, jimmied the works. But he was not in it for the short run like Byron Jasper. He really wanted Roebuck to succeed. It was his monument to permanence.

B-J said she had no difficulty picturing him with his principal residence out here on the first fairway. Another *pied-á-terre*—was that the way to say it?—in the south of France. Get him out of that stuffy Charleston snob world where he couldn't be himself and he was all mired in social ritual.

Chase gave her a manly smile. "Good old B-J. Everybody's a detractor but you."

He said he was negotiating in good faith with his wife. Barring any more irrational demands on her part, the separation agreement would be worked out soon. She'd be a lot happier without him. Believed she might come out of the closet and admit she was a lesbian. But he had a big immediate problem right now.

He sighed.

The long and the short of it was cash flow. He had been working with Grady Troxler on a way to get a transfusion into Roebuck Phase 2 so they could build the second golf course.

B-J said Grady Troxler? That boy has got the emotional range of pig iron. Not to mention he owed her $50,000 on a bet she won fair and square and everybody was a witness to. The man had sworn no pissing and moaning.

Chase said well, yes, he was working on bringing Grady in line on that. Just be patient and rely on him.

B-J said Chase was just one act of generosity after the next. Had been since the day they met. But she did have bills like everyone else.

Chase agreed that was true. He didn't want to spoil their afternoon by talking business . . . but he'd be grateful if she'd drop by Seagrass tomorrow to learn how helpful she could be in all of it.

There it was. His bad side showing its ugly face. A major integrity break-down was coming up next.

She said, "Now how could I do that?"

He hesitated.

"It's kind of complicated, but from your point of view simple. Just sign some paperwork. Help us get over this pre-tax profit drop."

Whoa, girl, she thought. Here he was just sliding away all remote from the truth.

B-J got all animated, teed up her ball on number eight and smacked it straight down the middle of the fairway. Picked up her tee, smiled at Chase and said she was just an amen chorus of helpfulness. Being in a position where she could do nice things for Chase was like a dream come true. She hoped she could just keep going and build on it. She just knew they were a team that could pull the upset.

"Good old B-J," he praised. "Whatever fundamental differences remain between the sexes, you bridge them all. I feel whole when I'm with you."

Chase addressed the ball and hit it smack into a cavernous bunker.

B-J said tough luck, but didn't this course sure have a challenging variation of holes. All those sissy courses with the perfectly mowed fairways had just killed off the art of shot-making.

One thing about Bobbi-Jean Kincaid, she had a sound grasp of who she was. Didn't need grief workshops. Never got anywhere near an identity crisis. Never checked into Heartbreak Hotel. And characteristically, she could find the bright side of things.

If Chase was going to turn into a stinker, then he'd just become a target of opportunity like the rest of those bozos.

The love affair had been about half-wonderful, but now it was absent, learn to live with it. Just like not being able to hit a high-draw one-iron. No pissing and moaning.

She should have known they were incompatible. All those practice swings he took, then waggling the club head back and forth would drive her crazy over the long haul. Pacing off yardage on the greens. And that 60-degree wedge he had in his bag—the thing looked like some kind of kitchen tool. The boy was just not a shot-maker.

■ ■ ■

Tamzie thought the limit been reached when Jacquilla Gillyard get the gout from eating so well. First, she got to drive the woman to the Medicaid clinic, then go get generic medicine which still cost way too much, then back home, the woman screaming at every bump in the road.

Tamzie thinking why don't you cry silent so I can feel sorry for you.

Jacquilla say she's bereaved thinking of how her house burn down. She's worried about her goat and thinking the white neighbors might poison him. She say she's feeble and dizzy and need help getting back inside the house. Making gargling noises like she about to croak.

All this was a power play in case Tamzie had any crazy ideas she could dump the woman in a welfare shelter and leave her. Or buy her a Greyhound bus ticket and just shove her on it for Kansas City. Once back in the house Jacquilla take her teeth out, settle in with a stiff vodka tonic and watch TV without any pain at all.

That's it, Tamzie's thinking. Omar can just come retrieve

his auntie. He's the one stand to inherit all that valuable real estate the Roebuck folks want so bad.

Luevenia Parsons see her out the door saying they was a special on beef ribs at Winn Dixie. She say it stand to reason. They the beef people after all. And she's right fond of that Cajun barbeque sauce too. Also, the toilet paper was kind of scratchy. Could she move up to Charmin?

Tamzie got to Legendre Street about dog walking time in the evening. Omar usually took them out in two groups, so if she missed one shift, she was sure to catch the next. She parked the Saab up the street, walked down and just casually ran into him. Trying to think how she's going to lead into this.

Omar had eight corgis on leashes, four on each hand, and a big black Labrador retriever walking loose.

He said good evening and get over here, Maverick, you know how to be a good boy.

Tamzie say nice night ain't it.

He ask how was golf course living? She said you either love it or you're so-so on the subject.

Was she enjoying lady of leisure status? Well, she'd read there were folks who'd pay $20,000 for a custom-designed Christmas tree, have it delivered to the house and team of workers with stepladders put it up. But she ain't met any of them yet.

He said things had been quiet here downtown and come on now, Cleopatra, leave Rathskeller alone. Be a good dog like you know you ought to.

Tamzie look out at the night with the lights in the big

houses. She couldn't figure out how keeping dogs for a rich white woman could make a man so complacent.

Then kind of shy, Omar said everybody who work downtown was mighty proud of her freedom march and what she was doing. The Reverend Peebles even deliver a kind word from the pulpit, say maybe Sister Tamzie done learn something about herself and Christian charity. Pretty soon the prodigal return to the fold and buy them a new "Sunshine Bus of Promises Redeemed" for driving the old folks to church.

Tamzie said she won the inaugural, but they sure break you with aggressive play over the long haul. Right now, she was wore out and used up and feeling at an all-time low. His Auntie Jacquilla was the biggest trial since Job got all those boils and sores.

He said she sure marshal impressive evidence to the contrary. As best as he could estimate she looked about twenty years old and going on nineteen and under.

The corgis were biting each other. The big retriever sniff Tamzie's shoes and then up to her crotch.

Tamzie didn't think on how Omar was dodging the bullet, trying to deflect what she was up to. Instead it was the compliment that strike her, and a bunch of sadness well up inside her throat like oatmeal in a double boiler.

Tamzie's money had promised happiness that didn't come to pass. Nobody had said anything even approaching nice to her in she didn't know when. It was all share the wealth and gimmie what you got 'cause I'm more deserving than you.

At that moment if she could have just been whisked

back to Cannon Street, the no-account Section-8 people vanish in smoke, and her crawl into her old bed she would have done it and been happier than a kid staying up late with the adults on New Year's Eve. Tyrone Davis' "Turn Back the Hands of Time" played in her head.

"I want to come home," she said, her voice kind of catching. "At least on a interim basis."

"Do what?"

About then the Mercedes SL came cruising by slowly, two ski masks inside, shotgun poking out of the passenger window. Like the dudes thinking they gang-bangers out in L.A. or somewhere. Fucking Doctor Dre gangstas.

Headlights went up in their faces blinding them.

Tamzie was thinking oh shit not in my car!

She gave Omar a shove that sent him sprawling among the leashed dogs.

BA-DAM!

The big retriever dash at the car maybe thinking the gunshot mean retrieve something, maybe trying to attack the front tire. Whichever, he get himself smacked by the front bumper and bounced high in the air.

It was only after the car had squealed off that Tamzie climb up off the ground shaking and stricken with terror at almost getting smoked. A big white gash was ripped out of a tree where the tight buckshot pattern slash through. It's not easy to picture what a shotgun can do until you see it, realize you've played the role of a deer in season.

Omar was unfazed, talking to those yapping, snarling corgis. Trying to calm them down and stop them biting the blood out of each other.

"Imbecile!" shouted a white woman's voice.

Her heart pounding, Tamzie jerk around to see Isabelle Fanseau with a frantic face on her like the mother in the *Exorcist*. Tamzie's back hurt, she thought she had a ruptured disk. A near-death experience had just flash by and rip up a tree. She need a Bible to pray on. She need a rug to chew up. She need a hospital to keep her under observation. And now the woman calling her imbecile.

Isabelle Fanseau run out into the street, kneel down and cradle the dying dog's head on her lap. The woman was crying.

"Imbecile, Imbecile!" she sob.

She seem upset at the dog for running in traffic, kill himself like that.

Tamzie really want to lie down for her health. Satin pillow. Doctor prescribe total bed rest.

First though she want to order a set of Ginsu knives off that 800 number on TV, throw them every one into Vineyard Dupree's sorry murdering hide.

After that the bath oil and bed agenda.

34

Being both a black and a Jew would not be an easy burden for most men to bear. But for the Charleston police chief, there were heavier loads in life. Like Izzie Fanseau and her pack of yapping corgi dogs filling up his office at a time when he was trying to get the department nationally accredited.

For Bracey, being dragged along was an even more dispiriting encounter. The dogs were yapping and tangling with each other, seeming to vent Izzie's frustration for her.

Izzie expressed incredulity at the lack of progress that had been made on her case. Fugitives still at large. How many Mercedes SLs were there in the region?

The Chief said he had no license number and eight different body paint colors out of three witnesses. Even given the notorious unreliability of crime scene witnesses, it was something of a record.

Izzie said America's social fabric was deteriorating daily. The judicial process had become a mess of whitewashes and cozy plea bargains. The chief agreed with her. Said he had written a book on the subject.

His back story was how in the last century, a Russian Jew had married a black woman in Texas and begat the line that resulted in the Chief. He roller skated, rode horses Western style and kept the law best as anyone could in a port city with a one-a-week murder rate.

Izzie sat among her barking dogs like the center of a controversy.

Was there no implicit guarantee of safety to the citizens? Could he afford a widespread rebellion of the taxpayers?

He didn't have a response to that one.

Bracey closed her eyes and tried to be somewhere else. Ever since Blake Huston's deposition, Izzie had made her life a living hell. It was the knowledge that he had received $3 million for that big chunk of Roebuck Island when she had so many immediate pressing needs. The money remained with a broker at Smith-Barney/Robinson Humphreys despite Herculean efforts on Izzie's part to separate him from it.

Contractors had found $200,000 in urgent repairs that simply must be done on the house. New roof. Crumbling piazzas restored. It was one of the most historically significant in the city and couldn't be allowed to deteriorate further.

Her jewelry collection was woefully incomplete. Krogan's had the most darling 18-karat-gold scarf pin with three diamonds set in it.

They needed at least two more servants. She couldn't go on doing everything herself.

She simply had to get away. A cruise to the Greek Islands would be perfect.

The final bombshell Izzie dropped on the Chief without

warning. It was an emotional decision, but one she had to make. She was going to become actively involved.

Involved?

Izzie claimed her dogs could track the killers.

The Chief said killers? Izzie said surely he had read the investigating officer's report. Imbecile was dead.

■ ■ ■

"I've sure always wanted to have a horse farm," said Bobbi-Jean all agreeable. "Maybe in Tennessee outside of Nashville the way the country music stars do. I'd be right good at it. I like animals, and they seem to like me."

"It's a natural," Byron agreed.

Grady Troxler sat behind his big desk, that narrow lip mouth like a crack in cement. Not saying a word. Letting Byron do all the talking like maybe he figured nothing could be pinned on him later if he kept dead quiet. He still hadn't paid his gambling debt, and B-J knew it was going to be a bitch getting the money out of him.

"All those miles of white fence," she said. "It would just be so lovely. Some big handsome manager named Rafe or Dirk like in the Harlequin Romance books. If that awful mistake boyfriend of mine Travis came around Rafe'd just run him off."

Byron rolled his eyes. "Yeah, right." Each day Travis Swails didn't show up made him more dubious.

"Just think of it," she said with awe. "Three million dollars." She looked around at the marble office. "Where does all that money sit? Is it right here in a big vault or something?"

"It's electronic," Byron said. "It just comes in over the phone lines. We call up a mutual fund in New York. Say how much we want. Set a rate of interest that's attractive. It comes down here in deposits of less than $100,000 so it's all insured with the FSLIC. Nobody hurt if the loan don't quite work out."

"How can we get $3 million if it's less than $100,000?" said B-J, all wide-eyed innocence and awe at their higher finance.

Byron stared at her, not quite believing what he had heard. Then real slow and patient, he explained you broke it down into hundred thousand units. It was like long division. Remember back in third grade?

"Where do you think my horse farm ought to be?" she asked, just as sweet and serious as could be.

Byron almost blew up. Said who gives a flying fuck? Instead, he got a grip, tried to keep his voice calm. "It really doesn't matter, sweetheart. Well, it does, for the sake of the paperwork. The loan documentation and all that goes in the files for bank auditors. But there isn't going to be a horse farm. You, Bobbi-Jean Kincaid, are going to turn right around and lend the money to Roebuck Plantation. The same day. Maybe a gap of two days. Turn-key operation."

"I can't have a farm even for a little bit?"

Byron bit his tongue. "No. Not even for a little bit."

She made them go over it so many times that Byron was just throwing his hands up in the air and openly saying you dumb bimbo how can you be so smart one minute and so damn dense the next?

After close to an hour of this, B-J said well they were all smart businessmen and knew what they were doing so she guessed it was okay. She'd always done her part to make things go smooth. Byron knew that.

He said yes that's true. She was one of their steadiest profit producers and just as sweet as spice apple jelly to boot.

But there's just one problem.

Byron said what's that?

She said, "I just can't think about all this complicated big business stuff until I get that Clemson bet paid off and out of the way."

35

Vineyard said, "When stuff don't go right early in a love affair, it makes things kind of retrograde."

Tamzie felt like adding some volatility upside his head. Instead, she told him to just sign the damn title papers and let her get on with trying to negotiate something with the car dealer to sell it back. They were in the sales office of Autobahn Imports out on Savannah Highway where the car dealerships string out for miles. Acres of shiny Mercedes and BMWs around them and big American flags flapping.

The day before interview with the cops had taken her back to her marriage to the armed robber Debone who later died of gunshot wounds. She said she thought the car was either red, green or blue, she wasn't sure which, but worrying about it was giving her an ulcer. She was sorry she couldn't be of more help.

The white cops looked at her like she was some lying jigaboo covering up for the gangsta dudes. They didn't know the half of it.

The car salesman asked Tamzie was she a nomadic sports fan? If so, he could take her across to their adjoining lot, show her a real value in a Recreational Vehicle. Tamzie said he could change his thinking on that. All she wanted to know was how much it was going to cost her to get out of this deluxe sports vehicle.

"I concede I'm really disappointed," Vineyard told her. His pen just hover there not wanting to sign the title. "Things look bad, but we got some upset opportunities here. We remake the financial situation. Roebuck becomes a contender for a big money gusher."

Tamzie told him he'd sprained a tendon in his brain, and if he didn't shut up and get on with it, he'd need a health maintenance organization in a hurry.

He said sure, Vineyard-bashing was real popular right now. Tamzie, his wife Shereese, both of them on his case. But once he started winning, there'd be plenty of gals want to jump on his bandwagon. Frenzied female fans just coming down out of the stands to swamp him. He was thinking of buying a six-person hot tub to get ready for the joyous event.

Tamzie said, "You'll have to pardon me if I don't follow that fad."

Tamzie had thought about the problem in detail and decided she had to get her money out of that car. That was more important than the cops hauling in Vineyard and the white dude for shooting at them. Drive-by shootings were a fact of life. Poverty you could avoid.

She had enough on her plate as it was. She had gone to the HUD people to try to evict the Section-8 tenants. This little pipsqueak HUD lawyer come around personal to accuse her of racism.

Tamzie hold her hands up, turn them around one side then the other, say the man maybe going color blind but she don't think so.

He say, "Have you ever heard of xenophobia?"

Tamzie say not as she could recall.

He say it's self-hatred. The reason all the black Barbie dolls get left on the store shelf at Christmas.

Tamzie say maybe he ought to get his head outten the ass of whatever parallel universe it's stuck in and face up to reality. She's getting her teeth kicked in by welfare scum.

Little son-of-a-bitch GS-something bureaucrat lawyer. Not a real lawyer like down on Broad Street. For-true lawyers made a pile of money and understand the problems of the propertied class.

Out on the car lot there was a sudden sound of dog barking and wailing. Tamzie looked through the big showroom window and saw Izzie Fanseau and Omar holding onto the leashes of about fifteen dogs. The dogs were jumping and yelping and tangling with each other fit to beat the band, all lunging at the front bumper of her car. They were smelling the dead labrador.

Cops were out there too, pointing towards the showroom. Then they were walking their way. Vineyard said oh shit.

The cops got right to asking Vineyard would he like to come down to the station and have a chat, maybe take a polygraph, and yes, whatever he said could be a problem for him later on in a court. He got all huffy with them.

"You trying to kill the momentum of my day? What is this shit? I'm gonna give you a merchandise certificate? Prize for your big win here today?"

The cops said nothing. Just stood there stoneface the way cops do.

Vineyard said he knew what was coming. Him hand-cuffed and doing a swan dive onto the pavement smack on his face. He called on Tamzie to come along as a witness, be his Rodney King video camera.

Then he saw the Chief who was considerably darker than him. Which kind of blocked that avenue of accusation.

Vineyard backed up and started over. He said, "I'm feeling confused and out of sync. Every lawyer is an officer of the court. Is this respect I deserve? I can't disguise my upset. Getting rousted in a car lot before all these customers. Why not a football stadium capacity crowd?"

The Chief said, "Why don't you just read my mind. It shouldn't be hard."

"Chief, you ain't as smart as advertised getting sucked into these false charges. There's folks say you're mistake-prone. I always take your side. Say, the man's playing catch-up after centuries of white cop racism."

The Chief said, "You don't have me completely stalled by that fancy argument." He take him by the arm pushing him towards the cruiser.

Vineyard was whining. "You being sarcastic with me? Now you're bringing huge doubts to my mind about the equity of Charleston's police force. Getting your whole reputation marred by this injust travesty. I hear there polls what list this city as number four nationwide as a destination point. When the tourists see me being manhandled on the Fox network over satellite, they'll go straight on to Florida."

It dawn on Tamzie the cops would be impounding her car for their crime evidence lab. She asked the car sales-man could they still do a deal, buy the SL back but kind of hold delivery in limbo until the cops were through? He said he wasn't a communications specialist but read his lips. N-O spells no.

Tamzie said real disgusted, "I got to take my hat off to this piece of good luck."

Vineyard was yelling as they put him in the car. "There's old buildings down in Saint Augustine for them tourists to go look at!"

■ ■ ■

"I ask you, did you ever hear of a man beating his wife because he had smoked a pack of cigarettes? No, it's always a case of beer." Sparky threw his lit Marlboro out the window of the Cadillac driving down Meeting Street past the Visitors Center where all the tourists were milling around.

Vineyard Dupree had gotten clamped on by the cops that morning which ordinarily would have put Sparky in high spirits. But now he was kind of pissed the way Doris was starting to tell him what to do. Letting him know she couldn't stand him smoking, the taste of it on him, the dangers of second-hand smoke, all that happy horseshit. She found it offensive, she said.

"I've never said a word about your drinking," Doris added. Her mouth puckered up like she had tasted a persimmon. "Even though it is kind of demeaning for a man of your potential to be shit-faced drunk so much."

Sparky said the whole smoking, drinking thing was controversial. All the data wasn't in on whether it was smoke or booze that caused early heart attacks because so many heart attack-prone people both smoked and drank.

Doris said if you thought about it, you'd quit both. Or cut down at least. Sparky said he had some real bad news. She could grade him an F-minus if she wanted, but he wasn't quitting.

Doris said, "If you had more of an unbiased mind on the subject, you'd see I was just trying to enhance you."

She sniffled a little bit like she was tuning up to cry. Sparky hated it when she did that. Once she got teared up, you couldn't argue, negotiate, nothing. He was thinking he really ought to cut her off the bone for a day or two. Make her beg for it like she used to.

Here just a week ago, he was thinking when this Roebuck job was over, maybe he and her would drive over to the Mississippi River, go on one of those gambling boats for a week of screwing and screwing around. Then down to New Orleans. Stay in a big hotel with room service. Eat creole crawfish.

Now it was all piss and moan and bellyache. His dick work was only getting mild applause when it used to bring screams of "fuck me fuck me!" joy.

What popped in his head was how women talked about having a dog "fixed" when they were going to get its nuts cut off. Like it was a repair job. Put it in a normal state.

Then Doris said, "It's just that things have gone through kind of an evolution. Not just our relationship. But things."

Sparky said okay, okay, what is it you want me to pull out of you? I'll wheedle and say please tell me. Whatever sacrifice I'm supposed to crawl on my belly through.

"When I love a man," said Doris, "I want him to take my love straight. No chaser. And I want to be at the forefront of promoting his interests. Not keeping him as an alternate source for when others've made a mess of things."

Sparky was thinking, Jesus, women could be wordy and confused and he was sure there was national statistics to confirm that. He said what's your god-love-it point?

"Them using you as their auxiliary police force. They've got all these limits and control over your actions. They have a travel and vehicle policy, but you've got no car. You're always off doing stuff for them which doesn't give you much availability to see what they're up to."

She kind of pouted like a wife nagging her husband to go in and tell the boss he demanded a raise. Sparky didn't like the wife image. You could never underestimate that all women got into that routine sooner or later. Using your little perceived inadequacies as welcome ammunition until they pretty much had their way on things.

Doris went on, saying she heard things. Grady had so little respect for her, he just talked in front of her like she was a post. Or a mule. But it sounded like with all the recent disruptions and setbacks putting things at a crisis stage they had kind of re-engineered the plans. It emerged that they were on the brink of initiating a flat-out looting of Seagrass.

Sparky said, "No shit, Shakespeare. I mean this may not be the most scientific thinking, but that was the whole idea in the first place. Well, more or less. Everything Byron Jasper gets his fingerprints on is a rip-off. And from what you've been telling me, Grady Troxler ain't exactly Little Bo Peep."

"Well, it's just that I've discerned the mechanism through which they'll be pulling it off."

She said it was a tough topic to get out on the table and perhaps she'd live to regret this, but they were going to hang it all on that poor, silly Bobbi-Jean girl. Sparky said that was fair enough with him. If that were their true wishes, then so be it, he'd endorse the plan. Yes indeed, they'd get no veto out of him on that one.

Doris said, "But what I'm wondering is if they feel you're kind of an inconvenient deficit drain on them?"

Sparky was having a nice fantasy of seeing B-J doing her dumb routine in front of a woman judge who didn't give a shit about the size of her boobs. In fact considered them an insult to modern right-on feministhood. Judge saying she was going to give some relief to America's taxpayers by sending a message to the criminal element. Thirty years.

He said what? What kind of a drain? Doris said well primarily an extra cut out of the pie. She said she was afraid instead of splitting three ways they were about to split bye-bye. Say see you around. We'll mark your name down for future reference. Leave Sparky sitting in the cheap seats. Or worse. Maybe leave him looking across the landscape of America from behind a barred window.

She said it wasn't pleasant what she was thinking, it was just kind of like reality. What had to be done. But think about it. Who among them all had the most potential to send Sparky to the electric chair? And would crack in a skinny minute under cop questioning. Roll over on somebody to cut a deal. Who had been under cop questioning that very day and was now out with cops watching his every move?

Sparky didn't have any trouble figuring that out. He hated it when women were right about something. All that subtle intuition gift they were supposed to have. Making him feel he was outcoached and outplayed.

He put Doris out on the corner of King and Broad and told her to get a cab home. He said he was going to go erase an albatross from around his neck.

Vineyard Dupree was sitting in his office in the People's Building looking like he'd been bit by a dog. Which in a way he had.

Sparky said, "Tell you what, podnah, I been doing a nuts and bolts analysis of the business and wondering how much money you got in your trust account. I mean the cash Byron and them gave you to pay off property sellers."

Vineyard was in no hurry to answer. A smell of the city jail hung on him. That stink just jumps on you when you're sitting in there waiting to make bail. All those big dudes with a lot blacker skin saying can I have your lunch if you ain't eating it?

Sparky said wasn't that Vineyard's bank downstairs? And looking at his watch, it was nowhere near five o'clock.

"Go away," Vineyard said, his face in his hand. "I got no time for you."

Sparky said what he had in mind wouldn't take long. They had been playing a game with each other. Now they were going into a sudden death overtime.

36

Bobbi-Jean Kincaid was saying to Bracey, "You know it's just fascinating how the media is trying to present the idea that there's no such thing as a slut. The theory is it's okay for a woman to have a man's sexual appetites. The new equality and everything, I guess. You see it in all the movies. But it never really quite works as a device. Men are scared of it, and women really do believe in true romance. Look at how *Bridges of Madison County* did so well."

"It's nice to be abreast . . ." Bracey hesitated, looking at B-J's enormous bosom. The girl wearing something so tight it must have come from the preteens department ". . . of these trends."

"Not that I haven't been a slut from time to time. But I try to not make a habit out of it."

"I'm sure that's wise," said Bracey. She forced a smile, trying to remind herself why good manners were important. This chatterbox person had come up to the house on Legendre Street, rung the bell. Bracey had to invite her in.

"Everybody in Georgia always said my momma was just a passionate lover-gal, and I turned out just like her. She thought so too. Used to say 'B-J honey, you are nothing but love-trouble come down the pike'.

"You meet men with their line of bull. You know it's just a line, but it always sounds so reasonable. They're pretending they know how to order wine in restaurants when you're sure they live off beer and pork skins. They take you out on the town and behave like Jaycees up in New York afraid they'll get ripped off.

"Still, a girl hears all this big bank balance talk, and she just wants to believe. You're always saying what if this or what if that or the other. You're just pulling the lever. That crank handle on the big slot machine of cash."

Bracey couldn't figure what she was listening to exactly, what the underlying point was. Her mother wouldn't have cared. Would have just ushered B-J out with a routinely scathing negligence.

"You know how men are," said B-J. "They get to breathing all hard and heavy, and the next thing you know your clothes are off and you're giving them hip-movement like Soul Train.

"They want you in garter-belts and doing it in bed while wearing four-inch high heels. If they can't get it up, they expect you to use a vibrator or water-pik on yourself, let them watch. The old ones always sound like they're having a heart attack. Afterwards they just have that kind of empty, bored look of men who are sexually drained. Same as the young ones. They never change. Same old same old.

"So you just kind of ignore your own trashiness and get on with it. B-J's easy steps to fake orgasm and total male satisfaction. Wear a porno outfit with a nippleless bra. No man ever had any trouble picking up on those hints."

"I suppose," said Bracey, "it satisfies consumer demand." God this was appalling.

"If I can't really find a decent man to pour all my love out on, it seems like the next best thing is to be rich. Be like Liz Taylor and have a perfume named for me. Sleep with Russian ballet dancers like Lauren Hutton.

"You're so lucky to have such a good-looking husband. Your Chase is just a darling. And so funny. He'll get all serious and say 'I don't need this continuous punitive action'. Or sometimes a real mouthful like 'What's personally disturbing to me, and don't believe I'm not truly concerned with it, is the emerging economic and regulatory landscape'."

Bracey noted B-J was wearing two citrine bracelets on her wrist. Where would she have bought them? Izzie had complained for a week that hers had vanished. Was convinced the maid had stolen them.

Suddenly, it dawned on Bracey. This scatterbrained creature had come to tell her she was co-opting Chase Jeffcoat. Check out the house. Maybe measure it for new curtains. Like all men, Chase was hesitating to break the news, so she was pushing the agenda along.

The thought that Chase was this stupid gave Bracey an odd sense of calm. She could imagine herself confronting him in a pivotal scene of matrimonial crisis. Saying I'm not resigned to your infidelities, but at some point, the ridiculous becomes sublime.

"I draw the line at being a whore-lady," said B-J. "But how can I help myself around your man as handsome and rich as he is?"

Bracey smiled indulgently. "Chase? He's not rich. He doesn't have a pot to pee in." Bracey was amazed at her own vulgarity.

It didn't throw B-J at all. "He doesn't? I kind of suspected that. The way all those old boys are clutching at this golf tournament with skin magazine gatefolds. Those beaver shots are just so tacky. Don't you agree?"

Bracey said, "Beaver . . . ?" Then checked herself. Said it does raise fundamental questions. She said her mother owned the house, not Chase. They were living off the money of a crabby old blackmailer in a wheelchair.

B-J said oh my Lordy. Well her daddy was in prison for insurance rip-offs. She didn't know if he'd ever get out because the Georgia Insurance Commissioner was convinced he was masterminding a big fraud ring from inside the state pen. It made her feel kind of guilty living on a golf course and having fun day-in and day-out.

"Do you get out to Roebuck? It's kind of a make-believe atmosphere out there. You're far enough away from city lights that you can see all the constellations. Just sit there at night and meditate. I'm right there on the seventh fairway. Chicadee Villas?" She said it as a question like maybe Bracey knew the place.

Bracey realized she had to draw a line. She wasn't going to fall into some let's-all-be-friends routine. Come out and visit. Give her blessing to the new union.

She said, "I don't feel any great sense of urgency about this conversation. If you wanted to continue it another time . . ."

B-J just sat there not moving. Then she delivered the bombshell.

"Now don't take this the wrong way, but I'm fucking your husband. Tomorrow night? If that's of any interest or use to you?"

"How very thoughtful of you to keep me informed."

"Normally, I tend to practice before I preach."

When she left, Bracey sat thinking for awhile. Then she picked up the phone and called the 800-hotline of the American Birding Association.

In a calm and distinct voice, she said this is Bracey Fanseau Jeffcoat of Charleston, South Carolina. I've been a subscriber to *WildBird* Magazine for a decade. I guess I'm trying to tell you I have credentials.

"We're prepared to believe you," said the voice at the other end.

"I've sighted a Barred-tailed Godwit."

The voice cleared his throat. "I'm not trying to be contentious. Just a cautionary note. That's all. But that's a Siberian bird. It nests on the tundra."

"I'm only too aware of that."

"There is a European version. A rare migrant, but occasional migrant just the same."

"Mine has the more heavily mottled rump. It's the Siberian."

His voice rose sounding exhilarated. "Well, I guess I can speak freely. This is going to cause a lot of excitement!"

Bracey said, "I fully expected as much."

■ ■ ■

"Your auntie done test me to the maximum," Tamzie insisted, trying to explain the urgency of the matter. "Second them two get wind of some purchase of food or liquor they in there doing some voracious eating. They got like a timetable to get through it all before sundown."

Omar untangle some of the dogs, say he really appreciate her rescue mission. Her good works don't pass by unnoticed. The Reverend Peebles had in front of the entire congregation praise her taking in the devout worshipper Luevenia Parsons. Omar had personally said amen to that, brother.

Tamzie said that's fine for a while, but she ain't devise an exit strategy. Now the feral cats moving into the condo. Lounging all over. Scratching and tearing the furniture. Peeing on her brand new Nouristan rug. Making the whole place look and smell like some impoverished community. Which was what her bank balance was. She had hocked her Tahitian pearls, got her Versace in a consignment shop.

Omar said it sound like a right colorful situation, but who among has the right to judge a kindly action to animals?

Tamzie just let it all out. Explain this was the time of year when she would get ready to kick back and watch them Georgetown Hoyas, daydream of being a few years younger and meet up with and evaluate them young studs. A little fantasy makes life without men bearable.

Instead, she got gospel coming at her nonstop. Luevenia had throw out her near-priceless collection of original James Brown records calling them "demeaning-oriented rap music."

"And here they listening to Little Richard sing gospel like they don't know what he is!"

Omar say when morals collide, you get some mighty big shock waves.

Tamzie said, "Here I done save your ass 'bout to get shot off! Let you keep that bright face to show the world!"

He suggest she try to use some psychological mechanism on them. Maybe get them interested in the bingo tournaments at the county home.

Tamzie said she ain't got space to think in that cat-fight pandemonium. All she can do is go off and have a whisky sour and a nervous breakdown.

Tamzie knew for sure she should have paid more attention in church when the man preach about how the first will be last and that camel going through a needle's eye.

37

Bobbi-Jean phoned Buddy Burdett's Pool Hall in Mobile, Alabama and asked to speak with her old friend and mentor Bass Renfrew. Bass operated his gambling and venture capital office out of there on the pay phones and could be right helpful when he was in the right mood. When he came on the line he was in that mood, saying he wished somebody'd invent TV phones because Bobbi-Jean Kincaid was a one-woman School of Visual Art.

B-J said Bass was just a catalog of good deeds, and speaking of pictures, she wanted him to take a gander at a photo, see if he knew the man. He said fine, fax it to me right here. She said you got a fax? He said sure, it's my office.

That meant she had to hang up and drive to Kinko's to send the photo of Grady Troxler clipped from a newspaper, then phone again. When he came on this time, Bass said, "B-J you are one heartfelt item and a half. I'm having me a fit of public disorderly conduct just hearing that sweet voice."

She said, Bass, you replenish my well of joy. When you're through being loud and boisterous, tell me who's in the picture.

Bass said, well, the quality had faxed pretty poor, but it was hard to miss old Gerald Tackman. He said she'd find a front-and-side view photo of him down at the post office hanging right there on the wall. Wanted for inter-state flight from everything you could name.

"Man of a thousand faces old Gerald, and every one a swindler. I mean he don't even give you a sporting chance."

She asked did he ever work with Byron Jasper? Bass said does a bear shit in the woods? They had looted some banks in Texas back in the '80s when Republican deregulation made it so easy to do that kind of thing. Byron was the "who me?" boy who'd pose as the honest but now bankrupt property developer. Play dumb and just sit there. Never get anything to really stick. Gerald would take off. Pop up somewhere else with a resumé sporting a Harvard law degree or an MBA from one of those Stanford-type places or a background in engineering projects in Saudi Arabia.

B-J was trying to think of something she wanted to ask but had forgotten. She could actually hear the clicking of pool balls over the wire. She asked who was playing. He said Skeeter Jackson. She said eight-ball?

"Round-robin fuck-your-buddy Shanghai."

"Is that something he just made up?"

"Pretty much."

"Who are the marks?"

"Couple of insurance salesmen. Boys think they know the ins-and-outs of billiards."

Then she remembered. "Is Grady or Gerald whatever, the kind of guy who would have had an ant farm as a kid?"

Bass said you mean like a live bait place? She said no, a nerd thing that you put in the window. Watch ants do their thing.

Bass said, "You never know with people. But I mostly think of him as a quiff hound. He once owned a strip show in New Orleans. It was like an outlet from taking orders from his mean-ass wife. Not your mirage quality vision that woman, but tough as boot leather. And the brains of the outfit. What's Doreen calling herself now?"

"Doris."

"She would. It's close enough. Make a slip-up, say folks called her both. Her angle is to play a victim role. Wife of the abusive spouse. That co-dependent horseshit. Actually was on a talk show one time. Oprah or Sally Jesse. One of those. Right after that televised hen-fest, she clipped some women's lib group for their entire treasury. Have you ever heard her 'I've got the pussy' story?"

B-J said she had.

Bass said, "It's a sure-enough hum-dinger, ain't it?"

■ ■ ■

"You bought those citrine bracelets to get even with the bank trust officer," Bracey told her mother angrily.

"That's pure nonsense. I know you've told that little story to just absolutely everyone. Don't think I don't hear what you say about me."

It was just past midnight and Bracey and her mother were having their usual war of wills even as they broke into Chase's office on Broad Street. Izzie insisted it wasn't really breaking in. He was her son-in-law. They had every right to be there. And Chase giving the citrine bracelets to Bobbi-Jean had put Izzie way up on the moral high ground.

When she used the crowbar on the locked file cabinet, it popped open with a horrible screeching noise. Bracey was astonished at her mother's skills, and yet she shouldn't have been. The woman had had a lifetime of prying and snooping into other people's business.

Using a flashlight, Izzie began rummaging through the files. Bracey's news of infidelity and disaster had perked her up, given her a sense of mission.

Bracey sat down at Chase's Biedermeier desk. Fingered a cup and saucer of Spode china in which he served coffee to his clients. Moonlight filtered through a Palladian window. It all spoke volumes of his ambition, as though banking were a matter of competitive opulence.

Chase's requirements had been a building with "strong architectural character" and a "near-residential design" for the office furnishings. At enormous expense he had gotten solid wood paneling and fabrics in subtle shades of green. 19th century paintings of alpine landscapes.

He had used a lot of contrived decorator's language. A hint of grandeur. A sober restraint. Timeless sense of style. Antique furniture that you can live with. No one should be intimidated by it.

Bracey suspected Chase had slept with the interior decorator, a blowsy divorcée who drove an antique Triumph sportscar. And girls he met on his business trips. Maybe bored wives in Charleston. And now this pneumatic bosom B-J creature comes chattering with yackety-yack nonsense that bordered on eulogy of his prowess in bed.

Bracey said, "I can't believe she just came out and told me. That little trailer-trash girl Bambi-Jean whatever. That heavy lidded sex kitten look."

"They'll do that," said Izzie. "She's had her territory staked for some time. Now she's formally laying claim to it. Think back to the signs. When did he start wearing those Paul Stuart suits?"

"I don't need to revisit the past. Particularly when it's occupied by little pert-butt cornsilk blondes with shiny mouths."

"It's crucial to practice a modicum of feminine artifice," Izzie lectured. "You don't win in your country tweeds and sensible low-heeled sling-backs when the competition looks like it just crawled out from between the sheets of a man's bed."

Bracey looked at her pleated wool skirt and matching jacket. "I won't do raccoon eye make-up and hair teased up at the crown. Besides, I've had quite enough of Chase's repression."

Izzie had no sympathy with women independent of men. "You were never a model of appropriate develop-ment. It's like your whole ambition in life was to go off track. You never sparkled on social occasions. Totally self-destructive. Then you marry a man from Orangeburg. There was always an air of wholesale gluttony about him."

"I was looking for alchemical magic," Bracey answered furiously.

"Your marriage is not what I would call a happy collab-oration. I would have warned you against him, but chil-dren have to be allowed to make their own mistakes."

Bracey ground her teeth. It was a perfect moment for her mother to indulge her passion for nastiness.

What Izzie was looking for in the file cabinet was evi-dence of Chase diverting money to Bobbi-Jean Kincaid that rightly belonged to Izzie Fanseau. What she found instead was much more sinister—the trail of Tamzie Jerome's money into Seagrass, thence to Roebuck and finally to Blake Huston for the Phase 2 land.

Izzie took the file and tucked it under her arm. Bracey said what was she doing? She said she was taking it away to study and probably destroy. Thorny legal issues were over her head, but she could imagine Tamzie might have a claim on the money if she got her hands on the records.

Bracey said that's disgraceful. Izzie said it seemed like fate to her. Money management was clearly over Tamzie's head. It had been merely a question of whose hands it changed into. Besides the girl had had a perfectly good job with Mary Canty Ralston.

Bracey told her mother she was as crooked as Chase Jeffcoat. Izzie replied, "I'm afraid there's only room for one judge of what's right and wrong in this family."

Bracey said fine, she'd move out of the house. It was Izzie who had pressured her to live there. Izzie said why would that make her any less a member of the family?

At that point, what might have been just an ordinary night of being bullied by her mother turned into a watershed moment.

Bracey sniffed the air and said what was that smell? It's a stench. Like feces.

Izzie was making disparaging remarks about today's janitorial help when Bracey shone the big flashlight over behind a Venetian screen. A pool of yellow light showcased the body of Vineyard Dupree.

Bracey got a nervous attack. Her hands were trembling,

voice quaking. She kept saying he's the attorney for Seagrass. He's the attorney for Seagrass.

Izzie said they do that when they die. Sphincter muscle cuts loose. She was expecting that from Blake any day. Really, it was no worse than cleaning up dog mess.

Bracey felt like she was going to be sick. She said they had to phone the police.

Izzie said no, this is an off-the-record visit to Chase's office. A little girls-together thing. No men invited.

38

"Everything that comes up, I've got to tell them how to do it, then show them how, then finally get in and do it myself."

Chase was buck naked and brewing the morning coffee in an espresso maker he had bought Bobbie-Jean while complaining about his difficulties with Roebuck. He was catching a lot of heat from investors. They couldn't remember how early and often he had warned that this was high risk.

B-J agreed all investors have selective memories. She kind of covered a yawn and thought about going back to bed.

He waved his hands in the air. "So I get vilified."

What B-J wanted was for him to put his hands on her great big naked breasts and give her some more intensive care management. He had sure done an adequate number on her during the night. Just got right down to it with none of this what's wrong with America bore you to death stuff.

She wished awful bad it could be a satisfying love story but knew for sure it wasn't. No matter which way the double-crosses were running—and there were always double-crosses when fast-draw con artists like Byron and

Grady looted a bank—Chase was involved somehow. He had pushed her to borrowing that money from Seagrass. The only question was he just thinking it would go into Roebuck? Was he dumb enough to not realize Grady and Byron had a track record of taking the whole hog?

At least she had her $50,000 out of Grady Troxler. He had choked up a check that hadn't bounced. Probably loaned it to himself from Seagrass.

Chase was saying, "I take kind of a low-key approach, try to allow Byron and Grady maximum latitude in decision making, and what do I get? All their excuses ring hollow."

Chase got on his marriage next. His wife and mother-in-law were compulsive spendthrifts. He said they'd fit in well with the Democratic party, but he was very suspicious of economic programs where you spend yourself into prosperity. He claimed each time he entered that big mansion on Legendre Street he whispered a little prayer that he'd survive to morning with his 'nads intact.

Chase revealed his income was way down and he was pretty much living out of Seagrass. A series of short-term notes. One of them was due, and Grady said all friendship aside it couldn't be rolled again. $25,000 he had to come up with.

He was looking at her all manly and restrained but biting that lower lip. Sure enough, he was exceeding her bad expectations. He knew she had the money out of Grady, and he wanted it.

B-J said wouldn't his mother-in-law give it to him? After all, he supported her. Did all that good deed stuff of managing her money. Surely she owed it to him after all his kindness and generosity.

Chase snorted, "Izzie Fanseau." She was sure one to teach you about the absence of charitable giving. He told her his marriage was a theater of the absurd with no audience empathy.

B-J looked out the window and said, "Well, whatever empathy is, you sure got an audience."

Sure enough, a sellout crowd was on hand. The entire condo was surrounded by folks in lawn chairs, maybe three-deep. There must have been a couple hundred of them.

Chase stared with horror out the window, realizing that disaster had struck. Ran to other windows to see that the ring was complete. "I'm fucked!" he said. "Jeezus am I royally fucked!"

B-J agreed that about summed up his predicament. She was too polite to say it, but she was kind of in awe of what Bracey had rigged up. The girl could sure fire play a smash-mouth, right-at-you game of hardball.

Chase was ready to snatch his clothes and go hightailing out. But his clothes weren't there. Someone had actually been inside the apartment while they slept and made off with them. B-J's leaving the door unlocked had aided in this, but he didn't know it.

They spent a half hour with Chase going through her clothes trying to find something that would fit. Only thing remotely suitable was a Frette terry bath robe. She said it was from a fancy hotel in Boca Raton, Florida. It came as part of the room price because they knew the guests would walk off with them anyhow.

Chase got real stiff. He said, "At this point I do not think it imperative that you lecture me on old boyfriends you've humped just because they rented swanky hotel rooms."

There it was. The dark underbelly of a man's personality. No more lingering hopes. He'd be stealing the citrine bracelets back next. Trying to figure how to break her loose from the BMW. Well, she had foxed him there. Used part of the Clemson game windfall to pay off the loan and get title. Basically, Chase had paid for three-fourths of it.

B-J looked her now ex-boyfriend in the eye cooly and said it was a real nice hotel with indoor swimming pool, masseuse, and solarium. Probably the only place better she had been was the Mauna Lani Bay on Hawaii. She really grooved on Pacific Rim cuisine.

Chase jerked his hands shoulder-wide apart and opened his mouth to shout at her, then choked it back.

She looked around at her little place a bit sadly, knowing she'd soon be leaving it. The field stone fireplace flanked by built-in bookshelves. Cross beams in the vaulted ceiling with the skylight up above. Seltzer-water colored walls. Bright floral fabrics on the furniture. Well, they're all the same, she thought. Faux-this and faux-that. Golf course houses come out of a plan book. And there was a whole big world out there waiting full of champagne and roast duck with tamarind mustard glaze.

Outside, they were having coffee and breakfast off a van. The event was catered. Group interest was still lively. Most of them had binoculars trained on the condo.

"They look like a bunch of goddam bird watchers," growled Chase with total disgust. "Binoculars. Damn L.L.Bean-looking clothes."

Chase put the robe on. Then white rimmed sunglasses, a pair of rubber boots and a pork pie rain hat. All it achieved was making him look like Chase Jeffcoat in a pervert costume.

At that moment, Bracey Jeffcoat walked through the door. It had been left unlocked after all. She was wearing a cable knit Aran Isle sweater and blue jeans.

Chase took the big gulp of a man caught without his pants. The pace had quickened, and the process was even further out of control.

Bracey looked B-J over as though her naked body were everything she had been expecting and more. She said, "I doubt this would qualify me for the Pulitzer Prize in investigative reporting, but offhand I'd say you've been sleeping with my husband."

■ ■ ■

"You doing some home-based work?" said Sparky, walking into Byron Jasper's condo without knocking.

Byron looked up a little startled. He was nursing a hangover and cleaning his short irons. He drank some coffee from a John Wayne mug, said, "Oh man, I feel like a turd dropped out of a tall cow's ass."

Sparky glanced in the bedroom. Nothing in there but wadded up sheets and empty liquor bottles. Rebel flag bath towel. NASCAR posters. "Rough night?"

"They got music in these bars kids play today, sounds like the trump of doom with a rhythm section. I think I'm meeting B-J, and she don't show. I got to sit there and drink for hours with that ruckus. Now I got enough cotton in my mouth to weave a pair of sweat socks.

"That little cock-teasing bitch. If I don't get in her pants, I'm gonna die of blue balls. Holding them tits in a constructive trust. Lying about some killer boyfriend fresh out of prison who'd get all jealous."

"Why don't you tell her eatin' ain't cheatin'?" Sparky suggested.

"I been through all that. But she keeps me in the sideline seats. I got a lingering tendency to tolerate her shit, but it ain't lingering long."

"They say envy will eat you like stomach acid."

"My personal pride is taking a nose-dive, and I'd just as soon not memorialize that. Dick hanging down awaiting the call to action. The job at hand's turned into a damn hand job. I end up tying a big drunk on because I got nothing else to fill the hours of darkness. PowerChest gals ain't here yet. I'm making a career out of choking the chicken."

"So how's business?"

Byron drank coffee. His eyes flitted. "Fine. Just fine."

"You're sure now?"

"Yeah I'm sure. I got to buttress the argument with something?"

Sparky said it was just that there were some rumors going around that maybe things weren't fine. Byron said that was a real pie in the face. He said sure he's beat up, but they got the bridge loans to see them through to Spring. Phase 2 would open then. In the meantime, the golf tournament was coming up. Get national attention. Bring in some buyers.

He said, "Roebuck plantation ain't gonna fade from

contention. The competitor in me says we've got to beat this thing."

Sparky rubbed the back of his neck. Said it's always nice to run the option. Shift things about according to what defense you run up against. Generate a big play.

"That's the heart and soul of what we do in land development," said Byron. "Make no bones about it."

Sparky sat down on the couch with a glass top coffee table between him and Byron. Stretched out his legs and crossed his cowboy boots at the ankles. All relaxed. Said, "Savvy veteran like Grady Troxler ready to get down with some serious embezzling. Right cool boy. Right tough. Yet we got to look at the fact that I'm boffing the man's wife right in his house. Driving his Cadillac and using his gas charge card. The moral of the story is does it look like I'm particularly intimidated by him?"

Byron got surly. "I don't need no in-your-face style. You got a threat, why don't you come out and heave it?"

Sparky sat up and leaned forward, forearms resting on his knees. He picked up Byron's five-iron, kind of toyed with it. He said, "A little bird keeps telling me ugly bedtime stories. I'm hearing hints of dark depths. Double-cross by old buddies. And they say the trickiest time lies ahead."

He smacked the five-iron down hard on the glass top coffee table. WHAM! Little glass shards flying in all directions!

"Sum-va-bitch!" yelled Byron jerking back. He brushed glass off his trousers. "Dammit dammit! What the hell are you up to, you crazy dam' mully-fucker? You gonna create a family history of premature heart attacks for me!"

The thick sheet of glass was broken right down the middle. Sparky looked down at the coffee mug fallen to the floor spreading a big brown stain on the indoor-outdoor carpet. He nudged it a bit with the golf club, then put the head of the club up against Byron's chest, pushed him back into his chair.

"Winning is always meaningful," he said. "But hanging around with bankers like I'm doing now, banker's wives, I get particularly attentive to ethical issues. They some real masters of duplicity, bankers. Right behind land developers. With this in mind, I wouldn't want any sudden departures by you and Grady. No rabbit runs. It might create a real serious work-family conflict . . ."

Poked him with the golf club again for emphasis.

". . . and I'm not sure you'd survive the fury of all that infighting."

39

"What's past is past," said Chase Jeffcoat calmly. "We can't put the toothpaste back in the tube. Unring the bell."

Bracey thought Chase was as cool under fire as ever. Just came right home, put on a fresh suit, and called a conference with her and her mother. He saw them as a unit to be dealt with expeditiously.

He said, "So we all take a little breather here. Go sit in time-out. I'll cite family pressures as an excuse. Our marriage was strained. We'll try to put it back together. It's a far cry from a lasting peace but the best we can do at the moment."

Bracey thought, what does that mean?

Izzie said she saw the problem as one of finances. Marital rifts were to be expected in life.

Chase was critical even of this concession. "You're always after current income instead of waiting for something to grow. Short maturities. You set targets that are too high, and I've been forced to lower your sights. You think that stunt out at Roebuck with your birdwatcher creeps was a brilliant pre-emptive strike? Think again.

"I've leveraged my reputation, everything on Roebuck. It was like stepping up to a roulette wheel and putting it all on black. I've clarified my position. I know what business I'm in without writing some freaking mission statement to gain focus. The battlefield is in marketing. Once the tide turns there, I'm home free."

Izzie said she wasn't eager to impede his success. But she had reservations about his judgment.

"I can't claim every penny was well spent. We've made mistakes, sure. It's inexact. I'll grant that emphasis. Calculate the math. It's the only solution."

Izzie insisted she wouldn't know where to begin to reduce her personal expenses. She had been round and round with the bank trust officer over that. She had moved her money into Chase's management to avoid draconian measures.

Chase said, "So go out and buy a low-fat cookbook. You want to travel, stay at Motel 6. Any money that comes in in the next months in going to the Chase Jeffcoat Benefit Fund. This family is getting out of the democracy business. I'm claiming exclusivity in decision making."

"We're all interconnected," Bracey insisted, trying to get a word in edgewise.

"Of course we are dear," said Izzie. "We're a family"

"I mean humanity and nature. The wetlands cleanse the earth, filter the poisons out. You intend to use every inch of ground on Roebuck Island and then some. You'll fill the marsh ten acres at a time to dodge EPA regs."

"You take all progress for granted," Chase argued. "Sure, go back to rotary phones. Carbon paper. You think that's an antidote to what's wrong with the world? I'm trying to give people a decent lifestyle. I'm giving Phase 2 a Norman Rockwell look. Neo-traditional urban development."

Bracey said, "You really think it will happen? Phase 2?" What she was thinking of was Vineyard Dupree lying dead in Chase's office. A corpse waiting to be discovered.

"Of course."

"You're getting along with your associates? No profound disagreements?"

"My associates are utterly committed to the project," Chase said smugly.

■ ■ ■

"The three of us'll be sitting in Caribbean sun pondering a life of ripping folks off," said Grady Troxler, looking just about as pleased as a tight asshole like him ever can look.

"What?" said Byron. "We can't stick around and just act innocent? Remain established as substantial citizens?"

Grady said suit yourself. Everybody thinks white collar crooks get off light. Well some do. But if the feds want to know where the money went, they're got a real cute stunt. They transfer you continually between federal facilities. You spend your life on a bus with wire on the windows. Handcuffs. Leg irons. And some low-grade moron coon as your seat mate. After six months of that you'll tell them anything they want.

Sparky laughed. "Yeah, and I tell you, the meatloaf in jail will sure make you puke."

They were sitting in Byron's Oldsmobile—Sparky in the back, the other two up front—across the street from Nations Bank waiting for Bobbi-Jean to come out. The deal was they wouldn't be seen with her making the enormous deposit.

This was the first of what was to be about six visits over a couple of weeks. She'd shift the money one move at a time among the bank accounts of a variety of shell corporations. What she wasn't told was she'd never know what happened to it. When she asked, they'd act dumb too. Or maybe pissed with her. Accuse her of stealing it. Thinking they might kill her would get her on the run and hiding out. A red herring for the federal cops to chase after.

Sparky was wondering how many of the accounts Grady had signature authority on. Claiming it was just the last one must be a lie. That Grady just had double-cross written all over him.

Byron looked at his watch. "I tell you what. This crime of the century stuff is a breeze. We take all that money, I'm hardly sweating."

Grady looked at his watch. Said what's she doing in there so long? It had been close to an hour. The account was set up. All she had to do was deposit the loan check from Seagrass.

Before she went in, she had driven them nuts, making them go over it and over it until all three of them wanted to scream. No human being could be as dumb as she acted. Like she couldn't get it through her head that she wasn't really borrowing the money for a horse farm.

She kept saying I can't believe it. I'm an overnight success story.

They waited some more. A small pile of cigarette butts lay on the pavement outside Sparky's window. She didn't come and she didn't come. At last Sparky said fuck a duck and got out to go look in the bank floor.

He came back out and reported she was nowhere in sight. They sat thinking about that.

Grady got on the car phone—big clunky thing that sat in the console—and called the manager of the Nations Bank branch. Identified himself and said he had a big loan out and needed to check that it had been deposited okay to the account of B-J Enterprises. The manager said, yeah, the money went into the account and then got wired somewhere, but he wouldn't say anything else. It was a privacy issue. Federal regulations. Yes, Miss Kincaid had gone out the back door of the bank.

Grady kept smooth-talking the manager, asking him did the money get transferred to Kincaid, Inc? The manager said no. Grady went through the whole list of shell corporations. No, it was none of those. Otherwise he wouldn't say.

They sat letting this development sink in. B-J had pretty much flipped them the bird.

Grady did some lengthy and serious blue-streak cussing. Byron said there had to be a logical explanation.

"Yeah," said Grady all sarcastic. "Why don't you make plans for a fucking full-scale study."

Byron said he found Grady's brains about as underwhelming as his charm.

Grady said it was Byron who got led around by a stiff dick for that little bitch which had led directly to this logistical debacle.

Byron said Grady was a factory-direct asshole. And if social ills was the topic under discussion, it wasn't any wife of his being grudge-porked by another man right in the family boudoir.

Both of them stopped the bickering at that point like the thought of Sparky in the back seat had sobered them.

Sparky rubbed his jaw. "I'd say the opening gambits in this operation ain't been too good. I'd like to give some special thanks to both of you for letting me be a part of a monumental fuckup."

40

Bobbi-Jean said to Byron who was standing looming over her table, "Why would I run away? The big golf tournament is coming up. I wouldn't miss playing in that for the world."

Byron Jasper sat down and pulled up a chair in the fancy East Bay Street restaurant and said, well, flight had crossed his mind seeing as how she hadn't answered her phone for three days, hadn't slept in her bed and hadn't made the appointments with her business associates she was supposed to.

B-J just looked him right in the eye and said of course she had done what she was supposed to do. She had bought herself a horse farm.

Byron was trying to be poker-faced, but he looked like he had been kicked in the stomach. "You spent it all? Ever' penny?"

"Well they're not cheap. I'm sure that's why Mister Troxler lent me so much money in the first place."

"You spent it all?" he said again.

"Well you know the major reason for small business failure is undercapitalization. I've heard you say that a hundred times."

The waiter brought B-J's lunch. Hydroponic arugula with bean sprouts and a wedge of unleavened bread. Byron stared at it, said you know I could probably drop by a public school about now, have chili or maybe taco salad with diced tomato and grated cheese. Cornbread. Milk. An ice cream sandwich.

He stared some more, told the waiter to get him a double Black Jack on the rocks. No, straight up. And put it on her bill. B-J said could she go ahead and start eating? She had to be somewhere. He said please do.

Byron told her he was glad he had caught her here alone. Give them a chance to talk without Grady.

B-J agreed. She said she sure didn't need him sitting there glaring contempt at her. All his little tart commentary he thought was so fetching.

B-J held out her wrist for Byron to sniff. She said it was Gardenia Passion. Real floral smelling. Did he like it? He said it was just positively delightful. But let's meander back to the subject at hand. She said sure.

Byron hooked his arm over the back of his chair and put on a pleasant voice. "Dahling, I'm gonna make you a good faith offer. If you're lying to me, I want you to admit it and tell me where the money is. And in return, I solemnly promise to not break every blessed bone in your body."

B-J said she knew he wouldn't dare hurt her because it would make her boyfriend Travis so mad. But why would she lie to him? It hadn't been hard to pull off once all the loan paperwork had been done for her. That was the part really over her head. But once that went through, she just relied on trusted business associates. They handled the rest.

Byron said, okay, who were they?

She said Bass Renfrew, Buddy Burdette, Skeeter McCutcheon, Doc McEachern. A few others.

Given the business Byron was in, these names were familiar. He said they bought you a horse farm? That pack of con artists and swindlers? Where was it? Ocala? Camden? Bluegrass Kentucky somewhere?

B-J said well they didn't actually buy her a farm per se. What they did was spread the money among professional horse raisers who need investment capital. Thoroughbreds. Quarter horses. Tennessee Walkers. When they sell the horses, they'd give her a return on investment minus their expenses.

Byron's drink came, and he slugged it down. Wiped at his face with a cloth napkin. Said, "I ain't no shrinking violet when it comes to facing up to the truth. I can take pressure pretty well. Make the play in crucial situations. But I can't believe—no, I cannot begin to believe—that you are so dumb as to give so much money to so many crooks with so many ways for them to steal it."

B-J just sat all round-eyed innocent. She said, "Well they told me there were all kinds of tax-break angles I could capitalize on."

■ ■ ■

Your serious bird watchers have got considerable tenacity and had no problem hanging on for days in hope of a glimpse of a Barred-tailed Godwit. They camped out on the land of an old black woman named Jacquetta Gillyard on Roebuck Island. Roebuck Plantation didn't like them being there, but title to the property was clouded, and Roebuck couldn't evict them. Bracey felt terrible about lying to them and developed a dread that they would figure it out. Anxiety grew to a near panic attack.

Where things began to turn around for her was when she drove the Range Rover out to the airport to pick up a late arrival. Hank Harder looked like a potato dumpling with thick glasses, navy blue Gore-Tex Maine Warden's Parka hung with binoculars and cameras. He waved good-bye to the pilot and crew of his Gulfstream III.

Hank took off his Ragg Crusher hat like a gentleman and said he was sorry to be late. He had been in Socorro, New Mexico to watch the sandhill cranes. 14,000 of them. An awesome sight. Had Bracey ever seen them? No? Had she been to Laguna Atascosa?

"Atascosa?" she said.

"South Texas. Yellow-green Vireos have nested there three years running. It's an easy hop from there over to High Island for the spring migration. You need a plane of course. There are plenty of small dirt strips used by geologists, oil prospectors. They work fine for short-range take-off like the G III."

What it turned out was Hank had a mammoth inherited fortune that money managers fought to manage and a Park Avenue duplex he only used once a year for board meetings of the Audubon Society. He lived on his buffalo ranch in Wyoming and a thousand acres of rain forest in Costa Rica. Or wherever his travels took him. India. Indonesia. The Arctic Circle.

He was an artist and naturalist and collected rare bird books. His complete set of John Gould, the 19th century naturalist called the British Audubon, was worth a cool two million. He had published a book of his own entitled

Birds of the South Atlantic (1993, Methuen Press), the result of three years living in Patagonia and the Falklands. The illustrations were also his.

On the drive he asked about migratory piping plovers, and Bracey said more were being discovered passing the entire winter on the beaches. Any tundra swans sighted in the bays? Bracey said she grew up calling them whistling swans. Hank said he preferred that name too. He was sentimental he guessed.

When Bracey turned to glance at him, Hank's eyes seemed very large through the glasses. He was looking with approval on her spruce colored L.L.Bean's Alpine Classic Anorak and worsted wool pants. His gaze rested on her 7" rubber-bottom Bean boots. Her feet were a very petite size. It was probably her best feature.

When they arrived in the woods, Bracey noted that Hank's feet kind of splayed out in his Gore-Tex Town and Field boots. Nonetheless, he became a man in charge. Every move he made was made with authority. He was not very impressed by the notion of a Barred-tailed Godwit in South Carolina and thought the roof of a condo a highly unlikely place.

"No," he said, "what I see here is an environmental agenda. Is that closer to the truth?"

"Yes," Bracey admitted in a very small voice.

He adjusted his binoculars and scanned the treetops.

"What I imagine we'll find here is an extraordinary plant community making it one of the more important natural areas in the state. Good lord, was this place a landfill?"

Bracey admitted as much, asked how he knew.

"Because it's survived this long. Plus all those big dead trees. The dump makes them grow rapidly, but when the roots get down deep, it kills them. And look what we have here. An endangered species. There. Red-cockaded woodpecker. They like diseased pine trees." He handed Bracey the binoculars.

Sure enough, the little bugger was tapping away at the bark. Bracey thought her heart would leap out of her throat.

Hank said, "We'll be getting in immediate touch with the Sierra Club, the S.C. Conservation League and the Office of Ocean and Coastal Resource Management."

"U.S. Fish and Wildlife Service?" Bracey suggested helpfully.

"Yes, and probably the S.C. Department of Natural Resources."

Bracey said her husband wouldn't like that very much.

Hank said that was predictable. He didn't seem to pick up on the "husband." Was Bracey in Newfoundland for the Pink-footed-geese that got blown over from Europe?

She said she didn't get to travel much. Hank said if you were isolated geographically, the Lowcountry was about as nice as you could ask for. What was left of it.

He said, "Do men tell you how attractive you are in a slash pine forest setting?"

"No," she said. "Not a whole lot."

Hank casually reached out and unzipped her Anorak to reveal the plum heather chamois cloth shirt underneath that her tiny breasts barely pushed out.

He said, "I'd like to have you in a cabin in the Adirondacks curled up before a roaring fire wearing a plaid brushed flannel nightshirt from Land's End. Your legs and feet bare and tucked up under you. I'd slide my hand up under the shirt and find you were wearing no underpants."

Bracey didn't have any trouble getting "it" wet. In fact, "it" got so wet she thought "it" would drip all down her leg.

They slept together that night in a double Lite Loft cold weather bag in a spruce colored Woodlands Tent among the cluster of other tents of the bird watcher colony. About three-quarters of the way to orgasm, Bracey suddenly lost control and began groaning and moaning and finally screaming tumultuously.

In the morning she was mortified to have to face the others. An old woman from Connecticut came up and asked if she suffered from night terrors. The woman said her little niece had that problem and the only solution was hot milk at bedtime.

41

Rannie Ralston said, "I've got a client, stone cold killer. Goes on the run for two years. Finally captured in Atlanta. Meanwhile three other dudes in the robbery had been brought in. They all finger him as the trigger man. Kneeled the 7-eleven clerk down and shot her dead, her begging for her life. Jury takes about fifteen minutes to come back with a unanimous guilty verdict on my boy. You know what he says?"

"What?" said Bobbi-Jean.

"He says it's not fair that just because he was the last one to get captured, he didn't get a deal. All the others got 20 years to testify against him. He gets the electric chair. It was like it was being held against him that he was better at evading the police."

B-J sat there in this red-haired lady's law office saying these kind of folks can sure make you a little skeptical. Like that Grady Troxler. Did Rannie know him?

Rannie said sure she knew the misanthropic bastard. He was living proof that apes and men are all descended from a common ancestor.

B-J said don't let him jam you alone in a room with that trash mouth of his. Personally, he scared the dookie out of her. Did Rannie know his picture was hanging up in the post office? All kinds of major felonies listed underneath. Seems like the boy just steals repeatedly and with no remorse whatsoever.

Funny how you can live near a hoodlum like that and not realize he was what he was. Like in *America's Most Wanted on* TV. A gal's live-in boyfriend turns out to be a serial rapist from Idaho. It'll sure negatively impact your digestion. You watch that show and there's like this it-could-happen-to-me creepiness about it. It's like somebody's shook up a Dr. Pepper can and exploded it all over you.

Rannie was listening and thinking. Wearing brown mascara because she had such red hair. A rosy stain of lipstick.

B-J said, "I mean here the poor girl's been sleeping with the man. He loves her green bean casserole. He's gone shopping with her. Helped her pick out a vinyl jacket and skirt. How does she wear the thing now? Does she just chuck it out? You say, okay, enter a professional treatment program. But it doesn't help. She's still all wore down mentally."

"Hey, message received," said Rannie. "And I'm sure Grady'll pay dearly for embodying everything that's wrong about banking today. And for having crossed your path."

B-J said men sure seem to be just a game of roster roulette.

Rannie said, "I've got another client, he gets charged with neglect of his baby. Left her alone in front of a space heater for four hours. He said he was just next door. And he was. He was busy burglarizing his neighbor's car and house."

B-J said, "I hate a neighbor like that. You're always having to keep an eye on him out the window. You think he's working on his motorcycle in the yard, the next thing he's stolen your wheel covers."

Rannie went on. "Back in college I read a historian who said life in the Middle Ages was nasty, brutish, and short. But I ask you, what's changed?"

"*Déjà-vu* second time around," B-J agreed.

Rannie shifted to look out the window.

"I never pass the buck. Can't really when you're a solo practitioner. I play as tough as the guys, throw a few elbows, they say I'm too aggressive. But basically, I'm widely respected as one of the better players on Broad Street."

"Are you trying to tell me something?"

"You mean is there a moral here? Probably. How about this? You don't win men with tits that'll fit in a champagne glass."

B-J said she wouldn't dispute that. Privately, she was thinking Rannie wasn't lacking in the tit category, but it probably wasn't polite to say that. Downtown Charleston was such a gentrified place she wanted to put on her best manners. Even wearing her Talbot's clothes, carrying a Spiegel pocketbook, she felt kind of underdressed.

Rannie said, "You're . . . what should I call it? Visually imposing? It affects their chemistry in a profound way. Come in with a big set of lungs, and they're capering around like goats in spring. It's a testament to widespread bosom appeal. Gives a girl clout in a fickle world of momma's boys and men who won't commit."

B-J shrugged. "You know the old expression 'if you're going to get fucked, lay back and enjoy it?' Sure you do. Well, they say the best position for a woman to get an orgasm is on top."

Rannie gave her a slow smile of appreciation. "I know you're an act," she said. "I'm something of an actress myself. I do my routines. Ball-buster bitch in civil cases. Junk yard dog on debt collections. Maybe Delilah to some meat-head Samson that comes along needing to have his locks shorn."

B-J said she bet Rannie did those just first rate.

Rannie said she had a detective doing some checking on the roles B-J played. He had turned up a sizeable number. She opened a manila folder that seemed to hold his report. It was right thick with pages.

She licked a finger and leafed through. "You seem to have got your start at a little muni course in south Georgia. Learned the usual tricks. Vaseline on the club face to make the ball go straight. Talk during the opponent's backswing. Cast a shadow on the putting line. It didn't amount to much. Everybody cheated so it cancelled out.

"Then when you were sixteen, you clipped the club pro for $2,000 by stringing side-bets together. It was a career defining moment. You made your mark as a gambling amateur, then went on to bigger and better promotions. One success breeds another. Golf is a song and dance man's dream.

"Out at Palm Desert you switched sleeping pills for a hotshot CEO's blood pressure medicine. He staggered through the back nine barely able to keep awake. Kept dozing off while riding in the cart. Dropped $75,000. A straight eighteen in hole play with the rest side bets he could never quite keep straight."

Rannie leafed through the folder, picking out choice ones.

"There was the Saudi Prince at La Costa. He was such a sorry excuse for a golfer you had to play for three days with a left-handed set of clubs to convince him you were bad enough he could beat you. I think you took him $10,000 a hole."

Next page.

"A loud-mouthed Oklahoma oil man out of Tulsa. Forearms like logs. Power hitter. Great long drives. You told him he could hit three drives off every tee, take his pick of which one to play. He grabbed that bet right up. By the twelfth hole, he was so exhausted he could barely swing the club. Triple-bogied the last seven. Dropped $35,000. That was at Tennison Park in Dallas. I believe it's called 'Hustler's Park' by those in your trade. Fool should have never played there."

B-J gave it her best baby-doll stare, all round-eyed innocence. She sounded right puzzled. "Are you sure you have the right person?"

■ ■ ■

Chase Jeffcoat had laid off the one clerical employee at Chase & Co. and didn't often go into the office himself. With all his eggs in the Roebuck basket, there wasn't much need. When he finally dropped by, the body of Vineyard

Dupree had been decomposing for a week and stank so bad, Chase staggered back out onto the street to vomit.

Naturally the murder and office break-in were big news. A party or parties unknown had rifled the file cabinets and gunned the attorney for Seagrass S & L. A $15,000 check found on his person seemed to link him to the murder of a man named Omonio Reese. Vineyard's trust account had been cleaned out shortly before his death. It was all a huge mystery.

Grady Troxler was on TV speaking reverently of his former in-house counsel. He said, "It's difficult to accept Mister Dupree's no longer part of the team. There are times when I look over there in the corner and he still seems present. He was a fine attorney and a credit to his race. Our lives are works in progress and we got to move on."

Chase went on the local radio show "Feedback America," putting his spin on it. "Battling Bob" Dawtrey threw him soft lobs and let him hit them out of the park.

Bob began, "It's said the past catches up with everybody. Was there some suspicion of the shady in Vineyard Dupree's past?"

"I don't want to come across as an overearnest weenie here," said Chase. "He was African-American; I'm Caucasian. Okay? I thought I could trust the man. I put some sweat equity into our relationship. But frankly there are disturbing reports of his involvement in a drive-by shooting just days before he was himself killed."

"You think he was hit because he knew something?"

"Some folks are decrying this heinous crime and saying Charleston's a murder capital full up with repeat offenders. To them I say this is a fine city to live in and do business around. I'm proud of its features and assets that make it one of the fastest growing metro-urban areas in the Southeast if not the nation. It's a pleasure to live in for the young, and we have excellent golf retirement communities for the old."

Chase was a lot less sanguine about the halting of Roebuck Phase 2 by a whole variety of conservation agencies demanding an endangered species management plan.

He said, "So often I'm dismissed as a tree-hugger. When I urge planned growth, people accuse me of favoring the environment over jobs. I tell them we're creatures of this earth just like rabbits and squirrels. Carcinogens are a danger to all of us. Public health is our health."

Bob interjected, "Allow me to say at this point that your position on a healthy environment is a known and respected one."

"Thanks, Bob. I appreciate that. Truly. Now to find myself in this bind of halting a work in progress and be accused of environmental crimes—I just take exception to that kind of innuendo and character assassination by implication. Sure, down the road we can institute some gradual, far-sighted changes in the master plan. But I don't see squandering all we've accomplished because of scaremongering."

"Are federal regulations what are driving the entrepreneur to the wall?"

"Bob, you have to admit I have a unique understanding of the financial underpinings of a major land improvement like this which . . ." He trailed off helplessly.

"Which pointey-headed D.C. bureaucrats don't got?"

"Exactly. Civil servants are fine people, but they lack

both the leadership skills and the vision to take this nation of ours to the next level. I'm truly disappointed, not just for Roebuck Phase 2, but for all the people who believed in it. I'm dejected, but I'm also buoyed up because when we prove our case, it will not just be a victory for Roebuck but for all the . . ."

Bracey reached out to turn off the radio and snuggled back in the sleeping bag with Hank Harder. They were both naked. The synthetic-fill insulation and breathable lining was perfectly adequate against the cold. It was advertised for –15°.

She hooded her eyes and said, "Turn-ons: sensitive men who seem vulnerable when you take their glasses off. Turnoffs: fatuous husbands on the radio."

"So you turned him off," observed Hank.

"God, you're a wit as well. Ooo, feel of this. You've gone all priapic."

"Let me go deep with my concerns," he said.

Her lips were wet. "And a locker room poet."

Bracey did more than feel the earth move through the compressed foam core of the Therm-a-Rest mattress. She climaxed so many times she nearly passed out.

42

"What is this?" yelped Tamzie. "Some kinda 'freeze moth-erfuckers' routine?"

Just at five p.m. closing time, fifteen federal marshals and ten officers from the thrift take-over squad in Washington, D.C. flashed their i.d. badges and took control of Seagrass S & L. They locked the doors, secured documents, counted cash in the till, filled boxes with files for removal.

The Board had been meeting on the Skydeck, Grady Troxler hammering at them about his stock options and openly threatening legal action against them for breach of fiduciary duty.

The marshalls ignore Tamzie, ask was he Grady Troxler? He said he was and who was this line-up of clowns busting in when he was grappling with challenges?

They said who they was, read him his rights and then a long charge against him.

"If two or more persons conspire to commit any offense against the United States, and one or more of such persons do any act to effect the object of the conspiracy, each person is guilty of a felony blah blah . . .

. . . whoever corruptly influences, obstructs, or impedes the due and proper administration of the law under which

*any pending proceeding is being had before any depart-
ment or agency of the United States, or the due and proper
exercise of the power of inquiry under which any inquiry or
investigation is being had by any congressional committee,
shall be guilty of a felony* and so on and so on and blah
blah blah."

Grady reacted up right fierce with some confusion and
alarm. "These dark inuendoes and half-truths do nobody
any good. I don't see any point in emphasizing default
instead of examining how we can turn this around. If I
get unencumbered authority to straighten things out, do
a little more short-term bridge credit, specify some outlay
reductions . . . I grant you we needed a reality check."

It was a right poor beginning and didn't get any better.
The old cocky grin fade away to a flat, confused nothing.
Thrift employees were coming into the normally forbid-
den Skydeck. Their fear of the man had died a quick death.

The timid little accountant was shaking and shivering
all over he so pissed off. "All the dirt we had to eat in here,
the fear and the groveling, it's like it became part of a common experience."

"Y'all are a real topography map in ingratehood," said
Grady. "I come in this hick town with zero skepticism.
Provide foresight and vision. Make a world of happy faces
brightly shining. Now that the engine slows down a bit
you bite the hand that throws pearls before swine. A damn
Kermit the frog with a CPA thinks he can tell me what for."

"You're a real asshole category unto yourself," Tamzie
told Grady. "We, and when I say we, I think I speak for all
the folks present. We done had about enough of your shit.

For just a brief moment here, we gonna control our own destiny."

"You buncha liberal goo-goos!"

Tamzie could be formidable looking most times. But now she was seething. It was visible in her face and shoulders. She said she was trying hard, but she just couldn't contain herself. She went on to say, "I'll goo-goo you!" and proceeded to knock Grady down and kick the daylights out of him. The accountant and other employees joined in.

Jubilation pretty much took over from there.

■ ■ ■

When Bobbi-Jean got to her condo the answering machine had a half dozen messages to call Bass Renfrew at Burdette's Pool Hall in Mobile. It was an hour earlier down there, and Bass had just finished whipping up on some young dynamos in billiards. He said he was going to need him an audit director to keep track of all the money he was making.

B-J said those young fellas must have outsourced their brains somewhere to think they could beat him.

Bass said the reason he called was Byron Jasper had been phoning down there to Burdette's poor man's country club wanting to know about horse investments. Bass had picked up on the storyline easy enough and done what he could to assure Byron that all the boys were helping B-J in her horse flesh bargain-hunting.

B-J said along with a peck of gratitude, Bass could expect to receive her love and affection.

Bass said a profit-sharing check would go down even better.

B-J related how things were moving at warp speed up in Charleston, and the intense media coverage was just kind of amazing. On the verge of being arrested, Grady Troxler had been beat half stupid by bank employees he had mistreated over the past months. But in the confusion, he just upped and escaped. It was amazing but apparently in character.

The federal marshals had found racks of tape recordings of conversations stored in the Skydeck. The whole thrift was wired from top to bottom like Richard Nixon's White House. Speakers, amplifiers, bugging apparatus, the works. She said she wasn't much of a psychologist, but she figured Grady was love-starved and tried to make money and power a substitute.

Bass agreed that Grady had long needed to be under correctional supervision. Then he said, "Now, B-J, you got to admit you've always found me polite and full of useful advice."

B-J allowed that was the truth.

He said then she'd best remember what he'd taught her. In property development, everything hinges on either selling the whole kit-and-kaboodle to a sucker—or else moving to the next phase so the new loans fill in what you've stole.

B-J said those complexities sure abound. The feds had already found an awful lot of Grady depositing money into personal accounts contrary to what the loan documentation indicated.

Bass said she'd better pay heed to what he was driving at. She'd just busted the piggy bank that was keeping the cash flow going at Roebuck. And from what she was telling him, there was no sucker to buy in.

B-J said that was a predictable glitch.

Bass expounded he'd been asking around about Byron Jasper. Turned out he was hooked up with a character name of Sparky Truluck who's like trained personnel for the rough stuff. Leaves a trail of shallow graves behind him.

B-J said she knew the boy.

"Well he's guaranteed to let the blood out of anybody Byron points the finger at. And as to Byron his ownself, well he might seem like a big old court jester, but there's something a whole lot meaner there. You give that boy some fundamental change in the landscape—go jacking around with him—inconvenience the sum-bitch—well, the boy will dominate any way he can."

She said she thought that was a little overly alarmist.

Bass said he remembered when B-J was barely out of high school, her clipping a Saudi prince for a whole lotta change out at Palm Desert. He said he had never been prouder of her. Those were the high points that stick in a coach's mind over the years.

She said from way back in the beginning she'd tried to have a work ethic. Never wanted to be viewed as lacking in commitment. And Bass had always been a tough critic and demanding teacher. He was the best. Really.

"Dahlin' we got to remember that you've cruised through life with a Barbie-doll physique. Or more like an action figure Barbie modeled on Dolly Parton. Anyhow, maybe you're just a victim trapped in big jugs. Or maybe to your credit you're right sharp and analytical for the normal woman wearing Dolly's bod.

"What I'm trying to say is I'd sure hate to get a taste of the national media covering your premature demise. There's a lotta old boys down here are strong candidates for your love."

B-J said they were all just as sweet as apple turnovers.

Bass said, "Well, I think I'll go stalk me an old girlfriend. I been winning initial approval for getting back in her good graces. Maybe if I get to her before I'm drunk tonight, I'll manage to score."

B-J said, "Well, like you taught me, try to gain every edge you can."

Bass kind of hung there on the phone seeming wistful. "You proceed with caution now, Bobbi-Jean. Y'hear?"

She said every day she was learning a lot and trying to give it her level best.

43

In the newspaper, Byron Jasper said he barely knew Grady Troxler, couldn't understand all this federal regulatory mess. He said, "Financial discrepancies? Alls I know is the economy got a way of eating its young."

Roebuck Plantation was getting an early Christmas present in the form of the PowerChest Pro-Am Golf Classic, and he was extending invitations to everybody to come on out for good times for all.

The provocative Bobbi-Jean Kincaid was shown with three other women with big hair, all them wearing eroticism like a fish skin. The *Post & Courier* reported the tournament straight. Local newspapers never cast a skeptical eye on anything.

Bracey got so tired of answering the phone to hear a stiff Charleston voice say Chase had led them down the road to financial ruin. He had played a crucial role in denying their children a college education. He had stripped them of their European vacation, their summer home, their retirement. Headmasters of prestige private schools raged about drastic drops in student enrollment. Why didn't Chase just open a car theft ring? The losses would have been easier to contain.

Bracey's mother was talking about having sclerotherapy for the spider veins on her legs. You injected a hypertonic saline solution which caused the blood vessels to collapse inward. It required injections over four months and sometimes a brown mark lingered where the syringe had gone in.

Bracey asked why she didn't just wear dark stockings.

Izzie put on lipstick, blotted her lips with a Kleenex. She said Bracey would get stretch marks if she didn't control her rapid weight swings.

"Thanks for the warning," said Bracey. "I'm fortunate I have a mother to tell me these little things. That way I don't have to discover them painfully on my own."

Unprompted, Izzie began to list the current problems in her life.

"I've been thrust into a role I never asked for. I was raised in the days when being a lady still meant something. Now I find my son-in-law has hopelessly tangled my assets in Roebuck Plantation leaving us in a ruinous state."

Bracey said she'd be happy to keep her on a budget.

"Don't imagine," warned Izzie, "that because you gave me some feeble warnings you now have enormous leverage over me. It was my own natural inclination to distrust anyone from Orangeburg."

Bracey said, well call her a cock-eyed optimist, but she thought things were looking up. She was going out to Roebuck to watch the wet T-shirt contest, see if she met anyone interesting.

Izzie said what on earth was she talking about? Bracey said nothing at all really.

What Bracey was talking about was sleep-overs with the loin-stirring Hank Harder that had her feeling better than a month of step-aerobics. The man satisfied all her primal urges.

Skip Rightenberry nearly blew Bracey off the road in his blue Oldsmobile, then smashed through the striped barrier at the front gate of Roebuck when the guard tried to stop him. By the time Bracey pulled into the parking lot he had cornered Chase and backed him up against a golf cart.

"You made representations to me, and I took you at your word!" He sounded like he had been prepped by a lawyer.

Chase was backpedaling to get out of harm's way. He was an ex-football jock, but Skip was big and in a righteous wrath.

Chase said, "Everybody acting like I'm in some ethical crack-up. Opprobrium. Social stigmatization. I've got Bracey Jeffcoat née Fanseau to thank for the bulk of it. Ms. Sheena of the songbird jungle who thinks nature is her personal play toy."

Skip turned to stare at Bracey.

Chase went on with his accusations. "All your little environmental theories that masquerade as science. You know there's severe disagreement on how much nesting is actually going on out there. This whole confrontational line—you want to make Roebuck a pawn in the domestic spat you and your overbearing mother brewed up."

Turning on Bracey was an easy alliance for them. "We walk in the same shoes on this one," was how Skip put it. "We're talking jobs here. Putting people before tree toads."

Bracey said, okay, say for the sake of argument, economic growth was good. But she had just one question for them. What was the magic threshold, the level of market activity—the number of people devouring resources—that was needed for unemployment, human misery, poverty, drug addition, whatever to vanish?

Logic never stalled them for long.

Chase said, "There's a human dimension you refuse to examine. I've got three hundred employees down here. Heating bills are rising. They're worried about stretching their food budgets. Someone has to take their side."

"The net effect of your wilderness management," said Skip, "is a program with something to hurt everybody."

Bracey laughed. She knew debate never swayed anyone. She was just so pleased with herself. She had actually talked back to them. Two great big, overbearing, blowhard men, and she had posed a question they could not answer. And been cool about it.

They weren't listening to her laugh. Instead both of them were staring at a crack in the parking lot pavement where a little yellow flame wavered. It was like a candle one second, would enlarge to a gas cigarette lighter size the next.

Bracey said, "Methane gas."

44

Bobbi-Jean heard Byron Jasper say, "Don't react to the gun now. Listen to what I'm saying."

He and Sparky had caught her headed for the first tee on the day of the big PowerChest tournament. Her tee-off time was one PM. Byron was wearing a navy turtleneck under a white v-neck alpaca sweater. The little shiny handgun was in his waistband. He showed it to her, then put the sweater back over it.

Bobbi-Jean gazed around at all the people drifting past. She was looking just provocative as hell in her short skirt and tassel golf shoes and was all excited about being paired with Hoover "Rebel" Seaton who played a game that was steady but so boring he put sports writers to sleep during his backswing.

Bobbi-Jean knew that other than the bowl games, Byron was over football season. That was because he had started to use basketball imagery. He said, "Honey, I been hard-fouled under the basket. This was my retirement money. I saw myself out in a Stratos 201 bass boat. Standing up there casting in my declining years. But instead I find I'm walking off the field at half-time with zeroes on the clock."

Whups, there he was back to football. B-J said she'd

have no comment about all that money business until after the match.

Byron said, "Dahlin,' I don't think you fully grasp the current reality. Either you cooperate to the utmost or you're going to develop respiratory problems and stop breathing."

B-J said well, to be completely honest, she had been lying about the horse investments. Byron said it's nice to consolidate the truth, now where was it? B-J said it was tee-off time and she had to go. Her partner was waiting right over there. She stood on tip-toe and waved at him. Yoo-hoo. Hooo-ver!

Byron said interrogating her was like peeling onions. Get through one layer and just find another one. He told her he wanted the whereabouts of the money or he'd knee-cap her. Leave her a golfless cripple. Only those pre-verts who went for gals with prosthetic legs would date her.

She said she'd be glad to help him, but there was just one problem. Byron said what's that? She said she'd wagered the whole amount on the golf match. She had always wanted her own championship purse. The little $70,000 put up by Roebuck seemed so piddly. So she kind of arranged it on her own.

"You bet on yourself?"

"Well it didn't seem right to bet against myself."

Byron was starting to unravel. He waved the gun in her face, said he swore to God he'd be exonerated on a murder charge. Not a jury in the land would convict. And goddammit all to hell he had had one corncob too many shoved up his ass in one day!

Sparky told him to put the dam' gun out of sight.

Byron was babbling. "We got to acknowledge there's a situation here. Having got that out in the open, it's our mully-fucking task to deal with it."

Sparky told Byron to shut his ass. Asked B-J how she laid off so much money on a rinky-dink, big-tit golf tournament. She said she spread it around in small-to-medium wagers. She had the help of some friends. Like that old Beatles tune. She sang, "get by with a little help from my friends, help from my friieeends."

She could see the name Bass Renfrew going through Byron's head. Skeeter Jackson. Lance Wallace. Doc Burdette. All of them.

He put both hands on his heart. "I'm gonna need a life-support system."

Sparky asked what were the odds. She said she got as much as three-to-one on average. She could see their simple brains doing the math, $9 million if she won.

Byron said, "you prolly figure I'm choking like a dog. Not true. I'm under control, both physical and mental."

All the way to the first tee, Byron had an iron grip on B-J's arm. Told her caddy to get lost, peeled off some bills to pay him off. Said he was going to be right there, stroke by stroke. Trying to turn the negative into the positive in his very own, down-home way.

He was real loud. "I swear my Bobbi-Jean is just as wholesome as fresh baked goods, and I can't stay away from her. Woo-ee! We are here to go for the win, ain't we though?"

B-J told her playing partner Hoover Seaton, "I don't want to put any undue pressure on you, but I've got three million dollars riding on us winning."

Hoover gave her a look. "You're kidding, right?"

"Well, some people think I am." She turned and struck her tongue out at Byron. "The old meanies."

■ ■ ■

"This is just darling," said Bobbi-Jean. "All these nice people out here today are like a barometer of support."

Sparky basically knew fuck-all about golf, but he knew some. There are four major stud tournaments that define what great golf is all about. The Masters, the PGA, the US and British Opens. The PowerChest Pro-Am was not part of this rich heritage. It was as low down the food chain as you could get and smack in the middle of the year-end period known as golf's "Silly Season."

First off, it was only a one-round 18-hole event, which made it really rinky-drink. If the $70,000 check wasn't pathetic enough. Most of the no-name guy players seemed to be there because they had nothing else to do and wanted to meet girls with big gazongas. Some of them were on their way somewhere else and liked the free hotel rooms that were part of the package.

They could, however, play golf in a way that seemed pretty respectable with no Nicklaus or Calcavecchia making them look like the low-level goofs they really were.

When it came down to winning, the girls were the wild cards. They could play after an erratic fashion, but their flubs would screw up the best of the male scores and make the whole thing an unholy, unpredictable mess. If Bobbi-Jean was on her game, she and Hoover would walk the dog around those eighteen holes with the winner's cup being engraved with their names by No. 12.

The real danger to a Seaton-Kincaid victory was a Donna Kandy McBride who had been *Penthouse* Pet of the Year a couple of years back, married and divorced a pro golfer, but in the process put in a lot of hours on courses developing what turned out to be a natural talent. She was paired with a pro from one of the zillion country clubs in Houston, Texas.

B-J acted like the nonchalant, could-give-a-shit, ding-bat Sparky knew for sure she was. When she right off screwed up the 1st hole by four-putting for a double-bogey, she said, "I really don't understand all this hoop-la craze over Zinfandel wine. Personally, it gives me a headache."

Byron's eyes rolled back in his head. "I'm cut down in the prime of life," he moaned. "I'm reamed. I'm racked. I'm gutted and hung up for skinning."

Sparky got the crazy notion she was trying to kill Byron with a quick heart attack before strutting her stuff.

When she stepped up to the 2nd tee, a par-3 with a little slime-covered pond just below the green and sand trap to the right, Byron was babbling. "Come on now team. We're hurting ourself more than getting hurt by the competition. Let's have a nice drive and then a little two-putt here. Just a fine drive and then glide in a two-putt. Par is just fine, no need for birdies or eagles. We'll get to those later."

Hoover told Byron he wouldn't raise no major objections to him getting his tongue under control. That was about all he said all afternoon. The boy had all the personality of a toilet seat with the top lid down on it.

B-J said that was a real eye-catching outfit on that girl over there in the gallery. She wondered where she had bought it. Then she snap-hooked her drive into the sand trap, blasted it from there over into the rough, then caught the very far edge of the green on the next one. She three-putted for an absolutely unheard-of triple-bogey.

Byron was staggering like a drunk. He said he thought he was having a stroke.

B-j said this really wasn't a very challenging course. Now you take Augusta with those lightning fast greens. And every tee shot going up hill. That's a golf course.

On the 3rd, B-J hit a spectator which knocked the ball into the fairway instead of the salt marsh where it would have been gone forever. She said she sure hoped Roebuck had liability insurance because she didn't carry any personally herself.

She came in at par. Hoover birdied it.

"Stay competitive now, team," Byron urged. "Nothing wrong here a couple of birdies won't cure."

When she bogied the 4th, Byron said he had an irregular heartbeat. He asked if anyone could recommend a good undertaker.

The light came on in Sparky's head. The lying bitch hadn't made any wagers. This was her idea of a money laundry. Tell them she was awful sorry, but the three million was just lost and there was nothing she could do. Like they were two retards born yesterday and new in town just off the turnip truck.

That numb nuts Byron would believe anything. Wave a big twin set of kowabongas under his nose and his mind just clouded over.

Both B-J and Hoover birdied No. 5. That had Sparky scratching his head. Of course, he had never seen tightly controlled golf hustling before.

"Come on now team," pleaded Byron. "Let's just stick to this winning motif." Huge sweat stains spread out under his armpits. He kept sniffing of them and nearly gagging at the added reek of fear. He was like a man losing bad in a toad-eating contest.

B-J getting a three-putt bogey on No. 6 gave him cause for renewed cynicism and despair. He waved his hands up around the level of his head. "You stoo-pid fucking bitch, can't you do anything right?!!"

B-J adjusted her glove, said, "That's not just man-chauvinistic but really very irresponsible. Adding to my stress here when I'm just all a-jangle with nerves as it is."

On the 7th, both B-J and Hoover pulled off birdies.

On the 8th tee, B-J paused and watched across to the thirteen green which was real close. Donna Kandy was putting. Elbows out. Huge tits hanging down like they'd drag her to the ground. Pert butt up in the air.

When B-J finally teed up her ball she seemed to be thinking hard on something. She hit it a humdinger though, just plumb bisecting the middle between two bunkers that looked like the Sahara and the Gobi trying to grow together.

On the green, she sank a 15-foot birdie putt. But she was thinking hard. You could see the wheels turning.

On No. 9, playing back into the shadow of the clubhouse, she pulled Byron aside and asked him sotto voice how much money Roebuck had in the current bank account. He said he had a payroll to meet on Monday, contractor bills crying out, mechanic's liens on every goddam thing in sight and what mully-fucking business was it of hers anyhow?

The boy was right tense at that point.

Real cool, she said she wasn't born yesterday and knew full well he intended to cut and run with all the money they had lent her from Seagrass. Since she was increasing their capital to three times its original size, she figured she was entitled to an equal share and not just bag holder for the cops to arrest.

Byron chewed on that development and said what's your angle?

B-J said, "I'm about to develop some inventiveness in shot-making. And I'm pretty dead sure of winning this thing. What have you got to lose anyway if you're about to go on the lam? Up the prize here as much as you can. It's money in our pockets. Get our career earnings up as much as possible."

Byron went off and checked the leader board and found out that the closest teams were fourteen and sixteen strokes down. That meant only Donna Kandy to beat so what B-J had counseled made good horse sense.

Hoover had played even par, bogey here, a birdie there so far. And if B-J ever got her game together they'd smoke them.

Gathering up some TV media, he swung into one of those patented wild man routines of his jumping around like the old one-armed paper hanger with crabs. What a day it was turning out to be and woo-eee man wasn't it just slicker'n eel (bleep). Weren't these just the greatest guys and gals anyone had ever seen. Just proof positive of the (bleep) women's golf (bleep) explosion and how women were breaking through that old glass ceiling like it was a (bleep) defective condom.

He was right there on the spot exercising his executive discretion to show his plumb gratitude and raising the purse to $250,000, and here was the new check to prove it.

The press all applauded, and a bunch of drunks whooped.

When Byron came back to join them on the 11th, he was urging, "Let's get driven and methodical here, team. Driven and methodical."

He tried to ignore the fact that B-J had double-bogied No. 9 even as he was raising the purse. She had made par on 10. There was hope. There was light at the end of the tunnel.

Hoover hit the only piss-poor drive he did all day. Byron stayed on B-J's ass. "Heart and guts now team. Heart and guts."

A big roar out of the crowd back at the clubhouse signaled some right bleak news. The Houston pro had birdied, and Donna Kandy made a par on eighteen. They had finished strong.

The numbers came up on the leader board. They were 1-over-par 141 team total for the round.

"I'm gonna need an appendectomy," said Byron. "I'm gonna need a heart bypass."

B-J said, "Maybe just once you could think about somebody other than yourself"

Byron set his face in a crazed grin. "We need faith and strength now," he preached. "Got to repair that social fabric. Once you've lost it you can't get it back."

B-J threw a pinch of grass up to test the wind, told him, "I long ago realized I have to calculate and accept my personal limitations. Play within my own private self. Get the basics right. Stance, address position, grip."

"You stupid bitch why don't you play the goddam game!" Byron raged at the top of his lungs. Then he bit down on his hand hard to keep himself from screaming in agony at the money he saw flying out of his reach.

"Yeah, ditto, you twat," said Sparky. There didn't seem much he could add.

"Well sure," she said. Then she hauled off and smacked the bejesus out of the ball which took off on a clean, low-level mission an F-15 pilot flying under the radar into Baghdad would have admired. And damn if she didn't magic-wonder birdie the hole.

B-J was on her game. She was fucking on it!

"Let's not misdirect our focus, here team," nagged Byron. He was on his knees when she tapped in an easy three-foot putt on No. 12 for a par. "We got to get control over our golf destiny here. Got to get control. Golf destiny."

It was all going through his head like pin-ball lights. $250,000 was nothing. It was the nine million they could make. The nine million they could lose. The three million they had given the thieving cunt and she had put at risk and it could all get flushed down the commode.

When she made par on 13, Byron did a little jigging dance like a man that had to piss bad. "I'm shocked into surprise. In the groove now. Sparks are flying upwards. That big bluebird's singing like Bing Crosby."

She birdied 14, 15 and parred 16. Hoover Seaton did his steady par.

Byron looked like a man who had gotten dragged all the way down to the electric chair and strapped in before the governor's pardon showed up. His eyes were glazed over and his jaw hung slack and drooling.

Then she fucking flat-out eagled the seventeenth!

Byron was slobbering and foaming. "I ain't yanking the welcome mat. Not giving you no big cold shoulder. We got a moral issue here. Got to do what's right and not what's wrong!"

The par-5 18th green looked about as far away as New Orleans when you're broke busted and hitch-hiking there from Pensacola.

B-J and Hoover both nailed their drives rock solid and airborne exquisite. If B-J's ball had been hit into a night-time sky it would have joined the constellations.

Out on the fairway she dithered between a two and a three iron. She said well this certainly calls for a first approach shot.

Byron begged yes baby please baby. Think mental. Mental game. B-J said speaking of mental she thought playing thirty-six holes in a day was a bit much. The men who do that kind of rigorous play—when they went on golf vacations and all—must be trying to prove something about themselves that she couldn't understand. Then she turned to address the ball, paused again and asked Byron if he had played Hound Ears up at Blowing Rock?

Byron said, "No, I mean yes. Yes I have. But please please baby think think what you're doing. Nine fucking ball-busting million dollars." Tears were streaming down his face. Byron was actually starting to cry.

Her shot kicked to the back of the green and sat there staring, at them. A thirty-foot putt for an eagle. It would win the match.

As she lined it up, Byron's arms and hands were vibrating, and it spread into his whole body.

The putt went straight then curled out and rested two inches from the lip of the cup.

They would now play sudden-death hole-by-hole.

Byron bent down like he had an excruciating hernia or had racked his balls or something. He said he was going to start taking prozac for depression.

B-J walked to the ball, gave it a negligent tap . . . and *missed the hole*. She tapped it again and it went in. A par.

B-J said now that she'd won this money she'd like to go down to Georgia, play the St. Simons Island Club.

She had finished a 2-over-par 72. Her partner Hoover Seaton had an even par giving them a team total of 142.

Byron straightened up and said you goddam shit-for-brains cunt-mouth bitch, you can't do third grade math?!!

She looked at him, said, "You got a dick like a bread stick. Bottom line—if the stress is going to prostate you so, you need to stay away from gambling."

Sparky told B-J there was nothing conclusive in his mind, but he was pretty sure a random shooting or two was in the offing. He'd be happy to do it personally or load the gun if Byron wanted the honor.

B-J said oh ye doubting Thomases of little faith. Then she called over some of the official types in red arm bands and told them she hated to disrupt the celebration, but she was pretty sure she and her esteemed colleague had won.

They told her her claim was bogus.

She said they were playing the Rules of Golf, weren't they? Everyone nodded and agreed that was practically a truism. She said she had seen how on No. 13 Donna Kandy had put her ball down at her partner's mark by mistake and made a putt. Then when he pointed this out to her, she picked up her ball and putted from her own mark.

"You might want to check Rule 20–7b/1 and Rule 20–1 which I just hate to say it looks like she violated the hell out of."

Byron was whimpering. He sounded like a puppy locked off in a kennel in a rainstorm.

They thumbed through the pages and found Donna Kandy should have holed out after realizing her error and taken a two-shot penalty. Then she compounded the heck out of the problem by putting from the original mark. Additional two strokes. Donna Kandy and her Texas pro were 5-over-par 145.

The press was crowding round, and B-J had already gone into her victory speech. "It was probably about number twelve when it turned around. All of a sudden, I get sense of—is self-esteem overused?—then of self-determination. I ask myself should I just quit and become a cheerleader? The community of women train and sacrifice their lives for this. I got to forge on."

"I need a straitjacket. I need a padded cell," Byron mumbled. He was lying flat on his back down on the grass holding his nose tightly at the bridge to stop the bleeding. Somehow, he had managed to punch himself in the face.

"Sorry-ass rip-off son-of-a-bitches," Donna Kandy commented on the ruling.

B-J told the golf writers, "I swear these moments, it's impossible to hold back the floodgates of tears and laughter. All day I had my caddy verbally and physically abusing me. I have spoken to him about his behavior, but I swan he was one major obstacle 1 had to overcome."

As the reality of the money sunk in, Byron rekindled his pleasure in the ancient sport of golf. He suddenly bolted upright and was just grabbing B-J up hugging and squeezing. "You are the best little shot-maker bar none! Didn't she do it! Didn't she shoot out the goddam lights! You just a hum-dinger, sweet-meat, darling bitch, is all you are!"

She said all beaming, "I think we brought in a better return today than the stock market."

45

Bracey Jeffcoat watched in the crowd as Bobbi-Jean Kincaid, all perky and cute, made one of those meaningless post-game talks to the press.

"Well, me and these lucky ladies out here today ain't virgin territory."

That drew a big laugh out of the reporters.

"But I'd say overall we got real good heat. Real depth of talent out here. Donna Kandy's got a very consistent swing. She really pressed me, had me and ole Hoover here scrambling.

"Golf is a super-healthy sport. Nothing pretentious. We had some gaffes; we had some glory. Didn't relent. Played smart. Sometimes not with a lot of poise. Pretty much epitomized what this day was all about.

"Video analysis has been a big step in improving my technique. And I know for sure when Alice Cooper and Eddie Van Halen, all of Hootie and the Blowfish are playing golf, well it just shows those 24 million American golfers know something good when they see it."

Big round of applause. Whooping from those already drunk.

She held up the check. "Now I'm going to scamper right

off and consolidate these ill-gotten gains. Easy money. Tootie-fruitie, party-down!"

To Bracey, what followed next seemed like maybe eight hundred lunatics dedicated to drunkenness, distemper and pawing over women with large bosoms. She had been to a fraternity party at the University of Virginia once, but otherwise had never seen men get so drunk so fast.

A loud galoot in a lime green sports coat, sleeves pulled up over his elbow, started pushing a bottle of Wild Turkey at her. He was shouting, "Found this in old Bubba's golf bag! He died of heart arrest on the eighth green last year out at Wild Dunes! Fuckin' subpoenaed his ass to the big courtroom in the sky! He would have wanted us to finish it for him!"

Bracey pushed him off, but he kept coming back at her grinning lopsidedly.

"Like I always say, an over-sized driver and a dick got a lot in common. The bigger the head, the bigger the sweet spot."

Another drunk caromed off her. "Fuggin' dirt dobber . . . slick shootin' . . . low-ridin' . . . unparalleled dip-shit . . . mother . . ."

All flushed with success, B-J was drinking and telling stories about herself. "So I said, 'You call me back when you grow a dick,' but he had already hung up the phone. Wasted a perfectly good line."

All the men were laughing and trying to rub up against her. At least the ones who weren't rubbing up against the other girl golfers.

B-J sure had a shape and attitude. Bracey could have

imagined her wanted for home-wrecking and marital discord in all fifty states.

Byron Jasper was drooling drunk. He seemed to be saying, "Fuggin' shit-faced is what I am is all!" Then he said what sounded like, "Hubba-dubba razzmatazz hullabaloo! Knee-Knocker, toad-stabber, cunt shit whupped their asses. Aww-rat boogaloo! Lemme hug on you bebby!"

A man in coordinated burnt orange dragged Byron off B-J and they shouted abuse at each other. Bellied up all bellicose and threatening. That led to a little pushing and shoving, a couple of flat-hand slaps, and then they were dragged apart.

Unbridled discord got on with its reign.

A drunk who was soaking wet like he had walked fully dressed through the shower tried to stuff a hundred-dollar bill down Bracey's blouse while discussing interstate speed limits.

"I tell you these goddam speed limits fuckin' imposition on taxpaying drivers goddam siege mentality locked up in your car. It's inattention that gets you ever'time. Let us fuggin' get up to speeds where you got to pay attention to what you're gobble goob poormouth freedom information . . ."

Everybody wanted her to meet a good friend. Or go someplace quiet with them. Or admire the coconuts on "thet trash-talkin' little high-test performance-review over there in the corner."

"You dam-ole burned-out, dope-sick vagrant!"

"That gal gimmie fuggin' hypothermia by predesign!"

By the tidal movements of the party, Bracey kept bumping against Bobbi-Jean who was stuck to real close by that hick-looking character Sparky Truluck. He was giving her a predatory look, but it was not sex he was interested in.

"You're gonna dance with the ones what brung you," he said, a plastic cup of beer in his hand.

She said to him, "There's just not much trust left in this mean old world, and sometimes I just get to wondering what are things coming to here at the end of the 20th century?"

He was looking her right in the eye. "There's liars so tangled up in lies they'll believe their own sick selves."

She said in a sing-song, "Sick minds like sick faces are often found in public places."

Irremediably plastered, Byron was babbling, "Fuggin' rodeo . . . ring-a-ding . . . lasso . . . Golfer's Bill of Rights . . . pro-life get-down . . . midnight tequila afterglow . . ."

"I'm sticking to you like a duck on a June bug," Sparky told B-J.

Then Byron said something almost coherent through a thick lolling tongue. "Laying off fuggin' Seagrass loans . . . horse piss . . . cow tit . . . three into nine high-low double-press wager . . . come in a full-ash winner . . . nine million buck-a-roonies . . . loverly big-kahunas golf playing bish . . ."

Bracey might have learned more, but events came to a catharsis at that point when Skip Rightenberry lit a cigar in the locker room of the club where methane gas had been building up and blew the building sky-high.

That's an exaggeration—there was no flaming debris or the roof lifted off—but the resultant blast ripped lockers from the wall, destroyed the ceiling tile, blew out the doors, and travelling concussion shattered every window in the building. It was a big boom.

Skip came shrieking out missing his toupée, eyebrows singed off, his whole body gray like he had crawled in pencil sharpener shavings. Since his shirt was on fire, him responding with a St. Vitus dance, a bunch of men grabbed him and heaved him into the swimming pool where other drunks were carousing with their clothes and golf shoes on.

The explosion didn't end it. Methane tends to continue to burn, and flames were licking their way up the inside walls of the club. The catering crew, who hadn't enjoyed the big boom, liked the fire even less and came out of the dining room yelling and hollering along with a lot of guests.

The staff were all black men and women off the islands who still spoke Gullah, a total foreign language to people not from the region. They seemed to be saying demented things like, "Hog fat, pig toes, sump pump!"

"Catch-a-boolie, jabber-nobs, rabid-dog!"

"Potato-head, plum-down, hand-job!"

Bobbi-Jean gazed at all this action and said, "Well this certainly spoils an otherwise big day."

During the pyrotechnics, she slipped away. Bracey watched her disappear into the crowd. Saw Sparky searching for her frantically.

"I'm gonna put you in the rehab room!" he shouted in pure frustration.

46

Sparky said he knew from the get-go the slippery little bitch would rabbit on them.

Doris said she still couldn't believe he let her get away. She said, "You are one substandard dam' product."

They stood out in the far corner of the Seagrass parking lot in the dark, Doris' Cadillac parked next to the vacant Buick LeSabre of her husband. One light showed in the bank lobby where a couple of federal marshals sat as night guards.

Doris said, "Grady's in there with the wagons circled. The secret chamber I told you about. Ducked in there during the confusion of everyone whipping his ass. Once we get the bank account numbers, we pull up stakes and take this circus to where the money lies."

They walked at a blind angle up to the building and sure enough found a steel door painted the same color as the cement. You wouldn't have given it a second thought if you didn't now it was the passage to the secret chamber in the Skydeck.

Doris had a big tote bag with South-of-the-Border printed on the side. Pulled out a ring of keys. Sparky said did you bring along hot dogs, chips and drinks? She said very funny. She said it was beyond the call of duty for her to even be there. Dealing with Grady was a man's job.

Sparky said, "I gotta insist on a clarification here. There's not much comfort in thinking he's in there maybe armed, hearing every entry noise we make."

Doris said of course he expected them, she had got off the phone with him not an hour before. Sitting in there in a lock-down mode for them to show with a fresh car for the getaway. It was part of the plan. Her voice started carrying a harsh tone. "You want specific guidelines? You shoot the shit out of him. You never killed an unarmed man before? You disappoint me."

Sparky said, "That's your criterion for man's work is it?" He was thinking Doris was as morally dangerous a bitch as he'd ever gotten tangled with.

"Pure and simple," she said.

Sparky had bought a silencer with the last of his money. You could score one from spades right on the street in North Charleston. They got stolen off the military bases. As he screwed it onto his .40 Smith & Wesson Taurus automatic, he felt like James Bond.

Doris opened the door, and they stepped inside in the dark. Closed the door. In pitch blackness they felt their way up circular metal stairs, Sparky first to spearhead the thing. Tong. Tong. Tong. Sparky knew for sure they could be heard. Probably by the marshals down in the lobby.

Grady unlocked the door and opened it, a bar of light jumping out. That move didn't pay off too well.

"No hard feelings now," said Sparky. He shot Grady three

times. Poff-poff-poff. Grady flung backwards like a rag doll and flopped onto an already messed up bed.

Sparky inspected his handiwork pretty pleased. Those 180-grain jacketed hollow points will sure enough do a man in. He unscrewed the silencer and put it in his jeans pocket. The Taurus he stuck in the back of his pants.

Doris didn't stand around lamenting the loss of her husband. She said she guessed when the press phoned seeking comment, he wouldn't return their calls. Under a pool of light from a desk lamp lay a computer print-out of bank account numbers. She folded the paper four, five times and shoved it inside her bra. Then she pulled a handgun out of the tote sack, a big .44 Ruger with cherry-wood grips. Held it with both hands. Cocked it.

Clik-click.

Sparky said, "What the . . . ?"

Doris started screaming at the top of her lungs.

"EEEEEEEEE!!!"

Sparky was one to react quickly to change, and he sure jumped awake at this. The gun she now pointed at him was more hard evidence that the scenario had changed behind his back.

In the closed space the boom of her gun deafened him as it blew him back against the wall. He clawed for his Taurus in a last-ditch effort to nail the cunt, but she shot him again. His gun flew across the room and he pitched over to one side and lay still.

No "spray and pray" about the woman. She had aimed for and hit his chest twice about two inches apart.

When the federal marshals came through the door she had opened to the Skydeck, they heard Doris say, "I've got the pussy."

Both of them swore those were her exact words.

■ ■ ■

The $250,000 check to the winners of the PowerChest tournament bounced like a rubber ball, and Hoover Seaton went home without a dime. Roebuck's many creditors put the corporation in involuntary bankruptcy. The worst case possibility had arrived.

Rannie Ralston had come out early and loud against Seagrass and Roebuck. Now her voice mail was clogged with callers and her office jammed. Nearly everyone with over a million dollars in assets in the city of Charleston had been injured in some way. For Rannie, money and vengeance held a seductive musical appeal. Knowing the precise details of financial disaster in Charleston's best families was also attractive. The decline of others had long held a fascination for her. She likened it to endorphins, the body's opiates that flow after vigorous exercise or sexual orgasm.

The Federal Savings & Loan Insurance Corp was facing an outlay of millions and needed a lawyer to also sue the officers and directors of Seagrass in an attempt to recover some pittance. Rannie's brother, state Senator Collier Ralston, swung some influence with congressmen who moved the federal bureaucracy to hire Rannie. Some big law firms in town, irate at the loss of business, huffed about the multiple conflicts of interest, but the FSLIC never responded.

Everyone was in agreement that the outside auditors were the deep pocket, and Rannie Ralston should nail them for every penny and then some. Suing the Big Eight accounting firms had become a popular national sport, and there seemed no reason why Charleston society shouldn't get in on it. The auditors had been grossly negligent in allowing Seagrass to go so long with such shoddy bookkeeping.

Rannie was particularly pleased, however, to be able to go after the directors as co-defendants. Among that hapless crew, her special favorites were (1) chief bandit Chase Jeffcoat, (2) the odious Skip Rightenberry—an area realtor currently in the skin graft ward at the Medical University—and (3) an uppity former maid of her mother's named Tamzie Jerome. Her otherwise detested brother Senator Collier Ralston was exempt.

"This is a leadership issue," she told the clients. "Follow my advice and counsel or get off the bus."

To those who pressed for an explanation, she said the Seagrass directors were so pathetically dumb that a jury was liable to take pity on them. Her brother was needed to testify to their willful sloth and deliberate cupidity. He hadn't done anything wrong anyway. Senatorial duties had kept him from the bulk of the Board meetings. And it was absurd to think he had ever been Chairman of the thing. That was an error in documentation.

Any who still resisted, she brow-beat, tongue-lashed, and generally gave the full range of her emotion. They emerged from her office looking ready for a trauma ward. But they all signed a waiver of liability for her brother. Even the FSLIC.

Rannie was fond of saying that in big cases the clients first rush to one side of the boat or the other but eventually settle down in their seats.

Izzie Fanseau said she felt almost relieved at hiring Rannie to sue her former son-in-law Chase Jeffcoat. Through an almost obscene exercise of undue influence he had clouded her mind and spirited her assets away from the trust department of a reliable commercial bank. Following a face-lift, she took her husband Blake Huston off on what she called "a long delayed" cruise of the Greek Islands. As her skin was still bruised from the operation, she wore dark glasses and swathed her head in a scarf.

Bracey drove them to the airport, said good-bye, have a nice time. Izzie said don't purse your lips. It will wrinkle them.

When no murder charges were filed against her, Doris Troxler said she felt about vindicated as hell and drove out of town in a motorhome towing her Cadillac. A long cigarette hung from her lower lip. She seemed to have taken up smoking. Or to have resumed smoking.

47

"I'm afraid I've never shared your enthusiasm for the animal kingdom," Chase Jeffcoat said drily.

"Strange," said Bracey. "You seemed to enjoy snuffling like a pig with that Kincaid creature. Or was it just your mammary obsession coming to the fore?"

He raised an eyebrow. "Did you take photographs? I have no independent recollection of the event."

It was not a pleasant interchange. Chase was loading the BMW with suitcases, moving out of the big house on Legendre at Izzie's orders. Her exact words had been, "I have no more need of your inconsistent performance."

He was taking the pigskin luggage Bracey had bought him for the honeymoon in Rome which she had also paid for.

Roebuck was on the ropes. The explosion of the club house detracted severely from the otherwise successful PowerChest Tournament. OHSA was all over them, citing them left and right for not coordinating hazardous activities. The string of denials out of Byron Jasper—claiming that safety was "a daily worship service"—didn't stand up well against the raw facts. Byron's face twitched a lot on TV like he was suffering nerve degeneration. He swore he had no knowledge that landfills gave off methane or that it could ignite spontaneously in air. He hadn't been a physics major at Texas Christian.

Chase turned away in disapproval of everything about his wife and shoved the last suitcase into the car.

"Well, good-bye lordly manse. All its pretense of opulence and grandeur. You were never home-sweet-home." He blew a kiss. "Farewell crusty matriarch watching me depart from a high window. Your daughter won't have me to help her get dressed anymore. The one she asks if a particular dress makes her look fat or not."

"Mother's in Greece," said Bracey.

"One small blessing in a world of injustice."

"You've certainly turned out to be a misunderstood hero in this drama," said Bracey sarcastically.

"Yeah, you're a real abuse-survivor yourself. Now why don't you run along and shave your head in protest. Chain yourself to an old-growth tree and zealously guard it."

As he drove off, she realized he had taken his shotgun in the pigskin gun case. A $12,000 Beretta, stock measured for his arm length. Exquisitely engraved with game birds. In the flush of their honeymoon, she had bought it for him in Italy, both of them envisioning him as Lowcountry gentry. Hunting with the Middleton Deer Hunt. Shooting quail. Maybe flying to Idaho with friends for partridge.

He had never once used it.

Did he intend to hock it? Or did he have some use for it finally? She didn't care if he blew his brains out.

■ ■ ■

"I'm gonna put your ass back in Medicaid Motel!" Tamzie yelled above the din. The CD player was blaring gospel rap at top volume so the two half-deaf old biddies could get with the rhythm.

"Get down wit the man
The Mon with a plan
For life eternal
Jesus our Man."

Tamzie shut off the CD and they look around blinking at her like they coming out into sunlight from the dark. She said it was time to listen up good. They were exacting a social cost on her income that her, an ordinary American, couldn't be expected to stand. House full of starving cats looking skinny and waiting for a chance to bite someone.

Luevenia Parsons said to not get all morose and uptight with her. She had looked a grave challenge in the face before, and her rectitude was up to the task. She was living her life in the Lord's name, and He wouldn't lay nothing on her He didn't think she could handle. She could mine that vein and pull that plug.

Tamzie said, "We got a situation where since the weekend you go through eight bags a' cat food, two-three cases of beer. Maybe more. I don't know. I stop counting after that."

"You don't inspire whole bunch'a confidence yourself," said Jacquilla. "All kinds of bankruptcy folk coming round to look at the house with eviction in they eyes. All distant manner and high-hand. You know what I'm saying?"

Luevenia agreed it shook her up bad and made her have to lie down a whole lot more than usual. She go on to say the place was awful crowded, and she had read that mirrors would open up the space.

Tamzie said she was back to her initial assessment. County home for both of them pair starting tomorrow. Get packing. Time for some kick-start initiative. Kick them both out.

Luevenia said, "That don't allay my anxiety none too much. I gots to lie down."

Jacquilla chime in, "We done lay that proposition to rest last week. We ain't goin' nowhere soon. We both in shock and can't take no sudden scenery change."

Tamzie stormed out of the house. She never knew what kind of mixed message of insanity was coming at her next. Major mishap when the golf club blow up. Grady Troxler and Sparky Truluck shoot each other dead in some gunfight in a secret room at Seagrass.

Tamzie walk and walk all over the golf course where the methane turning the grass to brown.

Angry voices among the trees sounded like the voices buzzing in her head.

She tried to get a fix on who was talking.

"I am sickened and angry!" a man was shouting. "You had your orientation session! Weren't you paying attention?"

"You still haven't caught on have you?" said a woman in a much calmer voice. Tamzie knew that voice. It was Bracey Jeffcoat. The girl whose momma had all those dogs Omar Gillyard looked after.

She stepped out into the open.

Chase Jeffcoat was holding an over-and-under shotgun, staring daggers at his wife. "I'll brook no opposition on this! The tail's not wagging this dog!"

Bracey Jeffcoat said, "You've been dragged down in your debt-ridden mess. Go ahead. Juggle the books. Borrow some more. Do some downsizing or rightsizing. Whatever you call it. But the game's up."

"Honey," Tamzie warn Bracey, "the benefit of the doubt's a good thing, but there may be none left here. That ain't no crocheted placemat the man's holding."

"It's okay," said Bracey her eyes fixed on her husband's. "He couldn't identify a red cockaded woodpecker if his life depended upon it. And I'll give you a hint, Chase. It's got a red cockade and it pecks wood."

Tamzie didn't like what she was seeing the least bit. His hand was shaking. The man was ready to kill more than woodpeckers.

"You are perilously close . . ." he threatened.

Tamzie lunged for the gun barrel.

BA-DOOM!

The blast echoed through the woods.

No one was hurt. She had knocked it aside.

Chase Jeffcoat was staring at the gun like he had a sudden big awareness of what he had nearly done.

Cool as ice, Bracey told her husband, "It's time for you to get religion."

48

"We need to have us a bilateral talk, sweetheart," said Byron Jasper. He caught Bobbi-Jean leaving her condo in the real early morning with a thin mist rising off the ground. She had the door to her BMW roadster open.

She slung a set of golf clubs into the little space behind the seats, said, "Oh Mister Jasper. It's just so fine, Clemson going to the Peach Bowl. Sure, everybody admires Virginia and how well they did, but as you never tire of telling me, bowls are in the business of selling out the tickets."

Byron showed her his handgun, told her to get in her dam' car and start the dam' engine. She got in. Put one arm across the seat and said if this was some kind of a duress threat, well her boyfriend Travis wouldn't like the pointing guns business worth a shit.

Byron rolled his eyes and said here we go with that dam' ol' *déjà vu* deal again. He climbed in the passenger seat.

"I can't pretend I know French too well," said B-J. "But old Travis has sure as heck showed up. The bad penny routine, I guess."

"What I'm trying to get across," said Byron, "is this *ad hoc* boyfriend Travis is a pure fiction of your imagination, and we're going to put him behind us."

At that point, he sat on something hard and pulled out a dagger in a sheath with a Nazi insignia on it.

"That belongs to Travis," said B-J.

He rubbed the side of his face with the dagger, said, "Let's closure the debate on that issue."

She started the engine and drove off. Byron directed her down the sandy path into the trees winding all around here and there with the marsh beyond. Across a broomsage field lay the burned house of Jacquilla Gillyard.

Byron tossed the dagger on the floorboard. He said he wasn't going to bear the brunt of B-J's little rip-off escapade. They were getting a unity on the money instead of it being a point of divisiveness. Down where it was private and quiet, she'd tell him where the book of her bets was located, or else he'd end their partnership permanent like.

She said well it's good they weren't having to split with that Grady Troxler person. That man sure could project a combination of nastiness and sleaze.

Byron said, "Grady—God rest him—wanted to redshirt you. I said, no, you was first string. I came in with that mentality, stuck to it all the way. Just underestimated the detrimental impact of your treachery. But now, fortune's about to take an upward leap. The gun making you nervous?"

She said she was responding pretty well to it. But she wondered was he feeling okay?

Byron said he had himself 12 milligrams of Dexedrine and a shot of Wild Turkey. He was feeling just fine and alert so don't try nothing. And don't pull some enticement with those big tatas of hers. He was immune to that.

She said, "Well, I just wondered. They say holiday

depression is a common problem this time of year. And you look kind of beat-down."

She stopped the car at the edge of the marsh. Byron said he was a real fault-tolerant guy, but this was the end of the trail for tired cowboys.

B-J said, "Now, Mister Jasper. Do you really want Travis to cut your 'nads off?"

Byron said they been over that Travis shit, and he was something made-up. Whatever she might think, he hadn't abdicated his brains. She said then who's that in the trunk of the car?

Byron jerked around like he thought somebody was sneaking up on him. B-J said Travis had come up to her house the night before, got drunk and started smacking her around to make up for the beatings he hadn't given her while he was in prison. This had forced her to subdue him. Then lock him in the trunk for safe keeping. She had been getting ready to drive him to the police and charge him with parole violation when Byron came up and interrupted her plans.

Byron was shaking as he got out and held the gun with two hands like in the cop shows. Pointed it at the trunk. Took one hand off the gun to pop the lid, them slapped it back on the gun.

There was nobody in the trunk.

He said, "You sorry, lying B-word . . ."

At that moment a five-iron crashed into the back of his head giving him a hemorrhage that had him dead in minutes. All the bleeding was internal so there was no blood or hair on the club for B-J to wipe off. Since the Nazi dagger had Byron's fingerprints all over it, she gingerly picked it up with the hem of her skirt and dropped it beside his body. It would add a little air of mystery to the whole thing.

Some buzzards had been circling high on an updraft. As she drove off, they came down for a closer look.

B-J drove back to Charleston and stopped off at Seagrass S & L where the federal bank examiners were spending taxpayer money trying to sort out the mess their lack of regulation had allowed. She got ushered into a chair and crossed her legs, said she believed she was what was called a whistle-blower. You see, her boss Byron Jasper and Grady Troxler, the one who got shot dead in the secret room, were up to something awful odd. She didn't understand it, but perhaps they would. She said at some point she began to worry, well not really worry, but there was an edge of concern. That was why she had come by.

The federal examiner asked wasn't she the winner of the PowerChest Pro-Am, and she allowed she was. She said she was looking forward to promoting other events. "I'm psyched. Really."

■ ■ ■

Tamzie couldn't quite figure why, but the fight over the shotgun in the woods foster parent a kind of kinship between her and Bracey Jeffcoat. Together the two sit back and watch a week of adverse publicity for Seagrass and Roebuck Plantation. A lot of records were missing, but the accountant and key witnesses were cooperating fully. Chase Jeffcoat got indicted by the grand jury for making straw man loans.

They took Chase's Beretta shotgun and spend a week shooting feral cats. Tamzie said she had never actually shake hands with a red cockaded woodpecker, but she figure they were having a harder time holding onto life than stray cats of which the world had a gracious plenty.

It was in the process of cat hunting that they come across the body of Byron Jasper half eat up by buzzards, a gun and a Nazi dagger lying nearby. The forensic lab couldn't place the time of death real well, and the speculation was he had been killed by other parties in league with him and Grady Troxler. Bobbi-Jean Kincaid had showed the feds where $3 million had gone through a series of bank accounts and then disappeared without a trace somewhere in Alabama.

Back out in the woods, Tamzie told Bracey how her ex-husband Debone got ex through being shot dead. The man was poisonous as nuclear fall-out. Kept getting his ass in the slam. Then a tight pattern of hot lead give him that constricted feeling in the chest.

Bracey asked if there was another man in Tamzie's life.

Tamzie huffed, "Christmas is for children. I done decanted my belief in Santa Claus"

Tamzie said it wasn't easy being a black woman of means. She didn't have no Shaquille O'Neal come courting her. Just a bunch of thieves and outlaws needing new cars and dental work.

She could see Bracey looking at her not having the least idea who the Shaq was. But she went on railing about how soon as black men get money they go taking up with some white bitch. Dennis Rodman humping that Madonna.

She say, "Excuse my mouth, but you know what I mean. Seems like the black woman always got her ass in a crack between a hostile environment and a hard place."

Bracey said she though Tamzie was sweet on Omar Gillyard at one time.

"What you know about that?" say Tamzie kind of resentful at that invasion of privacy.

Bracey said, "Black folks aren't the only ones who watch and listen."

Tamzie said the man walk dogs for a living. Ride a bicycle with fat tires and a big basket on the front. Bracey said as opposed to inheriting a freed slave's diary worth a few million.

Tamzie say, "What is this? A tough love session?"

Bracey said you don't need a draft planning document to figure out if you're attracted to someone.

Tamzie then ask what's got the inside track on her heart?

Bracey thought on that and said, "What I'd like to do is fly around on jets and see rare birds." She caught Tamzie giving her a bug-eye look. "Sure, you think it's silly. But it's what I want. I've come to grips with myself in that regard. I've learned to set my own goals."

She added, "And I've found a man."

Tamzie said she hate to admit it, but a man does help a woman construct a sense of self. You get all pissed off at one, and the next one come along with recuperative powers.

49

Hank Harder said, "My wife is going blind. She's having extremely delicate laser surgery in a desperate outside chance at saving her sight. The children are very upset at the situation. My daughter is border-line suicidal."

Bracey was seeing him off at the executive airport. "You don't have to use so much overkill," she said. She had worn her most beguiling scent in vain. Elixir of Love No. 1 by Caswell-Massey.

"Okay," he said. "My wife is fine. She plays championship croquet, winters in Palm Beach. I have no intention of leaving her. It's not just the expense of a divorce, but the time out from things I like to do. However, I'm going to Iceland in July. I'd like to stop by and pick you up."

Bracey looked him up and down. The expensive private jet lent him a stately backdrop. "I'm available," she said.

All of Roebuck Plantation was in bankruptcy. The federal D.A. basically bought Bracey's story that she had been forced into doing the straw loans. And if you stepped back from criminal charges, what you had was a loan from Seagrass to Bracey. And a loan from Bracey to Roebuck. To make the deal look legitimate, Vineyard Dupree had actually done what he was supposed to do and filed a mortgage on the property. Bracey was the sole mortgagee on Phase 2.

It was certainly a tangled web they'd woven, but if she could find a way to pay Seagrass whatever the FSLIC would settle for, she'd own Phase 2. All of Blake Huston's old property excluding Jaquilla Gillyard's little plot of ground. She could put it in a conservation trust, try to preserve some fragment of how nature had once been. Even if it was just a landfill.

It gave her a lot to think about as she waved good-bye to Hank. He looked like such a nerd in those thick glasses. But he had been awfully good in the sleepingbag. And it would be nice to go to Iceland. She had never seen puffins.

■ ■ ■

Lacking the money to meet the outlandish fees that criminal lawyers always charge, Chase Jeffcoat had no choice but to plead guilty to a variety of federal bank fraud charges. He was one of three from his class at the Darden School of Business to go to prison that year.

Chase told the press the whole process had been a valuable experience. He had learned a great deal about himself and about Christian charity. The tutelage of a religious counselor media specialist had helped him find Jesus. He was taking each day at a time and always looking forward to the future. After he had served his time, he hoped to travel the country raising awareness of God's divinity and at the same time raising funds for good works.

■ ■ ■

Thinking on that missing $3 million cause Bracey to remember what Byron Jasper had been babbling drunk about at the post-PowerChest party. She confide this in Tamzie who drop by to see an old man name of Dewayne Porteous Gilyard known on the street as the "Night Dean."

The Dean was playing checkers at his taxicab company on Sylvania Street which was his front. In reality, the Dean run light dope, numbers, and other forms of gambling in Charleston. Tied in with a wire to the big bookie with the mob financing up in Columbia. The man was unfettered by conscience on what he call "victimless crimes" and even more unfettered if you don't pay up on time. Tamzie's now deceased husband Debone had done collection work for him years back, and Debone could sure enough whip up on you when the mood take him.

Tamzie asked a few questions, and next day she drop back by for the answers. He tell her he done a fuzzy study of the issue, but there do seem to be a whole mess of small wagers out there on the PowerChest. Three-to-one odds on the two-some what turn into the ultimate winner. Didn't hurt no bookie bad a-tall, but it was certain some big money done gone down in a sure enough brazen experiment.

Tamzie said she had a willingness to believe in the truth of that, and thanks for his expertise. It would foster learning and communication.

The Dean said he was there for his expertise and time. Hold his hand out. Tamzie put a twenty in it. He said he had give her a better litany than that. She slide him another. He kiss that Andrew Jackson and stick both in his back pocket. Go back to playing checkers with some old men.

Afterwards Tamzie and Bracey Jeffcoat go over to Bobbi-Jean Kincaid's condo where she had just finish packing up the trunk of a BMW roadster with suitcases and golf clubs. Locked the door of her condo and got behind the wheel of her car.

Tamzie got in the passenger side. Said, hi, y'all, it was a nice day for riding in a sporty car like this with the top down. Little cold, but B-J seem to be dressed warm.

B-J said she'd sure like to yack, but she was overdue to be on the road. As the boys had been so fond of saying, Charleston was a beautiful city and a growing market, but she had to order an abatement of all this fun and get on gone.

Bracey climbed into the little narrow back seat. She said, "You know, Miss Kincaid, you've done so well around here . . . and I have to ask myself what's the best use of all that money? And then it came to me. You need a support system. To let you just tackle the problem all on your own . . . well, it borders on the unthinkable."

B-J just sat there smiling, revealing very little.

Tamzie come in with, "What it come down to is I figure we got to make us some tough decisions. But it's a whole sight easier when you realize how you can divide nine million by three. I can do that level of math."

B-J took the news real calmly. She said, "I hate to disappoint you, but I'm not really into sisterhood. Group girl activities. That kind of thing."

"That's okay," say Tamzie. "We ain't exactly manless. Fetch all that money, and they'll come around same as always."

About the Author

MARGOT SINCLAIR played front-row volleyball at Ashley Hall and studied ornithology at Cornell. She spends her winters in Barbour coats and Bean boots, owns her father's Purdey shotgun, and can pole a boat over a marsh at flood tide when the clapper rails can be seen among the Spartina grass.

Her grandparents were part of the Second Yankee Invasion of the South. Between roughly 1888 to 1940, Northern industrial wealth purchased vast tracts of worn-out cotton land, cut-over timberland, and abandoned rice fields. They restored old plantation houses or built new ones, and turned their estates into hunting preserves for duck, quail, turkey, and deer. The railroad brought resort towns to Pinehurst, Camden, Aiken, and Thomasville—golf, racehorses, polo, and quail.

Each winter, the Sinclairs migrated from Tuxedo Park, New York, to Run-a-Gate Hall on the banks of the Cooper River above Charleston. Margot's father was born there as she was much later. She is so much a part of the Lowcountry that she considers herself a valid "ben-ya."